SWEDE SHADOW COOPER

SEALs of Honor, Books 4-6

Dale Mayer

SEALS OF HONOR, BOOKS 4–6
Beverly Dale Mayer
Valley Publishing Ltd.

ISBN-13: 978-1-988315-50-8
Print Edition

Books in This Series:

Mason: SEALs of Honor, Book 1

Hawk: SEALs of Honor, Book 2

Dane: SEALs of Honor, Book 3

Swede: SEALs of Honor, Book 4

Shadow: SEALs of Honor, Book 5

Cooper: SEALs of Honor, Book 6

Markus: SEALs of Honor, Book 7

Evan: SEALs of Honor, Book 8

Mason's Wish: SEALs of Honor, Book 9

Chase: SEALs of Honor, Book 10

Brett: SEALs of Honor, Book 11

Devlin: SEALs of Honor, Book 12

Easton: SEALs of Honor, Book 13

Ryder: SEALs of Honor, Book 14

Macklin: SEALs of Honor, Book 15

Corey: SEALs of Honor, Book 16

Warrick: SEALs of Honor, Book 17

Tanner: SEALs of Honor, Book 18

Jackson: SEALs of Honor, Book 19

Kanen: SEALs of Honor, Book 20

Nelson: SEALs of Honor, Book 21

Taylor: SEALs of Honor, Book 22

Colton: SEALs of Honor, Book 23

Troy: SEALs of Honor, Book 24

Axel: SEALs of Honor, Book 25

About This Boxed Set

Swede

This is the 4th book in the SEALs of Honor action and romance mystery series. It is Eva and Swede's story.

Swede watched the other SEALs fall one by one, even as murder got in the way of love…

But his turn for love had yet to come. Swede hoped that he'd be lucky enough to find the perfect partner but knew it wasn't going to happen while deep in the wilds of Mexico hunting a rebel training camp. Until a group of civilians showed up in the middle of their operation and he found out that the one person he'd known to be the wrong woman for him – was right in the middle of it.

Eva had always loved animals, especially those in need. When a friend requested help moving a large group of horses from Mexico to their new homes, she jumped at it. And landed in trouble. With Swede, an old frenemy determined to extricate her.

As he worked to keep her safe, she struggled to protect her heart.

Only the rebels had plans of their own – and it didn't involve a happy ending for either of them.

Shadow

Shadow's life has been an uphill struggle. No wonder he's so damn good at dealing with the hard, the difficult, and the dangerous.

Shadow's all about being a SEAL. The one world he's comfortable in. He knows what he can do, when to do it, and how to do it … until he sets off on a mission to rescue Arianna and her family, and his world goes from controlled action to chaos. Who knew women like her existed?

Arianna struggles to deal with the foreign world she's been plunged into. Kidnappings, beatings, threats. *SEALs.* The only good thing is the darkest, most dangerous-looking saviour she's ever met. And he doesn't know what to do with her.

Well, she has a good idea, but will they get that chance? Not if the kidnappers have anything to say about it.

Arianna has been marked for extinction, and it's up to Shadow to save her ... before it's too late and he loses something he had no idea he wanted in the first place ... but now he can't live without.

Cooper

The doctor saved Cooper's life and his sanity – but she stole his heart.

Being a SEAL means everything to Cooper, so when the doctor who saved his life is kidnapped, he's the first to volunteer for the mission.

Dr. Sasha Childs has devoted her life to helping others – until she finds out her husband is helping himself to her best friend. Disillusioned, she volunteers her medical skills to a Syrian refugee camp crying out for medical aid.

She's completely unaware that a war is brewing around her – until she's caught in the middle of it…

Cooper has his hands full rescuing Sasha from foreign hands the first time, but when the war comes home, it becomes damn near impossible to keep her safe a second time.

He's been blessed with one miracle in his life, now he needs a second one – before the woman he loves becomes a casualty of war…

Sign up to be notified of all Dale's releases here!

https://geni.us/DaleNews

SWEDE

SEALs of Honor, Book 4

Dale Mayer

CHAPTER 1

SWEDE HUNKERED DOWN behind the massive tree. Who knew they grew to this size in Mexico? In this rebel infested part of the woods, he and his team were after a new breed of terrorists. One that was possibly linked to the Middle East. Like hell anyone needed that. It was a good thing Mexico was cooperating with the US on this one. Joint efforts were always more effective.

No one wanted to see terrorist training camps set up on this continent. Better to destroy them while still young and unorganized.

Voices off to the left had him sliding deeper into the brush. Footsteps approaching followed by raucous laughter and snarky comments about several women in the compound. Swede frowned.

He hated to think of any woman forced to be in there with these assholes. Still, the team needed to make sure they captured the top man alive. He had valuable information.

The two rebel soldiers walked closer, their conversation easy to hear.

"Horse rescue. What bullshit."

"Hey, they can come rescue us. We could use the distraction."

"Don't let the commander hear you. We're supposed to be in hard training."

"I know. We have thirty men training here. We could

use a few more women. Who's going to miss a couple of do-gooders like the women at the hacienda?"

A new voice joined them. Harder. Colder. Angry. "Not happening. No one is to know we are here. Kidnapping a couple of women, when you already have several available, is not in the cards."

"Sorry, Sarge, we were just joking," the one man said in low tones.

"And for that ill placed humor you will report to the commander this afternoon for special orders," Sarge said, his cold voice turning soft, lethal.

Swede winced. Yeah, these first two men were low on the hierarchy and likely knew little but the other man…now he could be useful. But the one the team really needed was this "commander."

The voices marched away as the men straightened up and hurried back to the camp. Swede knew they'd been watched for days now. A second infraction and they'd likely go for a short walk in the woods, and no one would know what happened to them.

The sarge's voice changed as he made a phone call. Swede listened as the sarge followed the men and made a report. "No sir, they are on their way back. I know the hacienda is out of bounds, but there are a number of horses there and strangers." He nodded then added, "You can't stop the men from thinking about the women."

Silence.

Swede looked through the bushes.

"Right," the soldier said. "It would make a good training exercise." With that, he shut off his phone.

A single raptor cry sounded overhead.

Swede tilted his head to the side and smiled. Hawk was on the move.

Swede pulled back and waited for the next signal.

When it came it was not what he expected. The first cry was repeated followed by two short bursts of the same raptor cry. Frowning at the message, Swede eased back several more yards. They were supposed to be grabbing these assholes, not retreating.

Under the cover of heavy growth, he waited until Shadow slipped to his side.

"What's up?" Swede asked in a low voice.

"Hawk has learned something about a group of civilians close by who are trying to round up a small group of horses being shipped today."

Civilians? What the hell. Swede closed his eyes. Damn it. They couldn't pull off the op if civilians were in the area. It was bad enough the rebels already knew about the civilians, the women, but he didn't want these people to know about the rebels. Or about his team of SEALs. That was not in the cards.

"Is the op cancelled?"

"Stalled while we figure out how close the–"

Just then the sound of running hooves raced toward them.

And galloped past at top speed.

Swede wanted to cheer the horses on, except the horses were in rough shape. Ribs visible and bony skulls covered by rough hides that looked dull and sickly. Shit. These horses *needed* the rescue. He couldn't imagine where they were going or who was a part of this, but he hated to see any animal in trouble. Even exhausted and worn out these animals could cover a lot of ground fast.

An odd crooning cry rent the air. More like a cowboy call to the horses.

The horses calmed, circling around Swede and Shadow's hiding spot, their panic stilling, their movements slowing. Two mounted riders came into view, corralling the horses between them and persuading the animals to turn back the way they'd come. One of the riders continued to croon to the horses.

Swede and Shadow stood in silence, letting the horses do their thing. They weren't in danger and both were animal lovers. Hell, Swede was bigger than some of these poor things.

He grinned. This was a new one. As operations went, all kinds of things could go wrong, but a band of horses hadn't happened before.

Another mounted rider broke through the dense brush. A woman. Her gaze was intent as she checked out the trees, looking for any horses that might have been missed.

Her gaze floated past both Shadow and Swede. Swede recognized the moment she realized something was different, and her gaze zinged back to stare at the spot both men stood.

"Swede?" she asked in shock. "Shadow?"

Ah shit.

Swede felt Shadow's start of shock. It was damn near impossible to see the two men on a good day, but when they were hidden like this – there was no way she should have seen them. That she not only saw them, but recognized who they were…

That was seriously bad.

Especially when neither knew her.

The woman, a hat pulled low, scarf up over her chin and nose, nudged her horse closer.

How the hell had they been seen?

"It is you, isn't it?"

The men melted farther into the shadows. The horse she rode bucked slightly, not happy with the situation.

The woman gasped. "Oh shit. I'm so sorry. I'll leave

now."

She spun her horse and urged him away. In seconds the horse and rider had disappeared into the trees following the same path as the other horses.

Swede turned slowly to look at Shadow.

"Did you recognize her?"

"With the scarf, hat and oversized shirt – hell no."

CHAPTER 2

EVA KEPT HER head down as the branches whipped past, catching at her hair. She'd given the horse its lead, knowing he'd take her back to the ranch. She could only hope the other horses were moving toward the correct destination. They had three trailers lined up to haul the animals to special flights that would take them to two separate locations in the US. A special horse rescue on a large scale that would help these animals before someone felt it was a kindness to shoot them instead.

Her body relaxed into the saddle, but her mind…oh good Lord. She couldn't even begin to fathom what she'd seen, who she'd seen and why.

She must have mistaken it. Knowing they were a long way behind her by now and she shouldn't be able to see them any longer, but unable to help herself, she twisted in the saddle and looked behind her.

No sign of them. Of course not. She'd been traveling in the opposite direction for the last fifteen minutes. One thing she did know – if she'd seen what she'd seen – if those two men were really here – her brother, Hawk, was here, too. And that combination meant trouble for someone.

Someone in this area. Crap.

Why here? Why now?

She wanted to be a long way away from them. At home, when Hawk and his brothers in arms came to

visit – that was a different story. When they were working, doing what SEALs did, she wanted no part of them.

Just thinking about the reasons why they could be
here made her skin crawl. She urged her poor horse into a
gallop. Anything to get back faster.

Up ahead was the hacienda she'd arrived at yesterday.
She'd come as a volunteer to help move these animals.
With over thirty being moved, extra hands were a help.
And she'd known April, the coordinator and a vet herself,
for years. She'd been facilitating animal rescues around
the globe for just as long. She was as worldly as Eva was a
hometown girl.

But they'd become fast friends. It was because of
April that Eva had done the little traveling that she'd
done. It was good for her and she'd enjoyed every minute
of it – but she loved that moment when she walked back
into her house and realized she was home again.

There was also the problem of leaving her own rescued animals at home. The Bangor brothers, Peter and
Paul, often stepped in. While Mia, her best friend who
lived on the property, was around she helped out when
she could. This time however, Eva was planning to be
gone a little longer. She had hoped to fly the horses to
their new homes and help them settle. There were
multiple veterinarians on this project to help the horses
stay calm and minimize the stress of their new world. So
she wasn't as necessary to the success of this project as
they were. And there was no doubt that the animals were
being well cared for, yet Eva had been involved in this
project for a long time from afar. Finally getting to meet
the animals had been great. Now she wanted to see this
through to seeing them all settled.

Still, having SEALs in camouflage outfits in the
woods just a few miles away terrified her. Why were they

here? And had she blown their cover?

She hoped not. That was major. A lot of time and planning went into each and every operation. Operations that were highest security, yet somehow she found herself in the middle of one.

She'd seen the surprise on Shadow's face when she'd recognized him. He always lived in the shadows even in society. Always quiet. Always off to one side in social settings. Not an introvert but reserved. The strong silent type. Unlike the mountain, Swede. He always had a girl on his arm except for the time he came to the ranch with two. That had pissed her off. She'd love to like him as a person, but his relationship style kept getting in the way. The rest of Hawk's team were great though. And Hawk was around a little more now that he and Mia, her best friend, were an item. The two of them had been through a hellish nightmare during which time Hawk saved Mia's life and in the process they'd fallen in love.

Eva could feel her heart choke up over what her friend had been through. Mia had recovered – and faster than anyone had expected. With Hawk being very attentive, it was no wonder. And they were ideal together. Eva grinned thinking about the shy quiet Mia who, because of her search and rescue job, forced herself into caves, even though she hated them, paired up with her big strong tough brother. But it worked. Eva had always hoped for such a relationship for her friend and never thought it would happen for her brother.

But it had.

And reminded Eva she was alone.

Not alone as in no friends and family, but alone as in there was no one "special" in her life. And she wanted a partner. Not just anyone though. She didn't want to settle for second best. Hell, she didn't want to settle. She wanted what Mia and Hawk had. What she knew several of Hawk's friends had.

She had no illusions. She wasn't looking for a Cinderella scenario. But she'd like someone to stand beside her in the tough times and to rejoice with in the good times. To be there for her when she was down and turn to her when he needed cheering. A partner in all ways for all time.

What a joke. She wasn't ever picked for the volleyball team either.

Neither was life in the habit of dropping huge gorgeous men in front of her.

Especially ones that looked like Swede.

Unfortunately.

BACK AT CAMP, Swede listened to the others discuss the options, but his mind was caught on the profile he'd briefly caught a glimpse of, barely seen under the hat.

Surely it wasn't the one woman who came to mind. She should be home at the ranch. He glanced at Hawk. Now he'd eased back into a settled quietly happy state of mind these days. It was both sickening and awe-inspiring. Swede knew he was losing his buddies one by one, but at the same time he was gaining some incredible women into his inner-circle. None of these new relationships had impacted the men's brotherhood. Good thing. The team had always come before the women, in many ways they still did, but it was different now.

He understood, but not having the same kind of relationship, he didn't *really* understand. Inside, deep inside, he admitted he'd like to.

But didn't it figure that he'd still be alone. Maybe

because he couldn't identify what he wanted. Except as he stared at the men and remembered their partners, all he could say was he wanted exactly what they had – *as in yes please, can I have one too.*

He couldn't identify the type because he'd never met it until his buddies had. They'd recognized their partners in some inexplicable way. How could he describe something he didn't know or understand? All he could do was wait in line and hope he was served up a perfect partner of his own.

Then his mind caught on the one element he'd missed in today's encounter. Her muffled voice. That tone of voice. The lilt to the voice. The way she raised her voice at the end. And he realized it *had* been her.

He spun around and stared at Hawk. "Where is your sister?"

His voice, the question so at odds with the current discussion, shocked the others into silence.

Hawk raised his eyebrows as he studied his friend. "At home, why?"

"Call her," Swede said urgently. "Please."

Shadow made a strangled sound in the back of this throat. "Holy shit, you're right."

Hawk leaned back and stared at the two men as he fished his cell phone out of his pocket. "He's right about what?"

"She was the woman who recognized us," Swede stated. "It took a while but I finally got it."

Only Hawk was shaking his head in denial. "No. Can't be. She's at home." Still he pulled out his phone and called her number.

They all listened, waiting in tense silence. If it was her, the game had changed.

They could hear the ringing from the phone as it

echoed around the room. Finally, just when they thought her voice mail would kick in, she answered. "Hello? Hawk? Is that you?"

"Hey, Eva." Hawk settled back with a smile. "How are you?"

"I'm great," she said in a jovial voice.

Swede leaned closer. Her voice was forced. Fake.

Hawk heard it too. "Are you all right? Alone and safe?"

"I'm fine," she said lightly. "At least I think so. But tell me, did I really see what I saw this morning or am I getting old before my time?"

"What did you see?" Hawk asked curiously, his voice straining to stay calm, his gaze roaming the table and connecting with everyone sitting with him.

"I thought I saw Shadow and Swede."

The others groaned softly. Hawk glared at the men. "Where the hell are you, Eva?"

"In Mexico," she said indignantly. "And I'm not following you. We're moving this large group of horses to several ranches in the US. I came down to help." She paused, then said, "I told you about it."

"You mentioned it in reference to next month – maybe."

"Well, April said that Isabella wanted the horses to be moved now, so plans changed a few days ago."

"April, of course," he said sourly. "Can you hop a plane and go home?"

"No, I'm not going to leave the horses," she cried. "If there is a problem, you should have warned me."

"When was I going to do that when I had no idea you'd planned to come?"

"Well, I hadn't planned on meeting you here either..." She paused. "Okay, so what do we do now?" She laughed and Swede swore he could hear her smile through the phone. "I know, you guys can wait on your op until I get the horses safely out."

There was a collective snort from the men.

"Yeah, I hear you," she said softly, obviously having heard through the phone. "Not going to happen."

Swede listened in, grinning. He'd always liked Eva. She had spirit. But she was Hawk's sister and that was a no no.

Too bad. Then again, she seemed to have something against him. So maybe not. Or he could work to change her mind.

"How bad is it?" she asked, her tone low, worried.

"Bad. And that was before we heard men talking today about grabbing a couple of women who were looking after the horses as if they wanted something new to ride," Hawk said crudely. Deliberately. Swede figured he was hoping his sister would get the message and run back home.

"Of course. They are men after all," she answered coolly. "With any luck we should be gone by morning. Three trailers are leaving now. Two more tomorrow and I'm in the last one in the morning."

"I want you out today," Hawk ordered. "Do you hear me?"

"I hear you, but I can't," she snapped, her voice easily reaching through the phone. "I'm here with April. We're leaving with the last trailer in the morning."

"You need to get the hell out."

"I won't leave the others," she cried. "If it's dangerous for one of us, it's dangerous for all of us."

"Fine, then all of you get loaded up now and go. It's dangerous and going to go to hell very soon."

"Shit."

And she hung up.

Hawk stared down at his phone in disbelief. "Eva? Eva!"

No answer. She was gone.

"So does that mean she's going to leave today?" Swede asked. He hoped it did but doubted it.

"Knowing her," Hawk snarled. "Not likely."

"I think she's gone to assess the situation there and see if she can move the schedule forward." Shadow spoke from behind the table. He stared out across the land. Always on watch. Never sleeping. Always living in the shadows. "She's not foolish."

Swede was the same as Shadow except for one big difference – he came into the sunlight to play – a lot. It was what kept him sane. Let him keep doing what he was doing. He loved his job. The people he worked with. But it wore one down over time. By walking in the sunlight as much as he could, he knew he could do more, work longer.

That brought his mind back to the men with the new loves in their lives. *Loves unlike any relationships they'd had in all the years they'd known each other.* Was that akin to living in the sunlight and visiting the shadows – the opposite of what he and Shadow and Cooper were living. Cooper was still on limited duty from an injury, but he was involved just enough to have watched the men partner up.

Something none of them could have predicted or understood, but something they all wanted for themselves. Now that they knew it was an option.

"What do you want to do?" Shadow asked Hawk.

"I want to kidnap her and put her on the next plane home where she'll be safe," Hawk said in exasperation. "But as that isn't going to work…"

"We'll have to keep her protected and safe until she pulls out."

"We don't have a man to spare," Mason said quietly. "Otherwise we could assign one to watch from that location."

Swede stared at him. "It's not a bad idea. We could set up a secondary base. Whoever runs the ranch might have some idea of what's going on with the training camp."

"Or they might be involved, and that's going to not only blow our cover but get one of us killed." Shadow added, "Especially considering the latter part of the telephone conversation we heard regarding the hacienda and training exercise."

Swede nodded. "And it's likely to get Eva killed if she mentions this to anyone right now."

Silence.

Hawk bolted to his feet. "I have to keep her safe."

"You can't go," Mason said. "Anyone can research you and find out who you are."

"But I'm her brother."

"Right. Better for a lover to go. At least that's a plausible reason."

"No more plausible than a brother stopping by to help out."

"No reason for you to either. However, Shadow here has the magical touch with animals. He could go."

"Or Swede," Shadow said quietly. "He's also magical with horses."

"That's because he's as big as a horse and they consider him family."

That brought a round of laughter lightening the air.

Swede studied Shadow's face. He could have gone easily. But he seemed to want Swede to go. Why?

"Swede?" Hawk asked. "You up for it?"

Swede nodded. "Sure. You might want to warn your sister I'm coming."

Hawk narrowed his gaze, then grinned. "That's a great cover. You two had a spat last time you saw each other, didn't you?"

Swede shrugged but slouched back. They'd had an argument but he couldn't remember what it was. He knew he hadn't been able to stop bugging her until she'd finally snapped at him. Even now he questioned his behavior and the only logical reason that had come to mind was that she'd ignored him the whole time he was there. Which was stupid as he'd been there with two female friends. He'd not shown his best colors, but there was something about her that had gotten to him. In a big way. Every damn time he saw her.

He owed her an apology.

So maybe this was a good way to do it.

He stood up. "I'm going now. Call her and warn her. She needs to talk to no one, including April."

"Too late," Shadow said. "She's likely already spoken to her."

CHAPTER 3

T HERE WERE A half dozen people in the barns when
Eva joined April. She tried to get her friend's
attention but there appeared to be a horse down. Two of
the vets were in discussion over the mare's condition. Eva
worried they'd put her down instead of trying to help her.
The poor thing appeared anemic and unable to stand.

Catching April's eye, Eva motioned to her and the
outside corral. April nodded and walked out into the
sunshine.

Giving the mare one last look, Eva followed her
friend out.

April was standing on the far side, her arms crossed
and leaning on the fence rail.

"What's wrong with the mare?"

"Mark is looking her over now," April said sadly. "I
can't help but feel I should have gotten here a month
ago."

Eva winced. How many times had she said the same
damn thing with one animal or another? It was too often.

"Let's hope they can help her."

"That doesn't mean she'll be strong enough to make
the trip and if she can't travel now…"

"Right." It's not like they could just arrange all this
for one horse next week. They could but it took money. A
lot of money.

Funding rescues was a constant battle. Some months

were better than others. Some projects easier to raise money for. People loved helping horses, but that didn't make it easy to raise this kind of money a second time so they had to do the most they could with the money available.

Still, that wasn't why she'd brought April out here. Eva glanced around behind her, uncertain how much she should say. "I guess there's no way we can all leave convoy style today. It would be good to have everyone out at once."

"I wish we could." April looked around nervously. "I'm not normally given to nerves, but I've had a feeling that we're being watched all day."

"Yeah, me too," Eva said in a low voice. "That's partly why the suggestion. Do you think we could?"

"Given the one mare, I don't see how?"

"If she's on her feet, we could travel with her."

"They won't take her on the plane if she's not walking and won't be allowed into the US if she's not ambulatory. I have no idea on this one. We'll have to make a call soon."

Eva didn't want to leave the mare. But a dead or dying mare while in transit would be a nightmare.

There was a deep rustling in the trees beside them. Both women started. Eva grabbed her friend's arm. "Let's go back. I'm not sure either of us should be alone here."

"I don't like the way you say that," April murmured, but with a last glance around at the heavy woods, she followed Eva to the barn.

"I know but it's the truth, even more so now," Eva said darkly, wishing she'd never seen her brother's friends this morning or talked to him just now. It was a beautiful day in Mexico, only now there was a dark edge to it. And that she didn't like. How much danger were they in? Back inside the barn she was relieved to see the mare on her feet and being walked around in a circle.

"Will she be able to travel?" she asked Tom, the vet standing closest to her.

He nodded. "Yes, she will." Eva grinned. "That's great. I'd feel terrible leaving her behind. She looks like she needs to get out of here the most."

Tom nodded. "She's going to need some nursing on the way home, so I'll stick close."

That was the best thing. Mark and Tom were here on their own nickel just to help out. They were cousins and from fairly wealthy families which helped fund ventures like this too. Thankfully. Then they'd been born and bred into money so knew a lot of money people to call on. And their friends were used to it.

"I think we should all leave today and travel convoy style to the airport. Load up and head home together."

"And you know we can't do that. There are too many horses traveling in different directions." He shook his head. "No, best we do this as we planned."

She felt more than saw his searching glance. "Do you want to leave today?"

Hell yes, she did, especially now that she'd heard her brother's warning, but that wasn't going to happen if it meant leaving the others behind. "I'd like to go home period, but we did it this way for a reason so we'll stick with the plan for now."

He grinned and nudged her shoulder. "Think of it as a holiday."

"I might if I didn't get the feeling we're being watched," she muttered half under her breath. She caught his sharp gaze, but he didn't say anything. Maybe he'd think about it though. Who knew? Her glance landed on the Mexican woman whose beautiful hacienda they were staying in. She walked closer to her. "Thank you again for your hospitality, Isabella," Eva said warmly. "It's lovely here."

Isabella laughed. "That's because no one is here. It's just God's country and us."

Eva laughed too. "So true." She glanced around seeing trees and rocks for miles and tried to forget all that wasn't visible at the moment. "Do you have any neighbors?"

"No. Not for miles. It's the way we like it."

If Eva hadn't spoken to Hawk this morning it never would have occurred to her to question Isabella. But now she was dying to push the issue. "Aren't you ever lonely?"

"No." Isabella smiled. "A lot of my family and friends live in town. I visit about once every week or two and get my fix of people that way."

"I'm the same," Eva said. "I prefer the company of animals. People in small doses."

"Exactly." Isabella pointed at the horses. "These horses have been running wild for a long time, but they weren't born to it. As people couldn't care for their pets they drove them out here and released them. All fine in theory, but there isn't much for them to eat. They didn't know how to fight for their survival. They have suffered."

"Well, their suffering will stop now." In truth, many of the horses Isabella had been caring for came from other places as well. She'd been rescuing horses out of the goodness of her heart, but the struggle to find homes for larger animals was never ending. The cost became too much and the available space too little. Over half of the horses they were taking back were ones she'd been caring for because others couldn't.

This project would give the horses a better life and ease Isabella's burden too.

And if it wasn't for who she'd seen in the bushes and her brother's phone call, Eva would be enjoying herself immensely. Now, she wanted to go home – fast. But she wasn't about to desert anyone.

SWEDE WENT OVER the approach in his mind several times. And realized with a shock he was nervous. He of the hundred women – okay so that was an exaggeration – was nervous about meeting Eva again. Hawk was supposed to prep Eva for the upcoming scenario, but Shadow, a thread of humor in his voice, had suggested that if Swede went in without giving Eva any preparation, then she'd have a more honest reaction.

Hawk had agreed, damn it. How was Swede supposed to use the cover of being an all-important ex without her blowing it and blowing him off?

Right. He had to really mean it.

Grumble. He didn't play games. Then he was SEAL and there was nothing he couldn't do. Yeah right. When it came to computers he could make them sing. When it came to terrorists, he could make them scream. When it came to women, well he was no slouch there, he could make them scream – with pleasure too – but he didn't play games well.

The ranch appeared deserted when he arrived. From the looks of the typical Mexican hacienda, the owners weren't poor. It was large and of course white and sprawling. There were several stories on the one side and appeared to go forever on the other side. He parked and walked through the gate and thought he heard noises down the long walkway to the back of the property. Coming around the corner he saw several barns and corrals. And a group of people working on loading up several horses. He paused and studied the horses. Skinny and bruised but still gallant, they walked where they were led. Not defiant but not beaten. Nice for those on the other end of the rope.

Swede had been on that other end of the rope with a different story many times. Then these horses likely didn't have much fight left in them. They'd been beaten and abused. Although some looked like they'd just been let go.

It happened.

Still, he didn't want to startle the animals and cause the nice orderly system to turn to chaos.

"Excuse me, sir, can I help you?"

Swede watched the young woman approach. Maybe early twenties, Mexican, long hair in a thick braid down her back. Hired help from her clothes and mannerisms.

"Yes, I'm here to see Eva Loring." He gave her a winning smile. "She's my fiancée. And has no idea I'm here. So it's a surprise."

The young woman's face lit up. "She's in the back with the horses." She turned around and called behind her, "Come with me and I'll take you to her."

He'd hit the right note. Of course the thought of romance often won a young female heart over. Good thing in this instance. He followed her through a winding path that followed the fence to where the group was working.

The woman stepped back slightly and pointed to the far side. "See, she is over on the right."

And she was. Looking as animated as he'd ever seen her, talking with a tall man at her side. He almost growled. That man was a little too into her for comfort. Swede wasn't ready to accept that Eva might have someone else in her life. Maybe in the back of his mind he'd always wondered if he could be that man. He especially didn't want to think of her hooking up with anyone down here.

Long distance relationships never worked.

As his mind kept dreaming up the reasons why she should have nothing to do with the other man, he wanted to laugh at himself. Like what the hell? If that was any other woman, would the same reasons apply? Of course not.

He was an idiot.

And he had a fucking job to do so do it. Let her sort out what she told the man at her side. It wasn't his problem. He approached quietly, his footsteps almost silent as he navigated the pathway. He passed several horses on his right, their heads hanging over the fence rails as he walked by. He loved horses. Loved all animals. Usually they loved him. Shadow dealt with the wild variety better than Swede did, but there wasn't a domestic animal he couldn't sweet talk into behaving.

It came in handy with guard dogs.

And maybe at times like this. He worked his way around toward Eva, keeping an eye on the orderly movement of horses.

Until Eva saw him. He knew the moment she registered his presence. There was a startled gasp and she froze. As in mouth open, eyes wide type of frozen. If someone knocked her over, she'd have fallen like a log. He grinned at her, almost enjoying his next move.

As if she saw something in his gaze she took a step back and then another one, her gaze widening to impossible orbs, and she started to shake her head, her hands up to ward him off – like that would work.

He laughed and reached her with his next step.

"Oh no," she gasped.

"Hell yes." And he reached out and snagged her up

into his arms and twirled her around in a big joyous arc, and when he placed her back onto the ground, he lowered his head and planted a hard possessive kiss on her mouth that said, "She's mine" to anyone watching.

And for that moment he meant it. He had no idea where that possessive streak came from, but it was there. And he couldn't stop the waves of longing that coursed through him.

And then there was the response…

Shock, disbelief, curiosity – he liked that one – and maybe passion, but it was hard to tell. He'd have to try this again at another time when they were alone. The thing was, she wasn't exactly responding like he was a returning lost lover and he needed her to.

So he cranked up the heat.

By the time he lifted his head she was a liquid puddle of female in his arms. Now that was the *right* response. He grinned. Lowering his head he whispered, "You need to pretend I'm your long lost fiancé who couldn't be apart from you and flew down to join you. We had a recent spat but I'm here to make up."

He watched the concept and suggestion fire through her mind, catch, get discarded before forcing herself to take another look and reconsider. She was smart. Damn smart. Always been at the top of the class but did she *get* it?

He hoped so.

She sagged against his chest, and he cuddled her close. "Are you okay," he murmured.

She nodded and straightened. "I'm fine," she said brusquely and shoved against his chest. To no avail. He didn't release her from his embrace. He studied her carefully then said, "I'll let you step back if you keep up the act…"

"And if I don't?" she whispered in a spirited voice, but she kept it low, private.

"Then I'll throw you over my shoulder and drag you the hell away from here regardless of your feelings in the matter."

"But that's kidnapping."

"Like I care." He stared at her calmly, coolly, but giving her no way to misunderstand. He'd do what he needed to do and she could holler all she wanted, but she was not going to change his mind or stop him from doing what he felt was the right thing.

And finally she got the message. She slowly nodded. "Fine. But remember, you came to apologize, to make up for being such an asshole to me," she snapped. "And I'm not convinced. So you'd better make it good."

She spun and flounced out of the way.

Leaving him staring, flummoxed behind her.

Somehow she'd turned the tables on him and instead of making him mad, he was…fascinated.

CHAPTER 4

SHE DIDN'T KNOW how to feel. There was so much heat coursing through her veins it was amazing she'd been able to speak at all. Hopefully she hadn't given her reaction away. She groaned at that. He couldn't have missed her response to his kiss. Holy shit. Was he for real? What had she missed out on all her life? She'd had relationships, lovers. Almost made it to the altar right out of high school but looking back she realized that "almost" was a good thing now. She wasn't the same person she'd been back then. A lot of time and experience had passed. She wanted different things now. Different people.

And damn, apparently she wanted different kisses.

She'd always had a different view of Swede. She'd put her attraction to him down to the fact that he reminded her of her brother. Big, capable, determined. Like her brother.

So she'd done her best to ignore him. Or jab at him to hide her anger at his life choices. Because she couldn't be a part of that. Unfortunately, Hawk had noticed and had commented a time or two. She'd brushed him off saying Swede irritated the hell out of her, but he was Hawk's friend so as long as he behaved around her then he was welcome.

She was an idiot.

It was only now that she'd been kissed by him – a fake kiss at that – she realized the women had been right to hang on his arm. She'd do the same in different circumstances. But she *didn't* have different circumstances. She was here and now and his suggestion was ludicrous.

But her twist on it worked.

She grinned. The onus was on him to make things right. Which gave her a chance to appear more natural. She'd damn near failed drama class in school because she couldn't pretend.

She was all about reality.

And often reality was a bitch.

"Hey, Eva, who is that guy? I didn't know you were in a relationship?" April looked behind Eva at Swede, her attention caught, her eyes assessing. Eva studied her friend and realized that for the intensity of her gaze and the interest therein, it wasn't personal interest. More as in she was concerned for Eva.

"I didn't say anything," Eva muttered, "as we got engaged then had a fight." She glanced behind her at Swede. "Now he wants to make up."

April nodded slowly. In a low voice she said, "He looks like he gets what he wants."

"To a certain extent," Eva said. "But I'm a little different than his stream of ex-girlfriends." She directed her glare at Swede who gave her a hot melting look that damn near made her stutter. He quickly approached.

When he turned on the heat, the man was lethal.

And she'd better watch out that she didn't fall under his spell.

She couldn't afford to believe the fantasy was real.

"I wouldn't have you any other way," Swede said easily, placing an arm around her shoulders and tugging her up close, his words letting her know he'd overheard her comment. He reached out his right hand to April and said, "Nice to meet you. I'm Swede."

April shook his hand, her own disappearing into the big mitt. "Nice to meet you." She slid a sideways look at Eva. "I can't believe you didn't mention him."

"That's a good thing," Eva said, refusing to let Swede outmaneuver her. "As the things I'd have said recently wouldn't have been very nice."

Swede's hand on her shoulder gripped her gently. "And that's why I'm here. Misunderstandings require some reassessment. However, I know what's important."

He beamed at her, a devilish twinkle in his eyes. "And you're it."

She wanted to roll her eyes at him because she knew better but damn if the weak female in her didn't want to believe. In a low voices, she said, "I bet you say that to all the women."

"Only you, honey, only you."

His voice was so serious, so caring, so real, she was shaken. She didn't dare look at him. She wanted to see the sincerity for her in his eyes and not for this ludicrous scenario they'd fallen into.

That he could make her want him so fast, to yearn for something other than what she thought she wanted, said a lot for her confused state of mind.

This had to change. He was here for a reason. To that end, she smiled at April. "I'm going to show him around the place, we'll be back in a few moments."

April nodded, the tilt of her lips saying so much more than her words. "Have fun."

This time Eva did roll her eyes.

SWEDE GENTLY TUGGED her toward the horses milling at

the other side of the pasture. They should be able to talk there. And make it look like a lover's conversation without too much effort. He hoped. Depended if she was planning on cooperating. It looked more like was she planning on making him pay for melting her bones.

If that was the case that was fine with him. He'd had little choice but could understand her position. And honestly, he was damn glad he'd kissed her.

Who knew Eva was the hottest thing around?

Ever.

Even now he couldn't get the feel of her lips out of his mind. The taste of her. The feel of her slight frame tucked up against his chest. She'd felt...right. And that was bad news. Because right with her meant *not* right without her.

And he wasn't ready for that.

Not with her. No matter what his mind had been wondering earlier. It wasn't possible.

She was Hawk's sister and out of bounds.

He slid a sideways glance her way and frowned. She also wasn't his usual type. Black hair with creamy white alabaster skin was all good, slim and light was also good. Yet she was shyer, quieter than he was used to. He played with party girls who knew the score.

Eva was anything but.

And yet, she had something he couldn't quite let go of – including packing a punch in that kiss. He'd gone for gold deliberately, and what he'd found blew him away. And kept him wanting more.

"Why so quiet," she asked suddenly. "Are we in danger?"

"You could be." He wrapped an arm around her, intent on getting her farther away from the others, but she pulled back and turned to confront him. "What the hell is going on?"

He motioned to the others and said in a low voice, "I'll tell you but I want you to come with me quietly."

"I'm not going anywhere with you," she snapped. "Not until you tell me what the hell is wrong."

"I can't tell you much." He narrowed his gaze and wondered what he could say that would gain her cooperation without telling her too much.

"The truth, Swede," she said in an ominous voice. "Now."

He glared at her then turned around studying those around them. Maybe they were alone enough. He shrugged. "You saw us this morning so you know we're in for a reason. And that reason is very dangerously close to this ranch." He lowered his voice even more. "And the hacienda, horses mentioned as a possible terrorist training exercise."

"What?" She stared at him, her eyes huge endless orbs of horror. "We have to do something."

"Exactly," he said, motioning to the ranch and her presence here. "I'm trying to."

"Not just for me. What about the others? There are several good people here who volunteered their time to help these animals. And April is here."

"We know. We're monitoring the situation and will do our best to keep it under control, but you need to know how bad this is. And we need to know if anyone from the ranch is involved."

"Never."

CHAPTER 5

S HE COULDN'T KEEP the shock and indignation from her voice. "Isabella couldn't be involved in this. She's helping the horses the same as she's probably helped hundreds of others over the years."

"Which makes a perfect front for the rest."

"What's the rest? You're not saying anything, you're just implying. And none of it makes sense."

"We have to consider all options, and with this ranch here as it is, she must know about a rebel training camp only a few minutes away."

She stared at him, wordless. Then shook her head. "Not possible."

"Eva, are you okay?" Isabella asked from behind her. "I don't know this man."

Her voice was harsh, cold, and Eva understood. She was a guest in Isabella's house and her fiancé had arrived without warning and was now walking the place as if he had the right. And of course he didn't.

Apologetically, Eva turned to Isabella. "I'm so sorry. I should have come to you right away." And damn Swede and her brother for not giving her some warning to set something plausible up to explain Swede's presence. "Before I came down, Swede and I had a terrible fight," she said. "He came to make up."

Eva quickly made the introductions. Isabella shook Swede's hand but her gaze didn't release him. It was as if she was trying to see into the very soul inside.

Then she smiled. "I'm glad he has romance of the heart. It is always better to not stay angry at each other. Better for you to stay together and eventually get married."

"Thanks for letting me on your place. It's pretty spectacular," Swede said easily, his smile very much in evidence.

Eva envied him. He seemed to believe everyone loved him and of course they did. Maybe they did because he believed it. She'd heard that logic a time or two. Not sure she believed it yet though. And she never felt the same easy camaraderie on first meeting someone. She always held back, waited to see who was who before jumping in. She was cautious. Her brother would say overly cautious.

"You are welcome. If you are here to help save the horses then you are doubly welcome. We need more people to care."

"I do love horses. If I can be of assistance, then point the way."

Swede's voice was so smooth and friendly, so damn natural Eva could only stare at him in envy.

"Is that okay with you, Eva?"

Eva turned, startled to hear Isabella's apologetic voice. And realized they were both waiting for her to respond. Like she had a choice.

She slipped her arm through Swede's and smiled at Isabella. "I'm fine with it. Work might make him appreciate what he has."

She gave Swede a hard look, but he gave her a wide innocent look in return. Isabella laughed. "Now that sounds like an idea. If he's in the doghouse, then this is a good way for him to get back into your graces."

Swede wrapped an arm around Eva and smiled at

Isabella. "Lead the way."

With a gentle eye roll, Eva allowed herself to be led forward to the barns. The horses were all well cared for and not in need of any other assistance so she wasn't sure what Swede was going to do. Besides, didn't he have his own agenda to follow here? Like catch bad guys? Terrorist training camp. Really? That was so bizarre. And yet in a way almost normal. And that in itself was wrong. But being Mexico, it was as if so many things out of the ordinary were okay. And that in itself *wasn't* okay.

She watched the horses being brushed and the vet checking that their hooves were in shape for traveling. It wasn't long before the animals were sorted out. She watched it all in a daze. There'd been dozens of smirks and sly looks in her direction. The women were checking out Swede, and the men looked at her as if they hadn't seen her before. She put it down to the fact that they hadn't considered her as an eligible female until now. And with a man beside her, her desirability had apparently gone up. Odd.

And amusing. She straightened her back and tilted her chin. So be it.

"That's my girl." Swede tucked her up close, his voice low and quiet against her ear.

She glared at him. "I'm not your girl."

That white smile flashed her way. And damn if she didn't want to believe she really could be his girl. At least for a moment. And that was dangerous as all hell.

"I'm thinking there's a hint of regret in your comment about not being my girl. Do you want to be?" he said in a wicked tone.

Outraged, she spun on him, ready to blast him. At the last minute she caught sight of his big grin and came to a spluttering stop.

While she was still trying to figure out what to say, there was a loud cry.

She spun to see one of the horses rearing on his back legs. The gelding, startled and possibly hurt, the whites of his eyes showing as they wheeled in panic, was uncontrollable. He lunged backward and broke the lead the one vet had been holding.

He spun and raced around the small corral, his chest heaving and head down in a panic.

There were shouts from the others as they reached to control the animal before he hurt himself in the small space.

Stunned, she watched Swede vault the high corral fence and stand in front of the now rearing animal.

A voice called over the din, "Quiet…let him work."

Silence fell.

Swede stood calm and stalwart in front of the animal. If he was speaking, it wasn't loud enough for anyone else to hear, but waves of compassion and gentleness rolled off his shoulders. And the huge animal knew it. He finally stood, trembling and blowing hard in front of Swede. Swede never moved. Finally the animal walked forward and gently butted him in the chest.

Swede stroked the animal then turned and asked, "Do you have a towel I can rub him down with?"

Immediately one of several was tossed over the top rail toward him. He walked along the side of the horse and wiped it down, this time his voice, gentle and calm, could be heard in the silence.

"Easy, boy. It's all good. No one here is going to hurt you."

The horse kept nudging him, looking for more attention, which he gave. By the time the horse had been thoroughly wiped down, he'd also been well loved by

Swede, the big man seemingly unfazed by the scrutiny he was getting from his audience.

Eva didn't know what to say. Or think. He'd soothed that animal so easily and confidently that he'd instantly become an asset to the group. Talk about finding acceptance without trying. She'd have a hard time getting him to leave now. The others were going to urge her to keep him here even if only until they got the animals on the road. And maybe for the horses' sake she could.

But it would only be for their sake – right?

Shivers ran over her at the memory of his sure strong strokes soothing and calming the terrified horse. The animal had responded to that confidence and sure touch. Hell, so had the people watching him.

Damn him.

SWEDE DIDN'T KNOW if he'd helped or hurt his cover here, but the animal had been in need and he'd never been able to walk away from one of those. Even people.

From the corner of his eye, he could see Eva standing and watching. Animals responded to him easily. He'd volunteered at the local animal shelter as a youth, helping the animals through the traumatic changes in their lives. They were innocent victims.

He could see why Eva took in the animals that she did, but it was financially draining. Thankfully her land was paid for, but animals this size had to cost a lot in just maintenance. Then there were the vet bills…

But she was adamant about taking in as many as she could and helping those she couldn't as much as possible.

He admired that.

But wished she were anywhere but here.

With a quick glance at his watch, he realized time was wasting. He led the big raw-boned animal over to the others. "He should be good now," he said.

"Thank you. You know your way around horses," April said. "Glad to have the help."

"Ha, and here I was hoping to spirit Eva away," he said with a warm loving gaze in Eva's direction. He grinned as hot color washed over her neck and cheeks and her glare…well he'd be paying for this charade for a long time if she had her way. Too bad. It didn't even feel like he was faking it.

"Besides," Isabella said, "we could use your magic touch until we get the animals loaded and on their way. Surely you can put off the intimate reunion until later tomorrow. The horses will be on the road by then."

The low amused tone of her voice was picked up by the others, and with much grinning and sideways looks at the pair, Swede conceded, "I'm trying to get back on her good side. If this will do it, then I'm all for it. We can leave later tomorrow if that's the best option."

Inside he was thinking like hell. He'd spirit her out of here in a few hours if he could. Hawk was going to have a shit fit if he didn't.

"So, Eva, does that work for you? May I stay and help out, then take you away so I can convince you to give me another chance?"

CHAPTER 6

SOMEHOW SWEDE MANAGED to get everyone alongside in five minutes flat. Not only did they like him, they respected his ability with horses and now they were rooting for him to not only stay and help them in their efforts but in her giving him a second chance.

Damn he was good.

"Certainly your help will be welcome here," she said in a smooth no nonsense tone of voice. "After all, we need all the help we can get until the animals are on the road." She deliberately stopped there.

"And the rest," Isabella asked, laughing. "Does he get a second chance?"

The others laughed but April stared at her, eyebrows raised, her gaze confused. But then April knew nothing of Swede's presence in Eva's life and had to be wondering where he'd sprung from and why.

"I guess we'll have to wait and see tomorrow," she said in a saccharin sweet tone.

"Oh, she's going to keep you on your toes," Isabella said. "I'd be very good over the next twenty-four hours if I were you."

"I will be." Swede grinned. "Besides, I do some of my best work at night."

The others guffawed. Eva shot him a fulminating look. "Right. Now, but there won't be any opportunity for you to prove that as you'll be sleeping on the hammock outside." She turned on her heels and walked inside, still fuming at the ease he managed to have everyone eating out of his hand. And from the laughter behind her their supposed relationship woes were giving everyone something more to think about. Maybe that was good too. Lord knew they had enough to deal with right now.

She glanced at her watch. They had to get a move on. The trailers should be gone in less than two hours. Any later and it would push the transport logistics from difficult into stupid. The flights weren't bad, but the vets would have to keep an eye on how the horses reacted. Some horses took to planes no problems, others…well, she hoped no one would find out.

Just as she reached the kitchen she heard April calling, "Eva, wait."

Shit. Now she was going to have to come up with some kind of explanation. Too bad she didn't have one. She couldn't tell her the truth and neither could she make up lies she'd have to remember later on. Better to stay with a variation of the truth.

"Hey," Eva said, brushing her hair back out of her eyes and studied her friend's face. April was a vet but had sold her share in a practice to devote more time to rescues like this one. She had the simple all American girl look and glowed with health. "Are the horses going to be leaving soon?"

"We're hoping so. Likely another hour, maybe slightly longer. The guys are loading the personal gear right now. Everyone needs to have a meal before we go though so Isabella is arranging that."

Eva nodded. "That would be good. With any luck the group won't need to eat again."

"It looks like that boyfriend of yours could eat

though."

Eva winced. "Yeah, that he can." And he hadn't likely considered that.

"Not to worry, there's plenty here and if he pulls his weight, he's already been a huge help, then no one will mind sharing."

Eva gave her a wry glance. "No, and they'll love him all the while he's cleaning up the leftovers."

"So true." Her friend grinned at her. "So how come I haven't heard anything about this man?"

Eva sighed. "Because there's nothing to tell. He'll blow into town and my life then he'll blow right back out again."

"Ouch, a traveling man." She looked speculatively out the window where Swede was talking with one of the vets. "What does he do for a living?"

In a soft tone, Eva said, "He's career navy."

"Oh, a military man. Nice." And from the lilt of interest in her friend's voice, Eva could tell she had a thing for military men. Which of course many women did.

"Yeah, nice," she said in a dry tone. Maybe it wasn't all Swede's fault as women everywhere seemed to line up to fall at his feet. Could you blame a virile specimen for accepting what was so freely offered? And if he was single and unattached, whose business was it?

Not hers.

And she'd do better to remember that. Swede was a free man and she shouldn't judge him. So then why did it bug her so much? Men had been acting this way since time began. Maybe…because she wanted him to be relationship material.

Where the hell had that thought come from? Disturbed, she hurried inside to get a glass of water and to fan her suddenly scorching cheeks. She dare not let Swede see her. He was too perceptive.

The last thing she wanted was for him to have any inkling of what was rambling around in her head.

Sure he was big, macho, a man's man of the world, but he wasn't for her.

But he could be, her heart whispered. *He really could be.*

Shit. Shit. Shit. Blindsided by feelings she'd stomped on, she guzzled back a large glass of water and stared out in the afternoon sun. She so didn't need this. Especially not now. She was here for the horses. That was all.

Sure but while here, who knows what could happen.

No. No. No. Her mind and heart argued back and forth until she turned on the faucet and splashed cold water on her face.

April's anxious voice behind her asked, "Are you all right?"

She shrugged and muttered through her fingers, "He's making me crazy."

April laughed. "I can see that. He's a man and they all do that at times. But this one looks to be a bigger catch than most."

Eva stiffened. What did that mean? And was April seriously interested in Swede? She shifted so she could look at her friend and watch her stare out the window. Eva hadn't seen Swede approaching. That big body of his moving with panther-like grace. Maybe a panther was too tame. How about a lion? That suited his coloring and temperament – king of all he surveyed.

Knowing she wasn't being fair but hating the look in her friend's eyes as she studied Swede, Eva turned and walked toward the door.

She needed a distraction. The animals had always provided it before. Maybe she'd be lucky and they would again.

God knew something needed to stop her from throwing herself at her brother's friend and making a fool of herself.

Please.

PLEASE.

Swede walked into the kitchen. He'd seen Eva head there earlier and from her mad dash he'd been afraid she was upset. She wasn't delicate and had always appeared to be more even tempered than many women he knew but had a tendency to be acerbic around him.

He'd asked Hawk about it but his buddy had just shrugged and said she didn't like playboys.

At the time he'd laughed, then wondered if that was a serious issue. He didn't consider himself a playboy. He enjoyed what life had to offer, but he didn't go looking, and never aspired to the lifestyle. He really liked Eva, but they'd hit it off wrong and had stayed that way ever since. In truth it was because he liked her as well as he did that he'd been playing the suave playboy. She was the sister of one of his best friends. In the military that wasn't a good idea. As a SEAL his team were brothers. They were that close. And going after one of the family was not cool.

If he were serious then maybe but...? Still, he'd never forgotten her. The shy innocence. The natural beauty. Her soft touch and caring heart that was too big to be believed. She'd take in anything broken or hurt, and she did her best to heal them.

The last thing he wanted was for her to see *him* as needing *her* help.

How humiliating would that be?

Also, she didn't appear to notice him in any way –
except irritation.

He grinned. That could be shifted to something else
too. He might just have to work on it. Then again she was
Hawk's sister. That meant she understood the danger and
lifestyle they were in, and she knew about the traveling
and uncertainty. And the women. He frowned. Maybe
she'd seen too much of Hawk's wild lifestyle and judged
them all the same.

Still, whether she did or not didn't change the fact
that she was Hawk's sister.

Only his mind whispered through his psyche, *unless
you're serious.*

But was he? No. At least not yet.

He gazed at her out of the corner of his eye and sure
enough she was glaring at him. Her temper sparked the
devil within. Without giving himself a chance to second
guess his actions he strode to where she stood at the
hallway, reached down and snatched her up into his arms
and kissed her – hard.

Then lowered her and stepped back, checked out the
bemused look on her face and nodded. "Just in case you
were wondering – I missed you."

And he walked through to the main part of the house.

Leaving her spitting in his wake.

CHAPTER 7

EVA'S MOUTH WORKED but no words came out. The door slammed behind Swede. Nice exit for him.

April's shriek of laughter didn't help. She glared at her friend wishing she wasn't loving this moment quite so much. Or that there wasn't as much admiration and feminine interest in her gaze as she watched Swede walk down the long verandah.

Damn that man. Was she really so easily rattled that all he had to do was kiss her stupid?

April spun back to face Eva, her grin widening.

That's when Eva realized she held her fingers to her own lips as if to preserve his kiss.

"Oh my God, he's so into you," April said in a high swooning voice.

"Right. So into me. That's why he left." God, playing this game was going to be the end of her. She needed to leave and fast before she blew his cover. Hell, before she got sucked into the fantasy and started to believe any of it was real. She didn't want it to be real. Or rather…if she were honest she didn't want it to be real if it wasn't. There was a big part of her that really wanted this…him to be real.

But he wasn't and she had to remember that.

Lord, she was already twisted in knots over him.

And from April's shout of laughter, she realized she'd said that out loud.

"Damn it," she muttered and walked to the open doorway.

"Honey, I don't know what went wrong before, but he *is* into you in a big way. You two look perfect together," April said warmly. She placed a gentle hand on Eva's shoulder. "I highly suggest you see if you can find your way into forgiving him."

Eva stiffened. This was so difficult.

Just then Isabella called from the corral. "I think the first trailer load is ready to go."

Thankful for the distraction and even more grateful that the horses could leave, Eva and April dashed out.

They actually had two trailers loaded and a dozen horses now ready to go to their new homes. There was a smaller trailer loading up the next horse. That would mean sixteen almost ready to go. She checked her watch. Timewise, they were still on schedule.

Isabella came out with two other women and each carried large picnic baskets, thermos of coffee, and jugs of water for each truck. Nice way to send the troops off.

With lots of laughter and well wishes, the remaining group stood off to one side as the convoy started up and slowly pulled out in a cloud of dust and cries of "goodbyes."

Eva figured Swede would be delighted to see so many of their number safely off. But with her not being on the early trips, it meant he'd have to stay here longer. Being away from the team would chafe at him.

She turned to study the miles of acreage around her. There were too many places to hide. Trees, hillocks, bushes. If someone wanted to, they'd have no problem getting into the hacienda and getting out with everything they wanted.

And for the first time she wondered how Isabella

stayed safe. Or had she made an arrangement to keep her place protected.

Hating that suspicion, she couldn't stop her gaze from sliding to her hostess's face. But only joy showed on her older features as she watched the horses she'd cared for journey to a better place.

With low water levels in the area, the more the better and as soon as possible. This area was parched. Eva stayed quiet. She wanted the rest of the horses safely gone now too. Swede had infected her with his words and warnings.

As the trailers disappeared from sight she realized most of the men had gone in that trip, leaving mostly women behind. If Swede's concerns were correct, they'd just made things a lot easier for the rebels to do what they wanted.

Shit.

She might just need Swede after all.

Wouldn't he love that?

SHIT. HE HADN'T realized how the balance of the sexes were changing here and now. Six men left with the three horse trailers. That left two men, both older, and the rest were women. Unless Isabella had staff he had yet to see. He'd assumed several men who had been working around the horses lived here. Even now he didn't quite understand who belonged and who was leaving. Were the trailers coming back for a second load? That would make the most sense if the horses were being flown out.

That made for a long drive but more sensible maybe in the long run. Then again horses were flown around the world on a daily basis, so it depended on the handlers and the horses themselves.

"When are the rest leaving?" Swede asked.

"Two trailers are coming early in the morning from neighboring ranchers and we'll load up the rest," Isabella said. "These trailers came from Mexico City. One of the locals is doing a trip today and tomorrow to help out. We're dependent on everyone's good will to make this happen."

He understood that. It was great everyone was pitching together to save these animals. From what he'd seen they were in need of it.

Eva was studying the one mare that had trouble earlier. The mare was back on her feet and appeared to be eating well. He wouldn't doubt that Eva was planning on taking a couple home to her place.

The words were on the tip of his tongue to ask when he caught sight of something wrong out the corner of his eye. Gaze narrowed, he searched the corner of the barn where he was sure he'd seen a head pop around to take a look then disappear again.

Suspicion aroused, he sauntered over in a casual gait as if uncaring what direction he traveled.

"When we see him…" She glanced behind her as if to make sure they were alone and added, "You should tell Shadow to move from the horse training center over here to look."

Swede stilled then walked on casually. "You saw him?"

"Of course, at first just a man, but I quickly recognized it as him," she said in exasperation. "Just because you're all SEALs doesn't mean you're the only ones aware."

Apparently not.

Still, he wasn't sure he wanted her with him while he checked out the back of the barn. "You need to go back with the others," he said quietly. "I'll check this out. And stay together. Nothing is easier than picking you off one by one."

He disengaged her grasp on his arm and said, "Now."

With a fulminating look in his direction, she turned and hurried back to the others. Good, maybe now she'd finally realize he'd been serious. This wasn't the time or place to argue.

Not when there were rebels possibly looking to add to their stable of women.

CHAPTER 8

S HE COULDN'T STOP watching as Swede wandered close to the barn. It had been a subtle movement, but she'd caught sight of Shadow as he drifted around the other side of the same barn. Good. Then chances were the man wouldn't escape, and she could rest a little easier.

Hopefully.

"He's fine. Probably just exploring," April said beside her.

She turned to look up at her friend. "Sorry?"

"You can't take your eyes off him," April said, nodding toward the barn where Swede was no longer visible. "That's a good sign."

Eva couldn't help but laugh. If her friend only knew. "He's a good man," she admitted.

"There, see? You're almost ready to forgive him now."

"Ladies, shall we go in? The preparations for our dinner are underway." Isabella smiled at the two of them. "Then we'll need to do a final check on the remaining horses so everyone can leave as planned in the morning."

"And thank you so much for your hospitality in making this happen," Eva said warmly. "You've been most generous."

"They are my babies. I'm both sorry and sad to see them go, but it's good for them." Isabella laughed and motioned inside. "Come, the sun is much too hot to be out here now."

Laughing and talking amongst themselves, the remaining group moved into the cool hacienda. Tall drinks were passed around as they all settled into comfortable seats in the main part of the house. Eva's quick glance surveyed her fellow volunteers.

"Now that your fiancé is here," Isabella's eyebrows rose up, "and has a truck, will you be traveling with him?"

"Maybe." Eva nodded but she had no idea. "I'm not sure what the plan is yet."

"I would if I had a chance," said Mary, Janice's daughter, the second vet that would be traveling with the horses tomorrow.

That comment brought a twitter of laughter from the rest of the women. April added, "He is a male in his prime."

The other women grinned and nodded. Eva just slunk down in her chair uncomfortable with the conversation and hoping it switched out before she had to make up more lies. Lies she'd actually like to turn into reality not fantasy.

And that wasn't going to happen.

"Where is the man of the hour?" Janice asked. "I thought he was with you?"

"He's gone to take a look at the remaining horses."

"He's got quite a way with them," Janice admitted.

Mary laughed. "That's because he's half animal."

"And he's taken," her mother warned.

Eva wasn't sure Mary even heard the admonishment.

Still Mary's reaction to Swede was understandable. Eva would like to spend time with that animal herself. It was the aftermath she wanted nothing to do with.

She sprang to her feet. "I'm going to find him. Let him know the refreshments are here."

And she walked out. Whispers and laughter trailing in

her path confirmed that mother was telling daughter off. She laughed to herself. Swede was on a mission, he wouldn't be interested in either right now. Take their numbers for later, maybe.

But while on a job? She knew enough about SEALs to recognize they'd be focused on the job at hand. Everything else was secondary.

She wandered down the covered walkway along the outside of the main part of the house, feeling the heat after being inside the coolness. Holding a hand to her eyes, she shielded the reflection of the sun.

There was no sign of Swede.

Damn the man. Surely he hadn't run into trouble – had he? She stopped and listened but outside of the occasional swish from one of the horses standing and snoozing in the sun, there was no movement from anywhere.

She knew something hadn't gone as planned.

Instinct had her picking up her feet and racing to where she'd last seen him standing. And barreled around the corner of the barn only to come to a shuddering stop as she hit a wall.

"WHOA, SLOW DOWN." Swede picked Eva up and twirled her around to reduce the force of her impact. Then he stood her back on her feet. And grinned. She looked flustered. And worried.

His grin fell away, and he gave her a little shake. "What's wrong?"

"You." She glared at him. "I didn't know where you'd gone to. All the women are inside having drinks."

He relaxed. "Good. I was afraid something had happened."

"No. Everything is fine." But she didn't look fine.

"What's bothering you?"

"You. I wouldn't be so worried, but it occurred to me that we're a little short on males here now. Six left with the horse trailers. I think Isabella has two older ranch hands that live and work here, but if someone wanted to attack, well, there are four women without counting Isabella and her staff…"

"I noticed. Don't worry, the team is keeping watch."

"Thank God," she said with feeling. "I know I wasn't happy to see you earlier, but I'm delighted now. It feels empty with the other people gone."

"And it's also too damn convenient. Who arranged for the people to come and leave in this pattern?"

"I don't think it was a pattern but if it was arranged then it was Isabella."

Swede kept silent. He'd do a little digging into Isabella's background. He hated to be suspicious of everyone, but after his years in the military and seeing what people did to each other and often for little or no monetary gain, he knew better than to ignore something that was seriously obvious to him. Isabella had to know about the training going on behind her property.

She might or might not know something about the exercises going on here. And the women? Who'd know? Who'd care? The Mexican authorities weren't going to care too much. A case would be opened and the rebels would be blamed. But not likely in time to rescue the women.

He shook his head, his gaze at the corner of the barn. He couldn't let down his guard. As far as he was concerned, this ranch and all those who lived and worked here, could have ties to the rebels.

Having protection meant being left alone by the rebels, but that also meant they pretty well did what they wanted without any interference from her.

He pondered the problems of the other volunteers going missing in the back woods of Mexico and what the various governments would do. In this case with Eva being Hawk's sister, there'd be a whole lot more done than normal, but chances were good no one here knew about her brother.

If she didn't have that connection the volunteers would disappear and everyone would be warned again about the dangers of traveling in Mexico and that would be the end of it until they turned up again – if they turned up again.

Alive or dead.

A large bird flew overhead. Looked like a buzzard from the neck size and wing span. Not good. It was as if they knew there'd be bloodshed on the hacienda soon enough.

A long low bird call had Eva gasping and spinning around in his arms.

"That's my brother," she whispered, a huge smile on her face. "Wow, am I glad to hear that call."

"I told you they were all here."

"I know, but now I don't have to listen to your reassurances, I know it inside." She beamed.

"I have to meet them. Go back inside and give my excuses." He walked down the fence to a clump of trees off in the distance.

"Wait," she called out. "What excuse?"

"That you wore me out and left me to nap," was his instant response.

He heard her shocked gasp and laughed. He turned, flashed her a wide grin and added, "You and me – it's going to happen. And soon."

At her growl of frustration he turned and kept on walking. It was going to happen. He didn't know when or how but he knew it was. As he was starting to realize, his life wouldn't be complete unless it did.

Now all he had to figure out was if that was a temporary fix or if there wasn't going to be anything temporary about it.

He was starting to think the latter was the only option left.

Somehow she'd slipped under his guard a long time ago, and since then she'd been an irritant just waiting for him to deal with. To figure out what she was to him.

And what he wanted *her* to be.

CHAPTER 9

BACK INSIDE, FLUSHED from her furious race back to the hacienda and the heat, she strode into the room with the others and plunked down on the chair she'd vacated.

"Did you find him?" Mary asked.

Heat rolled over her cheeks as she remembered the excuse Swede had suggested.

That brought a snicker from April. "Apparently she did if her high color is anything to go by."

The others giggled and she blushed even hotter.

"I've said it before and I'll say it again, that man is going to drive me crazy," she muttered.

"In a good way apparently." April reached over and patted her hand. "Glad to see you've taken him back. He adores you. We can all see that."

"Unfortunately he does appear to," Mary said in disgust.

She was at least five years younger than Eva and looked to be barely out of high school and still into full on man crushes. Eva didn't think she'd ever gone through that stage. If she had, it had been short lived. Thankfully.

She smiled at the younger woman, seeing the dissatisfaction with life in that perpetual pout. She hadn't noticed it before as the woman was like many others her age – horse crazy.

The young woman, Lena, who worked for Isabella,

came with a large trolley of some kind laden with treats. Eva's stomach growled. She checked her watch. There really wasn't much else to do but enjoy the late afternoon and evening. Morning would be a repeat of today until they were on the road with the horses too.

Her mind flicked back to what Swede was saying. If they knew the men were gone today, then an attack would likely happen tonight.

Long shadows stretched across the interior of the open room. Overstuffed furniture covered with casual blankets made for several open seating arrangements. The kitchen was off to one side and down along the back of the hacienda on both sides were bedrooms. Isabella and her staff lived on the one side. Eva presumed that's where family would be if she had any. And that brought a frown to her face. She'd thought that Isabella had sons. If so, where were they?

Good manners kept her from asking, but she couldn't help wonder if everything was okay. That she was even worried about such a problem meant her instincts were truly aroused. Trying to shrug off her unease, she smiled at Lena and accepted a plate of some kind of mini cakes.

She didn't have much of a sweet tooth but these looked delicious. Deep fried breadsticks? Listening to the conversation around her, she realized they were calling the treat churros.

They were delicious.

Too bad Swede wasn't here. He'd love these.

The door opened suddenly. If she hadn't been already looking in the right direction she'd not have seen the flash of fear that crossed Isabella's face at the interruption. But the mask quickly smoothed over her face again.

Interesting.

Swede stopped just inside the entrance, his hard gaze

sweeping the room until it landed on Eva. She could feel the force of that gaze searching, willing her to be there, and the relief when he found her. She smiled at him. "Hey, decided you'd had enough of that heat, did you?" she teased him gently.

The air shifted with his arrival.

Feminine energy flared into light and instead of the calm passive relaxation of a few moments ago, there was now an atmosphere of sexual flirtation as Janice and her daughter instinctively primped. She looked over at April who thankfully was just smiling up at Swede as a normal male.

Swede strode toward Eva and took the seat beside her. It was too small for him, but he wasn't going to move elsewhere, apparently, as he pressed close to her.

She opened her mouth to say something but slowly closed it, feeling tension vibrating through his huge body. She couldn't believe how much larger he was than her now that he was sitting beside her. But given the muscle twitch flickering steadily in his jaw, something was up and she'd be very grateful for his size soon enough.

For the first time she wondered at the sense of staying here. Maybe they should leave for the rest of the day and night. It was a long drive to the next major town, but they could come back in the morning.

But how would she get the other three women to come with them? And she couldn't leave if Isabella and Lena were in danger here.

She needed about eighteen hours to get the last of the horses loaded and to see the hacienda in her rearview mirror. Were they going to get those hours?

SWEDE REACHED OVER and picked up Eva's hand.

He needed to talk to her in private and soon. He didn't want to cause a panic but based on what Shadow had found, there were men on the ranch that had been deliberately staying out of the day's proceedings. Why?

The volunteers could have used the men. Maybe none of them were equine vets, but they could handle those horses. Besides, why were there only women here now?

Maybe he'd been a SEAL for too long, but this was looking damn fishy. If all the horses had gone out today, that would have made the most sense. He couldn't let go of the idea that something else was going on.

"Come for a walk with me," he murmured, his voice husky, deep. He gazed into her eyes, willing her to take his lead.

One of the other women beside him sighed. He'd been around enough females to know the signs, but he didn't want to walk with any of the others. Or for them to get any ideas. He wanted to walk with Eva. He *needed* to walk with her. To talk to her. Bring her up to date. Hell, he just wanted to get his hands on her.

She studied his face then smiled. "Sounds wonderful."

And damn if her husky voice didn't catch on the words.

He stood up, her hand in his and smiled at the others. "If you'll excuse us, we'll be outside for a few moments."

The youngest woman sniggered. He caught the flush of color in Eva's face but ignored it. The charade was important. He wished it wasn't. That they weren't playing parts. That this was real between them. He wanted her. He'd always wanted her but hadn't had a chance to change her poor impression of him.

He knew he couldn't deal with that here and now and it was killing him to be playing the game.

"Food will be served in just under two hours," Isabella warned with a knowing smile.

Swede nodded, his mind already cataloging the various responses of the others and tucking them away in the back of his mind. He knew people. He knew animals, and his mind was similar to the damn computers he spent so much time on…and something here was off.

CHAPTER 10

OUTSIDE THE HEAT hit them in waves.

"You know we could've gone someplace else," Eva said, gasping and pulling her shirt away from her chest. "It's not going to cool down for a few hours."

"It's what it is," he said in a neutral tone, but his gaze never stopped moving as he motioned her to the horse barn.

Great, they could add horse flies to the sweltering heat. Why were they out here again? What had he found?

"Let's go. We have a bit of a walk." And he took the lead. But to where? And at the clip he was traveling, it wasn't leaving her any room for asking questions.

They strode past the horse barn, and she was more than ready to duck in and deal with the annoying flies rather than the heat, but he kept on going. He half turned, caught the wistful look on her face as she considered the barn, and shook his head. He held out his hand.

Damn. Under the pretext of their cover she placed her hand in his. Except…if it was all a pretend situation, why did her fingers tingle at his touch and her body temperature rise? It was all for show, right? Then her body damn well better not get any ideas.

Too late her heart whispered, *There are ideas aplenty here.*

He walked with a determined step and dragged her with him whether she wanted to go or not. After a few hundred yards they came to the stand of trees. The fence line crossed just in front of it.

She let out a startled shriek as she was lifted and tossed gently over the fence. She had stiles on her acreage at home. Apparently they weren't common here. She glanced along the long length of wooden rails. It went on for as far as she could see.

There was a lot of land here. Lucky for Isabella. Only the rough dry country was lacking in vegetation and water. It would take a lot of acreage to sustain one horse. Isabella had done well to keep the rescued horses as long as she had. At considerable cost.

She didn't know what Isabella did for funding but presumed she'd married money or had inherited enough to sustain her. Then again, Eva imagined that many people wondered about her and her own ability to survive financially. She did fine but rarely shared in what way her income books balanced – if they balanced. She didn't discuss it. Those who knew thought nothing of it and those who didn't, never asked.

Such was the way of people.

Swede tugged her into the grove of trees.

She stood and looked around, her breathing slow and heavy in the heat. "Why are we here?"

"Not here – there?" He pointed at another grove farther down. "Come on. Just another few moments."

Groaning she followed. Almost at the grove, she turned to look behind her. And thought she saw another man standing where she had stood.

Creeped out, she stayed close to Swede but couldn't stop herself from glancing behind her.

"Don't do that," he said in a hoarse voice. "I know he's there."

Shit. He pivoted her into his arms, his mouth coming

down on hers.

Blind heat washed through her as he kissed her, diving deep into the soul and draining her of the will to move. She was his to do with as he would. She should be upset at that but couldn't let go of the thought she'd only be upset if he didn't do more. If he didn't show her all there was to see.

Suddenly she was free.

She gasped, her lungs filling with life giving oxygen even as her mind filled with grief for her loss.

She was turned and spun around until she found herself tucked up against a tree where she was hidden. The branches hid her face as she registered his harsh order, "Stay here."

She couldn't have moved if she'd tried. Her head lolled to the side as she watched him disappear from her sight.

What the hell had he done to her?

IT WAS WRONG of him to take such male satisfaction in the foggy gaze and parted lips, the little whimper she made as he withdrew. He hadn't wanted to. Hell, he'd have thrown her to the ground and been inside her in a Philadelphia moment if they'd been anywhere but out in the deserted Mexican range land.

He adjusted his pants absentmindedly, his focus on the man skulking through the trees as if trying to reach where Eva was hidden. Like hell that was going to happen. The asshole was so intent on figuring out his pathway to Eva, he hadn't realized he'd been tracked himself. Shadow was on his ass.

There. Shadow took him out in a heartbeat.

"He's really good, isn't he?" Eva said in a small voice. He looked down at her in surprise. She'd come up beside him and had watched the whole thing play out. He hadn't even noticed. Shit.

"Shadow is deadly," Swede admitted. "He's a pro in so many areas it's scary."

"More dangerous than you?" she asked, studying his face intently.

He snorted. "We're all lethal weapons, but there's something about Shadow that just sets him apart."

"No," she said. "There's something about each of you individually that makes you unique."

He didn't take his eyes off the scene in front of them as Shadow dragged the prone man deeper out of sight. "Do you know everyone that well?"

"Everyone no, there are what forty of you at base at any given time? That's a lot of men. However, I have met at least a dozen of you over the last many years. And this team Hawk works with now is particularly easy to see and understand. You're all protectors. All big dangerous men, but you, in particular are the massive one amongst them."

He'd have snorted if he hadn't been trying to stay so quiet. Instead, he crossed his massive arms and frowned. So what if he was big. It wasn't like he could have changed it. Hell, his kid brother was bigger. Besides, the women seemed to like it.

Right? He'd seen the lost look in her eyes earlier, she was aware of him on a sexual level, but she didn't seem pleased by her own reaction if he was reading this right. And that just pissed him off. Why the hell not? He was a good catch.

Shit, she was going to make him crazy.

"Are the others here?" She spun around as if to look. "And the man that Shadow took out?"

"Likely a scout."

"Right." But her tone of voice said she was as confused as ever.

"The rebels have had a man watching the hacienda for days now. They switched the man out earlier today when the horse trailers left."

He didn't mince words. "Chances are good he was reporting back to the camp on the remaining numbers."

"Shit."

He agreed.

"Are they really after us?" The tremor in her voice got to him. He reached out to her but she didn't see it. He stroked her shoulder, his hand coming to rest on her arm as he tugged her closer. "It's okay."

"Is it?" In an incredulous tone she spun to stare up at him. "Think about what you've been saying since you arrived?"

"And you'll be fine. We're not going to let you out of our sight."

"And the others? The rebel training camp." She turned to look toward Shadow. "Are you supposed to be doing something about them?"

"We are," he said smoothly. "As we speak."

She sniffed. "Then why the hell did you bring me out here in the heat," she said in exasperation, wiping the sweat off her face. "I'd much rather be at the hacienda where it's cool."

"Shh." He dropped his arm. "There." And he pointed to someone coming through the stand of trees from the direction of the fence.

CHAPTER 11

S HE COULDN'T BELIEVE that Lena, the servant girl who had just handed them refreshments, was racing toward the stand of trees where Shadow waited – the man he'd taken down probably somewhere close by.

Why would the woman be meeting a rebel? Was that what she was doing? Or was it something else? An accidental meeting? Was she just going for a stroll, but then why in this heat?

She watched as the woman appeared to stand at the edge of the grove. Then she noticed the woman was speaking even though it was too far away to hear her words. Eva frowned. "Is Shadow pretending to be the rebel?"

"Not sure."

She could never read anything from Swede's face. He was so perfect at hiding his feelings it was impossible to know at any time what he was thinking – and that bothered her. In this instance it was fine. If they had a personal relationship – not so much.

After ten minutes, Lena turned and headed back to the hacienda.

The place was silent. She shook her head. "So you brought me out here to see that?"

"No." But he wouldn't volunteer any other information.

She spun around and said, "Then I need to go back.

Before our absence is suspicious."

His lips quirked. "Not long enough yet."

"Long enough for what?"

"For our interlude to be finished."

She didn't get it at first then her gaze widened as she realized that was exactly what the others would be thinking after he'd used that excuse last time. Damn. She checked her cell phone. "How long do you think we need to stay?" She couldn't help it, her voice was dry, amused. "Or do you have a set time you follow?"

He gave a shout of laughter. "No, but if it was you and me, then we'd need days."

"Days?" she asked, shocked. "Surely not."

"Oh I promise, it will be days."

She spun on her heels and stalked to the other side of the trees. He was impossible. But his words had heated what his earlier innuendo had started. Her body had worked itself into a royal state. She stroked her hands up and down her crossed arms. Shit. At this point, all she wanted was to get home. Her home. Not the hacienda. Back where her own horses lived and her dogs. And of course Mia, her best friend. If Hawk and his team were here, that would mean Mia was alone too. Eva wished she was with her. Mia was a gentle soul.

Eva had sworn to never date a SEAL…or any military men after hearing about some of the things her brother had gone through. Except they were something that so many other males weren't – big, strong, capable, domi-nant-*powerful* men.

After living with a military man, the rest just seemed so much less.

It wasn't fair to the other men… But she couldn't help how she felt.

Military men were dynamite, and the SEALs…like

wow. As in seriously wow. Still, it wouldn't do to have it go to their head. Not at this point. They had extremely healthy egos. Arrogant even.

And so damn sexy.

She groaned and barely held back an exclamation as Swede grabbed her arm. She turned to face him and found herself face to face with Shadow instead. "When did you get here?"

He shook his head and pointed at her to move forward through the trees. "Let's go." His voice was soft as a whisper but hard and brooked no argument.

"Fine." She dashed forward.

And right into the arms of her brother.

She cried out when she saw him. He hugged her tight. "Damn it, Eva, why the hell are you in the middle of this?"

Tears came to her eyes. There had just been the two of them for a long time. For his sake, he'd needed to leave the small town where they grew up, but she missed him every day.

"Damn it, Eva, what are you doing in the middle of this," she mimicked. "I came to help. That's all. Nothing dangerous and nothing that should be cause for concern."

"Except…it is dangerous and it is cause for concern."

She threw up her hands. "But I didn't know that."

"And now you do, there's no going back," Hawk said.

"I'm going back to the other women, one is my friend and the other two are mother and daughter, both volunteered to help the horses. No one deserves this."

"We'll help them all but we're after the rebels and anyone connected," her brother said.

"Understood, but that also means Isabella and her people are in danger."

The men looked at each other and a heavy silence

ensued.

She looked from one to the other. "No, I don't believe she's involved," Eva cried. "That's just not normal."

"There are some very unnatural women," Hawk reminded her. "And given the location of the rebel camp, she might have made a deal for protection or lose all she has."

"She might also not know they are there?" It was a faint hope, but she'd take what she could at this point. She didn't want to believe a woman alone would sell out other women but when up against a wall, everyone would do what they had to save themselves.

"I can't leave them," she said stubbornly.

"We won't. But we need to know you're safe."

"Ha, that sounds like no place is safe anymore."

"Not here. Not at the moment. We need more intel of those that started the rebel training camp. We don't want to just take it down or they'll just pop it up elsewhere. That's not the solution. We need to hit the organizers and even better the money men."

Eva nodded, still not convinced of Isabella's involvement but understanding that they were leaning that way. "So the girl that came from the hacienda is her lackey?"

"Or is involved with someone and selling Isabella out," Shadow suggested.

Eva brightened. "I like that idea."

"Maybe, but the girl is young, barely out of her teens. It takes a cold person to do something like that."

"No," Swede said. "Just a desperate one. She could be protecting a younger brother or already been abused by the camp and they are going to take her back if she doesn't find a replacement."

"You have a horrible mind set, you know that?"

Swede shrugged. "We've seen too much to overlook

human motivations. Whatever it is for whoever is involved, believe me it matters to them."

"From the intel we've received this is a trial run," Hawk said. "And if it goes well, it will be expanded to cover more military style training."

"I'm sure Isabella doesn't want that," Eva said. "That's not her."

"Maybe, but what if her brother is leading the rebel group? Or one of the men shanghaied into the camp is a son?"

Eva winced. "Not so nice."

Her cell phone beeped. She pulled it out and looked at the incoming text. "It's from April. She says it's almost dinner time." She deliberately refrained from reading out the last line about hanging Swede up wet for another session later. April was many things and crude at times was one of them. She tucked her phone back into her pocket. "I need to go back."

"I'm going with you," Swede said instantly.

She glared at him. "If you behave yourself." The innocent look on his face didn't fool her for a second. "I mean it."

"He'll do what he needs to do to look after you," her brother snapped. "We'll guard the hacienda, but we need him inside."

A cry overhead had the men spinning around. Swede slammed her against the tree trunk and covered her with his big body. And Jesus was he huge. She was completely hidden. And that meant if there was a bullet coming her way, he'd take the full hit.

She couldn't have that.

She couldn't live with that kind of guilt for the rest of her life.

She tried to wiggle free but it was impossible, the man

was granite. And tough as hell. She tried to push him and got nowhere. She managed to find some skin and pinched but he didn't seem to notice. Next she dug her nails into him. Nothing. Damn it. She sagged against the tree trunk and waited.

"The damn mosquitoes in these parts," he said from above her head, his voice heavily laced with amusement. "Crazy things."

That's when she realized he was talking about her. She opened her mouth and bit him. Only to realize she'd bitten into his chest and damn close to the nipple.

He picked her up and said in a low voice the others couldn't hear if they were still around, "If you want to play, I'm all for it. But we'll need to find a better location, sweetheart."

And he put her down beside him and started to run, dragging her along behind him.

Startled, it took a moment to find her footing and when she did finally she was hard pressed to keep up. The man's legs were twice as long as hers and the bunched up muscles as he ran said his power was way more than he was expending.

They passed one grove of trees and slowed slightly as they came to the other. She studied the trees expecting him to stash her in the middle of them again only he tugged her hand and pulled her along faster. They bypassed the grove and carried on toward the hacienda. The evening temperatures had cooled somewhat but not enough for a run. She was determined to keep up though and be damned if she'd complain.

He had a bad enough impression of her as it was. And she of him, although he'd done nothing but behave himself with the other women since he'd been here. Then again he was on a mission. That should mean abstinence –

right?

The fence line appeared almost in front of her. Swede vaulted the side as if he were doing an obstacle course without breaking stride. She on the other hand – yeah well – her tumble on the other side didn't do much for her dignity. She sat up on her knees slowly.

Swede picked her up, brushed her off, asked in a low voice, "Are you okay?"

She nodded. "I'm fine," she said in a brusque voice. "Just hadn't expected it to be so high."

"I should have slowed for you."

"Why, you had no trouble." She looked back at the fence. "At home my fences are higher so not sure why I missed this one."

It was galling to think she'd fallen to the ground like that.

A call from the hacienda had her turning to see Isabella waving at her. She smiled and waved back. "Looks like we've been spotted."

"Probably been on the lookout for us for a while," Swede said. "Remember, not a word to anyone."

HE'D HAVE LAUGHED at the disgruntled look on her face. Inside he was still feeling like shit for not having helped her over the fence. She'd been doing so well at his side he never gave the fence a second thought. And that was wrong. She might be long and lean but she wasn't used to the same physical activity he was.

"Don't you two look like you've been having fun," Isabella said in a coy teasing voice. Swede didn't take any offense, but as he glanced at Eva, he realized the fall over the fence had covered her in a fine layer of dust and the running had brought a film of sweat to her skin. Isabella's comment just brought the already high color in her face to a pitch. She looked well tumbled.

And he hadn't had a hand in it. Damn. He'd have rather kissed her until she sagged in his arms to have made the same impression. Still, as a cover it worked.

Although Eva, from the dirty look she shot him, didn't have the same appreciation.

"It's hot out here," Eva said. "If there's time, could I possibly sneak in a shower?"

"Dinner is served in thirty minutes so of course you can have a shower – if you can have a fast one." Isabella stared at Swede speculatively. "Do you wish to have one as well?"

The implication was clear. Swede laced his fingers with Eva's and said, "I just might. We'll be back down in time for dinner." He gave her a fat smile and nudged Eva into the cool building. "Eva love, let's move, we don't want to miss out on dinner."

She stayed quiet and led the way through the cool hallway to the room he presumed she'd slept in last night. Once inside, she stood for a moment staring at him. "Do you have to make it so obvious that we are together?"

Surprised, he turned to stare at her. "I'm sorry if it bothers you, but if it keeps you safe then I'm all for it."

While he watched, she ran her fingers through her hair, a tired look on her face. "What's really the matter?"

She opened her mouth as if to answer then closed it. "It's nothing. I'm just being stupid."

Damn. He wished she'd have opened up. But it was a lot to expect when she didn't really know him. He really liked her. And admired that she wouldn't ditch her friends, take the "me first" attitude he'd seen in way too many people over the years. Hawk was a hell of a good man and it appeared his sister was good people too. Honorable. Then he'd known that already. She'd drawn him back to Hawk's place more than once over the years and what he'd found had always held him enthralled a little more each time. He'd found excuses to go home with Hawk. Asking a few times more than he should about Eva. It was hard to acknowledge an interest where there shouldn't be one.

But what if the relationship could be something like Hawk had found for himself? Swede had watched that explode from nothing into something so perfect that the rest of the men had been left breathless with a want of their own. Now half his main team were hooked up with women Swede admired. And that was saying something. There were women everywhere. But not always ones he wanted to be with. He'd been in a bar one night where a group of women played a hand of poker – winner getting to take him home. Hawk had told him about it. Swede had gotten up and left. Like hell he was a prize for the winning hand. In fact, it wasn't long after he'd taken a close look at his life and had made a one-hundred-eighty degree turn.

That's not how someone treated another person.

If Swede ever screwed up in the relationship with Eva, yeah things could get seriously ugly. But what if he found that same unique special person that Mason, Hawk and now Dane had found for themselves?

It sucked to go to the same old bar with the guys and realize half your group had someone to go home to. The other guys had noticed too. Poor Cooper, he was still not on active duty and that had chafed him. He figured that's how the men had found their women. And he was mostly right.

Hell, Swede wished it were that easy. Go on a mission

and return with a wife. But it wasn't or he'd have had one by now. And he wanted what his buddies had. Hell, he'd wanted the same for himself a long time ago but had turned his back on the possibility knowing how that would go down with Hawk. He'd buried his feelings in a long line of beauties.

That had caused him trouble too. Eva had seen his single life. And she'd not been impressed.

He winced. If he'd seen her running through the long list of comparable men, he'd have been pissed. So much for that whole what's good for the goose is good for the gander thing.

He was an idiot. Still, he'd been alone for a long time now and celibacy sucked. Only Swede didn't plan to stop until he found what he wanted.

"Hey you?"

With a head shake, he realized Eva stood in front of him, wrapped only in a towel. Jesus. Talk about reality lining up with his thoughts perfectly. He swallowed. "What?"

"I asked if you wanted a quick shower."

With you? he wanted to ask but managed to keep the thought in his head. "We don't have time. I'll have one later."

She nodded and walked to the bed. "If you won't leave the room, do you want to go out on the deck or something?"

Startled, he looked at her and realized she wanted to be alone so she could get dressed. He grinned. "No, I'm good right here."

She shot him a look, gathered up her change of clothes and walked back into the bathroom and closed the door.

"Okay, okay you don't have to hide," he called. "I can

stand outside."

"Too late. And I'm not hiding, but I don't get dressed in front of strangers," she added sarcastically. "No matter how honorable they are supposed to be."

At the honorable comment, feeling like a shit, he sighed. "You're right, I should have walked out on the deck or at least turned my back."

The door opened, she came out fully dressed and grinned. "Yeah, you should have, but you didn't, so a chance to be honorable has passed you by again."

"Again, what do you mean again?" he said in outrage.

CHAPTER 12

EVA LAUGHED AT the disgruntled look on his face. "Well, you did let me fall over the fence."

His face fell.

And she realized she'd hit a sore spot there. "Hey, I'm kidding. I was fine. It was my fault."

"You might have been fine, but I should have picked you up and carried you over it with me."

The thought boggled her mind. Really? He could do that. What would it feel like to be carried around like a fair damsel in the arms of her knight? She'd never know. Then again, several hundred years ago where the fair damsel stuff came from, Swede would be considered a rake.

Of course reformed rakes were the best of all.

At the dresser she grabbed up her hairbrush and started trying to untangle the unruly mess.

After a few seconds of ruthless tugging, the hairbrush was grabbed out of her hand. In a dark voice, Swede said, "Let me do that. Even inexperienced, I'll do less damage than you are doing. And why are you acting this way?"

"Acting what way?"

"As if you're pissed off at the world," he said. He gently separated her long hair into locks and ran the hairbrush through them easily sorting the tangles out.

"I'm not pissed off." But she was and it was a little unnerving to know that he knew. It was also a little unnerving to be so pissed at him. He'd done nothing.

"It's nothing. The problem is me."

"When a woman says that, it's usually a man she is mad at."

He continued to stroke her hair in long strong strokes that tugged at her heart. It felt so good. She'd been alone a long time and to be pampered like this…well it was too addicting.

"So tell me, why are you upset? You know I wouldn't deliberately hurt you, right?"

She shrugged. "You have a lot more experience with women than I do with men."

"And that upsets you? This isn't about experience, is it?" He frowned at her in the mirror. "Besides, I haven't had a lot of experience in relationships."

"Ha, you have women falling all over you." She glared back at him. "Just look at the ones downstairs. They melt when you walk into the room."

And lo and behold hot color rose up on his neck. She narrowed her gaze at him. "You don't like that, do you?"

He shook his head but continued to brush her hair in silence. She continued to watch him and wondered if she hadn't done him a disservice all these years. "In fact, that bothers you," she said in surprise.

"Sometimes. If I want to find a woman then I go to a bar and it's a hookup where we both understand I won't be there the next day. But downstairs has more of a meat market feel to it. They don't want a one night stand. They want weeks and years."

"And you don't?" she asked curiously, seeing a side to him she hadn't expected or thought to see.

"I would like to. But I don't want it to be sexual only."

Wow. She didn't know what to say.

"If those were men down there, how would you feel?" he asked her.

She scrunched up her face. "Would hate it. If it was admiration but not thick or overdone, then it's kind of nice. Everyone likes to be appreciated, but if they were avaricious in their looks, then I wouldn't like it either."

"Good. Then we're in agreement. Downstairs is not for either of us."

She wasn't sure what just happened, but there was a sense of finality to something. As if they'd reached an agreement, only she'd missed the fine print as to what the agreement was. Feeling settled and yet she felt stupid for not understanding how or why. She took the hairbrush from him, and after gathering up her hair, she put it into a simple twist and clipped the mass with a large butterfly clip.

It felt strangely intimate with him standing there and watching. When done, she stood up and turned to face him. His gaze stayed locked on her face.

"Do I look all right?" she asked, frowning. What was in that gaze of his? She could feel her temperature rising inside and now flustered, she motioned to the door. "Shall we?"

He nodded silently. She gave him an awkward look then brushed past him. At the bottom of the stairs she was surprised to see the two men she'd seen working with the horses standing as if waiting for food themselves. Then why would she be surprised? They needed to eat as well. They'd worked hard today. She smiled at them.

Only their gazes were a little too warm for her comfort. Likely, only because of Swede's comment. She hurried past them when her arm was caught and tugged backward. She spun and found herself in Swede's arms. His head lowered and he whispered, "Earlier you asked if you looked all right. Their looks should be telling you the answer, but just in case you have any doubts and just in case they are getting any ideas…" He kissed her.

There were kisses, then there was this searing heat that burned her to her soul.

When he finally lifted his head, she realized there was only one way to describe his actions.

He'd branded her as his.

As she tried to collect her very scattered wits, she heard the titters coming from the room and realized Swede had timed his actions carefully. They were standing in front of the large open room where she'd left the ladies sitting earlier and the men, collected at the doors to the outside deck, could see her as well.

She shot Swede a veiled look. "Are you always so calculating in your actions?" she murmured as they walked inside.

"Only when it comes to keeping you safe," he admitted. "That was a little possessive of me, but I wanted them all to know they will have to go through me to get to you."

Only it would set the other women up as easier fish to catch. And she couldn't live with that either. Damn.

"Besides if we were alone and not having to play this role, I could be me," he said, his voice still soft, low. His smile was still intimate as it shone down on her.

"And how different would that be?" She doubted there'd be any damn difference. That man wanted the world to know she was his right now regardless of the truth.

"Then I would have made you mine for real," he said and with a hand in the small of her back he nudged her forward. "And you wouldn't have any doubts that I was yours by the time the morning sun rose again."

She quivered. Damn him. He'd turned her bones to jelly by his words alone. What could he do to her if they had all night together?

SHE DIDN'T SEEM to know how to take that last statement. Well, neither did he. He hadn't planned it. Hadn't meant to say anything even close to that. But now that the words were out, he had no intention of taking anything back.

Why would he? They were the truth and he was all about that. At least with her. Start as you meant to go on and somehow in the last hour or so he'd made the decision to go on – with her.

He could only hope Hawk would be okay with it.

Inside the room, he led her to a small settee and sat her down. She looked completely disoriented. Shit. Her vulnerability brought up his protective instincts. That it was due to his words brought up his caveman response. He wanted to drag her a long way from this place of guns and betrayal and show her what a relationship could really be. She might have had other relationships, but she didn't know her own power. He wanted to show her that. Hell, he wanted to know her that way himself.

They could have an incredible future ahead and having seen a tiny glimpse of it right now he couldn't imagine wanting anything else.

"Sir, would you care for a drink?" Lena stood in front of him, a large tray holding flutes of golden liquid.

He studied the young girl then shook his head. "No thanks, we're not drinkers."

He squeezed Eva's hand in warning. Knocking everyone out in this room all at once would make the rebel's job even easier. He intended to have his full wits about him if and when they attacked.

Hawk and Mason were back at the rebel camp on the assumption that if an attack was going to happen, then tonight would provide the best window of opportunity. Besides, the commander was coming in tonight. With any luck they could grab him and the rebels and save the women at the same time. A little over the top in terms of goals.

But over the top was what he and his team did.

They were SEALs. Nothing too big or too hard for them. They might die trying to make it happen, but at least they'd have done what they could and not given up in the process. SEALs didn't have a reverse gear.

Now that there was a chance of having Eva in his future, he wasn't going to accept any other outcome than the best one.

As long as he could get Eva to cooperate…then it would be all good.

Somehow he didn't think that was going to be quite so easy.

D INNER WAS FINISHED and everyone sat down on the sprawling deck in various pieces of furniture. Eva walked over to the large single chair that was left only to have Swede snag it first.

She glared at him, but he gave her a smug smile and held out his arms.

Damn, like she needed more heat. But like a moth to a flame, she couldn't resist and sank onto his lap. It was all a lie and likely a dangerous one at that, but there was one thing she couldn't ignore.

It was perfect.

She leaned back against his broad chest and let the sounds of the calm evening wash over her.

Isabella was preparing coffee for everyone and that would round out the perfect meal. Eva didn't know how Isabella lived so well, but she hadn't stinted on the meal. The traditional enchiladas matched to a spicy chicken dish and rice had been elegantly prepared and full of flavor. Delicious. And her stomach was seriously happy right now.

"Are you going to fall asleep on me," Swede murmured into her ear, his warm breath drifting just inside to tingle and tantalize.

"Maybe. It's beautiful outside." Cool and refreshing yet at the same time warm enough to not need a sweater for the chill. Darkness had fallen, giving a peaceful appearance to the surroundings.

"Mmmm."

She chuckled. "You don't sound like you're in any shape to get up and run a marathon either."

His laughter rumbled out of his chest like a volcano rumbling up warning signs. "No, no marathons. At least not at the moment."

"Good. I'm not going anywhere either."

And she closed her eyes, letting her breath ease back and the tension in her shoulders lessen. "See," she whispered. "It's all good."

He reached up and stroked her back, his big hand running down her spine and back up the sides, gently massaging the ridge of muscles on either side of her spine. His voice low and in warning he said, "No, it's not. Remember that."

She stiffened. He dug his fingers in deeper as a warning.

She relaxed slightly against him, but she was no longer sleepy and happy. Neither was he. She could sense the readiness in his muscles. The way they bunched up with each slight movement as if anxious to get into full movement. Then he was a warrior. He was born ready.

And how lucky was she that he was here ready to protect her. He'd be a force to get through, and he'd consistently put himself in the way to keep her safe.

Sitting here in his arms, it would be too easy to forget. Easy to let reality slide and let life be this dream. He was such a great man, but she knew her brother would have a fit regardless. Then again, he liked Swede, and he hadn't liked any of her ex-boyfriends.

Not that Swede would allow Hawk to run him off. Still, they were buds. In a big way. Something she'd never want to come between. The men were brothers in all ways that counted. And a woman in the middle was never good.

She remembered Hawk laughing about bros and hos at one point in time. She'd appreciated what he meant back then and understood that Swede wouldn't ever cross the line. She knew her brother would always come first — until Swede found that one special woman who would make him change his ways.

It could happen.

It had happened. To her brother. And that was something she couldn't let go of. Could she be woman enough for Swede? And would that make any difference if he wasn't ready to settle down? It had to be his decision.

"Don't you two look comfy?" Mary said in a mocking voice. "So cute."

Swede shifted slightly under her, but she kept her eyes closed and just ignored the bitchiness.

"Be nice," April said. "It's wonderful to see two people so in love like they are."

Eva stiffened at the *in love* comment, but Swede's huge hands gently rubbed her back up and down in a long soothing stroke, probably adding to the love bird look.

"If they are so in love, why did they break up?" Mary asked in a resentful tone.

Eva wondered what her problem was. She opened her eyes and studied the young woman. She had a petulant look that showed her dissatisfaction in life. Still, she was young.

"Have you ever been in love, Mary?" Eva asked, hoping to take the attention off of her and Swede. Their time tonight was special. Sitting like this was more public display of affection than she was comfortable with, but she was enjoying it too much to change. Because it was all part of the cover. *Right?*

"No," Mary said. "I thought I was a time or two but it didn't work out."

Her mother laughed. "That's the truth."

April grinned. "The older I get the more in love I always think I am."

Mary sniggered. "Love has nothing to do with it."

Isabella gave a deep throated laugh. "Ah, the joys of youth."

Eva grinned and snuggled deeper in Swede's arms. Arms that held her so close.

Just as she figured she could snooze, the horses erupted into a cacophony of shrill neighs and trumpets followed by wild running hoofs.

The group bolted to their feet.

"Fire," Isabella shrieked and chaos ensued.

Eva tried to run toward the horses, but Swede pulled her back out of the way and held her close. "Wait," he said.

Holding her hand in his, he walked to the pasture on the left. The others ran past in cries of horror. Eva tried to tug him forward, but he wouldn't be budged. She turned to glare at him. "What's wrong with you?"

He pulled her close, leaning down to whisper, "This is likely a diversion. Do not leave my side."

She stilled. Such a tactic hadn't crossed her mind, yet it made sense. And in the chaos if someone went missing then who'd know. And who'd find the missing person? She could see from where she stood that the horses were racing the perimeter of the pasture in a panic. They weren't hurt from what she could see, and although there was smoke, she couldn't see a blaze.

"Help, the fire is over here," yelled a farm hand.

She wanted to run closer. Only she couldn't hear any crackle. The other three women were already racing in that direction.

Overhead she could hear sounds of a hawk calling.

Was that her brother? Had he started a fire? If so, why? Surely he wouldn't do that. It was dangerous in this dry rough grass, almost impossible to stop. It could rip through this hacienda until there was nothing left.

Except the hacienda was made out of adobe that was so common to these parts.

Trying to calm down, she waited for Swede to tell her what to do next.

"Eva?" April called to her. "Come give me a hand, please."

Shit. With an apologetic look at Swede's hard face, she slipped her hand free and ran to April's side. "What's the matter?"

"I don't know for sure." April dropped to her feet.

And that's when Eva realized Lena was lying on the ground.

"Oh," she cried out softly as she dropped to April's side. "Is she alive?"

"Yes, but it looks like she has a head wound. Her breathing is steady but she's unconscious." April looked around, but the others were carrying water buckets to put out a small brush fire that had already been contained. "Ask Swede to carry her inside, please."

"Sure." Eva bolted to her feet, looking for him, only he wasn't immediately visible. Where was he? He'd just been at her side. "I can't see him."

"Well, it's not like he could have gone far," April said in exasperation. "Go find him."

With a last look at April and her patient, Eva spun around trying to determine what direction Swede would have gone. Had she seen him after hearing the bird cry or April's call? No, she'd dropped his hand and come running. But he had been right behind her – hadn't he? Two men milled around the smoke-filled area. She headed in that direction. And quickly realized Swede was nowhere to be found.

Good Lord, he could move fast. Still, they needed to get the young girl inside. She found the strongest of the men and motioned for him to come and help.

Returning to the barn, they found the still unconscious Lena – but no April.

"Damn it. Now where is she?"

The man only shrugged. Did he even understand English? This was a Spanish speaking area, and they didn't have many visitors so not much chance to learn. She motioned for him to pick the young woman up and take her inside the house. He obliged and she ran ahead to open the door. Inside she pointed to the couch. She ran to get a glass of water and a wet towel for the woman's head. Where the hell was April? Or Swede for that matter. Although Swede was less of a concern.

That man could take care of himself.

April on the other hand…

She twisted to look behind her, but she couldn't see into the living room. Lena was so young. Hopefully the injury was minor.

Turning back to the sink, she turned off the water and wrung out the cloth. Hearing a sound behind her, she turned with a smile. "I'm just getting water for her—"

The blow struck her in the temple. The force snapped her head back even as she sagged onto her knees. Her body refused to follow her commands. Her mind already noting that Swede and her brother had been right. Something much deeper, darker was going on here.

And she'd fallen into the trap.

Before the darkness took her, she whispered, "I'm

sorry, Swede."

Then she saw nothing more.

SWEDE TOOK ONE look at the paltry fire and immediately dismissed it. Although if someone had set it, they were taking a chance. The weather had been dry and hot, fire was always a danger but this side of the house was mostly sand and brush. Some grass would catch fire but not much would burn beyond the local spot. So maybe it *had* been deliberately set. There were more men around suddenly. Middle aged hand workers. Interesting. He'd seen more than he expected at dinner, but now there appeared to be a couple of new faces. Was this the group they'd seen hidden earlier? Were they ordered to stay out of the way? Could their absence be so innocent? He should have found out more about the hacienda and Isabella and her staff. Maybe there was something else going on here. Were they rescuers of a sort too, for humans? As in free room and lodging for work? Was Isabella really a big hearted person? He wanted to believe so, the horses would indicate that, but he couldn't resolve the situation in his head.

He could hear the cries overhead from his team. They were so natural and blended into the chaos so well he doubted anyone else would have understood they were here.

Still with the pandemonium, both human and horses, it was hard to sort out the people coming and going. He spun around looking for Eva. She'd gone to April's side. But he couldn't find April. For that matter he could no longer see Eva. Where had she gone? His gaze was intent as he searched the spot she'd been. The other horses had been let out on the far side to help them calm down. There was nothing like fire to spook animals.

He crossed to the other side of the barn, noting the dark coolness was inside. There were several stalls and tack rooms here. If Eva wasn't on the other side then he was going to start a room by room search.

Isabella rushed past him, fear on her face. Swede reached out and grabbed the older woman's arm. "Isabella, have you seen April? Eva?"

She shook her head. "Not April or Eva. Lena is lying in the living room unconscious. I think she met her new lover," Isabella snapped. "And he brought her home like this."

His voice was harsher than he'd hoped for but anxiety for Eva was rising. "Did you see him?"

Isabella shook her head. "No, he isn't local. But he is a fighter and takes what he wants. Like they all do," she said bitterly. And she tore her arm free and ran inside.

Instinct kicked in.

Barely holding back his panic, he sent out the call.

His phone rang immediately. Hawk.

"I can't find her," Swede said, hating himself at that moment. With fear choking his words he explained the little he knew.

"The men have the place surrounded. She's there somewhere," Hawk snapped. "No one has left yet and no one else has arrived."

That was good news. "I'll find her."

He hung up the phone and ran through a fast search of the barn, then moved to the second barn. Were all four women unconscious? That would make sense in that they couldn't scream for help. Eva would be quiet, biding her time. But the others…the young girl would scream.

The barn had several small rooms accessible only

from the outside. He made it through them and found nothing. Then moved on to the bunk houses. He was in and out of them in seconds and racing to the main house. The women had to be in there. There were no other buildings left.

He bolted through the kitchen door and into the living room. And came to a hard screeching stop.

Four men were in the living room, rifles in their hands. Four women lay unconscious on the floor in front of them, lined up in a row. And the young Mexican…? She lay on the couch still out cold.

Two more men moved into position behind him.

Swede crossed his arms and studied the men in front. Two were from the rebel camp. Two looked to be drifters, but the looks on their faces as they stared down at the women made his insides cringe.

A quick glance at Eva landed on the trickle of blood sliding down her cheek.

Hawk had better get here soon.

Or there wasn't going to be enough of the rebels left for him to tear apart.

CHAPTER 14

DAMN IT. WHY her head? She hated head injuries. How the hell had she gotten into this stupid scenario? She wanted to roll over and throw up, but since Swede had arrived, and boy was she glad to see him, she'd been too frozen to move. Now she needed to be ready to move and fast. Only she was afraid that if she lunged upright, her head injury would knock her back down. The rebels talked over her.

"And the women?"

"We can't leave them behind, besides we could use them."

Eva's stomach knotted. So Swede had been right.

Of course he had been. Being a SEAL and all. They weren't *always* right but damn close. She opened her eyes a slit, willing Swede to look down at her. Willing him to see she was alive and ready to follow through on whatever plan he had hatched. Please let him have a plan. *Please.*

He stood, his arms crossed across his massive chest and studied the men with an almost sleepy gaze. She wasn't fooled. He was pissed.

"What do you want with the women?" he asked in a cold voice.

"The men are complaining that the nights are too cold and they are alone." The rebel smiled. "Happy rebels are happy fighters. Happy fighters fight harder. Kill better."

"Rebels? Fighters?" Swede shook his head as if not understanding. "You have a group of fighters here? Why? There is no problem here. No uprising. No war? Nothing."

"There is war everywhere, and we need our men to be trained. I'm not telling you what or who for. We will take the prisoners to the camp. The commander will decide their fate. They can't be left behind alive. This is just the start. The men did good tonight. First real training exercise. Maybe the women will be their reward."

"I'd hardly call this well done. Amateur night maybe."

Eva shuddered at the slightly mocking tone in Swede's voice. These men had no idea what they were facing. Swede was not going to let her be captured.

"Too bad your commander isn't here. Doubt he'd be so happy."

"We're out of time here." One of the other men snorted as he shifted his feet. "He'll be happy with us tonight."

Eva kept an eye on Swede, waiting for the sign that would tell her to move. He wouldn't let these assholes take her. And her brother was close by.

She swallowed hard and tried to see the other women beside her – what condition where they in? Her hand rested on April's hand. She dug a fingernail in, hoping for a reaction. Nothing.

Damn that meant the other two were likely in the same condition.

Sounds of a truck engine in the distance filled her veins with ice. Shit. The rebels had transport coming to carry the women out.

"And Isabella?" Swede asked. "She's not here so I presume you only want the strangers."

The first man laughed. "No, we'd take all women but

Isabella makes deals to save her skin."

"But is not succeeding I gather," Swede added in a droll tone, but she wasn't fooled. He was searching for a way out of this mess. For all of them.

The two men who had been standing on the side of the room by her head, lifted their guns. "He's too much trouble. We should get rid of him right now."

"No, take him out back to where we're going to bury him. Look at his size. He's huge. We'll never manage to move his dead body."

Eva couldn't breathe. Dear God. How had they come to this? She bunched her muscles, waiting for an opportunity to create a distraction. One that wouldn't put a bullet in Swede or her.

Death was a little too permanent for her. She didn't want to lose Swede.

He shifted enough to look down at her.

She pleaded at him to do something.

And what did he do? He glanced at her and winked.

SEEING THE WOMEN lying unconscious burned his ass. They were not objects to be used and discarded. But in many parts of the world, women were just that. He'd seen it time and again. And it pissed him off each and every time.

To see Eva…like that…hell no. He'd make sure these bastards were dead if he had to choke the very life out of them himself. With pleasure.

No one was going to get away with abusing his woman.

If his mind stuttered at the wording, his heart didn't. When push came to shove and the chips were down, there was no fooling himself. He'd kept an eye on her for years. Waiting for the right time.

Now was the right time. He'd be damned to hell before he lost out on the one thing he only now realized was what he was waiting for all these years.

She'd been taboo until Hawk himself had shifted his stance after finding his own perfect partner.

Now Swede could claim his.

He just had to get rid of these assholes first.

With the goal in sight and without warning, he crouched, kicked out a leg, spun and grabbed the two guns held by the two men standing behind him. They went down in a heap, Swede was already on the move. Bullets spat in his direction, one hitting one of the men he'd knocked over. Swede was already behind the wall, their two guns as his trophies. Swede shot the second man who was trying to regain his footing. He started firing as he dashed into the room and took out first the gunman on the left then turned his rifle on the lone man still standing.

Standing behind but holding his gun on Eva. The only one of the women who appeared awake enough to stand under her own power. Swede took a deep controlling breath, his mind already cataloguing the options.

"Stop right there or I kill her," snarled the rebel. "She's going to get the first bullet."

Swede snorted. "I guess you can't count. Four of your men are already dead or dying." He waved his second gun at the man flat on the ground, his hands over his head. "And this guy is hoping you will think he's dead. Nice rebels you're trying to train here. First class men."

The leader glared at the man on the floor. And then did something Swede wasn't expecting. He shifted to stand a little to the left of Eva and with only changing the angle of the gun barrel, he shot the rebel cowering on the floor.

Swede swore. That wasn't good. That meant everyone was expendable.

Eva would be next.

He glanced over at her. She was trying to say something to him, but he couldn't decipher what.

"So what's it to be, big man?" The rebel jeered. "Feel like trying your chances against my gun?" He laughed. "You might not go down with one shot, but I can get off a half dozen shots before you reach me and you know you're not going to survive all of those."

Shit. He didn't trust this guy at all. The minute he put his gun down he was a dead man. He knew it. But his options were limited.

"Don't you dare, Swede," Eva snapped. "Just shoot the bastard."

He stared at her. He could. It was an option. But he'd have to shoot through her. Had she considered that? He doubted it.

Then she nodded. "Just do it."

Damn it. Hawk would kill him if he did. Then again, if Eva died…? She shifted her legs, widening her stance as if getting ready to run. She pointed her finger to the right. Was she telling him to shoot on the right or was she going to try to bolt to the right. Where the hell was the rest of the fucking team?

He didn't want to do this.

The gunman smiled. "How about I take out one of the bargaining chips?" In the next split second that he tilted the gun toward the other three unconscious women.

Eva leaned to the right.

Swede fired to the left.

CHAPTER 15

EVA FELT THE tug on her skin. But her ears were still ringing from the earlier gunshot and her gaze, hot on Swede's regretful face said something bad had happened. And the asshole who was planning on killing April? The gunman groaned, his gun still in his hand but his weight was now leaning on her.

She pivoted out of the way, and grabbed her side. The gunman fell to his knees. Then all the way to the floor.

Swede rushed over and kicked the gun away from the gunman before he spun her around so he could see her wound. He lifted her shirt. She slapped at his hands.

"Leave me alone. I'm fine," she said. "I'm not hurt."

"Ah, you are more than fine, and it's way too late to leave you alone."

"What?" She stared at his face, wondering at the caring look in his eyes. For her? Really? No. No not likely. She shook her head and pressed her shirt down over her side. "I don't have a clue what you're talking about."

"Yes, you do. At least your heart does. Your mind hasn't quite made the jump yet, but that's okay. It will."

She shook her head, feeling the room start to spin. She wondered at the injury. Had he really shot her to get at the gunman? Surely not. But anything was better than watching her friends or him get killed in front of her.

"I'm not feeling too good," she muttered.

"Reaction," he said cheerfully. "Good thing you're

not hurt."

"I'm not?" She searched his face in surprise. "I thought you shot me."

He raised an eyebrow. "I only grazed you. Don't you have any faith in my abilities? I'm a better shot than that."

Relieved she smiled. "Then I won't look at it. It's only going to hurt more if I do."

He laughed. "Come on. Let's find a bandage to clean it up."

She shook her head, not wanting him to touch it. It was going to hurt like crazy if he did.

"Hell no. We have to help these people. And there are six dead men here, remember?"

"I can hardly forget," he said. "But I only killed five."

"And that makes a difference? So what…you only clean up half the mess."

"Not worried about the mess at all. But I do want to know where the rest of the people are. Especially Isabella."

"I'll stay here, you go look."

He raised an eyebrow and shot her a look saying that wasn't happening.

She groaned. "We can't leave the women, and we can't be separated so that means we both have to stay here and who knows what the hell is going on out there?"

"Except the women are unconscious and no one is going to be dragging them anywhere right now."

"You don't know that. We heard a vehicle in the distance, remember."

He rolled his eyes. "I'm not asking you to leave them but to come with me to make sure the others are safe."

She stood undecided until April moaned.

Eva dashed to her friend's side. "Easy, April. You were unconscious, so wake up slowly."

Her friend's gaze focused on Eva's. "What happened?"

Not wanting to alarm her more than necessary, Eva said, "It looks like Isabella's place was attacked by a rebel group."

"Oh my God. Is she okay?"

Eva watched as shocked awareness slammed into April's foggy gaze. She lifted a hand toward Eva.

"We don't know," Eva said holding her hand. "We haven't found her yet."

April struggled into a sitting position. "Go. I'll be fine." She looked around the room, her gaze landing on the two women at her side. "Oh my God. Them too."

"Yeah, that's why we're a little worried about the others," Eva admitted.

"Go." April waved them off as she crawled over to Mary, her hand immediately checking for a pulse.

Swede tugged Eva back. "April, stay here with the women, we'll be back as soon as we can."

Dazed April looked around, saw the men collapsed where they'd dropped. "Yes. You need to make sure this is over. Oh, I can't believe this is happening."

When Eva stood uncertainly looking at her friend's face, trying to make sure it was safe to leave her, April pointed to the door. "Go. Always have to make sure it's safe for the rescuers before the victims can be taken care of."

And on that truth, Eva turned and headed for the front door, calling back, "Okay, we'll be back as soon as we can."

"Just make sure you catch the assholes. Or kill them. I sure don't want to see any alive."

Swede tugged Eva down the hallway toward the back room. "There's nothing visible out there but if there are men watching and waiting they will be looking for you there."

"Did they hurt my brother?" she asked in a tight voice.

"I doubt it," he said calmly. "There were shots fired outside but I'd bet on my team any day."

"If they did…" she threatened, ignoring Swede's grin.

"He and the others can take care of themselves," he said. "We're SEALs, remember?"

"Yeah and those were real bullets, remember?" she snapped. "Even SEALs can be shot and killed."

"So true," he muttered in a low voice as they approached the kitchen. He leaned his head against the door and listened. She waited.

She was so damn grateful she wasn't alone. She'd already have been carted off to the camp these men were using. How horrible her life would be then – especially if no one reported them missing. People at home would eventually – maybe. Hawk would come running to find her, and God help the men he found her with.

She'd had a close call, and it was only now settling in. She'd taken life for granted. Her safety here as a given. She'd come to help but hadn't thought of all the contingencies.

She snorted under her breath. How could she? No one would think anything like this would happen – could happen. And yet look at where she was now. Besides, she had been warned and scoffed at the warning. Shitty things happened to good people all the time, even at home. Look at what her best friend Mia had endured before Hawk rescued her. She'd almost died several times.

So maybe this was Eva's turn. How horrible to think everyone was going to go through something similar in life. How could these people do this? Treat women like that. Treat anyone like that. As a casualty of a training exercise.

Her stomach started to revolt.

She closed her eyes and took several deep breaths. Her arm was grabbed and given a handshake. "None of that. We need to hold it together."

With a hard swallow, she nodded. "I'm fine."

"No, you're not, but you will get through this."

Bolstered, she straightened and motioned to the kitchen. "Well?"

He nodded and pushed the door open. She waited a long second for his okay then walked in behind him. The large room was empty.

She walked about the gleaming kitchen counters to the back door and stopped.

The bile slid up her throat.

"Oh no," she cried out in a soft pained voice. The cook, who'd worked hard to prepare the food she'd eaten since she'd arrived was pinned to the wall, one of his own chef knives through his throat. Swede tugged her past the dead man, his body hiding the horrific sight.

"What do these people want?"

"Anything and everything I'd say," he said in a hard voice. "This could be any number of things, regardless of what the rebels were saying, including a deal gone wrong."

He slipped outside to hide beside the huge set of shelving that stood on the porch. It was from days long gone for men to store their dishes or boots or some damn thing. It was odd, but seemed to fit the rest of the old verandah. She forced herself to turn and look around. Focusing on the shelving allowed her to get past the sight in the kitchen.

"Where do you think the others are?" she whispered.

From their vantage point, she watched the horses

graze in the far pasture. An innocent sight. Surreal when side by side to what was behind her. "I guess that means the fire is out."

"The fire was only a distraction," he muttered.

She watched him as he surveyed the corrals. It was dark and calm and almost...empty.

"Are they gone then?"

"Maybe, but if so they will be back."

A bird cry sounded overhead. Swede grinned. He stepped forward, cupped his hands around his mouth and sent out a similar call.

With a happy sigh, Eva listened to the calls being exchanged. She recognized Hawk's voice. They'd both practiced bird calls growing up. That he was okay had to mean the other men were either long gone or weren't going anywhere ever again.

She hoped it was the latter. She'd never have considered herself blood thirsty, but considering what these men had done...well, she'd have nightmares for months. If she knew for a fact they were all dead...it would be easier.

And home was the only place she wanted to be. Right. Now.

As they stood in the cool darkness listening to the night, she wished she could see someone, anyone. But the darkness was so black. "It is really dark out."

"It's late, the moon is up behind those trees, and it looks to be a waning moon so it's only a sliver. Perfect for an ambush."

The casual way he said that made her blood chill. This was what *he* did, but it was not what *she* did. Unable to help herself, she reached out and slid her hand into his much bigger one.

She felt his gaze but deliberately didn't look at him.

He squeezed her hand and tugged her close to stand in front of him, there he wrapped her up into his arms and held her against his chest.

"It's going to be okay," he said, his voice low, deep.

She nodded but didn't trust her voice. She was fine. The men inside weren't. And she had no idea the injuries the other women had sustained. How was any of that okay? Given that uncertainty, she leaned back and soaked up his comfort. "We need to find Isabella."

A muscle in his jaw twitched but he nodded. "Let's check the barns."

Holding onto her hand, he led the way to the first horse barn. Under the cover of the night, they managed to get from one end to the other without seeing anyone. "Now the other one," he said, his voice close to her head. "This one might have some unpleasant surprises."

"I know," she whispered.

He led the way as the crossed the corral to the entrance to the tack room. There were no lights on anywhere. Still, the room appeared to be empty. She watched as he gave it a cursory glance then led the way to the many horse stalls. All the horses had been moved out but they had doors letting them back in. A few stood head down as if sleeping. That should mean all was well. Then again, it could also mean they'd adjusted to whatever they'd seen and experienced. She was happy for them. The adjustment wouldn't be so easy for her.

Tugged along at Swede's side, she came to an abrupt stop as his arm shot out stopping her from taking another step.

On the ground, a bullet through her head, was Isabella.

NOW THAT HE hadn't expected. Swede had been damn sure Isabella had been part of this nightmare.

"Isabella," Eva cried and rushed to the dead woman's side. Swede watched as Eva reached out to check for a pulse. A common reaction even though she had to know Isabella was dead.

Eva looked up at him, big fat tears rolling down her cheeks. "Why her?"

He couldn't say. He stood up and tugged Eva into his arms, holding her close. Damn it. Eva shouldn't be here. They should have removed the women hours ago. This had gone from bad to worse in a heartbeat.

And what had happened to the vehicle they'd heard earlier? The road ended at the hacienda. Was it bringing the commander the others had spoken about earlier? That it hadn't arrived, he presumed the team had taken care of it.

Or maybe the commander had parked down the road and came in on foot cross country. Then finding all not to his liking, had cleaned up? Made sure no one was left who could identify him? That would explain Isabella.

Then what about the rest of the men here?

"Swede?" Shadow called from the far end.

With Eva close to his side Swede walked down to the end. "What did you find?"

"More destruction."

He reached Shadow and tucked Eva behind him. "This wasn't just a kidnapping…"

The two men stared at each other. "Gang style? Two sets of rebels?"

"Maybe. The rebel camp? Anything happen there?"

Shadow shook his head. "Mason and Dane are there. So far they haven't had any movement in this direction."

"Maybe the women were going to be taken to them anyway?"

"By a supplier?" Shadow nodded slowly. "That's possible. But this…" he motioned at the carnage around them. "This is something else again."

"Maybe they thought Isabella had somehow sold them out?"

"All the traffic here yesterday? The horses." Shadow looked out to where the remaining horses grazed. "Not that the horses are much to look at."

"No, but they just need long term care," Eva said quietly. "They aren't sick as much as worn out and run down from lack of food and care."

Shadow frowned and nodded. "Then why take out Isabella?"

"For someone to take over." Eva took a deep breath. "It's not a castle but it's a really nice place."

"Could be," Shadow said noncommittally. He wasn't so sure. But then people had killed for a lot less. "Depends on who owns it now. There are laws that have to be taken into consideration."

"It's not our problem," Swede said. "The authorities need to be called and we need to get the hell out of here."

"And the horses?" Eva asked. "We need to get them out of here. They have new homes to go to. A new start. They need that." She glared at the silent man at her side. "We don't know what the new owners will do to them. And they aren't their property. All the paperwork has been taken care of already. They need to go."

Swede looked down at his watch. "It's already past two in the morning."

"Meaning?" Eva asked.

"Meaning it's almost morning." He smiled at her. "Aren't the first trailers supposed to be here at six?"

CHAPTER 16

E VA DIDN'T WANT to leave now that the worst was over. The authorities were on their way and would need to speak with her. Swede was here as were the rest of the SEALs. She had no idea what to do next, so with a nod to the men deep in conversation, she said, "I'm going back to the women."

"Wait, I'll take you," Hawk said.

She rolled her eyes at her brother's protectiveness. "I'll be fine."

In fact, with the early morning sun breaking over the horizon and the silence of the last few hours, she figured they *were* fine now. The rebels were gone and life could resume in the horrific aftermath and continue as usual.

Lifting her face to the sun, she walked back to the main house. She'd texted April a few times. The other women were just now waking up. The men had already dragged the dead men out to the barn where they were laid beside Isabella. The SEALs had also done a cursory look over the hacienda. Looking for some clue as to what and who just happened.

She reached out to open the door, but Swede's big hand reached around her and grabbed the knob before she could.

"I said I was fine."

"I know what you said," he murmured in that deep voice so close to her. How was it she hadn't noticed how damn sexy that voice was? Well she had, but she hadn't let herself dwell on what could never be. She'd been stunned by the man she'd kissed, and now everything she'd buried deep was rising to the surface and all the small details were making themselves known. That voice of his...what a number it was doing on her senses. She'd have dreams of him, she knew that now, but it would be that voice ringing through her mind that would send her back in time to this place.

It had been brutal. So how could there be anything good from it? She'd seen men killed. In front of her. Someone had tried to kidnap her, threatened to shoot her. Been shot herself – no, only a scrape. But still a wound – a scar that she'd take home with her. She'd avoided thinking about it, avoided looking at it, hoping the sting would finally leave. Instead as she grew more tired, it ached and bit at her with every movement – a little more each time.

But his voice, the memories of him would ease the pain, the horror. For that she was grateful.

"How's your side?" Swede asked.

She followed his gaze to realize she had slapped her hand over her side. "It's fine."

He snorted. "Obviously not. You're holding it as if that will minimize the pain."

"I haven't looked at it yet." She shrugged. "I should probably clean it."

"Clean what," April asked at the entrance to the living room. "Are you hurt?"

Not wanting to make a fuss, she said, "I'm fine."

"She has a burn from a bullet," Swede said, his tone stiff. "It wasn't bad, but it stings."

"Come sit. Let me take a look," April ordered. "I can at least clean it and put a bandage on it."

"You found some?"

April nodded. "I did. In the kitchen – once I could get in there."

Eva winced. "Right. I can't say I'm too eager to go back there again myself."

"He's gone," Swede said. "We'll need coffee and food soon."

"I know," she said. "It feels wrong somehow."

"Actually Lena has already gone to put on some coffee," April said with a bright smile. "She appears to be okay after her ordeal."

"She's awake? Since when?" Now Swede was all business. Eva looked at him curiously. What did he want with Lena?

"She woke up about twenty minutes ago. She got up, looked confused then started to walk away and I asked her if there was a chance of coffee." April shrugged. "Honestly she looked happy to have something normal to do."

"You stay here. I'll go find her. There're a few questions I'd like answered."

"I don't think she speaks English," April said.

Swede just nodded.

That's when Eva remembered her brother mentioning something about Swede speaking three, or was it four languages. She figured Spanish was one of them. And would be very helpful right now. She wished she'd learned something useful for a time like this. But all she knew were animals. Not exactly what was called for in this situation.

April tugged her farther into the living room and motioned for her to sit down on the couch. The other two women took one look at her and burst into tears.

"Oh my God. Is it true what April was saying? They killed Isabella and they were going to kidnap us?"

Eva winced. "I'm afraid so. At least as far as we can figure out. Looks like everyone else either took off or was shot. Except us."

"Even Isabella," Mary said tearfully. "That's horrible."

"Yes. She was shot in the head."

That sent the women off into another wailing session. She wanted to join them. Cry her outrage over all of this, but it wasn't going to happen. Not now. Not here. Not until this was over and she was home. Then she'd pull the memories out and examine them. When it was safe to do so. For now, she had to stay in control.

And…she couldn't help worry it wasn't safe yet.

"I just want to go home," Mary said. "Mom, please."

"We'll all be leaving soon," April said. "The horse trailers should be here in less than an hour."

"I want to go home now," Mary snapped.

Eva nodded. "So do I. But it doesn't much matter what we want at this point, does it?"

Mary was nothing if not persistent. Then again, she'd had a huge shock and much less time to come to terms with it than Eva had.

"And the authorities? They are on their way. Do you want them to contact the police back home to talk to you there?"

The young woman leaned back, then bolted forward. "Yes, I do. It's better than being here right now. Besides, then we're in our own country. What if we're arrested by the Mexican authorities?"

At that, her mother gave a small gasp and reached out to grab her daughter's hand. But her gaze was on Eva. "They wouldn't do that, would they?"

"There's no reason they would." But inside Eva had the same worry. There were so many things that were different here. They were in a foreign country and it didn't matter how she wanted to wrap it up – the rules – the laws – were different. Then she remembered the SEALs. "No, Swede won't let them."

Mary snorted. "If I were the authorities, he'd be the first one I'd arrest."

"Shh. Don't say that," her mother said.

Eva leaned back and closed her eyes. She might have had the same thought if he wasn't a SEAL. Hopefully, the team had permission to be here. So they might get detained, but it wasn't likely they'd be arrested. She hoped. But with that thought now in her head…

Lena arrived at the door pushing a cart ahead of her. It was full of coffee mugs and some kind of food. Muffins maybe. There was no sign of Swede.

The women let out cries of welcome. Lena gave them a wan smile and quickly served up four cups of coffee.

Eva thanked her and put it off to one side to cool. "Okay, April, take a look at the wound. Clean it if it needs to be cleaned then I can stop worrying that it's worse than it feels."

"Haven't you looked at it?" April motioned for her to lie down. "I figured Swede would have at least."

"He tried but I wouldn't let him."

The blood had dried on the material of her shirt making it tug on her skin as it was pulled away. She cried out softly.

"Sorry," April said. She poked then prodded. "It's not bad. But it's got to sting terribly." She stood up and walked to the table by the door. From Eva's position, she could see it held a few items. April returned with a bottle of peroxide and a bandage to wipe up the liquid. "This is old school and will bite, but it will clean it out nicely."

And sting it did. Eva bit her lip to stop herself from crying out. The other two women did enough gasping and moaning on her behalf.

By the time April was done, Eva was done too. She was desperate to have some food and coffee then she wanted to close her eyes and will this day to be over.

Unfortunately, it had just started.

SWEDE CHAFED AT the bit. Inaction drove him crazy. Lena had been of no help. He'd sensed fear and hadn't wanted to push her. But he wasn't leaving Eva alone. That meant he was on watch here. They needed to know what was happening with the rebel camp, so Hawk was on his way to meet Mason and get an update. Shadow had backtracked the attackers and ascertained that all had come from the rebel camp – and none would be returning. But it was the vehicle that had come for the pickup that he was currently hunting. Who had arrived? And had the same people left again? Or taken anyone new away. Swede knew Shadow loved the hunt. Dane was on watch outside the hacienda. Hopefully while he was out there he'd find out something.

No one had managed to find much and that alone was eating at him.

He spun and paced the long living room yet again. He was out of sight of the windows and yet could see all five women drinking coffee.

Eva had insisted that Lena stay and have the simple meal with them. She'd been grateful. Swede figured she didn't want to be alone after what had happened.

Eva was likely in the same position. And she was a smart cookie. After he'd taken up a position away from the window, she'd studied him as if wondering at his choice. He'd watched her facial expression change as she worked her way through it. Then the color on her face paled and she got up and moved to a chair deeper in the house. He'd caught her eye and nodded in approval. She'd been relieved and he'd been intrigued. Even tired and still in shock she was thinking.

And that was important.

It was when one stopped thinking that life bit you in the ass.

"I'm going to do a trip around the buildings again," he said to the women. It was his fourth pass. At this point they weren't bothered. Several never even acknowledged his comment but Eva did.

"Be careful."

He nodded and with a last glance at the coffee drinkers, slipped down into the direction of the kitchen. He did a fast survey to make sure it was all the same as it had been on his last pass, stopped for a moment to determine that nothing sounded out of place, that his instincts weren't screaming at him, then opened the large pantry and the small cooler to be certain no one was hiding. Nothing. He shifted to his patrol of the other buildings. He did a quick sweep. His gaze not missing but not lingering on the damage and death before him. They'd be dealt with soon enough. Although if they were in the US, the authorities would be here already. He wondered at whether the bodies should be moved to a more discreet spot, not lying inside a stall barely out of sight. He was contemplating doing so until sounds of an engine filtered his way. He moved to the side of the house where he could see the approaching vehicle.

Dane messaged him that the truck was hauling a horse trailer.

Good, they could start loading the horses. Fourteen to go.

So more than one trailer. He had to finish this pass of the outbuildings first. He quickly finished the circuit then made his way back to the living room. "Looks like the first horse trailer is arriving."

Relief washed over Eva's face. "I'm glad to hear that. We need to see these horses off to their new homes." She snagged up a stack of paperwork. "These are the documents for the remaining horses."

He frowned. "Where did you find those?"

"Lena pointed them out on the small table over there." Eva pointed to the side table beside the bookshelf. "Isabella had it all ready and waiting."

"Good. That will simplify things."

April stood up and stretched. "I'll be happy to get these horses loaded. We're supposed to go home with the last trailer, Eva."

"I hope our ride is on time," Janice said in a determined voice. "I need to get Mary out of here."

"I hear you. The sooner the better for me too," Eva said.

Swede refrained from commenting. The only way Eva was returning home was at his side. Regardless of what she wanted.

CHAPTER 17

E VA WALKED OUT to meet the truck as it pulled into the yard.

"Remember, say nothing," Swede said at her side.

"What's to say? I couldn't begin to explain this nightmare," she muttered. "But somehow we have to get the horses loaded and gone without arousing their suspicions."

"You let me handle that." Swede walked toward the truck. "You get the paperwork ready and the horses sorted. We can have this one in and out in an hour with any luck."

And somehow with Swede there keeping everything on track, and speaking Spanish like he was born to it, six horses were loaded, paperwork handed over and the truck gone before anyone knew about Isabella.

Afterwards, with the others standing in the dust, April said, "So where was Swede when we needed him yesterday?"

Eva snorted. "I know. Did you see how those horses did his bidding without a problem?"

"He's magic." April shook her head then paused. Her arm shot out pointing down the road. "And we have more company."

"Hopefully it's our ride," Mary said. "Are we allowed to leave if the authorities haven't made it here yet?"

Swede nodded. "Given the circumstances, they will

need to contact you at home if they have any questions. Otherwise we'll handle it."

Relief washed over both Janice and Mary's faces. "Great. Let's get this second load up and done. I want to go home," Janice said.

"Me too," Mary added.

It was fifteen minutes before the second trailer pulled in. This one wasn't so easy. There was a good deal of Spanish flowing before the driver was appeased. Eva heard the name Isabella a few times and some sadness on the driver's face.

She just hoped that whatever Swede said would be something close to the truth and was something the man could deal with. She held up the six sheets for the next six horses as Swede moved them to the trailer. April gave them a quick check over and they began loading.

One didn't like the trailer.

It took Swede several moments of calming him down to get him inside. Even then he wasn't impressed.

Still she stayed out of it. And that surprised her. She was normally in the thick of things. But Swede had this handled so easily he was a pleasure to watch.

The animals trusted him. Several that had been standoffish to date – or rather – when around her – now were rubbing their heads against him.

Interesting to see such an instinctive and heartwarming response. Swede stopped and tilted a muzzle toward him, talking softly to the nervous animal he was standing beside. It was almost as if he had a surreal connection to the animal.

"It's amazing, isn't it," Janice said. "He's got a pretty special way with horses."

"Yeah, he has."

"And you're pretty lucky. It's not often you get a man

like him in your life," she warned. "Be careful not to screw it up."

Then she walked away leaving Eva standing open mouthed in her wake. Her daughter stepped up and said, "Mom's right, you know. He's a stud."

And she followed her mother.

Eva snorted. Swede stepped out of the trailer at that point, the last of the horses for that load safely in and approved. "What did they say to you to put that look on your face?" he asked, a frown creasing his forehead.

"Oh nothing. Just you're such a stud I shouldn't screw up and lose you. Guys like you aren't common apparently." She glared at him, hating the wicked grin that lit up his face.

"And they are right. We are unique." He leaned forward. "So you better kiss me so they know you're not going to mess this up."

She almost growled in frustration. He laughed and scooped her up into his arms, then as he slowly lowered her to her feet again, he took her mouth in a possessive kiss that branded her as his whether she wanted it to or not. Oh what the hell. Doing what she'd been dying to do anyway, she threw her arms around his neck and kissed him back. His start of surprise was music to her. Good. Let him be off balance for a change. Lord knew he'd thrown her off balance for a long time. Damn him.

She poured out the years of wishing he'd been someone else. Wishing she'd been someone else. The right one for him. The man he was intended to be for her. Not her brother's buddy, not a SEAL. But her lover. Her love. Her one and only.

And in the face of her passion, he responded. His hands slid down her back to her hips where he pulled her tight against him. Hip to hip, pelvis to pelvis, his response was unmistakable.

Heat drove to the heart of her, and she could feel the need clawing for release. God she wanted him. She needed this. Him. Even if only for a short time. She had–

"Whoa," he said, pulling back, a flush high on his cheekbones. In a hoarse voice he said urgently, "If you don't want me to take you right here and now in front of an audience we need to dial this back."

She gasped, her body trembling from the shock of his withdrawal and the return to their surroundings. The only good thing was his big body sheltered her from those standing at the front of the truck.

Getting words out was beyond her. Forming them in her head didn't work either. What the…? When she found her voice again – she opened her mouth and blurted out the wrong thing. "What the hell just happened?"

"I have no idea," he growled. "But we're going to have to address it soon."

Mute, she shook her head. She spun on her heels and dashed into the hacienda. The cool air hit her instantly and chilled the ardor still driving her inside. Oh Lord. What had she done? She'd let her inhibitions go. That's what. Talk about shitty timing and shitting decision making. Whoa. She clapped her hands to her hot cheeks and sank into the nearest chair. She had to get a hold of herself and now.

The others would be leaving soon. She had to say good-bye. It was good they were leaving, but dear God, what was she going to do about Swede?

That man was impossible to be around before. How was she going to survive being with him now? And even worse, how was she going to survive being without him?

THERE WERE FEW times in his life he'd ever lost control. And never sexually. But to consider that the first time was with Hawk's sister, in a public place was daunting. He'd been tossed sideways by her response to his bantering. She'd dragged him into the hidden depths of a place he'd never been, and he'd gone eagerly like a puppy.

It drove him crazy that they weren't someplace where he could see this to the end. An end he knew would be something unique. He'd had a taste of her passion now. And he wanted the whole meal.

Damn she'd been hot. He looked down at his big hands, not surprised by the fine tremor that made them shake. Heat pulsed in his veins and blood still pumped into one very specific region of his body. Unfortunately. He was desperate to calm his body down before the women noticed. Hell, throwing Eva to the floor where she stood was still looking good. God, what the hell was that?

And wasn't that the same question she'd just asked? At least she hadn't been able to hide her response to him any more than he had to her. They were in this together.

Whatever "this" was.

"Hey, Swede." Mary waved at him. He took a deep breath and walked over. They were in the truck, the daughter in the back of the big rig, the whole seat to herself. "Take care of her. She's a little confused at the moment."

With a nod, he said, "Not to worry. I will."

"And April. They've both been through enough. I personally can't wait to get the hell out of here," Mary said. "We've got the paperwork. Tell Eva good-bye but we need to get on the road."

And with that, the big rig pulled out, six horses in the

back.

Swede stood in place, a silent April at his side, and watched the plume of dust rise behind the truck.

"Now it's just Eva and me."

"And when are you supposed to leave?" he asked non-committally. "I thought it was at the same time."

"No. We fly out this afternoon," April said. "I'd like to leave early if we can. Get the horses onboard and settled in as soon as possible."

"Can you do the trip on your own?" he asked.

She turned to him, her gaze searching, "I can easily. Is Eva not coming home with me?"

He shrugged, his gaze wandering the area. "She should. You both need to go home. And this is the fastest way now." He pointed at the big red truck they'd seen yesterday approach. "I presume that's your ride?"

"Yes." The relief in April's voice showed him just how hard this day had been on her.

"Good. Let's get you and the last of the horses loaded and I'll go find Eva."

"Is she okay?"

"Sure. Just tired." He paused and looked over at the remaining four horses, including the mare that had been sickly. "How did Isabella make money here? She had no horses of her own I believe."

"She gave her horses to the two men that were doing one of the trips for her. As payment. They weren't being used, and she wanted to make sure all the stock were taken care of," April said in a noncommittal voice. "They were two of the horses that went out yesterday. So we have four more to move."

"Weird. It's almost as if she knew she wouldn't be able to look after them," he said.

And her next comment caught him sideways.

"I think she didn't expect to. I know she saw a doctor many months ago for some condition but refused treatment. I never brought it up with her again."

"That would explain it."

"Then depending on the condition, the bullet might have been easier on her than a slow, painful death."

"No death is easy," Swede said. "But I'd like to think there is a good death."

April smiled up at him. "I don't know what went wrong between you and Eva. At first I thought the two of you were a complete mismatch, but now I'm not so sure."

Knowing some response was called for, he slanted his gaze in her direction. "And now what do you think?"

"I think she's intimidated. Afraid to be all she can be." April's tone was distant as if seeing something he couldn't see. "And maybe fail."

He rolled her words around in his head. Was she right? "I'm a big guy," he finally said, knowing it wasn't what she meant but not wanting to get into it further. He glanced at the living room where Eva had disappeared.

"In more ways than one," April said on a laugh.

He just barely managed to stop himself from adjusting his pants and bringing her attention to something he'd hoped had gone unnoticed.

"You're bigger than life, we'd say back East." She smiled. "You are a lot of man, and many women would find they lack the self-confidence to deal with that."

He stared at her.

She snorted. "And in typical male fashion you haven't a clue what I'm talking about."

She turned her back. "We need to get on the road. So much for being early. I'd say we're going to be hauling ass to get there on time. Do you want to go in and get her or shall I?" A sly smile took a hold of her face. "Never mind.

I'll go. Then I won't have to interrupt any sweet good-byes."

His eyebrows hit the roof.

"See, that's so sweet. You act like you know nothing of what I'm talking about." She laughed. "No worries. I'll go and grab her."

Jesus.

She walked into the hacienda. Swede looked around the other buildings, knowing Dane would be here.

Somewhere.

April came to the door a few minutes later, a frantic look on her face. "She's not here. Oh my God, where has she gone?"

CHAPTER 18

T HE ONLY THING that was good about being unconscious was the oblivion of what might have happened
when you were out cold. Eva had no idea where she was
or who had taken her. All she knew was she was lying
trussed up like a chicken in the woods somewhere with a
hell of a headache. Not pain but a weird grogginess and
thick head as if she'd been drugged. Why and how she
didn't know. The last thing she remembered was the
hottest most passionate interlude she'd ever had and with
Swede, of all people, and damn near in public. Like what
the hell had she done? Besides lost her head.

And what had it gotten her? Kidnapped and hauled
out into the woods by some asshole. She was here. Where
was Swede? She dragged through her memories looking
for answers.

Right – She'd rushed inside to calm down and to
avoid facing the others in the state she was in. She
remembered collapsing onto a chair, shocked at her
unbelievable response.

And then what?

Nothing. After that it was all a fog. She tried to shift
position but found herself only able to roll over. And that
didn't improve matters. She rolled onto her back again
and tried a different maneuver. With her hands tied in
front of her, she scrambled up on her knees. After a
couple of deep breaths, she managed to hop to her feet.

The brush was still higher than her head. She cocked an ear and listened but there was nothing. No birds, no animals rustling in the brush. Nothing. Why weren't there voices at least? She had to be taken by someone. So what did they do, dump her in the bushes for later? And what if there was no later? What if Swede or Hawk killed the asshole, stopping him from coming back for her?

That horrific scenario rippled through her mind in a never ending wave. Was one better than the other? She had no idea. She studied the knots in front of her. Surely there was a way to undo them? Maybe not her hands but what about her feet? Knowing it was going to take a lot of effort to get back up, but hoping she'd be able to do so with her feet no longer tied up, she plonked down on her butt to study the knots. With a little effort she managed to loosen the tie around her right ankle. It took another ten minutes of playing with the rope for the knots to fall apart. Yay. Her feet were free. Nice. She took another look at the knots on her wrists then got busy. Using her teeth, she could loosen up those knots too. Five more minutes and her hands were free. Thank God.

She pulled her phone out and checked for reception. Only one bar. She quickly sent a text to her brother and Swede.

Putting her phone away, she looked around.

Now to find her way back to the hacienda. The one truck had left while she'd been in the living room, she remembered hearing everyone calling out good-byes.

Then again, after her sprint inside to avoid the others – to avoid Swede – she couldn't blame them for giving her space.

But this much space was a little ridiculous.

Sigh.

She opened her mouth and in an echo of days gone

by she called out for help using her old Hawk cry that she and her brother had perfected while growing up.

She listened. No answer.

Taking a few steps forward, she peered through the brush. No one there. She was alone. Well, that was fine with her. But she didn't want to be here when her kidnapper returned.

She needed a new hiding place. She bent down and picked up the bindings. Maybe she could confuse her kidnappers by making them doubt the bush where they'd left her. She checked the trees around her to see if they'd left any markings. There weren't any that she could figure out. Still, it would make sense. Although she was horrible at navigating.

She did a quick check in all directions, looked at where the sun was above her and realized she needed to move in the other direction.

Emboldened by having gotten out of her bindings, she picked up her feet and started to run. She was leaving footprints but that couldn't be helped. She had to move and the faster the better.

Now to find someone or something that could help. Surely considering the sun was still high above she hadn't been missing for very long.

April should have noticed as they should be leaving soon, but if she wasn't there at the time of departure – then what? The horses had to go. They had to catch the flight. It was going to be a huge headache to reschedule. Not to mention once the authorities arrived how much more difficult it could be to get the horses out of there?

Damn it. Why had Isabella been killed? She was the one they needed to complete the horse rescue.

Frustrated and confused, more than a little scared, she kept on running.

Swede, please find me. And fast.

SWEDE DID THE fastest sweep of the house and outbuildings he'd done yet. His heart was pounding. How could she have disappeared? When? He had to believe she'd been taken. She couldn't be that upset with him surely? And even if she was, she wasn't a fool. And these horses meant the world to her. Getting them loaded and out of here was huge. So where was she? She was supposed to depart with this last load herself. She knew that.

April stopped him. "Look, I don't want to leave her behind, but I have to go as that flight is scheduled and even now I'm not sure I can catch it. If we miss it, the horses–"

"Go," he said instantly. "You need to move the horses. You know I'll find her. I won't have to worry about you in the meantime. I can't go after her and keep you safe."

He watched the indecisions on her face as her gaze went from the horses and trailer and impatient driver then back to him. "I hate to leave her," she cried out softly. "I feel like I'm abandoning her."

"Go," he urged. "I'll keep you in the loop."

She brought out her cell phone and gave him her number. "Call me. And if it's bad news…"

"Then there'd be nothing you could do anyway."

He watched as she, torn but seeing commonsense, walked to the front of the truck. "Make sure you let me know as soon as you find something out." And with a final glance at the hacienda, she shook her head and hopped in the truck. It fired up and slowly drove away.

"No sign of her," Dane said from behind him. "How

long has she been gone?"

"Maybe thirty minutes," Swede said, swearing. "I'm going to track how she was taken out of here."

"I was in the barn sending fingerprints to base," Dane said. "See if any of the men here are some of the ones we are looking for." He shook his head. "She didn't go through there."

Swede nodded. "Well, they are dead and we need to make sure that Eva doesn't end up the same way."

"She'd have been taken out by horseback. I doubt we'd have missed a vehicle."

Swede agreed. "Except there aren't any spare horses here. The last four just left."

In fact, the place had a desolated look to it.

"Everyone is gone now," Dane said. "At least it will be easier to focus on finding her."

Swede turned to stare at him. "Not everyone is gone. Lena the servant girl should be here."

Dane shook his head slowly. "I haven't seen any sign of her."

Shit. Swede bolted inside. "She's either taken Eva or she's been taken *with* Eva."

"How big and strong is she?"

Swede shook his head. "She's small and slight in stature. She couldn't have lifted Eva and certainly not over the back of a horse."

"Then she met someone or has been taken as well."

"Either way, we need to find her."

A few minutes later, along the back of the pasture, he found fresh horse tracks. One horse. Lighter when it arrived than when it left. "God damn it."

"Shadow is tracking the horse already," Dane said, coming up behind him and pointing in the distance.

"Do you think the horse has both women?"

"No idea, but as the rest of the house appears empty and there's only one set of tracks, it looks likely."

Damn. His phone buzzed. A text from Eva.

He read it quickly. Jesus.

CHAPTER 19

EVA KNEW THE heat was going to get her soon. That and lack of water. She should be able to survive for at least two days without water, but given that she'd bolted out of the hiding place in the dead of heat, she was burning through her energy almost immediately.

She needed to find shade and stay in one spot. Let the men find her.

The right men.

She couldn't see anything for miles. But someone had to be out looking for her. She stopped and leaned against a small bush to catch her breath, to cool down. She called out in her hawk cry yet again. She hoped someone who could recognize it for the call of help it was would find her.

Added to everything else, she was afraid she was starting to hear things. She peered around the far side of the tree. Was someone coming? This was a shitty hiding spot if there ever was one. Frantic now, she swiveled, looking for something bigger. But there was nothing close. Shit. Shit.

She bolted toward a clump of brush a hundred yards away. Believing her life was on the line, she bolted as fast as she could and dove into the center. She landed and knocked the wind out of herself. She lay there shuddering, waiting for someone to jump her. Frozen in place and petrified, she couldn't breathe as she waited.

Only no one came. Taking a risk she pulled into a tight ball and peered out between the greenery.

There was no one there.

God. She hung her head feeling like an idiot. It had to be the heat. Or the fear.

She leaned her head back. Her brother would come.

If he knew.

Swede would come.

If he could.

Tears filled her eyes at the thought of something happening to the big oaf. She shook her head and closed her eyes, willing her body to rest, her mind to calm down. She had to stay strong. She had to stay alive.

Then when she was rescued, she'd give them all hell. Especially Swede.

THE HUNT WAS on. The house and property were empty. No sign of the authorities that should have arrived hours ago and the bodies in the barn were getting a whole lot riper.

Hawk and Mason were looking for Eva from the rebel side. They'd meet in the middle.

Shadow was hunting as Shadow did best. He'd found the tracks leading away from the hacienda. He was still moving in the direction of the rebel camp, but there was no sign of her or the kidnapper yet.

Shadow was the best tracker. He'd find her.

Swede's fist balled up. "God damn it." He looked up at Dane. "Where the fuck is she?"

"Easy man. We'll find her." Dane motioned to the trucks parked in front. "Take yours or Isabella's?"

"Isabella's," Swede said, leaping toward it. "Mine's a

rental and might not stand up to what's coming."

"Got keys?" Dane asked, following behind Swede as he dashed to the front of the house.

"No, and I don't need any."

"I hear you there." By the time Dane had reached the passenger door, Swede had the truck hotwired and running. "There's still a half a tank of gas, we're good to go."

"I'll let the others know we're driving."

"Good," Swede said. "You keep the others in the loop while I find Eva." He drove the truck down the fence line just outside the property.

"So is there something you want to say?" Dane asked quietly. "About Eva?"

"Hell no."

"And what about saying something to Hawk?"

"No need." Swede shot him a hard lance. "He already knows."

At least he assumed he did.

"Even if he doesn't for sure, not much passes by him so if he didn't – then he does now," Dane said.

Swede nodded but he didn't say anything.

"Hawk has a different perspective on relationships now. It might be okay."

"And so do you," Swede snorted. "So are we done with all this heart to heart?"

Dane laughed, his guffaws rolling across the land.

Swede growled. "Really?"

"Oh, it's priceless."

Swede's growl started in the back of his throat.

"Like I'm worried." Dane sniggered. "Of course it's more fun watching it happen to someone else."

Swede shook his head. "Yeah but when does this horrible feeling ever calm down?"

"If you're lucky – never." Dane gave him a commiserating look. "It will get better, though."

"Yeah, when?"

They approached the first set of tracks. Swede shut off the truck and they hopped out to take a closer look.

"Same horse."

Swede concurred. They got back into the truck and kept driving in the same direction. The dry loose surface made the tracks visible and easy to follow. They drove another few miles following the line into the emptiness.

"We can't be too far from the rebel headquarters," Dane said.

"I was just thinking that," Swede agreed and hit the brakes suddenly.

"What–"

Swede pointed at tracks that headed toward a clump of stick pines. More brush than trees. The lack of water had stunted their growth, but it was big enough to hide someone and showed signs of mistreatment. Several branches had been snapped the wild grasses sparse along the dry ground were crushed. He parked and hopped out. They both walked the area, looking to read the story of what had happened.

And it wasn't hard to sort out. Dane walked through in the middle of the brush. "Rope fibers over here," Dane called out.

"She's walked out of here then…" Swede followed the tracks. "She's taken off running from this point." He gazed in the distance, following the tracks.

They climbed back into the truck, Swede driving and Dane updating the team. Swede drove along the side of the tracks. "She couldn't have gone far."

"She'll be here. We'll find her."

Swede knew they would. But would it be in time?

He slowed the truck to a stop to read the change in direction.

And saw something in the distance. He reached out and grabbed Dane's arm.

"Look…"

"It's Shadow."

They pulled up beside him.

He waved them on, calling out, "She's got to be close. Her footsteps are getting more tired. She's ready to lie down."

They surveyed the vast countryside. Up ahead were several stands of trees.

"Let's go."

With Shadow riding on the back of the box, they quickly closed the distance.

Swede was parked and out before Shadow had jumped out of the back.

Swede raced to the trees.

And found her.

CHAPTER 20

Eva could feel her body shifting. She struggled to hit the person holding her. And found her arms floppy, uncoordinated.

"Shh, easy."

That voice…She opened her eyes. "Swede?"

"Yeah, baby, it's me."

She stared in a daze. "Really? I figured you'd never find me."

"Of course I did. You know I'd never stop until I did."

"Thank God," she whispered. A water bottle was held to her mouth and cool refreshing water dropped in. She drank greedily. "Thanks," she whispered when she could, her voice raspy still.

"Have a little more."

She took a second drink and sighed happily. She smiled up at Swede. "Took you long enough."

Shadow's head popped up behind Swede. "Yeah, he's been mooning over you like a lost puppy."

Swede snorted and stood up. "Like hell," he said good-naturedly.

Dane picked it up. "Yep, he didn't want anything to happen to you."

"Yeah." She smiled. "My brother would kill him if that happened."

"Actually your brother might kill him anyway,"

Shadow said, a huge grin on his face.

Eva glanced up at Swede in shock. "Why?"

Silence. But the huge grins on the other two men had her suspicions rising. She studied the strong blank face in front of her. "Swede?"

"It's nothing."

She didn't understand what was going on but suspected it had to do with the attraction between them. She shook her head. "It will be okay."

"What will be okay?" Hawk's voice called out. "Glad to see you found her."

Her brother's warm caring voice washed over her as she was transferred to his arms and hugged gently. "Ah, Eva, you do get yourself into trouble."

She looped her arms around his neck. "I didn't get kidnapped on purpose." She was tired now. The heat and panic, the fear taking its toll. "Besides, I'd be happy to go home and live a calm boring life."

"Somehow I doubt that's going to happen." He hugged her tight. "Let's get you back."

"Back where?" She tried to lean back and stare up at him. "I doubt anything is left to go back to, is there?"

"Sure, the building is still standing." He glanced at the others. "But all the others are gone."

She blinked several times, trying to figure out what he meant. "April?"

"She left with the horses." Swede reached out and squeezed her shoulder. "We couldn't find you and the flight was leaving...so I sent her on alone. She didn't want to go."

"It's fine..." She yawned. "The horses needed to go. There's been enough death and destruction already. Let's save who we can."

"Trust you to make the horses a who and not a what,"

Hawk said. "But we have to get you to a doctor and get you home somehow."

"I'm fine. Hot and tired and well…" She smiled. "A little on the hungry side."

"Always."

She struggled to stand up on her own two feet. She understood her brother's need to hold her, she felt the same, but she didn't want to be a burden to the men. She needed them now. She had no way to get home. Her flight had left, and she had to make other arrangements. Somehow. And that was shitty as the flights hadn't been cheap. Being a rescue there'd not been any money to help the volunteers out so they'd come on their own nickel. The airline might give her another flight, but until she could contact them, there was no way to know what they'd say.

"We don't have anything here, but if we get you back to the hacienda there is food."

She made a face. "I have to go back as the rest of my stuff is there I presume, but damn it's not a place I want to stay." Her gaze went from one of the men to the other. "Please tell me that those poor people have been collected and taken to the morgue."

"The authorities hadn't arrived when we left."

"I was afraid of that." She winced. "You did call them, right?"

"Sure. But it's still hours away and if they need to pull a team together…" Hawk let his voice drift off.

"Or if the messages or team were intercepted, no one is coming at all."

"Oh someone will come," Mason said. "We've got our country involved now. The place will likely be crowded with people when we get back."

With her brother's assistance, she was helped to the

truck. "Where did you get this?" she asked as she struggled to get up into the cab. Her head spun and she was forced to grab onto the side.

Swede snagged her up and carefully deposited her on the front bench seat. "It's Isabella's."

"Oh," she said in a small voice. "So many dead and for what?"

"I'm not sure we know yet," Hawk said in a hard voice.

She looked around, realizing that the other men were gone. "Where are they?"

"They're heading back to see if there have been any changes at the rebel camp. Shadow is checking our tracks back to the hacienda to make sure we weren't followed on our way here."

"I'm sorry to take you away. I'm fine with Swede if you want to go with the others."

"I'll be sticking around." Hawk jumped into the driver's seat and started up the vehicle. He tapped the gas gauge. "Looks like we have enough."

"If we're going straight back we do." Swede sat on the passenger's door side effectively bookending Eva in the middle.

A place she was happy to stay. She was sad she was missing out on flying home with the horses but given where she'd been a few hours ago, she was just happy to be with the men.

She closed her eyes and instinctively snuggled closer to Swede, letting her head drop to his shoulder. She closed her eyes.

The rough ground they traveled on stopped her from being able to sleep. Yet knowing she was safe was such a relief she just wanted to savor the feeling. A particularly rough bump had her body lurching forward. Swede instinctively reached out and wrapped his arm round her shoulder tucking her close.

Like he'd done from the start.

"Thanks, Hawk."

"Thanks for what?" he asked, his voice casual, distracted. Likely from the rough ground.

"For sending Swede to look after me."

Swede stiffened under her head. She could feel the tension vibrating through him. "Now if I'd only managed to do that," he snapped.

"You did, several times," she murmured. "Just because they got to me eventually doesn't matter. Besides you found me."

"Yeah, big deal," the big man muttered.

She opened her eyes to see him staring out the window, a muscle on his jaw rippling in an aggravated motion.

"Hey, it is to me – so thank you."

He slanted that hard gaze her way and snorted. With a very precise, "You're welcome," he returned to glaring out the window.

She wasn't sure what was bugging him and turned to look at her brother, catching the amusement on his face.

"What is so funny?" she asked.

"Nothing."

She sighed. "Right."

"Hey, I've been there myself. Glad I'm not anymore."

She studied his words and didn't get it. She opened her mouth to ask when Swede gripped her shoulder in warning.

Disgruntled she subsided. "Fine," she muttered to him in a low voice. "You'll have to explain later."

His fingers squeezed then released.

She'd take that as a yes.

★

SWEDE WASN'T SURE what to say around Hawk. Somehow the relationship between his sister and him had changed. He didn't know to what, and she didn't appear to understand the problems this was going to create. Hell, it was already creating trouble.

Not that he was going to back down.

Not until he figured out if this was serious.

Eva had always been in the background. Always a nudging reminder that she was waiting for him.

"So, Swede, ready for days off?" Hawk asked, a thread of humor in his voice.

"It won't be for a while, surely?" Although that would be nice.

"Not until we get to the bottom of the rebel camp, no, but it's always nice to look ahead and plan our days, isn't it?"

What the hell was he getting at? And why? His sister? Hawk would be spending the days he had free with Mia. No way in hell he wasn't.

So how was Swede going to spend it with Eva and have Hawk's blessing.

He needed to have a private talk with Hawk. Somehow. But he wasn't looking forward to it. He wasn't even sure what to say. He didn't have answers.

There'd been no time. And she'd go home soon. Sure she wasn't far away but it was a few hours. Same as Hawk and Mia, although there was talk of Mia moving closer. The thought of Eva a long way away was a punch in his gut. He wasn't going to live that way. Long distance relationships were hell. Yet he could hardly move her closer. She had land together with her brother. And animals that needed her. She was country. He lived on base. Like so not compatible. He wouldn't leave the SEALs but neither could he ask her to leave the animals. They were both important.

In Mason and Tesla's case, the government was all over her. She could work wherever she wanted to. So the base was perfect for her and Mason's relationship. Hawk was working on Mia, and it looked like that was going to happen. Mariella, Dane's partner was already in San Diego so that was perfect. It was him and Eva that wasn't.

Then his head was in the clouds and he needed to get into the game. Not her.

He groaned and leaned his head back. And once again scraped the roof of the cab. He swore under his breath.

"Did you hit your head?" She asked sleepily beside him.

"Again, no worries. It's normal for him," Hawk said in a teasing tone. "The guy doesn't fit anywhere."

So damn true and never had he felt like he didn't fit the surroundings more than he did right now. And hated it.

"He fits everywhere," Eva said stoutly, shifting to a sitting position. "Besides he's special, we have to make allowances."

Hawk gave a shout of laughter. Swede glared at him.

And that just sent Hawk off in a series of chuckles.

Swede sank as much as he could in the seat and glared out the window.

"You should be nice to him, Hawk," Eva scolded. "He's your friend."

That just sent Hawk into louder laughter.

"Glad you're enjoying this," Swede snapped.

"Oh I am. Been there, done that, and so damn glad to be on the other side."

"Other side of what," Eva said. "What the hell are

you talking about?"

Swede watched as Eva got mad at her brother. Good, it took the heat off him. He listened in amusement as she ripped into her brother in defense of him.

Only it was having the opposite effect. Hawk was laughing out of control with every new scold she sent him.

This had to stop.

He dragged her onto his lap and said, "You're wasting your time."

Only she was too incensed at her brother to hear him. Swede sighed and figured there was only one way to stop her. He snagged her chin and sealed her mouth with his and kissed her. Long, deep and hard.

The fight went out of her instantly.

And him.

Whatever was going on here – it was already over for him.

She was his. Come what may, they'd just have to work it out. Because he wasn't letting her go.

Ever.

When he lifted his head, she collapsed against him and snapped in a voice that held no heat, "You have to stop doing that."

"Doing what?" he said in amusement.

"Scrambling my brains," she muttered.

"Never."

Hawk snickered at his side.

Swede tore his glance away from the woman collapsed in his arms to her brother and his best friend. As if waiting for the judgment. Waiting for the fury. Waiting for him to say the words that showed his disapproval.

Instead, Hawk, still grinning, managed to say, "Damn well time."

Eva straightened, opened her mouth to question her brother, but Swede pulled her back against him. "Enough," he said. "Leave it now."

She shot him a look. "Who died and made you boss."

He grinned and said with humor threading his voice, "Good thing I like spitfires."

CHAPTER 21

S HE SHOOK HER head. "You aren't making any sense."

Well, he was making sense, but she didn't quite believe it. And she wasn't sure she wanted him. Well she did, but she wanted the whole thing. The marriage, the white house and picket fence and the kids. She figured that if he ever heard that part, he'd book it back to the base and stay there. He was commitment phobic. Like her brother.

No, like her brother had been. And if Hawk had changed then maybe Swede could too. Only it was too damn confusing. All of it.

Hard pings slammed into the truck.

Hawk gunned it, but the truck ground to a hard slamming halt – as the engine died. She'd have gone tumbling if Swede hadn't grabbed her. He was out of the vehicle, her in his arms as he hit the ground running for the trees.

Belatedly she realized someone was shooting at them.

She peered over Swede's back to see her brother sending return fire as he raced behind them.

She clung to Swede's neck, petrified as her brother followed. They dashed into the trees, and she was slammed against a trunk with Swede standing protectively over her, a gun in his hand. Where had he gotten that one? She shuddered as more bullets fired in her direction, then Swede returned fire.

"Hawk?" she screamed. "Where are you?"

"I'm here, sis, not to worry," he said from beside her. "I'm safe."

"Oh thank God."

"Don't be too thankful yet," he said, "We're pinned down."

"Maybe not," Swede said. "I took one out for sure."

"I know I hit one but don't think it was enough to kill him."

"They'll likely finish him off for you," Swede said. "They don't seem to be worried about keeping any man who isn't fully functioning."

"Right. Soldiers are only good as long as they can fight."

"How far are we from the hacienda?" she asked. "Surely it can't be far."

"It isn't. It's just over the rise, but we still have to cross too much open ground to make it."

"And they have more men they can call on," Hawk said.

"We do too," Eva said. "There's Mason and Dane. And Shadow is out there somewhere."

An odd sounding single shot rang out in the hot afternoon air.

"What was that?" she asked in a panic.

"That," Swede said with a great deal of satisfaction to his voice, "was Shadow."

She brightened. A second shot rang out then a flurry of gunfire was exchanged at a distance.

Silence.

"Shit, is he okay?"

"Knowing Shadow he was long gone by the time the

bullet left the barrel."

"Maybe, but not everyone can stay hidden forever. He's been very lucky up to now."

"Luck?" Hawk said in a pained voice. "Do I have to remind you again, we are SEALs. Luck had nothing to do with it."

She snorted.

A bird's cry sounded overhead.

"Good. That's Shadow."

"So we're safe?"

"Yeah, he's taken out the shooters."

"What if others are out there we don't know about," she said nervously. Swede went to step out into the open, but she grabbed his hand and pulled him back. "Don't, it's not safe."

He patted her hand. "If Shadow says it's safe, it's safe. We trust each other."

"But he might have missed one. Everyone makes mistakes."

Both Hawk and Swede looked at her and rolled their eyes. She groaned.

"Fine then, I'll go first." And before they could stop her she stepped out into the open.

Swede grabbed her and slammed her back into the bushes.

"Ha," she snapped. "I thought it was safe."

He glared at her. "It is. But like hell you're going out there first."

Hawk laughed. "Come on, we're going to have to get her away from here. Then we're shutting down the rebel camp. Let's get her to the hacienda and the authorities."

Eva had been happy to walk out of cover with the men and had even taken a few steps in the direction of the hacienda when she heard his words. She spun on him. "What?"

Hawk winced. "Eva…" he warned.

She shook her head. "Oh no you don't. You're not leaving me to clean this shit up."

"That's not what I meant," he snapped. "And you know it."

With a glare meant to incinerate him, she said, "So who the hell do you think they are going to look to for answers when you're not there? They aren't going to listen to a word I say. They are going to throw me in jail and keep me there until this mess is sorted out." She wound up as she spoke. "Like hell you're going to dump me with them."

"Now, Eva, be reasonable…" Swede started to say.

She rounded on him and poked him in the chest with her index finger. "Don't say it. This is not a good plan. Hell, it's no plan at all. I'm still in danger and now from the authorities as well. I'm not…" she poked him again, "going to be the only one left standing…" she rose to her tiptoes to glare up at him, "to deal with them."

"She has a point. They'll try to keep her until the US government clears this up."

"Like that's going to happen." She turned on her brother. "Do they know you are here? Do they know what you are doing? Or is it all hush hush again?"

"Of course it's hush hush, but that doesn't mean we can walk into another country and do what we want without letting them know. All the countries talk. We have agreements and join forces a lot of the time."

"But that doesn't mean the local yahoos at the hacienda are going to know anything about it though, are they?" At the look on his face, she settled back. "Exactly. And I'm not the patsy who's going to try and explain this nightmare to them."

SWEDE LOOKED FROM Hawk to her and back to her brother. "She's right."

"I don't care if she is or not, I'm not going to take my sister into an op that's dangerous as all hell."

Eva snorted. "Too late."

She was right there. "Let's go to the hacienda so I can gather my stuff – my passport at the very least so I can get home safely." She took a deep breath. "Then stash me somewhere safe and go do your thing."

He glared at her. "It's hardly that easy."

She glanced at the damaged truck. "It would have been easier if there were still wheels so I could drive to the closest town and grab a room for the night." She shrugged and resolutely started walking back to the hacienda. "Regardless, I have to have my wallet and ID."

They could get her back in without it but having her passport made life that much easier. Given the circumstances they could do without it though. His prime concern was keeping her safe. Who knew who had been paid off at any level of the government? They hadn't arrived when they should have, and who knew if the ones coming weren't going to just shoot her on first sight.

And she had a valid point. How was she to explain the mess of bodies and exclude their presence? If the men coming didn't know about the joint operation – and they wouldn't – then of course they would look at anything she said with suspicion?

He fell into step. Best would be if they could get the stuff they needed and get her into town until they could return. If they didn't return she'd be able to get home on her own.

And if they did return then they'd take her back with them. With permission or not. He didn't particularly care at this point.

She was going home, and he was going to make sure she got there safe and sound.

CHAPTER 22

S HE CRESTED THE hill, more tired and worn out than she thought possible but using temper to keep her muscles moving forward. She stopped and looked ahead. It was there. A deceptively innocent look to the place. She shook her head. She wanted to go home and never leave again. This had been the trip from hell.

The back pasture looked the same as she'd seen it last time. With the men walking quietly behind her, she entered the first barn, grateful of the coolness of the interior and walked with Swede now slightly ahead through to the second barn. "Where have they been put?"

"They were here." He motioned to the stall up ahead. He leaned over for a look and froze.

"What is it?"

He spun and looked around as if to reorient himself. "They're gone."

"What?" Hawk said. "Really?" He reached the other stall and shook his head. He quickly ran up one side and down the other, checking on each. "There's no sign of them here."

"The authorities," Eva said. "They must have come and gone."

The men looked at her then at each other before bolting for the main house. She was right behind them. In the kitchen they stopped and listened.

Eva chafed at the bit. She wanted to race to her room,

grab her stuff and run. As in all the way back home.

She was tired, sore and desperately in need of some sleep. And her feet were killing her. She studied the runners never meant for hard walking in the brush. They were pretty much destroyed. And she had blisters on her heels. Still, she was alive and safe. She could live with a few blisters.

WHERE THE HELL were the bodies?

"They have to be somewhere," he said. "Unless like Eva said, they've been loaded up and hauled away."

"I hope so." Hawk led the way through the kitchen into the living room, Swede on his heels. There was no one there. Swede strode to the front door and stared out the window. "There are no vehicles here."

"Not now. Could they have been and gone and done what they needed to do in the time we were gone?"

Swede looked down at his watch. "Not in our country. This place would be cordoned off and we'd have teams of people for something this large."

"But we're not at home and we don't know that the authorities have even arrived yet," Hawk said looking around. "Where were the victims lying?"

Swede pointed to the bloodstains on the floor – at least he tried too. It was a wooden floor and from the looks of it someone had attempted to clean up the blood with some kind of hot steamer. The wood still had a moist look to the finish. "Someone is trying to make it look like this never happened."

Eva ran forward. "How? There were bodies here and here." She pointed out several other locations. "But it's all been mopped up."

Swede walked back to the kitchen. "The blood back here is gone too."

They looked at each other in confusion. "I have to find my bag," Eva cried suddenly. "If they cleaned up, did they remove my belongings?" She bolted for the upstairs, the men behind her. Hawk called out, "There was no visible blood in the stall either."

"No, easy enough to throw new straw on top of the old or take the old away with them. Another few weeks of this dust, and it won't be visible anyway."

"Straw is used specifically for soaking up messes like that to begin with so chances are good very little if any of the blood made it to the bottom of the stall."

"Which was dirt floor not wooden boards."

"So even less to clean up."

Swede stopped at the open doorway, letting Eva race inside. In a low voice, he muttered to Hawk, "We need to check on the women who went home."

"Right." Hawk moved off a few steps and made a few calls.

Swede turned his attention back to Eva.

"Is it here?"

"My sweater is not. My passport…" she lifted the mattress and checked the underside pocket of the sheet, "Is!" She pulled out her wallet that had a side pocket big enough to hold her passport.

"So they missed that," he said in an admiring tone of voice. "Nice."

"But the rest of my clothes and overnight bag are gone," she said looking around.

"But you hid your purse? Why?"

She smiled. "Hawk's influence to never be too trusting. With everything crazy going on, I didn't want someone to grab my ID and run off with it."

He nodded. "Good thing. But you're sure your clothes and bags…"

"They aren't here." She slammed the door shut then walked back to the closet she'd already checked. She spun around, looked at the single bed and dropped to the floor. "Someone tried to erase the fact that I was ever here."

"And the fact that anything happened."

She rubbed her forehead. "What the hell is going on?"

"I don't know. But we will find out." He motioned at her to come out. "We'll check the other rooms to make sure you weren't just moved to a different bedroom while Hawk makes his calls."

In a systematic way, they searched each of the other bedrooms. "They are all empty."

Eva turned to look at Swede. "Let's check Isabella's room. And Lena's. Surely that will answer some of these questions."

With Hawk's agreement they all headed downstairs. Swede had sent a message to the others letting them know what they'd found. Surely someone had answers.

At Isabella's room, they realized there'd be no answers here.

It had been stripped clean. Including the bedding.

With a horrible thought formulating in the back of his mind, Swede went through the motions of searching the room. But it had been cleaned out.

"Why?"

"Because they didn't want the men's bodies bringing up questions as to where they came from," he said softly.

She shook her head in confusion.

He didn't blame her. This was too bizarre.

Hawk stepped up into the room. "Apparently there was a lot of publicity involved with this rescue?" He quirked an eyebrow at Eva.

She nodded. "Some for sure. Not tons as Isabella wanted none of it actually. So we tried to keep it down." She smiled at the memory. "Isabella was quite upset when she heard that Janice had planned a media reception at the other end."

"Well, the horses arrived safely."

"Oh good." Eva's face widened into a big grin.

"But the women…" he took a deep breath and added, "are in the hospital."

She gasped, her hand going to her chest. "But they should have been safe. They were home."

"There was a car accident that took out both mother and daughter."

Eva stared at him in shock. "Deliberately," she whispered.

"Maybe." Swede wasn't surprised. He'd been afraid of just that the cleanup at the hacienda had happened while they were gone. "April?"

"No answers yet. I have someone trying to find her."

Eva collapsed onto the bed, big fat tears rolling down her cheeks. "Who are these people? What are they doing here?" She waved her hand around in the empty room. "This does not make sense."

"It does if this was a rebel stronghold and Isabella went over the boundaries of her agreement. Or maybe they just decided this would work as their new headquarters."

Hawk's phone went off. "Mason said the property doesn't have Isabella's name on it. In fact, no one quite knows who she is."

CHAPTER 23

THIS WAS TOO much. Eva tried to grasp what she was being told. "So the hacienda isn't hers? The hired hands didn't work for her?"

"I'm thinking this belongs to someone on the rebel hierarchy, and Isabella was likely family and part of the elaborate front to keep the goings on in the back here quiet."

Hawk growled. "This whole scenario could just as easily have been treated as a terrorist exercise once they realized they had a problem."

"With Isabella not wanting publicity but bringing all the strangers in here chances are she signed her own death warrant and didn't realize it." Hawk looked down at his cell phone. "We're sketchy on her background details, but it could be that the do-gooder in her figured the chance was worth it. Save the horses and no one would be the wiser. Or she figured it wouldn't matter. Or didn't care. Considering her health issues, maybe this was her way to thumb her nose at the rebels."

"But someone else had a different opinion." Swede filled Eva in on Isabella's health problems.

"What about Lena? Did anyone find her yet?" Eva shook her head. "What poor Isabella must have been through."

"That's a whole different problem." Swede held out a hand. "Let's check her quarters to make sure it's in the same condition as Isabella's then I suggest we take my truck and go to the nearest town."

"Lena called the police – or was supposed to," Eva said. "I remember the morning she brought coffee and the dead men had been moved. She looked exhausted but still so panicked."

"Makes sense. She's either involved willingly or un-willingly. But she kept you all here and calm until she was given further orders."

"But why?"

"At this point we can only guess, but you are still a woman alone. You were also the one person they could get the information on the others from. That they might have already hit Janice and her daughter means they found records of where you live in Isabella's papers."

At Lena's quarters they opened the door to a completely different scenario. This was fully furnished and lived in. Clothes and personal touches were everywhere.

"So she is still here," Eva said. "How does that work?"

"I'm presuming she's with the rebels and she'll have a place as long as she's needed. And help keep up the charade as they replace Isabella."

"That is way too much," Eva cried. "Surely that can't be."

"We don't have all the answers yet, but we can't stay here, in case they come back." He glanced around, his gaze seeming to miss nothing.

"I'd be more than happy to see the backside of this place." It had been terrible when there had been bodies here, but to know that they'd been removed and the place cleaned up while they weren't around was beyond creepy.

She wanted nothing to do with the place.

But she did want to know about Isabella. "Do you think they buried her here?"

Swede shrugged his shoulders. "Likely out in the middle of nowhere so they wouldn't be easily found."

"But buried and not just left for the animals, right?" she asked in a small voice.

"There's no way to know at this point. They didn't have much time and they had no heavy equipment," Hawk said. "So their options were limited."

She gulped. "Can we leave now?" She wrapped her arms around her chest and tried to warm up from the chill that was rapidly overtaking her. "Please."

"Yes, it's time."

"Someone is coming."

Swede nodded. "I'll check it out."

"Good." Hawk held out his hand for Eva's. "Come on. Let's get you out of here."

She was in full agreement. The faster the better for her. She wanted out and now.

It couldn't happen fast enough. But apparently it wasn't so easy. She waited inside the center of the hacienda with her brother while Swede checked out the new arrival. "It's going to be Mason. Don't worry."

She nodded at her brother. "Good. Then what's taking so long?"

And just like that, voices came from the front door. Swede's voice mixed with Shadow and Mason. "No Dane?" She asked.

"He'll be on watch. There is always one of us on duty. Always."

Good. She felt safer that way. Until this shit was over she felt more secure knowing that someone was watching. Swede walked around the corner, saw her and smiled reassuring at her.

He wrapped an arm around her shoulders and tugged her close. "Let's go."

With her wallet in her hand, she said, "I wish I had my clothes with me."

"We'll get something in town for you."

She nodded and let him lead her out of the hacienda. "Can we get food at the same time?"

"How about right after."

"Yeah, that works."

Outside, he walked her to the passenger side of the large truck he'd driven to the hacienda and helped her into the front of the vehicle. He stood and waited and watched as she buckled herself in. Only then did he close the door, locking her inside.

She slouched against the seat and waited for the others to get in. Mason was behind the wheel. Swede walked back inside. "Isn't he coming with us?" she said suddenly, realizing Swede hadn't returned.

"He is. But he's doing one last look first."

She let her pent up breath out slowly in relief. Thank God. She didn't want to leave him behind. She relaxed into the seat. "Hope he's not long," she muttered. "I'm thinking food should be next."

"Hungry?"

"Yeah, so very hungry." She laughed. "And tired. And desperately in need of a shower."

"All three are coming up."

"Good." She closed her eyes. "Tell me when we get there."

He gave a bark of laughter. "Will do."

SWEDE FINISHED HIS pass through the place and collected Dane and Shadow. They reached the truck to find the others waiting. At his nod, they walked over and opened up the doors. Swede looked at the front seat to find Eva sleeping. He peered at Mason. "How long has she been out?"

"Almost since you left. She was upset when you went back inside the building." He grinned. "Looks like another SEAL has fallen?"

Swede ignored him. Dane laughed. "Looks like she's fallen at least. Not sure about the big man here."

On that note, Swede reached across, unbuckled Eva's seat belt and picked her up to slide her across the seat. He slipped in beside her.

"Swede," she murmured.

"Shh," he whispered. "Go back to sleep."

She snuggled up against his shoulders without appearing to wake. He settled into place. Staring straight ahead he waited until Mason started up the truck.

But hearing the sniggers from beside him he rolled his head and looked at Mason. "What?" he barked.

Eva murmured at his sharp tone. "Shh." He stroked her cheek. "Sleep."

With a heavy sigh, the lines on her face eased back.

Swede caught the wide grin on Mason's face. He glared at him. "What is your problem?"

"Nothing. I have no problem." He snickered and turned the key in the ignition.

The truck was fully packed with Eva. In fact, it was too damn tight. He could hardly breathe. He opened the window and took several deep breaths. Eva slept long into the trip, the miles passing in an unceasing run of desolate landscape.

He knew he'd be back in a few hours. It was going to be harder to leave Eva in the hotel room. But they had to deal with the mission, and she should be safe at a hotel. No one knew her. No one would know her location.

There was no reason to suspect foul play. And the other good news was that April had been found and she was fine. There'd been nothing untoward on the way home. She was of course delighted to hear Eva was found alive and well.

Now if he could only keep her that way.

CHAPTER 24

EVA WATCHED AS Swede gave the surroundings a quick check, unlocked the motel room and stepped in. He did a quick sweep then motioned her inside. She couldn't help taking a long look at the large parking lot and the hedges on both sides of the motel before she followed him inside.

"You'll be fine here until we get back."

Sure she would. But it wasn't her choice. She'd rather grab her SEAL family and go home. But that wasn't an option. She tossed her wallet on the small dresser and said, "I'll be fine."

There was an odd silence. She looked at him sideways. He was studying her with a gentle look. She sighed. That this big man could turn her to mush so easily just by being himself was astonishing. And said much about the depths of her own feelings. Feelings she hadn't acknowledged before.

"I'll be fine," she reiterated in a firmer voice. The sooner he left to do his thing, the sooner he'd be able to return and they could all go home.

She walked over and sat down on the bed and motioned to the door. "Go."

But her voice trembled. Damn it. She was stronger than this. But she didn't want him to go. She didn't want to be left alone. With her memories. And fears. And unsettled emotions. She wanted to find the solid footing she'd had before coming to Mexico. A footing where she knew who she was and where she stood in life. Maybe it wasn't the life she'd seen herself living, but it's what she knew. What she had. If she'd yearned for more, well, some of those dreams seemed a little silly now. Nothing like facing the immediate possibility of your own death to make you reevaluate your life. And how you've lived it and what you've let pass you by.

One of those wishes she'd yearned for and had let pass her by was standing in front of her. She studied the bed she was sitting on. It was just the two of them. Here. Now. He'd shown her his interest. No way that could be mistaken. But this was hardly the right time for taking such a major step. And was she ready? She still had doubts. Questions.

Swede's phone went off. He answered. She listened with half an ear. According to the conversation, something unexpected had come up. When he closed the phone he walked over to her. "The men received information on a possible informant. They've gone to check it out. They'll pick me up afterwards."

She nodded. "Good. Anything that helps to solve this nightmare."

Then she realized that they had the perfect opportunity to sort out their own differences.

"Those girls…the last time you came home with Hawk…"

"Were good friends of mine." He made no attempt to misunderstand. "They were in a relationship together but weren't comfortable around strangers."

Lesbians. Eva rolled that concept and the two women she'd seen mauling Swede. No – mauling Swede and each other. Not overtly. And with him in the mix it had been easy to mistake. "I'm sorry they felt they had to hide their relationship."

"They just didn't know you," he said good-naturedly. "In fact, it wasn't long after that that I made a few changes of my own."

He sat down on the bed beside her and flopped backwards. He crossed his arms over his chest and closed his eyes as if ready to nap.

"You can't sleep after a comment like that," she exclaimed. "What changes did you make?"

A small grin peeped out then disappeared as he opened his eyes to study her.

"I stopped dating."

Silence. She leaned closer and stared at him. "Stopped?"

He nodded.

"As in none at all?" she asked incredulously. "That was what…a year ago?"

"Eighteen months, actually."

"And you haven't had…" She stopped and flushed. It was none of her business. But inside, her toes were tingling and her heart was swelling with joy. "Wait… Why?"

"Because I couldn't find what I wanted."

The words were innocuous enough. A zillion more questions bubbled to her lips, but it was the seriousness in his eyes that brought her heart to her throat. She opened her mouth, then closed it. Knowing it was important, and more than that momentous. Her mind still stuck on his earlier words, she choked out the question, "What did you want?"

He reached out and gently grasped her chin. "You."

Her eyes widened in shock and hope and she stared down at this huge man who could have anything — anyone – he wanted in the world…and apparently wanted her.

God she hoped he meant it.

He tugged her down on top of him, then rolled so he was propped over top of her.

They stared into each other's eyes for a long moment before he slowly, ever so slowly, lowered his head.

And kissed her.

HE SHOULDN'T BE doing this. Not now. He didn't have time to do it right. Things were unsettled between them. Only he needed her. Had wanted her for so damn long. And if he didn't drive his advantage forward right now, he didn't know when he'd get another chance. She'd pushed him away since forever.

Until now. She was responding with that same passion that had brought him to his knees before.

He couldn't get enough.

He suddenly realized that his hand was under her shirt and his mouth was moving along the inside curve of her neck. Too fast. Too sudden. His erection screamed as he tried to pull back.

She reached up, looped her arms around his neck and said, "No."

He closed his eyes and dropped his head to rest on her chest. "Sorry," he whispered, his voice tremoring with the effort to cool down. "I didn't mean to lose control."

His breath was coming in raw gulps.

"No. I didn't mean stop," she cried and tugged him down to her. "Don't pull away… Please don't reject me."

"Jesus. Never." He gave her the sweetest, most caring kiss of his life. As he lifted his head, her eyes were shiny, moist. Tears? He stared at her worriedly.

"Are you sure?" He propped himself on his elbows as he stared down at her, his heart pounding in eagerness. Please let her be sure. *Please.*

"I'm sure," she whispered and gave him the most breathtaking smile...

With his heart on overload he kissed her lightly, longingly, teasing her lips to open and let him inside. He kissed her deep and long, pouring his feelings into that kiss, his hips rocking gently against her pelvis, loving the rise and fall of her hips.

"So responsive," he growled. "God I love that."

His lips trailed across her cheeks, eyelids and temples. Then down to her ear and lower again. He tried to pace himself, tried to slow down and savor the moment, but it had been a long time. Too long.

"Love me, Swede, please love me now."

And he did his best.

He tried to go slow but she wouldn't let him. He tried to take her clothes off one piece at a time to savor the experience, but she wouldn't let him, jumping off the bed and stripping down to the beautiful skin he was desperate to touch, to taste. He tried to warm her up slowly only to find she was hot and ready. He tried to slow her hands so he could retain control and found he'd never had it.

He groaned when her hands closed around him. He cried out when her mouth found him. And he moaned in joy when she rolled him onto his back and mounted him. Dear God. Where had she been all his life?

When she sank low and seated him at her center, he knew he'd died and gone to heaven.

Until she moved. He lay in bliss as she set a pace that drove him nuts as he fought to leave her in control, to leave himself on the crest without flying over. To let this happen in its own time. And revel in it.

Dear God. It was so damn hard. His climax screamed to be released, yet he never wanted this to end. He was caught in a limbo of pleasure.

She stroked her hands down over his chest, her nails gently gliding along his skin. He slid his hands down over her ribs and belly to her hips and held her while he drove his hips up. She dug her nails into his skin adding pain to the pleasure and somehow making it all that much sweeter.

She leaned forward and kissed his collarbone, his nipples, testing her sharp teeth on the skin to the side, making him shiver in delight.

Then she sat back, her breath coming in low pants and started to ride. The graceful motion of someone born to the saddle. Faster and faster, harder and harder, his fingers firm on her hips, her hands braced against his chest.

With a harsh gasp, she arched her back, a long slow scream of release filling the room.

He sat up, tucked her close and flipped her onto her back…and drove to the hilt again and again, the release…right…there…and he was almost…

A harsh guttural sound as he collapsed down beside her.

But he wouldn't let her go. He couldn't. He pulled her up close to his heart and held her in a tight embrace. Then and only then did he close his eyes. But not to sleep.

He didn't want to miss one single moment of time with her. They needed to talk. And soon. But he didn't want anything to mar this moment.

And then his phone rang. And he knew it was too late…the interlude was over.

E VA WANDERED THE motel room aimlessly. She was alone. As in Swede had gotten a call, told her to lock up and stay inside and he'd be back as soon as he could.

Right.

As if she hadn't heard that before.

Still the hot kiss he'd planted on her before leaving should hold her for a little while.

How long would they be gone? Long enough for her to have a shower and not be interrupted? The place was clean and serviceable but was of the no frills variety – so no room service. In fact, she stared out the window, they were just far enough out of town she doubted there was food available to order in either.

Her stomach growled, reminding her she hadn't eaten all day.

She threw herself on the bed and groaned.

So what if she was hungry – she was safe here. She was no longer at that horrific hacienda. That's all that mattered as if they'd never been there in the first place. There were no longer bodies all over the floors or the ghostly fact that someone moved them. How horrible was that? And Isabella? Didn't she deserve a proper burial? She'd done so much for the horses that no matter what else she might have been a part of she'd had a caring, compassionate side.

The line of bodies laid out in the stall was hard

enough to forget, but the thought of these poor people…

She just wanted to go home.

Her stomach growled again. She rubbed her face and considered her options. They'd come back. She knew they would. But when was up for consideration. She needed a shower and she needed food. So first one then she'd have to consider dealing with resolving the other. Maybe there was a vending machine close by.

Dragging herself into the bathroom, she locked the door and stepped under the hot water. Too bad Swede wasn't in here with her. She hated to wash off his scent, but being clean was a gift…

Oh Lord that felt good. She scrubbed her hair twice then took the washcloth to the rest of her body. Her skin was so sensitive after Swede. After being out in the brush, the dust seemed caked onto her skin.

She kept at it until her skin glowed pink and the water at her feet was clear. Shutting it off, she dried off then wrapped the towel around her sideways. She opened the door to the bedroom a crack and looked out. "Hello?"

No answer.

More confident, she pushed it open and walked back to her bed. The room was empty and there was no sign that someone had come in while she'd been gone. She winced at the thought, and after giving her jeans and top a hard shake in the bathtub, she got redressed.

Her hair was not going to cooperate without a brush. She stroked her fingers through the locks then ruthlessly twisted it into a knot at the back of her neck and clipped it back up.

With her skin glowing after the shower but her eyelids drooping, no sign of food available, no room service button on the phone and Swede's orders to stay inside, she lay down, closed her eyes and slept.

She woke several hours later, darkness showing outside the window, disoriented. Where was she?

Rolling over, she found her phone. It was after two in the morning. Shit. She hated being awake in the middle of the night.

Outside she heard the sound of vehicles arriving and raised voices. She scrambled to the window and peered behind the curtains.

Soldiers.

Or maybe rebel soldiers were a better term. These didn't have a disciplined military look to them. They were arguing, but one man threw his arms out wide, pointing to her motel.

Her heart pounded. Were they looking for her? Or were they just looking for a room? Maybe they didn't know anything about her. Why should they? She grabbed up her phone and texted Hawk and Swede. *Soldiers in parking lot.*

She watched as two army rigs drove up. A meeting took place in the middle of the lot then the last two vehicles left. Good. As they drove away, the driver looked up and directly to the fourth floor – at her.

Shit. She bolted backwards, terrified he'd seen her. *No, not possible.* He couldn't have seen her. But what if he had? Should she leave?

Gathering up her courage, she shifted to the other window and peered out. Only the original two vehicles remained and the men who had arrived with them.

The parking lot was empty of people. So where had they gone?

Just then the manager came out of the office waving his arms. He motioned to the floors of the motel and his voice was indignant, but she couldn't understand what he was saying to the men who walked out behind him.

Questioning the manager? Booking rooms? The soldier reached out and grabbed the keys from the manager's hand and headed toward the floors below hers. Damn it. If she was ever going to leave, now was a good time. But where could she go? She was hardly inconspicuous. She had no scarf or makeup to tone down the whiteness of her skin. She couldn't speak Spanish and she was all alone.

Not suspicious at all. She snagged up her wallet, straightened the bedding then did a cursory check of the bathroom. Taking a moment to wash the dirt from cleaning her clothing, she stuffed the towels into the laundry bin and snagged up the keys. The hotel room was hers. If this blew over, she could come back. If it didn't, then she wanted to make sure she'd left it as if she'd never been here.

Just like at the hacienda.

She checked her cell phone for the tenth time, wondering why the men weren't getting back to her with instructions.

Then she realized they probably couldn't. They were on a mission. It was hardly normal to leave cell phones on during a raid.

She'd have to handle this on her own.

And her instincts were telling her to get the hell out – now.

SWEDE CUSSED LOUDLY. He'd ducked to the left and his movement should have been fast enough, but the gun tracking him compensated for his shift and a bullet nicked across his ribs.

Burnt like a son of a bitch.

"Quit fussing. It's minor."

Mason grinned as Swede bit off a few more choice words. "Girls will love the scars."

That didn't deserve a reply. Besides, there was only one woman in his life now and she wouldn't be happy that he'd been injured.

"What's the status," he asked Mason. "How many did we catch?"

"Looks decent. We got fourteen rounded up, four are dead and six more are injured. We've got one boss and he's singing prettily, but according to him, his boss is close by too."

He surged to his feet.

Mason held out a warning hand. "Hawk and Shadow are on it." He wasn't going to get far.

"And Dane, where is he?"

"Keeping an eye on the prisoners."

"Not smart to leave him alone," Swede growled.

Mason laughed. "They are right outside. I had to make sure you were okay first."

Swede was insulted. He strode outside to where Dane stood and gave his friend a reassuring nod. "I'm fine. Just too big to miss I guess."

Dane laughed. "It's a chore but what are you going to do…"

Swede looked at the captured prisoners. Mason was moving between the injured. The dead were off to one side. He studied faces, looking for anyone he might have seen at Isabella's. The last one…maybe…

He strode over and stood in front of the older man. In rapid fire Spanish he asked him, "Were you at Isabella's"

The man nodded. "I was taken from there to work here."

"How long ago?"

"Months. After training I was placed back at the ranch." He shrugged. "It's no life. But we have no choice."

He sounded sincere… But was he? Then he didn't exactly look like the rest of the young punks.

Swede could hear vehicles in the distance. Hopefully it was the Mexican task force.

He'd like to kick the ass of some of the prisoners. They had a cocky punk look like they knew something he didn't, and he was going to get his ass kicked for it. That was fine, he was ready to dish out some ass kicking himself.

"How's your chica," one punk said in bad English from behind his back.

Swede spun on his heels and reached out and grabbed the kid's jacket and lifted him off his feet.

"What chica?"

The men on either side of the punk shifted uneasily. Swede studied their reaction. Was it due to what he'd done or to the punk's words?

He gave the kid a shake then dropped him. The kid sprawled to the floor then bounced to his feet spitting like a viper.

Swede kept his gaze on him then deliberately turned his back. An insult he knew the kid wouldn't be able to let slide.

Sure enough, he heard the movement and waiting the half second he then pivoted, his own fist out and already in motion.

His fist connected with the kid's ribs and without a sound he dropped to the ground, unconscious.

"They don't learn, do they, Swede?" Mason called out.

"No." Swede shook his head. "I wonder if they are all

as stupid."

He took another look at the men standing and picked out one who looked terrified. He lifted him up like he did the first kid and asked, "What do you know about the chica?"

The words flew out the kid's mouth. "They know where she is."

"So what?" He held his own panic back. These guys had info they needed and the energy was going to change once the Mexican's arrived to handle them. He needed to know what the men knew now. He shook the kid.

"They've gone after her," he said trying to get the words out fast. "No one is to know about the camp. No witnesses. They kill everyone."

"Everyone?" Mason asked. "How many have been killed?"

The older ranch hand spoke up, "There were two at the ranch who wouldn't agree to the terms, so they were shot and buried as an example."

"And others?" Swede turned to face the kid he still held. The kid wasn't even shaving yet, he couldn't be more than fifteen at the most. And scrawny as if he hadn't seen enough food in a long time.

"If you don't want to fight, they kill you," said the man standing beside him. "If you fail in a job, they kill you." He shrugged. "If you don't want to be here…then your life is hell. If you are one of the best and like war then this is the place for you."

Swede dropped the kid and studied the man. "And you like it?"

"I like being alive. I watched too many die."

"And Isabella?"

He shrugged. "Our orders were to make sure no one survived."

"And yet, Lena wasn't shot?" At least he didn't think so.

"She's family to the commander. She runs interference and spied on Isabella." He shrugged. "She's got it made."

Nice. Not.

"So she's the one who got Isabella in trouble?"

The older ranch hand spoke up. "She's been in trouble for a long time. It was going to end badly anyway."

Swede could see that. "Well, do you realize that shooting her was a kindness? That she was dying anyway. And soon?"

The older man gave a slight smile. "She'd like to go out that way. Knowing she'd held out as long as she could. She wanted nothing to do with them, but they killed one of her sons and forced the other into the army."

So her son's life for her cooperation. He liked her better already. Not much a mother wouldn't do to keep her family safe.

"Is he alive?" Mason asked, reminding Swede that many young men had just died here today.

The older man shook his head. "I don't know. He *was* here…"

So he escaped. "How many others are missing," Mason asked, his voice hardening. "We'll need to find them."

"Let them go," the older ranch hand said. "If they managed to escape they won't be sticking around. They'll be heading home much wiser than when they left."

"Were many recruited willingly?"

The man nodded. "They were young and innocent when they came. Not so much now."

"Shut up, old man," snapped a hard edged leaner and mean version of the kid lying unconscious. "Some of us were happy to be part of something we could believe in."

His voice held the same disillusionment that so many young people had at the world they lived in today.

Swede nodded. "Ideology and all that aside, what was the plan here? Training for what?"

The fighter shrugged. "I don't know. I wasn't in with the commander. Isabella's son Paolo is."

"So maybe he escaped with the commander," Mason snapped. "That doesn't make him innocent and wanting to go home to his family."

The older man sighed. "No, but you don't understand. Paolo is just as likely to try and kill the commander for gunning down his kid brother and his mother. They were close."

That would be tough on everyone. But for the kid, yeah, if that had been Swede, he'd do his best to get revenge as well.

"And the women that were here?"

The fighter laughed. "Women have one use and one use only."

"And yet someone tried to kill the two female volunteers working with the horses when they went home again."

"Not us. Although we wanted to keep the women if we could." The fighter snickered.

Until his teeth flew out as Swede's fist replaced them.

He collapsed unconscious to the ground.

"They're dropping like flies," Mason said. "Who's next?"

The men shuffled uneasily. The young kid cried, "We don't know anything. The commander didn't tell us the plans. We know that any woman captured was to be brought to the camp, but more importantly, no one was to know they were here at all."

"That's too many people to silence," Mason said.

The kid's head bobbed. "Too many. That's why they were so upset with Isabella. She brought all the strangers in and when she was sworn to secrecy. The commander said they were suspicious of your presence after Lena said you had a military bearing." He shrugged. "They didn't want to take any chances and attacked last night."

Right. That made sense.

Suddenly trucks came into view. Men hopped out and raced over, guns drawn. Mason walked over to the talk to the leader. Swede sent out the word to the others. They were finished here.

He went to send Eva a message only to see a text from her. He read it quickly.

The kid leaned forward. "You have to save her. They know you took her to town."

Shit.

He raced to the closest truck, calling to his friends.

<h1 style="text-align:center">CHAPTER 26</h1>

EVA RACED TO the exit at the far end of the hallway. She'd gone up in a panic, then realized she'd be cornered up there and had slowly, checking out the windows at every floor, made her way down. Now she was on the main floor, but the closest exit had people milling in front. She didn't want to attract any attention, but she wanted to get the hell outside.

The door beside her opened, she jumped backwards but had no place to go. Thankfully the couple didn't appear to notice her. The man closed the door behind them, and they walked with their arms and lips moving on each other so passionately she had to wonder why they were leaving the room. Unless they were going *to* her room. So what room had they left? She eyed the door. This was a ground floor room on the back. Did they have a patio? An outside door? She crossed the hallway and opened the door in question. It wasn't a suite. More like a lounge.

"We're closed for the night," someone called out.

A private lounge. Kind of a sleazy location, but whatever. Then she caught sight of the poker tables. Oh, okay. She also caught sight of the exit. "No problem, I left something over by the glass doors."

She dashed across the room and unlocked the doors. She pushed one open, smiled at the man standing with cleaning rags in his hand wondering what she was doing and walked out.

Perfect.

The moon was up and shone bright on the back lawn behind the hotel. It was going to be a beautiful day. Later. At the moment, she needed to hide where the men she'd seen earlier couldn't find her and where she could watch out for her SEALs.

She had to believe Hawk and Swede had gotten her message and would be here as soon as they could be. She slipped over to the hedge and peered through the leaves toward the front yard. There were several new vehicles in the parking lot. What was wrong with people? It was the middle of the night. They should be asleep. Then so should she.

She stood for a long moment wondering if she was worrying for nothing. Had she been foolish to leave her room? Would someone have really kicked the door down to get to her? Surely not.

But she couldn't be sure. And damn it she wanted to be sure. Sure about something. Being wrong came with a horrific price tag.

She wanted to sit down and rest, have all this shit disappear. She looked around where she was standing and considered doing just that. In the shadows, hidden by the tall hedge, she could see through the bare lower branches. Maybe she was safe here. It was certainly not going to be the first place anyone would look for her, right? She glanced behind her, but she'd moved far enough away from the room she'd escaped through that even if someone did say something they'd be hard pressed to find her. Accidentally she appeared to have landed at a place that just might be ideal.

She crouched down and considered it. The sun wouldn't be up for a few hours. She could spend those hours here. If nothing untoward happened and there were no signs of anyone searching for her, then she could always try to return to her motel room. If it was the same as she'd left it then she was golden. She could nap until the guys returned. She didn't want to pay for a second night but might have to if they didn't get back before check out. She couldn't leave without letting them know.

They'd go nuts trying to find her.

No, that meant staying until they showed up.

She curled in a ball and leaned against the motel wall.

And closed her eyes.

"JUST BECAUSE SHE saw a soldier doesn't mean they are after her," Mason said. They were all in the truck and heading back to the motel. Tired and frustrated but with Swede and Hawk setting the pace, they'd been away from the ranch in no time.

Since leaving there'd been no sign of anyone else. The vast miles of countryside looked to be just as deserted as the first time they'd driven this road.

With any luck it would stay that way until they were at Eva's side. She was a bit of wild card. Swede wanted to be there as soon as he could. It was the only way he'd be able to reassure himself she was safe.

"Too bad it's too early for food," Dane said from the back seat.

"We all need a solid meal."

"Not until we get to Eva," Swede said.

Mason was driving with Hawk seemingly slumbering in the back, only Swede wasn't fooled. They all had the ability to doze off yet wake battle ready in a heartbeat.

He wasn't listening into the conversation but

wouldn't miss anything important.

"Right. So are you keeping her?" Mason asked, the devil in his voice.

Swede snorted and stared out the window.

Shadow sniggered in the backseat.

Swede knew this wouldn't be going in any direction he wanted to deal with right now, and he slouched down and closed his eyes.

"Let me know when we get there."

And tried to sleep.

Only sleep wasn't easy and his mind wouldn't shut off. Worry gnawed at him. Shit. After ten minutes of trying to sleep he sat up again and opened the truck window for a bit of fresh air. Either asleep or awake but he hated anything in between. When he was on, he was on. And when he was out...? Well it was rare for him to sleep deeply unless he was on days off. That sense of awareness was hard to turn off any other time.

And at times like this it wasn't going to happen.

"Bet she's not in the room when we get there," Hawk said from behind him.

Dane said, "I'm not taking that bet. I doubt she is either."

"Then where is she likely to be?" Mason asked curiously. "I happen to agree. She'd have seen the military and hidden."

"Interesting." Shadow smiled as he added, "But I would too."

"She's a smart cookie, and if things don't feel right then she'll go to the ground."

"And what will that mean in this case," Swede asked. "How much does she know to do?"

"She'll be outside. Hidden somewhere where she can see what's going on but not where anyone will easily spot her."

The men contemplated his words for a few moments. "Then again, that's what we'd all do too in the same situation, right?"

"Right," Dane said. "Can't get pinned inside so outside it is, but she needs us so she can't go too far."

Swede smiled. "Sounds like you taught her some things, Hawk."

"Didn't need to. Our daddy started that a long time ago and since he died, the two of us had drills we practiced all the time. She was a woman alone and that's not the safest."

It sounded like Eva had taken to the basics easily. Swede had already seen she didn't panic and could hold her own in the worst of situations. She'd been steady through this nightmare and had kept her priorities straight. The horses first then when they were all good, the men she cared about.

Which he already knew he was one of. She'd made that abundantly clear.

Now to lock down what that meant.

CHAPTER 27

EVA SNAPPED AWAKE and froze. Her back was throbbing, her arms achy at her sides. The skies were still dark, but light was creeping over the horizon giving the world an odd glow. Nice and mellow coloring crept over the land making her feel better except that she was alone.

Had the men come back? Were they planning on it? Could they come back?

With a slight groan she tried to stand up and almost cried out in pain.

Shivers wracked her frame. She rubbed her arms to ward off a chill. Crouching down, she peered through the brush at the parking lot. Had they come? If they had, she couldn't imagine that they'd not torn the place apart to find her. And if they hadn't – why not?

They'd been gone for hours. She glanced around. The place was quiet. She'd probably panicked for nothing.

She made a quick decision. She'd go back to her bed-room and lie down on a comfortable bed. Besides, she needed a bathroom. At least she would be where they expected her to be. Using her key, she let herself into the back door and used the stairway to get to her floor. The silence was eerie, yet comforting. She saw no one on her way to the room. She looked around to make sure no one was watching her as she reached for her door knob.

And realized it wasn't latched.

She swallowed hard. Shit. Had she left it that way? Had the men returned and were waiting inside? No, they wouldn't leave the door like this. She breathed silently trying to regain control. Gently, ready to bolt, she pushed the door open wide.

She stepped in and turned on the light.

And gasped. The bedroom had been tossed. The bedding was ripped off and thrown on the floor, the drawers from both the dresser and night table were pulled out and lay on the floor on top of the bedding.

Oh dear God. She was sick to her stomach. What could the intruders have been looking for? The hotel room had been clean. Empty. Obviously not occupied.

So why? It made no sense. But it did make her decision easier, she wasn't staying here.

Closing the door she crept back out the way she'd come. Her stomach churned. She couldn't forget what she'd seen. What if she'd been in the room when the intruder arrived? Would he still have entered the room? Or had she not latched the door and someone had noticed and came in looking for something worth stealing? But then why toss it? It wasn't difficult to search an empty room.

She couldn't stop shaking. Back outside she gulped large mouthfuls of air. There'd been enough death and destruction in her world. She just wanted this over.

The parking lot was calm. She wandered around the cars, hoping for daylight. And really hoping for a damn coffee. Lord she needed one. Was it too much to ask?

A bench was positioned outside the main office door. Groaning, she plunked her butt down. What a brutal night. She'd sit here until the men arrived. She pulled out her cell phone and sent yet another text. "I'm sitting outside the hotel. Are you coming soon?"

And waited.

As the sun slowly rose, she found herself lying sideways on the bench and staring up at the sky.

Harsh voices woke her out of her daze. She froze as the voices came closer. Harsh male voices and several of them were arguing. Once again she wished she understood Spanish. But the tone wasn't pleasant. And she was a woman alone. Damn it. She lay quiet, hoping she'd be missed.

Instead the voices rose and she could hear grunts and impact sounds as if there was a fight going on. That just made her situation worse. Could she slip away without being seen? She shifted over to the end of the bench and staying low she crept to the other side of the line of vehicles right in front of her and tried to hide.

She was snatched from behind, a thick muscled arm across her throat. A cold dark voice against her ear said, "Well hello there."

"WHERE THE HELL is she?" Swede stood in the open doorway and swore silently. The room had been destroyed and there was no sign of Eva. And neither was there any sign that she'd ever been here. There were no bits of clothing or personal items. She hadn't had much when he'd left her, but she'd had a few things.

"Ha, I win," Hawk said with a laugh in his direction. "I said she'd be outside."

Swede cast a final glance at the empty room. "She said she'd be outside the office and she isn't," he muttered. He closed the door. No one would be the wiser. All good. As long as they found her.

And fast.

Hawk was already leading the way to the lower levels. Swede followed. He knew Shadow and Mason were checking outside, and Dane had gone to speak to the manager at the office. If the man wasn't awake yet it was too damn bad – he was now.

Once outside they stood for a long moment in the cool air, Swede's eyes moving constantly, searching for a hiding place.

There were only the sounds of nature around them. No vehicles on the road. No people walking. Birds sang gently in the early morning. The sky was clear enough to see in every corner in front of him.

And she wasn't anywhere.

Dane came running out. "The manager said one of the waiters saw a woman sneaking out of the back patio doors a few hours ago. She was unharmed. They were cleaning up from a private party when she entered and exited without stopping. She mentioned something about having left something behind, but the server didn't remember seeing her at the party."

"Right." Swede considered the options she'd have. "Interesting that she didn't stay with them. Or ask them for help."

"But she might not have known she was in trouble. Maybe she thought she was making a big deal out of nothing or worse not wanting to put anyone else in danger."

Swede nodded. That sounded like her too.

"Let's split up and find her," Hawk ordered.

Swede took the outside of the building and quickly did a pass around the back, checking the hedges and trees. There was no sign of her. He met the others in the parking lot.

"Nothing," Hawk said.

Swede, his heart pounding, hated the thoughts clamoring inside his head. He knew all the bad things that happened to nice people. In this given situation, there were too many scenarios to consider.

"There's no way to know if she's been taken without having a witness who has seen something."

"Then let's roust them all and talk to them."

Knowing it was wasting precious time but not having much choice, they quickly started slamming on doors and speaking to disgruntled guests.

The motel wasn't even close to capacity so that helped.

Swede pounded on a door only to hear violent cursing from inside. He crossed his arms and waited.

"What the fuck do y–" The unkempt man clad only in boxers, stood and stared. Then backed up a step and in a much more polite voice, tried again. "Why the hell are you waking me up at this hour?"

"A girl is missing," Swede said shortly. "Did you see her at any time last night?" He gave a short description.

"I don't know, give me a minute." The man ran his hands over his face a few times as if to try and wake up. Push the hangover back was more likely but whatever worked. Swede didn't care.

"Yeah, maybe. But it wasn't last night. It was early this morning," the guy said. "My buddy and I were drinking heavily last night and got into a hell of an argument."

"Who is your buddy and where is he?"

The man pointed to the left. "He's next door."

"What did you see?"

"I'm not really sure. I think she might have been lying on that bench out front by the office and the parking lot as if she was waiting for someone. Then someone came, and she left with him."

"Who was the man? What did he look like? What vehicle was he driving?"

The man's whole demeanor changed now that he realized what was going on. Swede thanked him then went next door to wake up his buddy. The first man came with him and pounded on the door.

"Hey, Chester, wake the fuck up. The cops are here looking for a missing girl."

Chester, a tall skinny redhead with more beard than he'd seen in a long time pulled the door open. The two men talked but nothing more came out. He hadn't really seen the girl. Though it was a truck the guy was in. But wasn't sure. Thought there was a big army rig parked out there but wasn't sure. Thought maybe the girl hadn't gone willingly – but of course, wasn't sure.

"What are you sure of?" Swede asked in frustration.

"I was just so pissed off at Drake here that honestly nothing else really figured in."

Swede, realizing he'd gotten what he could, turned and bolted to meet Hawk in the parking lot. He passed on his message. The others had reports of the army truck but not the woman. Dane had returned from again questioning the manager. "The army doesn't rent rooms here. Neither do the rebels. The manager says he's seen the rebels around but knows to not ask questions. He added that they didn't get their supplies locally nor did they stop in town. Go through yes, but stop and spend money – no. However, they were here earlier asking about Eva – not by name but by description. The manager told them nothing but they took his keys. He never saw her with them."

"So we can't know for sure that she is with them but the other options are rapidly dwindling."

"The biggest problem is that she could have gone

with anyone anywhere. We can focus on the rebels camp, but that's no guarantee someone else hasn't snatched her."

The others nodded.

Swede joined them. "She was here," he pointed to the front bench, "and walked this far," he motioned to the side of a parking stall. "She walked on her own two feet. There are tracks," he motioned to them, "but she isn't stepping in a natural rhythm."

"Tied up?" Hawk snapped.

"No, I think someone was behind her and forcing her to the truck."

"So more than one?"

"She was pushed inside then he climbed in with her. The same tracks do not go around to the driver side."

"So two men."

"And a big truck." Again Shadow pointed to the tracks. "Duallies on the back."

"So likely army." Swede glanced at Shadow. "Unless you think we're talking a big truck like a one ton pickup."

"No. I'd say longer. The wheel base is bigger." He walked the distance showing what he meant. "See, it's big."

"Right."

"Direction?" Hawk snapped.

Shadow raced to the entrance onto the main road. Swede was on his heels. The only way to know would be if they took the corner tight or wide on the far side. The pavement had been washed clean but the shoulders were dirt and held the tracks beautifully.

"Here it is," he called to Shadow on the far side. "He went wide on his left turn and clipped the shoulder with the front tire." Closer inspection showed it wasn't actually the shoulder but more dirt on the road here. Good for them. The tracks clearly showed the heavier vehicle coming onto the road from the parking lot and heading back the way they'd come.

"Let's go," Hawk said. "They are hours ahead of us."

CHAPTER 28

EVA COULDN'T BELIEVE it. Her brother and his team were after the very same men who were driving her back to the same camp. They had hours of traveling ahead of them. Her mind kept spinning looking for options but came up blank. The men were armed. They were fit. They looked mean as hell. She didn't know if the passenger in the front seat was the commander or not, but he'd stayed inside when the man had forced her in the back of the truck. So had the driver. She was one against three. Nice odds.

Damn. She slumped back against the back seat. She could open the door and throw herself onto the highway. Likely break something in the process but as long as it wasn't her head she was good with that. If a broken leg was the price of escape she was also fine with that too. But a broken leg that wouldn't get treatment if she *failed* in her escape, and left her damaged and at their mercy…well she couldn't imagine.

No, she needed to keep her head and look for the perfect opportunity to escape. If they were back at the hacienda, she knew a few hiding places but if they were taking her to the rebel camp…well that didn't sound like a place she'd have an easy time running away from.

Damn it. Where was Swede and her brother? They were supposed to make sure this didn't happen to her.

There was light traffic on the road. She racked her

brain trying to remember if there were any places she might make a run for it and find someone to help her. She still had her cell phone on her. Interesting that they hadn't taken it away. She didn't know if she had reception out here though. And how could she use it to get help without anyone seeing her.

"What is she doing?" the big man in the front seat said in low tones.

"Looking for a way to escape."

Silence. "Then shoot her in the knee if she looks ready to make a run for it."

She gasped in horror. Oh dear God. Who were these people that they'd do something like that to her.

With her stomach rolling and heaving at his words, she realized with horror she was going to be sick.

She bent over between her legs and cried out as the bile climbed higher and higher.

"She's going to puke," the guy beside her said. He then said something in rapid-fire Spanish.

The truck came to a hard stop on the side of the highway. The driver hopped out and opened the door beside her. He grabbed her arm and pulled her out. She stumbled to the shallow ditch on the side of the road half expecting to be shot on the spot.

Her nerves gave up the resistance and she bent over and threw up. And threw up. And then again.

There hadn't been much food to upchuck but her body, reaction, fear, she didn't know, but it was attempting to empty right down to her toes.

Exhausted at the end, she kneeled on the side of the road and tried to control her breathing. No matter what she did, it seemed like everything was setting the vomiting off again.

She knew what it was. Terror. These men were going

to kill her. Given enough time, they'd do what they wanted to do to her first then they'd kill her. She had to stay alive long enough for Swede to find her. Her brother would be lost if they lost her. Only she didn't know how to help herself now.

She had to do everything she could to stay alive long enough for the men to rescue her.

The man beside her grabbed her by the hair and reefed her head back. She groaned and her mouth filled again. He let her go and danced backward out of the spray.

That was her. She was so dangerous she puked on her attackers. Too bad she hadn't thought of it earlier. She almost smiled at that. Almost. A vehicle drove by, the driver slowing down as he caught sight of her kneeling. Yeah, they probably thought she was being executed. And she was – slowly.

At the rebels waving them on, the driver picked up speed and drove away. She watched his taillights disappear in the distance. Was that her one chance of escape or had she just saved that man's life because she *hadn't* brought him into this mess. The soldier said something to her in Spanish. She shook her head. She'd picked up a few words over the years but didn't recognize any that were streaming out of his mouth.

Then she heard the truck door reopen. Shit. A bullet was next. She eyed the ground around her. There were lots of trees, but they were all over twenty feet away. She wouldn't make it.

Then again, she'd at least be doing something.

Just not what Swede and Hawk would want her to do. Stay alive. That was the bottom line. A bullet might not kill her, but chances were good they'd get several in before she found safety. And who said the trees would keep her safe. The men could run after her and then what? She'd have pissed them off.

"Get back into the truck," the man who'd sat beside her said.

She looked at him, wiped out from the vomiting, and nodded.

Stay alive. She had to stay alive. He turned and led the way back to the truck.

And she bolted for the trees.

HOW FAR AHEAD could they be? Swede chafed at the slow speed. Hawk was doing one-forty on the highway that allowed for eighty, but he was sure this truck could push one-sixty.

"Swede, I can't push it any further," Hawk snapped. "So stop looking like I'm doing a shit job here."

Swede growled and leaned back. "Have to save her."

"We will."

There was a long silence then Hawk asked, "I know, she's my sister and all, but are you finally going to put her out of her misery?"

Swede's eyes flew open. "Sorry?"

"She's so damn hooked on you. Has been for years."

"Like hell," Swede said good-naturedly. "She's seen me in the worst light."

"And fell in love with you anyway. The thing is…" he hesitated and Swede tensed. Here it came. Such shitty timing.

"If you don't feel the same, then don't go there."

"No place to go. She's already mine." Short. Clear. Succinct. Screw tiptoeing around the issue. "If she doesn't already know it, then she had better get the message fast."

"You keeping her then?" Hawk asked, amusement in his voice. "I already love you like a brother, but I'll be damned if I help you do something she doesn't want you to do."

"You just said she loves me."

Hawk's voice rippled with laughter. "That doesn't mean she's reconciled to that fact yet."

"She never looks pleased to see me," Swede admitted. "It's hot and cold all the way."

"Been there and done that," Dane said from the back seat. "Got to admit, it's a shit place to be. So it's up to you to convince her there's no other place she'd rather be."

"Yeah," Swede said. They'd avoided having "advice" conversations but at the moment, it was reassuring to know they'd been in a similar position. "The thing is, I'm not sure I can let her go no matter what she says."

"That's my boy, she's there. But she's likely afraid you will return to your wild days."

"My days were over a long time ago."

"You know that. We know that. She doesn't."

"Not an easy way to convince her."

"Tell her the truth," Mason said. "She's already in love with you. She respects you. Make her admire you too."

"I ignored her because of you."

"Idiot," Hawk said affectionately. "I could see what was happening between you two a long time ago."

Swede nodded. "Yep, but you were only okay with it after you found Mia."

Silence filled the truck cab as Hawk contemplated Swede's words. "I wonder… Eva has been alone for a long time. I hated having to leave her alone. But I couldn't stay any longer. I had to live my dream." He sighed. "She wanted to be a vet, you know. But wouldn't leave to go to school. She had the marks but figured she had to stay so I could live my dream. I only really figured out she had some kind of weird attachment to our old home recently. That it would be wrong to leave. Dishonor our father's wishes. The memories she couldn't let go of. It's not true, but it's something she and I will have to discuss."

"A vet?" Swede rolled the term around, thinking about what he knew about Eva. "It's not too late for her. She's young and loves animals."

"True, but I don't know if she wants that dream anymore."

Swede thought about the wistful looks she'd given the vets, watching as they worked on the horses at Isabella's. "I think she does, but she's relegated it to something she can't do anymore. Whether because of her animals or lack of money…or because she thinks the opportunity has passed her by."

"None are valid," Hawk growled. "But she always did the right thing and put everything else ahead of her needs. I've been gone just enough that I no longer know what those are outside of the basics."

"We have the property together, but if she wants to sell it that's always up for discussion. Mia hates to leave her behind too. I'd love to have them both close, but I do know that Eva won't leave her animals."

"She might not have to. I'm not sure if either of you would be willing to sell but you own a lot of land. I also don't know what property commuting distance to base would be worth comparably…"

Hawk laughed. "We'd go from owning a quarter section to owning a postage size lot."

"Not if you were out of town forty minutes."

Hawk was silent. Swede leaned back. It was too much

to hope that such a thing was possible, but hadn't he been wondering about the same problem. He knew there was a top notch vet school close by to where he lived. At least close enough to commute. But it was all premature. She'd have to apply, get references, etc. before she'd be accepted. And she'd have to have the marks. Even then it was a long shot as the competition was fierce.

Long shots were his thing.

But were they hers?

"Look up ahead."

An older model army rig was stopped on the side of the road. It appeared abandoned. The hood wasn't open and neither did there appear to be flat tires. Swede leaned forward as Hawk drove ahead slowly. The front of the cab was empty. Hawk parked in the front and the men exited. No one was in sight. Shadow set to work and quickly disappeared out of sight. Swede spread out looking for tracks. Had the truck broken down? Were the occupants picked up by a second vehicle? He frowned. Maybe, but he couldn't see any reason for the vehicle to be here. He opened the driver's door and hopped in. There were no keys in the ignition. That had never stopped him before. He bent under the dash and had the engine turning over in minutes. He backed it up. It appeared to be in good working order. So what was the problem? He turned to study the cab. No personal effects, but several empty water bottles, and yes, a rucksack. Typical canvas bag tucked into the passenger footwell. He shut off the engine and twisted to look in the back. And froze. There was a the motel rom key on the back seat. Eva's.

He snatched it up, grabbed the rucksack and carried both to Hawk.

The men exchanged grim looks and stared into the wild growth around them.

Hawk's phone went off. Shadow. He sent several texts. "He's found one dead man and has tracked a lighter set of tracks deep into the woods."

"She's running." Swede raced in the direction Shadow had gone. He had no idea what shape she was in, but she'd found an opportunity and had taken it. Now she had to keep going. There were men hunting her. Likely the dead man was the one who let her get away. Followed the same theme of *failure was not allowed.*

Swede wasn't dressed for a run, but he did twenty kilometers on his regular days and could double that when needed. Now he needed speed and agility. The ground was rough and his feet huge. Hard to be silent and fast but he was good at it. He caught up to Shadow, slowed to talk to him, but Shadow sent him on. The tracks were in a straight line. "We're right behind you."

That's when Swede realized someone was driving the army rig parallel to the tree line. Good.

He raced forward, his gaze on the mess of tracks. How far could she have gone? That she might have doubled back into the men chasing her made his heart pound and his feet fly faster.

He heard a faint cry ahead.

He adjusted his angle and added more fuel to the speed. And heard someone up ahead shout, "Just shoot the bitch."

Jesus. His eyes searched for their location and ways to approach without them knowing.

Only the trees were thinning, but there was no way he was going to slow down. He pulled his piece out and held it ready.

CHAPTER 29

S HIT. SHIT. SHIT.
Why the hell had she run? She'd seen a window
of opportunity and she'd taken it. Faster, lighter, and
more motivated than her pursuers she'd gained a good
lead right out of the starting gate. She'd hit the tree line
without getting shot and had immediately headed for the
deepest part. She'd run until she couldn't run anymore.
Now she was just trying to hide.

Until a bullet splattered, barely missing her head and
shocking her into screaming. She'd bolted again after that.

But her element of surprise had been lost and they
were tracking her. She'd left three men behind in the
vehicle but she'd only caught sounds of two of them. That
one might be the commander chilled her. He'd shoot her
between the eyes and never blink. She shuddered. Where
the hell was her brother?

Swede?

If she ever needed that big loaf it was now.

Footsteps raced toward her. She was buried deep inside a bush with several others around her. *Please run past,
please.*

The footsteps came closer. Oh God. She shuddered
and huddled in on herself.

"Where the fuck is she?" said one of the men from the
truck. So they spoke English?

"She has to be here somewhere."

"Where, damn it. We don't have time for this."

"We don't have time to not get her," came the more lethal voice. "Failure is not allowed."

She was close enough to the first man to hear him swearing under his breath. "God damn it," he whispered. "I'm not going home wearing a bullet like Leon."

She frowned. She thought Leon was one of the men in the vehicle. Had they shot him then? She wouldn't be surprised. As the leader said, failure was not an option.

Or maybe not as she heard sounds of another man approaching, someone big, heavy. Swede? Her brother? It wasn't out of the realm of possibilities. For all she knew they drove past each other earlier. She'd not been able to see much.

"Carlos?" one man called.

"Yeah. I'm here. But we're not alone."

Gunfire erupted from where the last man had spoken. Not toward Carlos and a long way away from her, but someone was shooting. Jesus. She had to be losing it but she thought she heard a truck as well. Had she almost reached a different road? She'd bolted far enough that it was possible.

Maybe she could sneak out there and get help. Or was it a road patrolled by Carlos and his men? In which case, she didn't want anything to do with it.

Carlos moved away slightly. She could see his back as he checked the bushes beside her. How long before he found her. Then he did something that made her heart go cold. He shot into the center of the bushes. And then again and again.

Her breath came out in short rasps as she panicked. Oh God, run or stay. Run, she'd get shot at. Stay, she'd definitely get shot at.

Not much choice.

Carlos started to fire again, only faster.

She slowly stood up so she could see what he was firing at, and a bullet whispered by her head.

She ducked again and realized whoever Carlos was firing at was shooting back.

She hunkered down, her fist in her mouth to stop her from crying out as bullets rained around – until silence descended.

Taking a chance she peered through the trees. Carlos was on the ground, blood dripping from a bullet to the head. He had to be dead. Thank God. But who was the mystery shooter. Or could this be the commander and he was cleaning up?

She waited, heard nothing, and taking a chance, bolted in the opposite direction.

Instantly bullets rained on her. She dove behind the trees.

"Eva?"

Swede.

Oh thank God. Tears poured down her cheeks as she realized they were here to save her. She'd done it. She'd stayed alive and now she was safe.

No, not quite.

She heard Swede racing in her direction still shooting at someone. Maybe he didn't know Carlos was dead.

Or maybe he didn't know about the commander. Shit. She watched Swede race toward her. She stood up, a huge grin on her face.

"Oh thank God," she cried. A movement behind Swede caught her attention.

The commander jumped to his feet and lined up his gun on Swede.

She screamed, "Look out."

Using a move Hawk had taught her a long time ago,

she dove forward and tackled Swede around the knees. Still powering forward, he ploughed over her head to face plant in the dirt behind her. The single shot plucking his jacket before embedding in the tree bark behind him. She threw herself on top of him. "Are you okay? Oh God, did he hit you?"

She was picked up and slammed around behind him as he pivoted and shot – the commander between the eyes.

Jesus.

She collapsed on the ground crying uncontrollably.

"Were there other men?" Swede asked, giving her a light shake? "We have three dead?"

"Dead," she whispered. "Oh thank God, they are all dead."

He rolled over onto his back and tugged her to his chest. "Where did you learn that trick," he said, his big hands sliding up and down her back in a soothing motion.

She lay on his huge body trying to calm down.

When she could, she lifted her head and stared down at him. "Hawk of course. He figured I might need it for self-defense."

"Ha," Swede said. "That's the only time I've been taken out by that movement, and who knew a pint pot your size could do it. Besides, you weren't trying to get away, you were trying to save my very large, however, very capable ass."

"Whatever worked," she snapped. "Besides, according to you what we have is more than a passing fancy so I figured I had to protect my investment."

"Your investment?" he asked warily.

"Your ass is a very nice ass. And no one is going to kick it but me." She glared down at him. His grin was a mile wide. "Right?"

"Damn mosquitoes in these parts." But he could hardly get his voice out he was laughing so hard.

She sat up and straddled him. "Ya think?" She didn't know where her bravado came from, but she'd damn well had it with running and hiding and being kidnapped and shot at. She was so done with living a half life. She'd wanted this man since forever and now he was there before her.

"And I heard all about Mia and Hawk and that talk about keeping her. A running joke between you SEALs. I know my brother is a big negative in this relationship stuff between me and any of his team, so I'm stepping in and putting you all in your place."

Swede was chuckling so much she could hardly sit on him anymore. God the man was massive.

"And just how do you plan to do that?"

"Because you can't keep me. I won't let you."

That stopped his laughter cold. In fact, a hard edge had entered his gaze.

She held up her hand to stop him. "Just so we under-stand. You aren't crossing any boundaries or shifting any lines or making my brother upset. This is my choice. My decision."

He glared at her, and she could see something she'd never thought she'd see in the eyes of this so very powerful and confident man – insecurity.

"And how do you figure that?" he asked in a casual I don't give a shit attitude that didn't fool her for a second.

"Easy," she said tartly. "Because *I'm* keeping *you*."

His gaze widened and widened and that self doubt and pain slid from his eyes and a smile like she'd never seen before took hold of her heart and gave it a shake before it crawled inside and wouldn't let go.

"I love you, you big oaf. I always have."

And she suddenly became aware that they weren't alone. The rest of the SEALs surrounded them. Huge grins were on their faces and their arms were crossed as they stared at Swede on the ground, her the victor sitting on his belly.

It was Hawk who broke the silence. "Well, Swede, does my sister get what she wants, or…"

The others chuckled.

Swede groaned. "I'm never going to live this down, am I?"

"Hell no. In Mia's words, you're a kept man now."

And the place cracked up.

Not that Eva minded because Swede had jumped to his feet, clutched her tight to his heart and was kissing her like he'd finally found what he'd always wanted. "You idiot," he whispered against her ear when he finally broke the kiss. "I've always loved you too. But I couldn't do anything about it because of your brother."

She shook her head. "No, you could have, but you weren't ready either. Now you know what you want and are willing to fight for it."

He stared at her and she could see the words tumbling through his mind.

"I might not have been a hundred percent ready but I wasn't far off. And neither were you."

"No, it just took being kidnapped to help me see my priorities."

"And now?" he dropped his forehead to hers. "Are you sure?"

She stared up into the most majestic blue eyes and still seeing a hint of doubt she whispered, "Never been more sure of anything in my life."

And this time she kissed him.

SHADOW

SEALs of Honor, Book 5

Dale Mayer

CHAPTER 1

J AMES MORROW, SHADOW to his friends, watched the lake come into view below him. He leaned forward to peer through the cockpit of the small bush plane he'd been riding in for the last half hour. This wasn't how he'd expected to be traveling. None of his team had. Mechanical trouble had brought their military helicopter to an emergency landing. Shitty timing. They were on a mission. To rescue a US senator and his family being held hostage in a remote Canadian cabin.

Instead they'd been the ones in need of assistance. They managed to land close to a small town, but without enough time to bring in a second military aircraft, and time being of an essence, they'd ended up in one of those small bush planes barely able to handle the weight of the four passengers fully geared. Dane and Swede were traveling with the Canadian unit in a different aircraft along with Markus and Evan, two other SEALs that were part of this mission. Good men. Shadow had worked with both before. Actually at this point, he'd been lucky enough to work with several dozen SEALs. It was just over time some were more memorable than others. Markus had lost his wife in his first year at Coronado. A loss that had hurt him deeply. It had been easy to empathize. That he'd kept his head down and his focus on his work, well, he'd earned everyone's respect then.

Evan was a bit of a wild card. Divorced and possibly

had a death wish with all his explosives training. Shadow was good, but Cooper and Evan rocked that world.

That didn't mean he was giving up his position though. Shadow was in the passenger seat for once – where he could see for miles. The others were in the cargo hold. Interesting switch. Then as a SEAL, he was accustomed to change. And being prepared. And adapting. One had to.

Hopefully the senator's family was holding up to the devastation in their life as well. There'd been no demands as yet. But the adult daughter had managed to transmit a blurry photo of one man to the senator's aide in Washington after they'd arrived at the cabin, and that had been enough for both countries to jump into action. The man was a known terrorist. In fact, he sat at the top of the top Ten Most Wanted list.

Not that Shadow cared about the list.

Shadow cared about the job. The work he did. This was his life. He was a remote cabin in the woods kind of guy. Take the city out of his world and he was at peace. Living on the base was a necessity, but he got away every chance he could. His friend and SEAL brother, Hawk, jointly owned a ranch with his sister several hours out of Coronado. Something Shadow could see himself doing. Only he knew Hawk and his sister were involved in heavy discussions about their options as they both had long term relationships to make work and the living arrangements needed some rethinking. Hawk had partnered up with his sister's best friend. And Shadow's best friend Swede had partnered up with Hawk's sister. Confusing, maybe, but it worked for them.

Then Shadow had seen that relationship coming. Hard not to. Only poor Swede, that big mountain hadn't.

Talk about being blind.

The way Swede had looked at Eva all these years but knowing it was a place he couldn't go…yeah painful. Still, they'd finally gotten there. Even if it had taken a rebel training camp and a mess of rescued horses to bring them together. Shadow grinned. It would take something like that for the big guy to make his move. But he was so damn happy now, it was ridiculous. That soured his mood instantly. Almost all his friends were happily paired up. It was almost sickening.

The small plane was buffeted by the heavy winds. Lightning cracked outside the window. He frowned, studying the thunderclouds around him. They should be close. The bush plane was rigged with floats, the plan to scoop down on the nearest lake and drop them as close to shore as Bob, the pilot, could get them to where the senator's family was being held. The storm gave them wonderful coverage for the landing. The plane engine would be lost in the crackle of the lightning and thunder. No one should be out in this nasty weather.

They were also landing further away from the cabin than the family would have arrived. They couldn't take the chance of alerting the kidnappers of their arrival.

Shadow looked at his SEAL team behind him, seeing that air of intense focus. That air of expectancy. That understanding of why they were here. That something could go wrong. Likely would go wrong. And they'd be ready. Whether it was Mother Nature about to unleash her worst on their small tin box in the sky or the terrorists holding the senator's family down below in the darkness — they had a job to do and they loved it.

So did he.

Being a SEAL had given him purpose. He'd needed that. He hated to admit it but joining the navy, coming from a small town to the city of the military had been tough. But he'd bore down and survived – thrived actually.

Yet there'd been always a sense of separation inside. As if the only way he could manage to get through this was to keep himself detached. Lock off the inner part of himself that was held inviolate. Foolish he knew. Particularly as he'd watched his friends go through such upheavals in their lives. They each let someone special inside. He didn't think he could. His walls were too strong. Too high. Too old.

The plane rocked wildly in the wind.

The pilot slowly descended, trying to bring the plane below the heavy cloud cover as visibility was nonexistent. And the plane wasn't equipped with the latest or the best equipment. Shadow half suspected that the old geezer beside him could fly this thing blindfolded. He had a special gift. A rare connection to his "girl."

Shadow understood.

He'd seen many an old-timer connect to a boat or car, or in this case a plane, in such a way that they seemed to have a surreal relationship. As Shadow watched, Bob coaxed the small plane down at a gentle descent. Shadow couldn't see all the dials on the dashboard but the one he could see, the altimeter, was spinning like mad. So the instruments had been affected by the storm too. He wasn't nervous. He was in life and death situations often. But not normally due to Mother Nature.

The clouds thinned enough to show the deep blue of a lake below, dancing in and out of their view as they descended. Good. This was the right lake. They'd be landing soon. He hoped the water was calmer than it looked.

It wasn't. As they got almost to the water level he could see white caps whipping up below them.

"Gonna be close," the pilot said with a huge tobacco stained toothy grin. "But you guys live for close, don't you?" His grin widened, but his gaze never came off the water as he carefully brought the old girl in to as smooth a float landing as possible given the circumstances.

Shadow respected the casual skill with which Bob set the plane down on the angry waves. This man had seen a lot of years in this type of wilderness in all kinds of weather to do what he'd just done. With no pier or dock to tie up to, the plane bobbed to the far end and Bob shut down the engines. The small plane rocked gently. Shadow looked at the shoreline and realized they were only about thirty feet out. Nice.

He turned to the back of the plane in time to see a small inflatable raft being lowered to the water and the first of his team climbing down into it. The raft was large enough to hold all four of them, but only just.

At the shore, they disembarked and turned to watch as Bob's winch rewound the rope still attached to the inflatable then he struggled to reload the boat in the cargo hold. Once done, he was quick to get back to the cockpit and turn on the engines.

The plane took off and disappeared into the storm clouds.

Good. They were alone.

Just the way they liked it.

Now to save the senator.

CHAPTER 2

ARIANNA STEPHENSON HUDDLED by the fire in the corner of the large cabin. Her baby brother had crawled half into her lap, his head nestled against her shoulder. At eight, he had just enough understanding of the world around them to know they were in big trouble. She'd always been fun and lighthearted with him, but there was no making light of this.

Her father, his head brightly colored after being battered by the kidnappers at the outset, sat on the couch, silent, his face pinched. But she didn't know if that was from the pain or the situation. Her beautiful stepmother sat beside her father, fingers and lips trembling and tears constantly pouring into the Kleenex crumpled in her hand.

Arianna might have more sympathy if her stepmother didn't look this way after most upsets, particularly when Arianna or Kevin refused to do her bidding. At his young age, Kevin had already taken more after his big sister's temperament than his mother wanted.

Yet if there was ever going to be a situation where her stepmother's reaction was appropriate – it was this one. And how stupid really. She'd been pulling that play for a decade now, and Arianna had come to the point of smiling sweetly and bringing her another box of Kleenex. Only this time it was for real, and Arianna didn't know how to deal with her.

Her father had been a senator for eighteen years. They'd had some security issues in the middle of that reign, but things had settled down in these last few years, at least she thought so. She hadn't lived at home for many years now so didn't live under the constant pressure she had when living there.

When they'd boarded a small plane to come to her grandfather's cabin in the Canadian wilderness, they'd had a very unpleasant reception waiting for them upon landing. They'd been marched from the dock to the cabin at gunpoint. As it was summer, and she wasn't due back at her teaching job until September, Arianna and Kevin had big plans to enjoy the unusual holiday. If she hadn't come, Kevin would be alone. Eight and having to listen to his mother bug their father every minute of the day. She was nothing if not contrary. Their father had done his best with Kevin when he'd been younger, but they'd grown apart years ago and now her father was always busy. She understood. The relationship followed the same pattern she'd gone through. She didn't want that for Kevin. She had lots of great memories of the land around the cabin she wanted to show him.

But who knew they'd be taken hostage? She stared out at the trees blowing wildly across the windows. A hell of a storm raged outside. Even considering they were under armed guard she was glad to be inside. She loved the outdoors as much as anyone but in a storm like this, it would turn nasty very quickly.

Except a storm raged inside, too.

She hoped her message had gotten through. Her phone had been ripped from her hands as soon as she'd hit send and crushed on the floor in front of her. All phones had been confiscated. So they had no way to call for the plane to pick them up early. It was prearranged for the same pilot to return on Monday.

But that was a lifetime away.

Her cheek still stung from the blow she'd received for sending the image. But it was nothing compared to what it could be. The leader had seemed to think her attempts more hilarious than anything. The terrorists wanted something from her father. His vote on something to do with oil. She remembered vaguely that there was an even split on the decisions that had been announced so far. Her father had yet to announce his decision. She wasn't even sure which side of the issue he was coming down on. Given his past views though, it was likely on the no side. He had no interest in oil pipelines anywhere across the country. Figured they weren't worth the environmental damage should something happen. But it was an unpopular decision for many as it would create thousands of jobs and of course that was a hot issue.

That's why she avoided politics like the plague. Her father had been approached with bribes, no…gifts, they called it, ever since his appointment had been announced. If he had been offered bribes for a vote in one direction or another then it made sense that someone would think he could be coerced one way or another as well. The old "if I can't give you a kiss then I'll give you a kick" sentiment. If she wasn't being watched so closely, she'd have laughed at her twist on the old attention getting action.

Still, she hadn't planned to spend her holiday facing guns. And what the hell kind were they anyway? Something like an assault rifle. They were mean looking firearms. And that was a whole different story. These guys were pros.

And she was stuck here waiting for a rescue.

Only she didn't do the whole damsel in distress thing very well. In fact, she wasn't sure she rocked the damsel thing at all. She was tall and lean and more athletically built than her women friends. As in missing the coveted junk in front and in the back. She was greyhound sleek, but her B cups didn't look as bountiful as her friends' chests. They'd been trying to convince her to get a boob job, but she'd laughed and said hell no. The men needed to take her the way she was or forget it. She didn't need a guy to want her for the silicone in her chest. And the concept of a butt implant grossed her out. She was what she was. And damn it, apparently that wasn't good enough.

Staring into the flames, stuck under guard, she realized how stupid it was to worry about her past lovers or physical failings – at least according to the men she'd dated – given her current situation. But it helped keep her mind off her worries. Another had wanted her to have curvy hips to shake on a dance floor, but he was out of luck there too. Why couldn't she attract marathon runners? After all that's what she was. She had no desire to return after an exhilarating run to someone still sitting on the couch.

"Love you, honey, be back in couple of hours." Then go run your heart out and feel the blood pumping through your veins like there wasn't going to be any tomorrow and come home to find the honey still sitting and playing video games? So not her style. Then, she didn't do video games either.

Kevin shifted in her arms. She smiled. She hadn't played them growing up. Her mother hadn't been a believer in any entertainment that required electronics. She'd learned to play video games for her kid brother. It was a great day when he could kick her butt on a game. He led a lonely life. And Arianna had done her best, but she couldn't be there all the time for him. Her stepmother was overprotective. Always afraid Kevin would get hurt. Of course, he had a hearing problem and speech impediment, but he was neither deaf nor dumb. But it made him a target by other kids. It helped to develop a tough skin early on.

Then kids were cruel and nothing protected anyone all the time.

Arianna was of the opinion that small hurts weren't a bad thing in the long run. Kevin's small hand snuck into hers. She wrapped an arm around him and tugged him so he was sitting between her legs and leaning back against her. He nestled in close. She studied the guard on the left. Bored to hell and stuck on his cell phone like so many people today. Did he have cell reception? Would his phone work to send out a message or just to play the correct flavor of the month game that everyone glommed onto?

She nudged Kevin, a budding techie, toward the guard's activities. She could see he didn't understand what he was looking at until his gaze landed on the phone and the information processing behind his thick Coke bottle glasses made his eyes glisten. Now he was thinking.

She squeezed him reassuringly. With a casual glance around she studied her father's grim demeanor and her stepmother's distress. They didn't look like they were going to be of any help. She worried about her father's condition. He didn't look well. He wasn't a well man to begin with. He had his first heart attack seven years ago, another small one a couple of years ago. Another man stood at the back behind them all. He caught her looking at him and raised the gun barrel to point at her. She flipped back around. She had yet to see the terrorist she'd managed to photograph again.

Her heart pounded inside her chest and it took

minutes for her panic to ease back. They'd been here close to ten hours now. How much longer until something happened? There was a four by four parked outside, but she knew the keys were in the pocket of the guy with the cell phone. Was there a second set to be found? She assessed the men. There'd been four at the cabin when they'd arrived. But there were more than that here now only she didn't know how many more. She'd thought it was only fly in and fly out access but old roads crisscrossed the area so it made sense that they'd have driven more men in if they could.

And that was encouraging. Road access also meant an escape route.

Kevin whispered, "I have to go to the bathroom again."

She sighed and stood up. She held out her hand. "Come on then."

He walked beside her until they got to the third gunman. "He needs to go again."

"What's his problem, he got a bladder infection or something?"

"Likely just nerves," she said quietly. The gunman moved to the side and let them pass. As the bathroom was right there, she motioned to Kevin to go in.

"No shutting the door," the gunman warned the same as he had every other time they'd been forced to come this way.

"We won't." She gave Kevin a little shove toward the bathroom. "Go on. It will be fine."

Kevin gave the gunman a worried look before racing inside. He shut the door just enough for privacy while she stood outside. She deliberately kept her gaze on the door straight ahead. She had an excellent memory, she was a hobbyist photographer after all, and she'd recognize this *type* of man anywhere. They even looked similar. They all wore khakis. They all had black hair and long beards. Each had dark eyes and larger slightly hooked noses. They all had mustaches. Their builds were similar. She didn't get it. All brothers of the same family? They were all roughly the same age. Or within ten years. And that made it possible. But…as she stole a sideways glance at the one guarding the bathroom, she realized their faces would have something unique to them. She struggled to find a way to identify the men from each other.

The man beside her smirked when he caught her looking at him.

Damn.

She didn't want him to notice her. But it was already too late. They'd been eyeing her since they'd arrived. She was casually dressed in jeans and a t–shirt with a heavy sweater over top. Decently covered but still showing too much for her peace of mind. Her stepmother was much prettier and more attractively dressed and barely a decade older. Why weren't they looking at her the same way?

Because she was the senator's daughter? She had to find a way out of this damn cabin before one of the men decided she'd make a great way to pass the time or to pressure her father into doing what they wanted. They probably didn't know that nothing would make her father change his mind.

The bathroom door opened and Kevin stumbled out. She reached for him. "My turn. Stand right here and wait for me." He nodded but his lower lip trembled. She gave him a quick hug and walked into the bathroom. She knew the guard had watched her last time, his position allowing him to see her in the mirror. She deliberately bent so as to keep out of his view as much as possible. When done, and wow had she become fast, she quickly washed her hands and walked out to her brother. He looked horrible. Fear had turned his eyes to huge orbs. He gave a tiny shake of his head to the right. She glanced over and saw the heated gaze in the guard's eyes as it locked on her. Shit.

With her throat too seized to speak she led her brother back to the fireplace. She had to escape. These men might have done this to force her father to help them on some stupid ruling, but they had no trouble seeing her as spoils of war. She had to get through the night and was very much afraid that it wouldn't be alone.

THE TEAM HAD been silent as they trekked through the wilderness. They'd checked the coordinates several times, but no sign of the cabin yet. The wet weather wasn't helping. With nightfall coming, they had no idea if the senator and his family were going to make it until morning. There were four family members here. The senator's third and much younger wife, their eight-year-old son, plus his twenty–five year-old-daughter from marriage number two. The senator himself was in his mid–seventies.

He had a reputation as being a square man. A bit old fashioned and stuck in his ways and if his cohort's reports came in a two hundred-page style, his tomes were usually five times that. Much to the consternation of anyone forced to read it. Long-winded maybe, but often with solidly made points.

And he had a reputation for being a good man. Un-swayed by popular opinion. A bit stodgy in his views maybe but he was thorough and pragmatic. Not someone who bent to pressure or could be bribed – apparently. But when a man's family was threatened, Shadow wasn't sure any man would hold out. If you wanted to maximize pressure on a person, take his family hostage. In this case, they'd taken the whole family. And that was the part that really confused Shadow.

Why? If they'd done this while the senator was home to do their bidding, they could have whisked the family anywhere in the world.

If the senator didn't survive this "holiday," it could be months before he was replaced. Or longer. It wasn't a simple process to appoint a new member to the senate.

Then why kidnap the family? Why not just kill the senator outright? He highly doubted the kidnappers had a conscience. But if so, maybe they were expecting the senator to do the right thing so they weren't forced to kill everyone. Because of course if they killed him, they'd have to kill them all. And no one wanted that.

Or was something else going on?

At a signal from Mason, they all stood up silently. Hidden under different trees they were close enough to be in contact but far enough that no one could see them all together. Cooper was closest to him. Now back to active duty, and not a moment too soon, Cooper was chomping at the bit for some serious action. He'd been sidelined with abdominal injuries that had stopped him from carrying the weight required out in the field. He'd healed but had been too overzealous and caused a setback with several pulled muscles. He bounced to his feet, appearing to be in glowing health now.

Moving in formation, Shadow leading, they hopefully were closing in on the cabin. The wind had picked up, making the going tougher. The undergrowth was wet and footing treacherous. With the dark of night settling in early, they'd need to locate the cabin and make plans when they saw the lay of the land. It was easy to make plans on paper but the terrain would have a lot to do with their next move. Shadow was completely okay to hike in and out, but he wasn't sure the senator was up to that level of physical exertion. And there was no point in saving him only to kill him on the way home.

Hat slung low over his eyes with the rain sliding off the brim to the left, he carefully assessed the way forward. Seeing the next step, he took a sharp right and picked up the pace. It couldn't be too long now.

CHAPTER 3

"ARI, I'M HUNGRY," Kevin whispered.

She hugged him little closer. "Sorry, bud. I don't know if dinner will happen."

He gave her long look. She grinned. "I know. For you that's going to be horrible."

"I haven't eaten since we got here," he exclaimed. "Surely they don't mean to starve us."

"There's food." That was the man with the cell phone. "But not what you're used to." He got up and walked to a box at the side. One of a good dozen boxes. Without any fanfare, he pulled out a jar of peanut butter and a loaf of bread. He tossed them at Kevin. "This is your dinner."

Kevin lit up. "Hey thanks."

The gunman looked at him oddly for a few moments then shrugged.

"Can I have something to spread the peanut butter?" Kevin asked in his guttural tone.

The gunman glared at him, then pulled out a plastic spoon and gave it to him.

Again the irrepressible spirit of a child on an adventure surfaced. Kevin snatched it up and opened the peanut butter. The spoon went in and he didn't bother with the bread – the first spoon went right in his mouth. If there was one food guaranteed to put a smile on Kevin's face it was peanut butter. Arianna rolled her eyes and helped him to spread peanut butter on several slices of bread. She slapped tops on both of them and handed them over to him.

He took one in each hand and had the first gone before she'd managed to make up two more. She nodded to their parents. "Go offer them some."

Still buoyed by the peanut butter, he headed to his father with a sandwich in each hand. Arianna watched as she continued making sandwiches. Her father was gruff and often distant but she knew in his own way he loved Kevin. However, he hated peanut butter.

Yet, with a resigned look on his face, the senator accepted the sandwich and whispered, "Thanks."

Kevin grinned. "I'll get you a second one too."

He turned to his mother. "Mom, do you want one?"

Arianna lowered her gaze. It was painful to see the other woman so out of her element. She'd not wanted to come in the first place, had made life for her father hellish for weeks and now seeing as what had happened, she could imagine what her stepmother was thinking.

"No, I most certainly do not." She turned on her husband. "See, I told you we shouldn't have come." She glared at him from watery eyes. "This is a terrible place."

He reached out and patted her knee. "We're here now and we'll make the best of it."

Kevin kept holding out the second sandwich to his mother.

Arianna watched, waited. Her gaze narrow, Linda stared at the sandwich like it was a viper about to strike and opened her mouth as if to offer a scathing report only to catch sight of Arianna's hard gaze. Her face pinched and she shot a glare at Arianna as if this mess was her fault, then accepted the sandwich. "Thank you, Kevin. Very kind of you."

Beaming, and seemingly unaware of the tension between the two most important women in his life, Kevin raced back to Arianna. "Two more please."

She nodded and handed him the next two sandwiches.

He reached almost instantly with empty hands. She had made four more by now. He snatched up two and walked over to the gunman who'd given him the peanut butter. "These are for you."

Silence.

Everyone in the room stared as the young boy held out the sandwiches to his captor. Arianna wanted to look around and see what the other men would do. Hell, she didn't know what this first man would do, but she hoped not beat the child for being impertinent. Instead, the gunman accepted the sandwiches and returned to the game on his cell phone.

After that Kevin went to the other three gunmen inside the house. She worried when he went down the hallway to the kitchen and back door where the fourth man stood.

Still he came back empty handed.

Then he realized the bag was empty and his face fell. He studied the two sandwiches left in her hand. One she'd been taking bites out of as she worked. She laughed and handed over her second sandwich. "That will teach you to give all the food away while you're still hungry."

"I might be a little hungry, but better that than everyone being really hungry."

Arianna smiled. She loved her kid brother. He said the most wonderful things. She had no idea how her stepmother had created him, and he looked nothing like her father or herself so she'd always worried he might not even be genetically related but knew DNA had been checked at his birth. He was family, but it wouldn't have mattered to her one bit if he technically wasn't. He was precious regardless.

They had to make it out of here. She wanted to believe they would. Her whole life functioned on an irrepressible positive good humor and outlook on life. Kevin had his whole life ahead of him. She did in theory too, but she'd do what she could to save him. She'd focus on that and work to make it happen. She didn't know what the kidnappers' plan was at this point – they'd been very sparse with their commands thus far, limiting their talking to clear orders.

As Kevin curled back up in her lap, she realized how late it was getting. She suspected there'd be no rescue this night. Unfortunately. She smiled. She'd hope for the morning.

Then the man who'd given Kevin the food said, "It's time for you to go to bed."

Kevin looked over at him, his body tense, his arm hooked around Arianna's. "The bedroom upstairs?"

The gunman nodded. "Two rooms. Two beds. You and your sister in one and your parents in the other. You first."

Thank God. Arianna hated to think that they planned to separate her from her brother, but with the looks they'd been giving her, she'd been worried. She got to her feet, knowing they'd be escorted. There was a bathroom up there as well. With one man behind her and her brother, they climbed the stairs to the bedroom.

Every step she worried the next would be her last. Her dad and Linda stayed below. They still needed her father for something. She hoped. Kevin gripped her hand so tight she knew he was terrified. Upstairs, their bags already in their room, they quickly grabbed up their toothbrushes and went to the bathroom. The gunman never left. Kevin didn't want to go to the bathroom while the man watched. She half covered him and persuaded him to get the job done then they could get into bed. Awkwardly, he finished and washed up his hands. Now it was her turn.

Kevin turned his back and stared at the gunman as if willing him to take him on. Then he crossed his arms and spread his legs in defiance.

The gunman laughed. But the trick worked. By the time the gunman's gaze had shifted back to her, she'd already finished and had approached the sink to wash her hands. In the mirror she caught sight of his disappointment. He was just pure slime.

In the bedroom the gunman had closed and locked the door. She hadn't even realized there was a lock on it, not remembering it being there last time. In fact, the knob was very new looking.

As in this had been preplanned and all contingencies worked out.

Then she heard raised voices downstairs and realized they were going to work her father over while they were forced to listen upstairs. She had to distract Kevin. He'd heard enough already.

Damn.

THE CABIN NESTLED deep inside the trees below. Shadow walked out on a ledge overlooking the tranquil setting.

Or what could be a tranquil scene if a storm wasn't blasting through the area covering them in rain and blowing branches into their faces. Still, there were lights on inside and that gave it a look of a haven from the storm. His team were spread out, taking up positions. They had work to do before going in on a blind rescue. As of now they didn't know how many men were here and if the hostages were even still alive. His radio crackled lightly. He adjusted the sound, listening to the conversation going on around him.

One man on east corner. Assault rifle over the shoulder. Two hand guns.

Shadow's lips turned down at the corner. The men were loaded for bear.

Grenades on a clip at his back.

Shit. Most kidnappers weren't equipped with grenades.

The radio sounded again. This time it was Dane talking. "Unit is a half mile out. Will be coming on foot from here."

The team traveling cross-country had arrived on schedule. Now to figure out how many terrorists they were up against – and to confirm that the hostages were still alive. It would be easy enough to pick off the one man outside but not until they were ready to move. Or the hostages would be sacrificed.

Second man on the southwest corner, came the low whisper. Mason.

That was two outside guards identified. Shadow studied the cabin. One single front door at the top of four stairs. A large lazy porch wrapping from the front to the left side. The windows long and low. So no traveling from one side to the other without being seen. He continued to catalog the house. Noting the light on upstairs on the right and the lights on in the main living room. Smoke curled lazily from the chimney. If they hadn't had the text from the daughter and seen the two guards, no one else would have any idea something was wrong.

But he knew.

The woods were alive with tension.

Upstairs a woman moved to the window and stared out. The daughter, Arianna. Long blonde ringlets, fully dressed, arms crossed as she stared out into the world. He pulled up his binoculars to see her tapping her fingers impatiently on her arm. Her mouth pinched with tension. A young boy arrived at her side. She took him in her arms and hugged him close.

That was the senator's son, Kevin.

So the two siblings were likely locked upstairs. Were the senator and his wife up there as well? He doubted it. The terrorists were "talking" to the senator now. Not good. The senator was known to be stubborn as shit and would take the beating, but at his age, that could be lethal.

He shifted his position slightly and set his sights back on the daughter upstairs. And gazed directly in her eyes.

She stared back at him.

Surely she couldn't see him. Her gaze narrowed and tingles slid down his back. He estimated the distance between them and realized that he could see her without the binoculars so in effect she might be able to see him, but not likely… She was in the light and looking into the dark. Still…

He raised a hand to her.

She froze. And damn if she didn't slowly raise a hand casually behind the boy's back and hold it palm forward.

Excitement drove through him. Was this possible?

Then she did something with her fingers. And repeated it over and over again. He locked the binoculars on her hand movement.

She was signaling for help using signals for the deaf. And then he remembered the senator's son had several disabilities.

Whether she understood what she was seeing or not, she'd sensed someone out here. Damn. Now how could he get a message to her?

He signaled right back, *Help is here. Sit tight.* And repeated it over and over. Inside he knew she couldn't see it. Damn it. He was too far away. And what benefit would it do to find a better location.

She continued to signal until the boy leaned his head back to her. And she smiled down at him and cuddled him close. Shadow glanced down at the binoculars in his hands. He'd been given a glimpse into her personality that he'd not seen in too many other people – if any. She really loved that boy. She was the sister, not the mother, although from what he'd just seen she could have been. The bond was that strong.

There'd been something so damn caring, loving between them, he felt…and the words eluded him as he glanced at the woods around him, the rain dripping from the leaves, the moon hidden high above. He knew exactly how the boy felt. How he always felt. Alone. On the outside. Not included. This setting only amplified that feeling.

Except for one very important point. He was not a young boy any longer. He was a Navy SEAL. This was his life, and if he didn't like it he could change it. But he wasn't prepared to change very much. He'd become comfortable with his life. Understood it. Knew how it worked. So even though there were other things out there for other people, he was good with who he was and the way he was.

As he returned his gaze to the window, he realized the room had gone dark.

Just then, his radio squawked.

Senator is in the living room. Two men working him over. Wife on the floor. Condition unknown.

And he realized something else. He was who he was and that was a damn good thing for the senator's son and daughter. Because of who he was, they'd get to continue being who they were.

He'd caught sight of an escape hatch for the kids. Saving the senator was a whole different story. But if they could get the brother and sister out it removed two pawns in the game.

He quietly told his team what he was going to do.

CHAPTER 4

S HE SWORE SHE'D seen someone on the hillside across from them. She knew it was likely to be her imagination, hope creating images where there were none because she was desperate for escape.

Her father's cries below had stopped. There was only the odd moan now. And that terrified her even more. She'd turned down the hearing aids in Kevin's ears. There was no way he needed to hear his father's last cries. She was so angry but knew she had to keep Kevin safe. Even if she could charge downstairs to save her father, she'd get a bullet. That might still be a kindness when compared to the possible outcome waiting for them. But she damned well hoped not. And she'd be no help to Kevin then.

She's been signaling off and on since they'd been locked in the bedroom. Hoping against hope that someone would come. Then she thought there had been an odd flash on the hillside and a weird awareness came over her, that feeling of being stared at.

Time was running out. The kidnappers had provisions for several days from what she could see, but she had no intention of being here with them. She'd been assessing options since they'd arrived. Being on the second floor with no balcony she knew it was a hell of a long drop to the ground. She might be able to tie the sheets and blankets together to lower them enough to jump the rest of the way but getting lost in the middle of the woods wasn't exactly an answer.

But it might be the only one available. If she could evade the guards outside. She'd seen them change out the guard every hour. What she didn't know was if they were stationed outside or if they were doing rounds on the property to keep moving and cover the cabin from all angles. She'd been staring outside since forever but hadn't seen any of them. That didn't mean they weren't there. She'd been looking with the light off for the last twenty minutes. After her father had gone silent. She didn't want them to think she was awake and listening in. Better to be oblivious.

She knew the chances of her father surviving this was poor, and grief clutched at her heart. She had no idea what they'd do to Linda either. The future looked like shit for all of them. She was loathe to run and leave the two of them behind, but if it meant saving Kevin…

She'd do it in a heartbeat.

She quietly tugged the window open. And stuck her head out.

When there were no yells or shouts for her to get back inside, she leaned out further.

And jumped back out of sight as a guard walked past.

Kevin clutched at her, fear twisting his delicate features.

She held her fingers to her lips to warn him to be quiet and leaned out again, looking for the man she thought she saw. There was no sign of anyone.

As she studied the height from the ground and mentally calculated the distance the sheets would hang she realized they were directly over the living room. If they dropped down to the ground here, they'd be seen.

Shit.

There were no balconies. There were no sloping roofs

to clamber across to the left or right. There was nothing helpful in that way at all. Huge trees rose beside the cabin and the branches higher up offered safety, but she had no way to get to them. The sheets were their only chance. Maybe if they were lucky they'd escape into the woods before being caught.

She slowly led Kevin back to the bed, her mind spinning but coming up empty. Kevin was counting on her. And fear was kicking in. Jesus. If the men killed their parents she and Kevin would have no chance. They were liabilities at that point. The kidnappers might try to use them for leverage, but her father had told her often he would never give in to extortion. If her father wouldn't do what he could to save them, then no one else could be bothered either.

Footsteps climbed the stairs. She closed her eyes in terror. *Oh God. Please not. Dear God. Help.*

Kevin dragged her down to the bed.

"Pretend to be asleep," she whispered.

It was as good a plan as any. Only it wasn't going to do the job. She knew that. But there weren't many options. She dare not strip the bed right now if someone was coming to check on them. But if they got a chance to leave after this asshole left, then they would.

Lying on the bed, on her stomach, hair across her face so he couldn't see her features well in the dark, she waited for the guard to come in. She briefly considered trying to kill him, but how. With what?

It wasn't possible – was it?

She swallowed when she heard a hand on the knob.

Then the key turned in the lock. With Kevin frozen and tucked up to her side, she lay quiet as the door opened, letting a sliver of light enter the room. The guard stood at the doorway and studied them. She kept her hand lax on Kevin's back and her breathing slow and steady.

If anyone touched them they'd know that the two of them were tense, muscles rigid.

The guard walked to the window where she'd been looking out. And she realized her one attempt to stick her head out had been seen. As she'd seen the guard, he'd seen her. Now someone had been sent to check.

God damn it.

She should have been more careful.

The guard looked down on the ground outside and studied the window and the view outside for a long moment then spun on his heels. And walked to the bed.

She lay so damn quiet, then realized it was too quiet. She made a snuffling sound and shifted slightly. They were lying fully dressed on the covers.

He stood and stared at her for a long moment. She could hear his breathing. Sense his interest.

Her skin crawled.

Then he reached down and touched her. His fingers sliding the hair back off her face.

She sighed and moved her head on the pillow as if something disturbed her and he stepped back.

After another long moment he walked through the door and closed it. When she heard the lock click inside she slowly opened her eyes, afraid that somehow two men had come in and one might be still there waiting for her to show she'd been faking it. When the footsteps continued downstairs, she sat up and got to work. It might not be the best idea but it was all she had.

They couldn't stay here.

IT TOOK PRECIOUS time to get into position. Even then he was thinking this was more foolhardy venture than good idea. But he did over the top rescues and this appeared to be yet one more. The reports coming in were rough. And they had to save who they could while they could. The minute the terrorists understood they had company, the hostages were going to be killed. If they'd killed the senator and his wife already, then there was no hope for the younger two members of the family. He had to get them out now.

Using the ropes from his pack and being a decent judge of distance, he'd climbed out on a low limb, but hopefully one still strong enough to hold the weight, and after tying several knots in the rope he lowered it down to the height of the window of the bedroom where he'd seen the brother and sister.

As there was no one in the window now to see his rope, he swung it gently forward to come up and lightly tap the glass. He knew his team was watching his progress.

The first swing fell short, the second was almost there. The third hit. A heavy enough thud, and he immediately pulled it up in case someone else heard it.

After a few moments, and lying full length on the large tree limb above, he swung it again. And it tapped the window lightly. Then he did it again. And again.

Damn it, where were they?

Afraid the two had been moved he tried one more time and watched as two pale faces appeared. Arianna wasted no time. She opened the window, did something to the brother and lifted him up to the windowsill. When Shadow swung the rope toward them, she grabbed it and had the boy grab high enough up the rope that he could stand on the knot below. Then she gave him a quick kiss and swung him out and away. She stepped back out of sight but he knew she could still see the boy as he hung on for dear life. Shadow carefully hauled him up. The boy was a lightweight. But it was still dangerous getting off the rope and over the main trunk of the tree where he wrapped the boy's arms around the trunk and whispered against his ear, "Hold on. I'll be right back. I have to get your sister."

Shadow returned with the rope to where the window was still open…and the young woman waited for him.

She peered out at him then darted back, slowly lowering the window again. What was she doing? Then he watched the guard on sentry duty cross the property line, his gaze automatically going to the bedroom window.

Shadow smiled in appreciation. He could kill the guard from where he was positioned and would love to – but only once he had the girl out and safe.

She needed to be rescued too.

He waited for the sentry to pass under him and go around the house, then slowly lowered the rope. This time when he swung it to the window he found her sitting on the ledge, legs out as if to jump. She stood up awkwardly, grabbed the rope as high as she could, and then pushed the window down behind her as she let go to swing out on the rope.

Smart.

He was liking her more and more already. She climbed up that rope like a monkey and as she made her way to where he was lying silently, he couldn't help but admire her. She was almost eye level, her gaze busy as she looked for a way to get up onto the tree. When he extended his arm, she reached up and clasped his forearm. He sat up and tugged, she landed in his arms. Very nice.

She lay there trembling for a long moment then turned to look directly at him. For a long moment their gazes locked. Then she said, "It was you, on the hill, wasn't it?"

He nodded. "Yes," he whispered. "Need to get the rope out of sight. Kevin is back at the main trunk."

She caught sight of her brother, carefully gained her footing and made her way over to him. Shadow, his hands busy pulling up his rope, looped it properly then stuffed it in his pack. He was surprised to see both Kevin and Arianna had backpacks with them. It was good but it had taken a presence of mind he hadn't expected.

He approached and with an arm around both of them he explained who he was and what they were going to do next.

Neither said a word until he was done. Then Kevin reached out and grabbed his hand, whispered in a hard to understand guttural voice, "Thank you."

CHAPTER 5

S EALs. Oh thank God. Even though she was still out in the middle of the wilderness with the terrorists down below holding her family captive, having SEALs here was a game changer. A big one. Still, they were a long way from being safe. Too early to celebrate. And then there was her father…

"The guard just checked on us. So our disappearance might not be noticed for a while, I don't know how often they will check."

"Right. Let's get you out of here," Shadow said.

Kevin froze. "Daddy?"

"We're going after them but that's for us to do. Not you."

"Do you want us to stay here until you come back?" she asked, looking around. They had to be a good thirty feet up in the air. They couldn't be seen from the ground and they were out of the rain. "This works. We're hidden and safe. We can settle on these big limbs until you get back."

"No, we should get further away. Stray bullets and all that."

She studied his lean face as he searched and assessed the area below them. His radio buzzed several times as the men communicated plans with each other. Suddenly there was some activity down below. Two men came out of the house and converged on the one guard who'd come back around again on his next pass. Raised voices and agitated movements said something bad had happened, but she had no idea what. She watched the SEAL as he studied what was going on.

Then a light came on in her bedroom.

"Shit."

That had been their window of escape. "How did they know?" she muttered in a low voice.

"It doesn't matter. They probably are checking on a regular basis anyway or maybe they saw something…" He surged forward to watch the men scurry out of the house and spread wide. "This is a good thing."

Immediately there were several pings and the one man deepest in the woods went down without a sound. From where she sat she could see another soldier in heavy combat gear step out from behind a tree and though the terrorists were big, this man was huge. He approached the terrorist from behind, and she didn't see what happened next but she could imagine. The SEAL shifted the man's body until it was hidden in the bush. So simple. So easy. For him.

They had a perfect view in front and below where they perched, but for the tree branches, couldn't see in other directions at all. So she had no idea what else was happening with the other men that had been inside. Surely they wouldn't have all come out on the one side of the house. That made no sense. But then maybe they had more men than she knew about. There were sounds of a powerful engine arriving. She glanced at her rescuer. "Is that yours?"

He shook his head. "Sounds like reinforcements to move you to a new location."

"Glad we're out of there then," she said with feeling. But there wasn't the same joy for their parents. She watched as both were escorted out of the cabin. Relieved to see both walking, although bent over and holding onto each other as they were prodded into the new truck, she was also dismayed to see so many new soldiers exiting out the back of the vehicle. This was not good. It appeared they'd brought another eight, possibly ten men. Why would they need so many? And these were dressed in the same khakis again. That made them easier to spot and easy to tell apart from the SEALs. Then again she couldn't see the SEALs. She had no idea where they were or how many were here. She glanced over at the man at her side, but he was studying three men sneaking up on a clump of brush to the side. She wondered what they thought could possibly be there when the SEAL beside her did a quick tie of the rope around the branch he stood on and dropped.

As in straight down.

On top of the first man and wiped out the second before a SEAL hidden in the bushes took out the third.

"Wow," she whispered.

Kevin beamed at her. "Yeah, he's awesome."

She'd never seen anything like it. Who could unless they did this kind of training? It was not something she ever wanted to experience again but the way this man moved, so graceful and yet wild, untamed. And he was so damn silent.

Looking down below them again she studied the ground looking for *her* SEAL. And couldn't find him. She shifted to glance at other areas through the trees but there was no sign of him. She wished she'd asked his name.

"Where did he go?" she asked Kevin in a hoarse voice.

He stared down below. "I don't know. He just…disappeared."

With no incentive to leave the safety of their hiding

place, the two hunkered down to wait. They watched the ground intently believing that their rescuer might return any moment. But nothing happened for at least an hour and by then she'd started to worry. What if he couldn't come back for them? He was only one man. Big and strong and obviously damn capable, but still, just a flesh and blood human like all the dead men down below.

Not that she could see any of them.

The vehicles were still parked outside the house, and their parents were still seated inside the back of the newest one. She studied the truck. It was a foolish thought but what if she could get into the driver's side… Could she drive out and get them to safety?

Had any of the men gone to guard inside the vehicle with her dad and Linda? Not likely as they weren't a threat anymore. Did the terrorists even understand that there was a bigger threat than themselves around here? Were they looking for her and her brother? Or were they going to assume the worst. Without the bodies of their fallen comrades that should throw them into confusion as to exactly what had happened. She'd rewound the SEAL's rope so no one else would know they were up here but as she stared at it, still tied to the limb they were sitting on, she couldn't help but wonder if there was something more she could do. More she *should* do.

Kevin made an odd gurgling sound. She studied his face, fatigue had bleached the color from his skin. Did he need his medicine? The shocks had happened so fast they had to be hard for him to deal with. She wasn't even sure what all his medications were for as his mother handled all that. But although he was looking tired, what he needed more than anything was to know he was safe and to see his parents again.

She didn't know about the last one. She hoped they'd

survive but was loathe to put Kevin in any danger. They were safe here. They needed to stay.

And that rope in her arms could stay right there too.

"HOW ARE THE kids?"

Shadow stared at Swede. "The boy is a kid but the daughter is twenty–five. Nothing kiddish about her."

Swede's huge grin split his face. Typical. Always a smile no matter what. But when you needed him, he was all business. He was a good man to have at your back. They all were. Cooper slid over to join them, Markus and Evan at his side.

"The senator and his wife are in the truck. No guards."

"Do we know that for sure?" Markus motioned in a low voice. "I can't see leaving the prisoners without a guard."

"Unless there are no prisoners," Evan said in a sarcastic tone. "A sleight of hand maybe?"

Shadow frowned. Why would they do that? The senator needed medical aid and wasn't likely in any shape to escape so they didn't need guards, but surely the terrorists had figured out that they were under attack by now. And stealing the truck was also a possibility.

He shifted position to get a better view of the confab raging inside the kitchen. He said, "All the hostages are outside. The terrorists are inside. We need to go in and take them down now."

Mason's voice came over the radio, low and clear. They were going in.

Shadow muttered back, "Is someone guarding the senator?" A short time later, Mason came back. "Two guards down. They were assigned to guard the truck."

Shadow confirmed he'd grab the truck with the senator and slipped between the trees. He was concerned that someone hidden was going to be looking out for the victims. But there were no drivers inside and no passengers. So just the senator and his wife. Unless there was a gunman hidden inside waiting. He took several steps forward until an odd sound registered. He stepped back and was tackled from behind.

He spun and grabbed and twisted his attacker to the ground and realized his hands were grabbing soft flesh, soft material, and there was nothing enemy like about the beautiful worried face beneath him. Arianna.

He reared back in shock, his mind trying to process what she was doing, when she whispered, "You can't touch the truck. We saw someone plant a device underneath. Looked like dynamite." Her voice was hoarse but defiant.

He didn't know what to say. He quickly withdrew and dragged her with him back into hiding. "Tell me again exactly what you saw," he said. His mind struggled at the idea that she'd left her brother up in the tree to come and save him. He had never expected such a thing and didn't know what to do with the information now.

She quickly related what she'd seen and her gut decision to drop down and save him. He stared at her again. "And your brother?"

"He's safe," she whispered, "He was in agreement."

He wanted to ask why but knew he couldn't. She explained anyway. "We couldn't let you be killed when you'd saved us. Besides we need you to help save our parents." Her grin flashed.

"It's my job to save," he said in low tones, turning his gaze to search their surroundings while he tried to process the information.

"And it's my job to save you when I could. Anyone would have in the same situation," she retorted. "You're welcome by the way."

And damn if she didn't reach up and kiss him.

Once again thunderstruck by her actions, his hand instinctively slapped his cheek where she'd kissed him. And he blinked at her in shock.

She grinned and reached up and kissed his other cheek.

He lifted his other hand to slap his other cheek then narrowed his gaze as he realized how silly he looked.

Then she pulled his head down and laid one on him. He couldn't help but respond. She demanded a response. One he couldn't hold back.

"Harrumph."

She broke away and spun to stare up. As in way up. Swede. Her gaze widened and she plastered back against Shadow. Shadow knew there'd be no end to ribbing now. He glared at the huge smirking Swede who was flanked by a wildly grinning Cooper. Behind were Markus and Evan with grins on their faces as well. Everyone at base had heard about their group's love matches. Hell, they were likely the laughing stock of SEALs everywhere. Unless you were jealous…

Several guys had asked to join their ranks on the next mission. Half joking but some were very serious. The type of work they did, it was tough on relationships and now that so many of his friends had seemed to find a magic formula the other guys wanted in.

"Thank you very much for saving my dear friend, Shadow here," Swede said in a gentle voice. "Don't mind him if his manners are a little rusty." And that smile of his that melted hearts everywhere appeared to melt Arianna's too. Still lying flat against him, she held out her hand and said, "At least now I know his name."

She twisted to grin up at Shadow. "And it's okay if his manners are a little rusty. His skills in other areas obviously…aren't."

And damn it, heat rose to his face. He had no idea who this woman was but he was…interested…intrigued. Hell, he was…no, he refused to admit it. Attraction was one thing. But this…whatever this was…had to be something else again.

Cooper stepped behind Shadow and chanted, "Another one bites the dust."

CHAPTER 6

ARIANNA COULDN'T STOP touching him. She was a toucher by nature, but when she'd seen the man who'd rescued her and her brother head toward the truck and knew he had seconds to live, she'd used the rope like he had and swung out and let go. And had landed on him. It had worked a little too well maybe, but she was down and he was fine.

And damn it, she ran her fingers over his features yet again, he felt so good.

"I'm fine," Shadow muttered, pulling her hands down.

The other SEALs had huge grins on their faces. She'd heard them called Swede, Cooper, Markus and Evan. What was it about the SEALs that made them all dashing and dangerous looking? She studied them. Swede was a blonde mountain, Cooper was only slightly smaller. Markus was dark, swarthy. Evan was the opposite, so blond his hair appeared almost white. Not to mention sexy. At that she turned to look back at Shadow, her mind immediately adding *very sexy*...

Shadow, and what kind of name was that, didn't appear to know what to do with her.

Hell, she didn't know what to do with her. He set her on her feet and turned to face the truck, his face leaning out as he considered the problem. "Swede, weight sensitive do you think?"

"I'm thinking so. Cooper, Evan, what do you think?"

"It would make sense but that's going to have been made here. Too touchy for that kind of travel." Evan said.

Cooper nodded but stayed silent.

"But they'd have been able to travel with the unit mostly built then add the mechanism here if that was the case," Arianna said absentmindedly. "They brought no equipment that I could see."

The group stared at her. "What? If I didn't see any bombs or bomb making equipment, then they likely brought it here with the truck." She spun back to look at it. "I wonder if the truck is stolen. Destroy it in the Canadian wilderness and leave it behind. A good way to make sure it's never found."

With Shadow still studying her, she turned warm under that intense light in his eyes. If he'd been confused before he was even more so now. She smiled up at him. "It's a hobby."

"Bomb making," he asked carefully, his gaze narrow.

She laughed. "No, mysteries."

With a confused look on all their faces, she explained. "I'm a mystery buff. Go to mystery dinners, read the latest and the best, not to mention every other one I can get my hands on."

"Cool," Cooper said. "That always appealed."

She turned to see Shadow's reaction, noting the dark gaze before it was turned back to face the truck that held her dad and stepmom. She wanted to call out but didn't dare bring any unwanted attention. She glanced upward to see her brother staring down at her. She waved.

He grinned.

Her hand was lowered and she was jerked back behind Shadow. She frowned at him. He glared at her. And she realized she'd completely forgotten that there were other men out here still and she wasn't safe.

She was an innocent, but he was keeping her safe.

She beamed at him.

His gaze narrowed on her then shifted to look at his buddies. Arianna caught the other men hastily hiding grins.

"Aren't you going to defuse the bomb?" she asked. "Anytime now would be good."

Shadow's eyebrows shot up to the hairline. But he stayed quiet – just shook his head.

"I'll check it out," Cooper said. Shadow moved the group back, keeping Arianna behind him and Swede. Markus and Evan split away and headed off to the sides.

She snuck up closer until she was plastered against the huge tree beside them as the men kept watch for Cooper.

Cooper slid over to the vehicle and lay down. He reached up and she gasped, her hand instinctively grasping Shadow's hand. Gunfire rained down around them. She cried out and covered her head.

Then suddenly Cooper was out from under the vehicle and racing toward them.

He joined them crouched in the bush. "Simple enough. No timer. No pressure sensitivity. Likely remote detonation just in case we did drive the truck away with the senator."

She squeezed Shadow's hand. "He's good."

When Shadow didn't say anything, she gave his hand a shake. "Isn't he?"

Shadow slanted a look her way. "They are all good."

She beamed. "See. Shadow thinks you're good too."

Cooper, his eyes dancing, said to Shadow, "Thanks, buddy. Your opinion means a lot to me."

With a snort, Shadow disengaged his hand and disappeared into the woods. Just like that.

"Where did he go?" she asked after several long moments searching the woods around her.

"He did what he does best, walks in the shadows."

"Hence his name." She nodded. "Did any of you consider that he does that because he's always alone? Thinks he's always going to be alone," she added in exasperation. "That's not a good thing you know."

Swede stared at her, a peculiar look in his eyes and said gently, "He'll continue to believe that until someone comes along and changes it for him."

Then he disappeared in the bushes too.

Cooper smiled down at her. "It's nice to see you already understand Shadow."

"I don't know that I understand him," she cautioned. "He saved my life."

"And you saved his," he said cheerfully. "Isn't there something to that old adage about saving a life and being responsible for that life ever after?"

"Then our scales would just cross each other's off as we're even," she said a little reluctantly, intrigued at the idea of having a man like Shadow feel a little responsible for her. Not totally responsible because that would feel like a ball and chain over time, and she couldn't handle shackles. Still…he was…all man. Sigh.

"Not at all. It would mean that he is to look after you, but that you are also to look after him."

"We're so different, that would hardly work," she said with a smile, speaking in light tones. Too bad Shadow wasn't still here.

"Oh, but you'd be caretakers of different parts of each other. Like you could look after the part of him that feels alone. Empty," Cooper added quietly. "Shadow needs to know that he has someone in his life besides his brothers." He tapped his chest. "He and the rest of our team."

"Doesn't he have any family?" It would be tough to be all alone. She didn't like her stepmother, had learned to deal with her gruff father, but she'd be lost without Kevin.

Cooper shook his head. "And he's very private."

She nodded, staring into the bushes. "Poor man."

"I don't think sympathy is on the menu."

"No, neither is pity. He doesn't need it either. He's survived and that's the best any of us can do sometimes." She tilted her head back to see the rope too high up for her to reach. "I need to get back up to my brother." She turned to Cooper. "Can you give me a boost up?"

The words weren't fully out of her mouth before she was literally tossed up into the air in the direction of the rope. She grabbed on and scurried up to where her brother sat anxiously waiting for her.

Her arms were aching, and her breathing uneven by the time she got to the top. But she made it, and with her brother tucked up close in her arms, the two of them safe against the trunk, and the rope once again looped around the branch, she closed her eyes and rested.

Shadow…an interesting name for an interesting man.

SHADOW STUDIED THE four men in front. They weren't as well trained as the other soldiers and stood talking as a group. Then he realized that his group hadn't been much better. And that was disheartening. Trust a woman to create such a situation. Hell, before she'd arrived he'd been doing well. Now he was scattered and confused. He shoved all thoughts of Arianna back inside. She was a job. That was all.

Liar.

But he wouldn't listen.

Swede joined him. Markus on his heels. Shadow glanced behind.

"She's with Cooper."

Shadow nodded but the thought soured his gut. Great. The only other single guy in the unit and one who was friendly and got along wonderfully with everyone. Wait, Markus and Evan were here too. Great. More men for her to choose from. Yet he shouldn't give a damn. She was nothing to do with him. Good for Cooper if he found someone. He'd had a shitty year. Then Markus deserved a relationship after losing his wife. And what about Evan's divorce? He could use a sweetheart himself. Someone like Arianna would be perfect.

And that made his stomach want to heave.

Suddenly the enemy in front of him were on the move, two to the left and two to the right. He headed right, Swede beside him. Markus walked the center line.

The two men went down without a fight. Shadow stared at an unconscious man at his feet. He quickly secured him and turned to see Swede already lifting the other over his shoulder.

They were collecting the men and keeping them on the other side of the hill under heavy guard. So far they'd managed to take several out without alerting the enemy.

But then the men had been easy to capture. And he wondered about that. As in they were *too* easy to capture. Shouldn't these men be more of a challenge?

Swede leaned closer. "Canadian team is suspicious. Says it's too easy."

"I agree." Shadow studied the collection of soldiers. "They don't look worried."

"We've disarmed them," Markus said adding, "at least our weapons stash is growing."

Then Shadow got it. He spun around behind him, searching for the enemy. "They are a distraction. While we're here worrying about them, the others are setting plans in motion."

"Time to get back to the cabin." Swede pivoted and blended into the woods. Shadow was close enough behind to hear his radio crackle and Mason's voice but too far behind to hear the words. He suspected they were all considering what was beneath this ploy.

"We need to make sure the senator is okay," he muttered to Mason.

"He's still in the truck."

"I'm not sure he is." Markus shook his head. "Like I said before, I think that's a sleight of hand movement and we fell for it."

There was an awkward silence on the other end. "That would not be good."

Swede, slightly ahead, turned and nodded in agreement at Shadow. There had to be some reason for the extra men to be scattered and easily caught.

Not to mention they were well trained soldiers. They were trained killers, weapons aside.

The truck came into view.

And lying underneath, trying to do something, was Cooper again. This time he had Evan helping him.

Then where the hell was Arianna? He spun and twisted so he could peer up into the trees above then shifted to look at others around him lest the enemy could see him and understand what he'd been looking for. He'd caught sight of Kevin's black windbreaker. Enough to know the boy was up there.

Cooper motioned to him with his hand. Shadow crouched down to see what the issue was. And found a second bomb. Jesus. He ran fingers over his face.

Just as he was trying to figure what to do, bullets circled the truck in a hail of gunfire, all coming from high up in the trees.

They were surrounded.

Shadow melted into the background. He hated to leave Cooper under the truck. If anyone chose to shoot the truck then the hostages, if they were still there, Cooper would be killed. That's why they hadn't had a guard down below. The guards had been above.

And that meant Kevin and Arianna were in trouble too. He spun in time to see Swede take aim and fire. A man gave a cry and fell to the ground twenty feet away. He landed heavy and didn't move.

Instantly, the area where they stood came under a barrage of bullets. But they'd moved already. Swede popped off another one as Shadow raced to the base of the tree holding the two family members. Gunfire spat all around him.

Realizing they'd been outplayed, he scrambled up the tree as Swede moved in and out of the bushes below him drawing the fire away.

In the distance he heard more gunshots. Not a good sign. Their captives had probably heard the gunfire and used it as a signal to overpower the men guarding them. The Canadian contingency had been right. This was too easy. Well, not any longer. Shadow climbed rapidly. He landed quietly on the huge branch he'd left Kevin on and found him wrapped around the tree, his eyes closed and trembling.

"Kevin, it's me," Shadow whispered.

Kevin's eyes popped open and he stared at Shadow. Then threw himself into his arms. Unprepared for the onslaught, Shadow had to quickly adjust his grip and position to handle the tiny tornado. But he held him close to his chest. "Where is your sister?" he asked, quietly searching through the tree. She'd been left with Cooper. Cooper was under the truck. He gave Kevin a shake. "Where is your sister?"

"Don't know." Kevin lifted a tear stained face to him. "She saw someone on another tree trying to make their way over here. She told me to stay here and she took off."

Damn, that means Cooper had helped her return to her brother then had gone to check out the truck. But if she'd stayed down below then chances were good that Kevin would have been spirited away without anyone the wiser. Holding Kevin tight to his chest, he searched through the branches.

And saw her crouching on a branch, the back of her clothing blending in with the greenery around her.

On a branch above her stood a soldier.

His heart pounded as he realized the soldier hadn't seen her. He turned and looked down at something. Shadow followed his gaze and caught sight of Swede moving through the trees. Shadow pulled out his gun and lined it up, but it was hard to get a good shot. As he waited for the right moment, Arianna rose up from her crouched position and with a large branch hit the soldier at the back of the knees. He cried out, toppled over, tried to save himself but she whacked him a second time and he fell.

Nice.

Arianna stared over the edge at her handiwork and then as if realizing she'd taken out one but there could be scores more she needed to watch out for, she spun around, ducking deeper out of sight. As that gaze of hers swung back toward Kevin, it landed on Shadow.

Shadow grinned.

She gave him a slow smile that seemed to light up the

darkness around them. Then she glanced past to check for more soldiers before zinging back in his direction. She shifted her attention, finding a path back toward them. Shadow kept an eye on her progress while trying to keep her safe from other shooters. But silence had fallen. Everywhere.

They were all in a state of waiting. For someone to make a mistake.

Arianna managed to make it to the tree next to him. She reached out to step over to another branch.

A single shot fired.

Arianna cried out and stumbled. She grabbed a branch and hung on.

Several more shots were fired and a lone gunmen fell from the tree.

Kevin called, "Arianna?"

Shadow pulled him back out of the way in case anyone else heard him. But there was no corresponding gunfire. His gaze tracked Arianna who was still standing but trembling. "You need to stay here and don't make a sound," he said to Kevin and left the boy hugging the tree.

Shadow quickly slipped through the boughs and made it to Arianna's side. He ran his hands over her body until he came to stickiness on her thigh. Crouching low he bent and checked out the wound. The bullet had gone in and through the top of her thigh. Painful as all hell but could be so much worse. He had to go by touch alone given the endless blackness around them.

Tiny whimpers sounded through her mouth as she tried to hold them back. Shock was the issue now. He pulled out his knife and cut the bottom of her t–shirt from under her sweater and quickly bound up the wound. Then wrapping an arm around her, he half carried her half supported her as they slowly made their way back to her brother.

"I'd really like to go home now," she whispered against his neck. "I'll never look at tree climbing the same way again."

"Too bad as you do it so well."

She gave a broken gurgle of a laugh. "No, I don't. Or I wouldn't have gotten shot."

"Ah, you see that's because you weren't supposed to play cops and robbers at the same time."

She gave a half snort that for some stupid reason he found wonderful. Back at her brother, he slowly lowered her until she was sitting on the thick branch. It was pitch black outside but the rain had slowed. "Any chance we can move back into the house," she said, her teeth chattering. "I'm starting to wish I'd never left."

Kevin wrapped his arms around her as if to keep her warm. "Don't say that, Ari, you know what they were going to do to you."

At the boy's words, Shadow swiveled to look at Arianna's face. She looked miserable, wet now, but she held Kevin close. Not wanting to ask for an explanation for Kevin's statement, he looked at Arianna, one eyebrow raised. She shrugged then nodded.

Damn. He hadn't really considered that. This kidnapping had a political overtone, but she was a beautiful young woman and rape was often meted out as a punishment and to control the victims. He was glad she'd made it out first.

"I'm fine, Kevin. Sorry for whining."

Whining? That wasn't close to being a whine but as long as she had Kevin to keep bolstered she'd do her best. And he respected that.

Down below nothing stirred. Off to the side he heard

a long drawn out hawk's cry. He quickly cupped his hand and gave a corresponding cry. He looped the rope back over his arm and studied the pair. "I'm going to carry Kevin down on my back. Then I'm going to come back up for you, Arianna, okay?"

"No, I don't want to leave her," Kevin cried.

"Hush, Kevin," she said, her voice soothing. "This will be fine. I'm safe here."

Swede came out from the bushes and held up his arms. Shadow tied the rope around Kevin's waist and dropped him down into Swede's waiting arms. Then with Arianna clinging to his back, he carefully climbed down the tree. When on solid ground, he helped her stand on her own feet. The color drained out of her face, she barely held back the cry of pain when she tried to put weight on her injured leg.

Before she could collapse, he swung her up into his arms and carried her back to the camp where they'd held the rebels with Swede at his side carrying Kevin. She looped her arms around his neck and snuggled in damn near breaking his heart. She shouldn't be so trusting. The world was full of assholes.

Cooper, now out from under the truck, raced after them. "I think I've got it dismantled. I need help though."

"I'm here." Hawk slid out from behind a tree. Evan shifted to guard the direction he came from then disappeared from sight. "Dane is at the camp and Mason is on his way. Evan is heading back. What do you need?"

"I think I can get the senator out from the back of the truck now. But I don't want the rebels to know that we have them."

Arianna tilted her head upwards and whispered, "Go help. I'm fine."

"You're not fine," he said shortly but his attention

followed the others. "They should have someone to watch out for them."

She gave him a push on the shoulder. "Put me down," she said. "Swede, leave Kevin here with me."

"No, ma'am."

"Yes. Those are our parents and we don't even know if they survived that beating. Save them," she ordered. "Kevin is fine with me. You'll only be gone a few minutes anyway." And she gave him a sharp nod as if to underscore the right actions for him to follow.

Swede grinned, glanced at Shadow, and said, "I think we've been told."

"She doesn't understand," Shadow said. "We have to get her and her brother to safety."

"And you have, several times, in fact, so far this night. Now get our parents and maybe we can all get the hell out of here."

She tilted her chin at him and narrowed her gaze.

He glared.

Swede laughed. "It's all good. Let's go."

He grabbed Shadow's arm and tugged. Markus, his gaze knowing, led the way. Damn.

CHAPTER 7

ARIANNA WATCHED THEM leave. With Kevin's arms once again wrapped around her, she leaned against the closest tree for support and took the weight off her leg. She could have kept going, but she was damn glad she didn't have to. And that just made her a softie. Her father would roar at her to buck up and take it.

Like he had.

But she didn't even know if he was still alive. Right now she wanted to be back home safe and sound and preferably in her own bed where her leg could heal and she could forget this nightmare. She was so far from being in that position tears of exhaustion came to her eyes. It had to be the injury making her so weak. She wasn't normally like this.

"How bad is it, Ari?"

She managed to smile down at him. "Hurts like the dickens," she said with a smile. "Going to make walking difficult, but as far as being badly injured, don't worry. I'm not."

He appeared to be satisfied with that, then again he desperately wanted her to be fine so something in his world was okay. She could only hope they found their parents and they were still alive. For all her and her father hadn't seen eye to eye, she'd do a lot to hear him rage at her once again. He'd always been gruff and loud but it was who he was. She'd hoped for something closer but after her mother's death, Arianna had gone inside to deal with her loss and so had her father. They'd rarely met in any meaningful way after that. After Kevin was born she'd made a point of telling her father how he needed to change if he wanted his son to love and respect him and to have a relationship with him. He'd been angry like she couldn't remember ever seeing, but for a while he'd seemed to be there for Linda and the baby more.

But in the last few years he'd gotten busier, colder, and Kevin had gotten older. The relationship between the two had stretched very thin. That Linda hadn't much in the way of maternal hormones had further complicated manners. Then she was raising Kevin the way she'd been raised. As a showpiece to be seen and not heard. That might have worked for her decades ago, but Kevin needed so much more than that.

Arianna had started taking him for weekends where they'd done zoo trips and park outings, she'd taught him to swim and snowboard. She sucked at baseball, but they'd spent many a great hour playing catch. She knew her time with him was going to change once he grew into a teenager and needed his friends around more and more. He had friends now, but he still wanted to spend a lot of time with her.

Hard footsteps raced toward them.

Kevin lifted his head, his grip around her waist tightening.

Shit. She tried to lower herself to the ground so she was hidden by the brush a little more until she caught sight of who it was. Shadow. He raced toward her.

"Are they okay?" she asked anxiously.

"They are alive," Shadow said in a low voice. "But your father is in bad shape."

She knew that. But he was still alive and that meant

he had a chance. Right? Shadow bent down and scooped her up, startling a gasp out of her. She wrapped her arms around him and held on. Glancing behind, she saw Swede walked silently carrying her father while Cooper carried her stepmother. Her father was unconscious, her stepmother had a large bruise on the side of her face and appeared to be in shock. The bruise probably meant she'd fought, hopefully to help her father. And for that she liked her stepmother for the first time in a long time.

Another man, nodded at her and disappeared into the bushes ahead.

"That's Mason," Shadow said in a low voice. "Hawk has gone ahead as well. Trying to clear a path for us."

"Why?" she asked. "There were two vehicles back there. Why couldn't we grab one of those?"

"Because we don't know if they have rigged them both," he answered in low tones, his gaze never stopping as they swiveled from one side to the other. "They also could have remote detonators. They could blow us up just when we thought we were safe."

"Right." She should have considered that. A sign of how she was really feeling. In fact, all she wanted to do was close her eyes and let this man carry her to safety. But then Kevin reached up and grabbed her hand. She squeezed his fingers. "I'm fine, Kevin. We've got Mom and Dad and we're heading to safety."

"Dad looks bad," he whispered just loud enough for her to hear. She stole a look behind her at her father's large but scrawny form in Swede's huge arms.

"I don't think Dad looks all that bad. It's just the giant carrying him that makes him look small and injured," she joked.

Kevin glanced back. "How come he's so big?"

"'Cause he ate his broccoli," she said with a laugh,

knowing that was a sore point with her brother. He glared at her, then dropped his hand and slowed until he was beside Swede. She watched as he asked the big man something and grinned when Swede threw his head back and laughed. Then he nodded and said, "Absolutely."

"That was unfair," Shadow protested. "I don't like broccoli much either."

"Well, you're likely as big as you're going to get by now," she quipped. "And it's not just broccoli he won't eat, it's pretty much anything green."

"Oh. Well, I do like spinach and kale and chard."

"See, all the good stuff." Behind her Kevin chattered happily with Swede and Cooper, seemingly happy to run along beside everyone. "Thank you," she said.

"For what?"

She caught his sideways glance and beamed up at him. "For not treating him any different."

She was lifted in his arms as he raised and lowered his shoulders in a shrug. "He isn't any different. He's a young boy caught up in dealings that had nothing to do with him."

"True enough. Same for me."

"You have a special relationship with him."

The sentence was delivered as a statement and not a question, but she couldn't help but feel that there was a question in there anyway. "He's alone a lot. So I try to step in."

"Your parents travel?"

"No," she said shortly. "They are busy."

"Right." And he fell silent.

She hadn't meant to shut the conversation down but what was she to do when the questions arose about how broken the relationship was between her brother and parents.

She sighed. "Linda is father's third wife. I'm a product of his second and my mother died of an overdose when I was little. I was raised by governesses until Father remarried. He chose another non–maternal type of woman, and I could see how Kevin was suffering. I'd moved out and he had a really hard time after that. So I stepped in to make his world a little happier when I could." She grinned as she glanced back to see him chattering nonstop behind her to the two men. "He's become remarkably normal in the meantime."

"You've done a good job raising him," Shadow said quietly.

"They raised him, I just helped to balance out the cold emptiness of living in that household. I remember it well."

"Your mother, was it deliberate?"

She didn't try to misunderstand. "I don't know. We'll never likely know. I was Kevin's age. And the cold front between my parents was already nasty. If she hadn't died, a divorce was in the immediate offing."

"Children are the real victims in a situation like that. It's not easy for anyone."

She studied his chiseled profile, detecting something long ago that had hurt him a lot. "Did your parents' divorce?"

"No." He gave her a smile completely devoid of any humor. "My father killed my mother instead."

SHIT, HE HADN'T meant to say that. In fact, he wasn't sure the last time he told anyone. It wasn't exactly ice breaker conversation.

And the last thing he needed was sympathy. If she

showed him any pity, he'd dump her on the ground so she'd have to walk the rest of the way. Although he couldn't, it wasn't in him to do something like that. But…he held his breath and waited for her response.

When it came it blew him away.

"You know, I often wondered if that didn't cross my father's mind a time or two. I knew he didn't kill her as in he didn't force feed the pills down her throat, but I'm sure he was hoping she'd do it herself sooner rather than later." By the end of her sentence, she'd lowered her voice to a husky whisper as she glanced behind them to make sure her father couldn't hear her.

"What happened to his first wife?" he asked curiously. If that woman had died then maybe someone should be taking a look at the senator.

"Nothing so gruesome. They divorced and she has since remarried. I've met her at a couple of functions, but she's so similar to Linda that I'm wondering if he hasn't been searching for his first wife all over again. According to her, she's the one that left him."

Shadow nodded. "It happens."

"Yeah." She looked behind at Kevin, who given the circumstances, appeared to be in his element talking to Swede and Cooper. "Your friends are very nice."

Shadow stiffened.

"Kevin is really enjoying being around them," she said. "It's really good for him."

"What is?"

"Acceptance," she said simply. "If you saw his relationship to Dad and Linda, you'd see Kevin can't do anything right for my father who has such high expectations that *no one* can reach them and his mother who coddles him because she wants to protect him from such a big bad world. All because he's different."

"And you, did your father have the same high expectations for you?"

"Sure, but I was a disappointment from the outset so the expectations were lowered immediately."

He glanced at her. "In what way?"

"He only wanted a son."

Several hard clicks split the air.

Shadow froze, his arms tightening around her, his throat closing up as six men, assault rifles pointed their way, quickly surrounded them.

"Arianna," Kevin cried and ran toward her.

And a gun fired.

CHAPTER 8

ARIANNA CRIED OUT. But she couldn't see if anyone had been hit. Shadow had shoved her behind a tree and covered her with his big body. A volley of shots fired. Then more shots. Hidden behind the big man and worried about her family, she stayed pinned in place, shuddering. Her injury had changed something for her. Instead of being strong and capable she felt weak, in need of help. And hated that. Sure she did need the help, but she wasn't a victim. If she didn't get out of that mentality she'd become a liability. She didn't know where her brother was, nor the men who'd carried their parents. Surely they'd have been better off going back into the cabin. Especially given her father's condition.

She leaned her head back, eyes closed and waited. *Please stop the gunshots.* Her ears were ringing and she couldn't hear any voices over the loud noises. Surely everyone had to be dead by now. She shuddered.

Shadow twisted to look and his gruff voice, low and harsh, asked, "Are you okay? Are you hurt?"

"Hurt? No, just my leg." She stared at him fearfully. "Did they shoot Kevin?"

"They tried and missed." He shifted position so she could see around him. "He's with Swede."

And sure enough she could see her brother. He clung to Swede's back as the big man still carried her father. Jesus.

"Shouldn't we try to go back to the cabin?" she cried out, her heart hurting at the look of her father.

Shadow shook his head. "No. Reinforcements are coming. And an air ambulance will land on the lake in less than an hour."

She stared at him in hope. "Really?"

He nodded.

"Oh thank God."

"It's only been a few hours since you escaped the bedroom," he muttered. "It takes a little time to get some things done."

She wanted to laugh. Hell she really wanted to cry. Neither was an option. Their voices were so low she didn't think they'd carry, but they were taking a chance.

Thunder clapped overhead yet again. She jumped in surprise. Normally she loved storms, but if that heavy rain came back to soak them she'd be more than miserable and that was without taking her injured leg into account. An air ambulance sounded so normal and lovely she knew she was losing it. Several single shots sounded from across the way but not far enough away to make her happy. "You've got him pinned down," she whispered. "Finish him off."

"Can't until he shows himself."

"Then go get him," she said in a hoarse whisper. "I'm not going anywhere."

"Neither am I."

Of course he'd refuse to listen to reason. She leaned against the tree and closed her eyes. He could leave her and be back before she got to her feet. And she slowly slid down the damn trunk. It was dark, wet, cold and all she wanted to do was curl up in a ball and forget that his night had happened.

"Go," she ordered. "Then come back." She sensed his surprise, felt his doubt. She waved her hand to send him away. "I'm fine."

"Back in a moment," Shadow whispered, but before she understood what he meant, he was gone. She closed her eyes again. In this weather, no one was going to find her. It was too dark and ugly to bother looking.

Only she didn't have a moment to rest before he was there hauling her up onto her feet again. She shook off his help and stepped on her own. And shuddered. Damn it. She needed to be able to stand or he couldn't do what he needed to do. He gave her an arm for support. Yet again, she didn't protest. She kept walking and hung on. Stupid system. Why couldn't the good guys have nice vehicles to ride in? Instead they had no cabin and no wheels.

She was ready to round on him and tear a strip off him for not having the right equipment when a boom split the night sky. She cried out, instinctively crouching down as the night sky lit up all around them. Shadow slid an arm across her shoulders, tugging her up close. Then his voice, a harsh but reassuring whisper in her ear, said, "That's why we didn't go back to the cabin. If they were prepared to blow up the truck with your parents in it, likely they weren't going to leave much else behind either."

"My grandfather's cabin?" she asked, her voice cracking. She'd spent many happy weeks up here. But even thinking about those holidays it was hard to feel anything but shock at the moment as she watched the smoke curl in the sky.

It was gone.

"Could it have been the truck?" She barely got the words out when the second small boom sounded and she assumed that was the truck.

"They don't want us using their truck to escape either, I gather."

"No. They think we'll be handicapped by the terrain."

She looked around. "I have to admit it would be a lot easier to handle if my leg wasn't killing me."

"Not an issue. It's less than a mile to the lake, but we've been moving steadily."

She shot him a look as if to say, *hell, no,* then realized that was really nothing of a distance and if they wanted to catch that plane…there wasn't much choice.

Except…as they slowly continued, the lack of light impeded their progress. How was the plane going to be able to land in this dark? When she asked Shadow, he said, "Dawn is only twenty minutes away. Bush pilot's don't live by the same rules that we live by."

"You? Rules? I don't think you follow any." She'd been trying to limp her way forward since starting again and now her leg was killing her, her breath coming out in harsh pants.

"Ready for some help?" he asked in a neutral voice, letting her know he'd noticed her struggle.

Shamefaced, she nodded. "Yes, please."

He swung her up in his arms and marched forward, his steps strong and sure in the dark.

She had to love that ability right now. Tired and sore and feeling very emotional for some reason, she gasped when she caught sight of the water twinkling through the trees.

"It's beautiful." Moonlight shone down on the ripples moving gently in the wind. She glanced back to see the progress the others had made. They were all close behind.

For all that he was tired and worn out, her brother was handling this adventure wonderfully. She was proud of him. "Kevin is doing really well."

"You both are."

She glanced at Shadow, her arms looped around his neck and shook her head. "No, we aren't. It's been a tough day for all my family."

He nodded but his scrutiny never strayed as he made his way to the water's edge. She loved that about him. Such focus. She could imagine he was the man to choose if you were alone on a desert island. He oozed competence. And that power that each of the SEALs exhibited was damn sexy.

But Shadow more so.

Knowing she shouldn't but unable to stop herself, she stroked his neck then leaned over and kissed his cheek again. She felt his start of surprise and had to wonder if he had much relationship experience. He always seemed so shocked at signs of affection. Every time she touched him, he seemed startled. As if not used to touch. Then again, this was a rescue mission, not a midnight tryst.

"What was that for?" he growled in low tones.

"Because I wanted to," she whispered. "Because it seemed like the right thing to do."

He gave her a slant-eyed look that said he didn't believe her. And just to be perverse, because she was being carried in a man's arms and probably not for much longer, and the experience was so new and different and, she admitted, quite surprisingly wonderful – she did it again. This time she kissed his jaw. Then dropped a kiss on his cheekbone. And one close to his ear.

A muscle in that beautiful chiseled jaw twitched.

And she realized something else. They'd been out long enough that he had a dark shadow growing along his neck and jawline adding to his dangerous look. It looked deadly good on him. How had she not noticed?

Shadow stopped and looked down at her. She smiled. "I know. You don't know what to do with someone like me. I'm different from other women. That's okay. Being different is allowed."

He shook his head. "And you talk too much." He slowly lowered her and pointed to the lake. Though she'd seen it peeking through the trees already, now the vista was open in front of her.

"It's beautiful. And I don't talk too much."

"Yes, you do." He smiled. "But maybe that's okay."

SHADOW SEARCHED THE rocky approach to the water. This was the most dangerous part of the rescue. With the new assault rifles the terrorists could shoot from hundreds of yards away allowing them to hide in the trees and pick off those standing on the beach – or worse, as they'd boarded the plane.

That they couldn't afford. They'd made it this far, now was not the time to lose focus. It could go perfectly or they could be slaughtered. Only one was acceptable. He studied the terrain. There were few places to hide on the beach. It wasn't sandy enough to burrow into, nor was it full of logs or large rocks to hide behind. Short and rocky, it was going to be hard to run across if that was their only choice. The trees were the enemies' best bet and that in itself was where he'd go. He needed to scout the line and see what the approach looked like from all angles.

He glanced at Arianna. She was pale but holding on. Good. The trip wasn't over yet. With a quick nudge of his head toward her, Shadow told Swede to watch her. Swede, still standing strong with the weight of the senator in his arms and the boy on his back, nodded.

Shadow, with a last look at the small group, disappeared into the woods. A hawk's call, long and lonely in the predawn light, told him Hawk was standing vigil on the captured soldiers. He'd barely heard what had happened but knew men were down. He just didn't know how bad. And the captives had another agenda. If they tried anything else, well they wouldn't be around for a third attempt. He quickly slipped through the trees.

The light was fascinating. Early morning, not quite night, not quite day. But getting lighter by the second. Hearing something up ahead, he slipped behind a large tree and waited. A huge buck stepped out onto the path. Shadow smiled. "It's okay, buddy, you go and get a drink."

The buck gave a light snort, his coat was damp from the night but steam rose off his back. He was on his morning trek to the lake for a drink. If he stayed to the one side he'd stay out of the path of the bullets. But if not…well Shadow would hate to see him get hurt.

The buck passed by, his gaze never straying from Shadow. After the big animal was gone, Shadow shifted his position to see if any unwanted attention had been attracted. But nothing moved. Uneasy but with nothing to show for it, he hunkered down and waited.

In the distance he could hear the hum of the plane as it approached. He tensed.

This was where it was going to get dicey. This was a Canadian military plane. It needed to be able to take the four family members out safely. No one could be left behind.

Swede gave a low cry. Shadow answered with the same series of raptor cries they'd perfected.

The plane's arrival had been noted.

He waited until the plane was visible. Still there was

no movement. Either the enemy wasn't here or they had been in position already. They were terrorists, but that didn't mean they had outdoor training and maneuvers or were used to the sheer vastness of the Canadian wilderness. He'd spent months in the Yukon exploring a countryside that was so different from anything else he'd seen. If anyone needed to remember their connection to nature, spending a week in the woods up there would do it. Like here, there was so much country it was daunting. And stunning. And full of hardship, yet also offered great rewards.

The plane came in low and landed smoothly, just barely enough light to make it down. Thankfully, the storm had passed and the water was calm.

The first out of the plane were two soldiers with a stretcher.

Good, now to transport the casualties.

Swede met them at the edge of the water. Transferring the senator to the first stretcher and loading him on board took time. Knuckle baring time. According to Swede, the senator wasn't likely to make it. He hadn't regained consciousness once, and his old frail body had taken a beating that left Swede thinking major internal injuries. There'd been nothing they could do for him out there, but Swede hadn't wanted the old man who'd given his life to his country in a different way – to die alone. So he'd held the injured man to the end.

Now as the senator was loaded up into the small plane, Shadow could only wish him well. Then it was the wife's turn. He hadn't had a chance to ask Cooper about her, but Cooper would have said something if it had been bad. He smiled as Cooper got wet carrying Kevin to the plane. Kevin turned to check on his sister's progress.

Shadow had finally caught sight of something.

The enemy. Sneaking up on Arianna.

He lowered his rifle.
And took aim.

CHAPTER 9

ARIANNA WATCHED THE plane land with wonder. It had actually arrived. The night had begun to feel endless. With the moon fading back and the sky brightening as the sun rose but a long time away from sunrise, she studied the area in surprise. It felt locked in time. Frozen by the years. She didn't think anyone had been here since her last visit. Her favorite rocks and hollows leading to the lake where she'd spent hours of fun swimming were undisturbed. But it was not a world she wanted anything to do with right now.

"We're up next," Swede said. "Can you walk?"

"I can. But go ahead. Get Father on first." She hobbled forward, hating the pain biting into her with each step.

They walked together as a group until she realized how slow she really was. "Go and come back for me," she said.

Indecision rode him then he nodded abruptly and ran ahead. As in he picked up his feet and raced to the water's edge. The plane had coasted in as close as it could. She watched as two soldiers hopped into the water and carrying a stretcher, made their way over to Swede. Catching her breath and trying to hold back the waves of pain, she kept moving forward. Her brother was almost to the water now. He'd gone with Cooper. She took several more steps and gasped. Then a couple more. She didn't have far to go. And that plane was looking mighty fine. She watched her father being transferred and then it was her stepmother's turn. They were safe. *Thank God.* Cooper had picked up Kevin and carried him into the water to the men. He turned and called back, "Arianna?"

"I'm coming."

Swede started back toward her. She grimaced, but managed a smile for him.

And saw his expression change. He grabbed for his gun. She tried to hurry, but her leg gave out and she dropped to the ground.

Shots rained around her as rough hands picked her up and threw her over a shoulder and raced back toward the woods. "No," she screamed, flailing at the man who carried her. "Leave me alone."

More shots fired. This time toward the plane. As she struggled to free herself, the man shifted his grip on her leg and from a different direction grabbed at her wound. She screamed in agony.

The pain continued to ripple through her. She couldn't stop sobbing. Oh dear God. She swore he dug his fingers into the bullet hole on purpose.

"Shadow," she screamed, then couldn't speak as the pain kept rolling in deep greasy waves. So much damn pain. At least her family had made it. They'd been worse off than her. Tears rolled down her face as the plane started up and pulled away from the firestorm. Damn. She wanted to be on that plane. She so wanted to be leaving with the rest of her family. Instead, she was being carried deeper into the woods.

Shadow would save her. Surely.

Please.

A single bullet sounded. A man on the left dropped. She didn't even realize what had happened to him until he didn't get up again. Good. Bastards. Picking on her like that. Hanging down over the man's back, she could see he was dressed in khakis, so one of the damn terrorists. Of course. Through the pain she tried to focus. How many men were with her? Four. Well, three now. Any chance they were the last four? Because she was damn tired of this. The men were racing in a tight group and moving fast. Every step made her stomach roil in pain, and she came close to losing the peanut butter sandwich she'd eaten hours ago.

Then her eyes caught sight of something important. Could she?

She reached down and without letting herself second guess, she grabbed the man's handgun from the hip holster and pointed it at the head of the man running beside her.

Pop. Down he went. She turned to the next and clenched her fingers and shot him. The man carrying her squeezed her injury again and she screamed. And fired and fired and fired.

She couldn't stop even after the hammer fell and fell and no bullets came out.

"Easy. baby. Take it easy. They are all dead."

Shadow's voice washed over her. He'd come. He'd saved her again. Crying out, she opened her arms. He picked her up and cuddled her close.

She burst into tears.

"It's okay. I've got you." He rocked her gently in his arms as Swede and Cooper raced to their side. She couldn't stop crying. Her leg. Killing those men. Seeing the plane and knowing her family was gone. To know she'd been so close to flying out safely and having it all snatched away.

Finally, she wound down, and just lay against his

chest. The odd sniffle still escaped but it was softer, faint. Then gulps of air as she tried to still the inside wretchedness.

Finally, she muttered, "Sorry."

He squeezed her gently. "Don't be. You needed that."

"Then how come I don't feel better?" But she did. She felt much better, but was that being safe again or being in Shadow's arms or from a complete breakdown in front of all the men? Then she remembered. She'd missed the flight. "They left without me, didn't they?"

"We sent them off. In a case like that, it's the best answer."

"I know." But she hated it. "I'm sorry I missed it."

"They couldn't wait. Your dad needs medical attention." Shadow hesitated. "He's in bad shape, Arianna."

She stared at him dry eyed. "He won't make it, will he?"

Shadow's lips curled down. She nodded. "I was afraid of that. He was always a stubborn old coot. But honorable."

"He's still alive, and we have to give him a chance so don't write him off just yet."

She nodded but inside she knew the chance was beyond slim. "Kevin and Linda?"

"Kevin is fine, although likely traumatized if he saw you carried off again. We're getting word to them…"

She winced. That would be hard on him. "The sooner the better."

"Right. And it looks like you're stuck with us," Swede said cheerfully.

"And what does that mean?" She tilted her head back to stare up at him and swiped her eyes. "Are we done here? Are there more assholes or did we finally get them all?"

Cooper coming up behind them laughed and said, "There are always more assholes."

"Any more around here?"

"Not likely. The man you took the picture of initially, have you seen him since?"

So much had happened she had to stop and think. Then frowned. "I'm not sure I did actually. He was here when we landed. That's when I snapped his picture. Then…" She shrugged. "I haven't seen him again."

Shadow nodded. "That would be my guess."

Leaning her head back against his chest, she thought about that man. "Are they going to come back after us again? After we get home?"

"You and your family? Not likely. Besides, they have pretty much decimated it already."

"Great," she said in sad tones. "I wasn't going to come, you know. I only came to spend time with Kevin and show him the great things to do here. The cabin was my grandfather's. My dad always used it as a getaway, but we haven't been here in years. I don't know what prompted it. Nor do I know why now. But out of the blue they made plans. I wasn't asked to join," she admitted, feeling the injury even now. "He wanted to bring Kevin, I think. Before the relationships with him and Kevin soured further."

"Was it bad?"

"Yes. I wonder if Father had been threatened before the trip." She frowned. "Maybe he figured getting away would save us."

"We'll figure it out. I know his house and office are being turned upside down as we speak to find answers."

Right. Of course they were. And her place most likely.

"Can we leave now? Or are we waiting for the plane

to come back and pick us up?"

"No, on the plane," Swede answered, "We have a truck back at camp. If you're okay to travel with us, we can take you back."

"Yes, please," she said in a small voice. She didn't have much choice but hoped it wouldn't take long. Her leg was killing her.

Still, she'd be with them, and Shadow. She'd take an extra hour with him. She struggled to try and get to her feet, with Shadow helping her to stand. Waves of pain rolled through her. She focused on her breathing, trying hard to keep it together. She hadn't even put her bad leg down.

When she could, she lowered her foot to the ground and gently put her weight on it. And whimpered. Swaying in place and still holding onto Shadow – or rather Shadow holding onto her, she lowered her head and sucked in deep breaths. She could do this. She had to do this. Why wasn't she on that damn plane?

Just when she was ready to break down and ask for help, she was swung up into Shadow's arms and told, "Now lie quiet."

She wondered at the lie quiet comment. Was that because of the enemy or because he was tired. Or to stop her from fighting the help. Damn she didn't know anymore. But he couldn't carry her all the way back. That was too far. "I'm too heavy for you to carry for so long," she protested.

He slanted a look her way and stayed quiet.

"Maybe you could take turns and that would ease the load for you," she suggested.

The only response was to squeeze her tighter.

She subsided. Fine. Let him suffer. She planned to enjoy the experience. Or would have if it didn't hurt so damn much. She closed her eyes and realized she'd tensed to the point of resisting him. And that she didn't want. She needed to relax. But given her leg and her fear that he'd shuffle her and hurt her more... Then she understood how he'd lifted her into his arms. With her injured leg crossed over her healthy one. So as to not hurt it more. And he couldn't grab it accidentally this way either.

As in he'd done everything he could to keep her safe and out of harm.

She sighed and relaxed against him yet again. "Thanks," she muttered.

"You're welcome."

She smiled and closed her eyes.

Damn, he was fine.

DAMN, SHE WAS fine.

And he was an idiot. But he kept remembering his panic when he'd seen her spirited away in the group of terrorists. They'd swooped down onto the beach sending out a hail of fire covering their movements and snatched her up. His heart had damn near stopped, but his feet were already on the move.

He'd raced into the trees following the beach to get her before they could take her out of the area and be lost forever. He'd seen too many people disappear in this life. And that wasn't something he was willing to let happen to Arianna. She was his. No, she wasn't his, but she was his. He rescued her once, or was it twice by now? Maybe three times. Who was counting?

He didn't dare lose her to these assholes. Who knew what they'd do to her now they'd lost the rest of the family. He remembered the look on her face when she saw the plane taking off in the opposite direction. To know she'd been left behind. It would haunt him forever. Then screaming in pain, her body twisted in agony as her leg was gripped to keep her under control. Did she give in? Hell, no. She managed to get that gun and kill three men all on her own. It was at the end when she just kept shooting he'd felt his heart break. She'd been doing her damnedest to maintain some control and then lost it.

He was so proud of her.

Now she lay curled up lightly sleeping in his arms. Like hell he was going to hand her off to the others.

Swede walked up beside him. "Do you want me to carry her for a spell?"

Sensing the humor in his voice and seeing the grin on his friend's face, Shadow shot him a look. "No. I'm fine," he said calmly.

"Better than fine from the way I see it," Cooper said cheerfully. "Look at that. The one man I didn't think would ever fall – has not only fallen but done an all-out tumble in front of us."

Shadow refused to answer.

Arianna shifted uneasily in his arms as if disturbed by the men's voices. Shadow glared at his friends for waking her.

Swede smirked and stepped in front to lead the way. Cooper, a huge grin covering his face fell in behind to bring up the rear. Their radio whispered in his ear. Mason and Dane were still at the camp looking for an update. Only half listening, Shadow kept watch on the surrounding woods as Swede reported that the plane had left with the senator, wife and son. That Arianna was injured and had been taken again. That she was back with them and four more of the enemy were dead.

There was going to be a hell of a cleanup done here.

The bodies all had to be collected and dealt with. He hoped the Canadians would handle that part. Mop up was a bitch. He needed IDs of the dead men, but that was the only thing he wanted from these men now.

They had just under a mile to go. Without breaking stride and on guard they trekked through the woods toward the rest of their team. As they came to a half mile out, Hawk joined them, his sharp look going from one face to the other then dropping to Arianna's wan features in Shadow's arm. "How badly is she hurt?"

"Gunshot through the thigh."

Hawk asked, "Not bleeding out?"

"No. It's stopped or had stopped until the bastards grabbed her."

Hawk didn't waste any time. He led the way into camp, letting the others know they were approaching. At the edge, Shadow stopped and stared, using the time to study what was going on ahead of him. He had no intention of entering if she wasn't safe here.

Mason walked over. Shadow clarified, "Gunshot to the thigh, missed the bone."

"Good. She's asleep?"

"Yeah, the last attack finished her."

"Tell me?"

Still standing, Shadow quickly explained what happened. Hawk and Dane joined them.

Hawk stared down at the woman in Shadow's arms. "She killed them?" he asked incredulously. "All of them?"

Shadow nodded.

Dane whistled. "She's a keeper."

Shadow glared at him. Hawk slapped him on the shoulder. "Let's lay her down on the back of the truck. We need to check out that leg. See if the bastards made it any worse."

That made sense, but it was damn hard trying to let her go. It took three tries with his friends watching before he could finally lower her down to the back of the truck and step back.

Finally he managed it.

Swede, a hand on his shoulder said, "It's tough, isn't it?"

"What is?" he asked, frowning down at the woman who had somehow gotten under his skin.

"Finding what you want and knowing it's yours but also knowing you don't have the right to keep her."

He lifted his head to stare at his friend and finally understood what he meant.

Damn.

Swede was right.

It sucked.

CHAPTER 10

WAKING TO PAIN sucked. Waking to horrific pain, sobbing, and with tears rolling down her eyes, yeah that topped her list of shitty mornings. Arianna tried to roll over to get away from the fire in her leg and couldn't. Not only couldn't she get away from the pain it seemed she couldn't move at all. And someone was blubbering over and over again. She couldn't think for the noise. She shuddered at the onslaught mental, auditory, and physical.

"Arianna, take it easy. We're working on your leg. You've just woken up. You're okay."

It was that last sentence that got her.

"I'm not okay," she snapped, bolting upright only to get instantly forced back down by Swede and Shadow. As she stared up at them, her breathing raw, she slowly realized where she was and why.

And that she was the one blubbering.

How humiliating. By this time she wanted to really bawl. Rail at the unfair world that saw her still in the wilderness being treated to field kit type medical treatment. Like really, wasn't she supposed to wake up in a hospital somewhere with nice white sheets and shitty food? Not staring at these two bad-asses who were holding her down.

Tears filled her eyes. Then someone lit her injury on fire and she screamed. Then whimpered as the waves of darkness pushed her back under. She could see oblivion. Escape was there – just out of her reach.

She reached for it – and fell under its spell again.

When she woke the second time it was to the cold. Shivers slid up and down her long frame like fingers on guitar strings. How had it become so chilly outside? It was summer, right?

And the sun shone overhead, didn't it? As she lay there shivering she couldn't help but think her world had completely spun out of control. She was so tired. And there were men all around her. She could hear the strange voices outside and could see some of them. Did they know she was here? She studied the face of the man closest to her, but she didn't recognize him. Her glance slid over to the two men talking together beside him, and she didn't know them either. Her panicked mind didn't know if that was a good thing or bad. Shaking so badly she could barely move, she huddled back against the side of the truck.

A man's voice reached her. "She's waking up. Where's Shadow? Swede? Even Cooper."

The man who'd been sitting closest to her reached out and gently grabbed her hand.

She snatched it back. She knew this man was dressed the same as the good guys, but her mind couldn't make heads or tails of any of this. Inside she couldn't seem to think or do anything rational. All she wanted to do was get up and run, but everything below her waist hurt like shit.

"Arianna, take it easy." In the background she heard someone say, "Get one of the other SEALs."

She partially recognized the voice, but she didn't know the man. She'd heard that voice last night, right? But then she'd been snatched up by a lot of men last night too. And been hurt by them.

Was this the man who'd hurt her?

She swallowed hard and stared at him saucer-eyed.

"No one is going to hurt you. Your leg is injured. We had to clean and bind the wound." He spoke slowly and carefully, his hand gently stroking her arm. "No one here is going to hurt you."

She shuddered. "Where are the others?"

He smiled at her. "They are coming. You'll see them in a few minutes. I'm Dane. You heard my name mentioned before, surely," he said in a teasing voice. "I know you did."

Another face slid into view behind Dane. She narrowed her gaze at him but didn't recognize him either.

"No need to worry. I'm Mason. Hawk is here too. The three of us were keeping a watch on the far side of where you were and holding the prisoners back," he said cheerfully. "Not a very glorious job this time but there was lots of communication. You're looking for one of the other three goofs. They went back to make sure there were no injured men after the bombs went off."

Prisoners? Communications? Bomb?

At the word bomb her eyes widened. "They blew up my grandfather's cabin?"

"They did. And their own truck apparently. Not sure about the other rig. We could use it right now."

Rig? Right, the terrorists had brought another vehicle.

Slowly the distorted memories filtered into her brain and arranged to a more or less recognizable pattern. She relaxed back slightly. She studied the truck bed she lay in. There was something beneath her, but it wasn't soft or comfortable. And she was so damn cold. Just when she thought it was getting better, a wave washed over her making her teeth chatter.

"So cold," she whispered.

"I can help with that," Mason said before he disappeared from view.

Like that was a help. But he returned a few minutes later with a big heavy coat that he laid over the front of her. "Now just rest. We'll be leaving here soon."

"Leaving?"

"Yes, we're driving you to a small town close by and will make arrangements to get you home from there."

"Oh." She didn't even know what to say to that. Drive to a town didn't sound great considering how she was feeling right now. A small town wasn't going to have a doctor or even a medical clinic. And arrangements to get home, although home sounded lovely that whole arrangement thing sucked.

But home was the nirvana she was looking for right now.

She snuggled under the heavy coat, loving the familiar smell to it, and closed her eyes.

"HOW IS SHE?"

Shadow walked into the camp and straight to the truck. He nodded to Evan who stood at the edge. Markus, who'd followed him back, veered off to talk to Evan. Always alert, always on guard.

Good thing. Too bad he didn't have good news to report. They hadn't been able to salvage either of the other two vehicles – or anything of what remained of the cabin. In fact, it was a hell of a mess. He hated to see it. The cabin had been prime in its day. Now it resembled charred toothpicks.

"She's awake. Cold, hurting and worried."

"Worried about what?" Shadow frowned at Dane.

"You, you weren't there when she woke up."

"And?" Shadow studied the men around him suspiciously. He was often the butt of the jokes in the group but no more than anyone else. Only when the others were grinning at him like he could see them doing now, well, that was guaranteed to set off his radar.

"She woke alone, she was scared," Mason said in a calm low voice. "And she was worried. About where she was and more so about where you were."

Shadow turned to look at his friend. "Worried about me?" He raised an eyebrow at the thought. In the physical surroundings he was the last person here she needed to be worried about. "She's just not feeling well."

"Ah, it's more than that," Cooper said at his side. "She's sweet on you."

Shadow shook his head. "Hell no she isn't. I rescued her, she's grateful, that's all." And he sure didn't want gratitude from her. Nor did he want her to mistake gratitude as being something more. It wasn't.

"Go and see her," Mason said. "Regardless of what's going on, her mental state is going to have a huge impact on her healing. She needs to know you're okay. So set her mind at ease."

With the others grinning, Shadow walked to the big rig and pulled the heavy canvas back. "Ari," he said, his voice soft, gentle. Damn men. Making him think in one direction as hope blossomed inside. But it wasn't to be. He knew that. He just had to remember.

"Shadow?" she asked sleepily from under the heavy coat. He stared at the coat. It was his. Trust the guys yet again.

"Yeah, it's me."

She sat up, and he couldn't help but stare. Tear

stained cheeks, red puffy eyes, but their vision was clear, direct and warm. Hell. She opened her arms. When he didn't reach for her, her lower lip trembled. Making him feel like an ass. Too damn bad if the men were watching. He opened his arms and with a small cry she fell into them.

"I was so scared when I woke up," she confessed against his neck, snuggling close. "I didn't recognize anyone."

"We had to go back and check out the condition of the cabin." And retrieve the bodies of the terrorists. They were stacked off to the side under tarps. There were only two vehicles here. Another was on its way. He moved so he could sit on the tailgate and hold her.

"Is it okay?" she sniffled.

"Well, it's gone if that's what you mean," he said quietly. "I'm sorry for that."

She smiled up at him. "Thanks. But I have the memories and that's what is important."

Pulling back slightly, she asked in a low voice, "Is there any update on my family? Is my father okay?"

He shook his head, hating to not be able to give her the news she needed to hear. "We don't know anything yet. Communication up here is spotty at best."

Her face fell, yet she nodded in understanding. He felt like he'd failed.

"It's okay. I know he's in good hands, and everyone is doing what they can for him. For all of us," she said gently.

He sighed. "That attitude will get you walked all over in this world."

"And sometimes it brings good things. I know there are a lot of growly bear people out there, scammers, and just really bad nastiness, but that doesn't mean there isn't room for people like me."

"And what are the people like you."

She smiled and snuggled close. "People who believe in heroes and unicorns, rainbows and chocolate chip ice cream at midnight." She yawned at the end, and he wasn't sure he'd heard her correctly. But when he went to ask what any of those things had in common and to ask if she understood unicorns didn't exist, he heard deep peaceful breathing and tiny delicate snores.

Damn.

He glanced out at the camp the men were tearing down. He should be helping them. But as he glanced down at the angel in his arms, he didn't want to leave her. In a voice just barely audible, he said, "I've never seen unicorns and haven't met any heroes, but maybe they are possible because until last night, I'd never met a real live angel, either."

And he dropped a gentle kiss on her forehead.

CHAPTER 11

W HEN SHE WOKE the next time, the pain had dulled to a deep agonizing throb but was no longer the hot searing rage in her leg. But she was alone. And that she was getting to hate.

She'd spent too much of her lifetime alone. In spite of her upbringing, she'd somehow managed to create that Pollyanna attitude that she'd have a good day if she could just believe in it hard enough. And for the most part she was content with her life. It wasn't awe shattering or full of excitement, but there was something comforting to it. And now she realized the comforting part was the familiar part. She was alone. Somehow that had become the norm, and one she had become satisfied with. She'd been happy in the few relationships she'd had until the men had wanted more. That hadn't been for her. At the time she'd just figured she hadn't been ready for the commitment.

And she hadn't been. In that she hadn't been ready to give up that comfort of what she knew – had known all her life – a solitary lifestyle.

What would it take for her to give that up?

The right man, of course. Because in that way she'd not be giving up anything, she'd be gaining.

Up until then though it seemed like she'd be losing.

So they weren't the right men.

Shadow stole into her mind. Was he the right man?

Not possible. Look at the differences in their worlds.

He wouldn't want someone like her. He lived in the shadows. She lived in the sunlight. She could take a walk in the shadows but only a short one. She couldn't live there. She'd have to take the rays of sunshine from her world to warm up the darkness in his.

In his? What was she thinking? He wasn't for her.

But he could be.

No. He couldn't be.

Yes. She wiggled with delight. She knew she was living a fantasy in her mind at the thought, but if there was ever anyone who needed her to bring light into his world, it was Shadow.

When his face appeared in front of her she figured she must be dreaming. She beamed at him. "Good morning."

His response was slow to come. "Good morning, how are you feeling?"

"If I don't move, fine. Thank you for asking."

He rolled his eyes, making her grin and prompting her to ask, "How are you feeling?"

"I'm fine," he said. "I'm not the one injured."

"No," she said cheerfully, reaching out a hand to cup the side of his face. "But you are the one who's feeling guilty."

And damn if a dark stain didn't wash up his neck.

Oh no. "You shouldn't feel that way, you know that, right?"

"I left you alone," he said curtly. "There is no other way to feel."

"You had more things to do than babysit me. You're a hot shot sexy SEAL and babysitting is not a required course."

Again that glance slanted her way.

"Sexy?"

She flushed. She had said that, hadn't she? Ah well.

"It's the truth," she admitted. "I'd say all of you are, but then you'll discount that you aren't and of course you're the sexiest man here."

Surprised and obviously discomforted, he said, "Do you always worry about other people's feelings like that? It's got to be wearing."

"It can be, but I am who I am. Sunshine and roses, remember?"

"Yeah, and what happens when you end up in moonlight instead," he asked curiously.

And because there was nothing mocking in his tone, she answered, "I usually get depressed until I can cheer myself up."

"And how'd you do that?"

She realized he was serious. "By listening to music, spending time with friends or Kevin, singing and dancing…" She shrugged. "There are lots of ways."

He glanced behind them at the work going on.

"What do you do when you get down?" she asked.

Startled, he answered willingly enough. "I tell myself to get over it and get back to work."

Someone called his name. And he left. Just like that.

She lay back down and realized they needed to get moving. And the sooner the better. She had no idea how long she'd been out, but as she peeked through the back the sun was still rising. Good. They hadn't been waiting for her. She shifted experimentally, wondering how mobile she was going to be as she desperately needed a bathroom. And of course there was no such thing available. She had no qualms about a walk to a secluded part of the bush except for that *walk* part.

Crouching down was going to be damn near impossible. And she needed to go. As she shuffled her butt to the edge of the truck, she realized she no longer wore her jeans. In dismay she stared down at the oversized sweat-pants. Donated by someone on the team most likely. But on her, yeah they were huge. Thankfully whoever had changed her left her panties on. And the leg did move easier in warm loose sweats. But she must look a fool.

She laughed. Oh well, better a warm fool than a cold one.

She lowered her legs over the edge of the tailgate and sat up. The place was full of activity. There were men sitting in another vehicle all handcuffed together. And dressed in khakis. She studied their blank faces, surprised to see any still alive.

The rest of the men appeared to be leaning over the hood of a truck poring over something. A map most likely. She carefully turned and crept down the back of the truck and hobbled to the front. There out of sight, and using the front grill to hold onto, she managed to lower herself on one leg. She quickly went to the bath-room. As she struggled back to the rear of the truck, Shadow stepped into her path.

"You know you could have asked for help."

She looked at him wryly. "Yeah, to what, wipe my butt?" She grinned.

He smirked. "If need be then yes."

She shuddered, and quickly said, "No thanks. I was fine."

"You were going to make sure of it, even if you weren't, right?"

A bit convoluted but she did finally get it. "Hey, if I can save myself that bit of humiliation, I'm all for it. You'd do the same."

"I would," he said immediately. "But if I couldn't..."

"Right. If I get that bad, I'll let you know." *Not*, she added mentally. It would be hard to be in that position.

She understood that everyone might need such assistance at one point in time but she'd hope that was at least eighty years away.

And she gave thanks to the world around her that she was in as good a shape as she was. With his help, she got back up on the tailgate so she could sit and watch.

HE'D WATCHED HER struggle to get down off the truck, her furtive glances to see if anyone was watching. He'd soon realized she'd needed a bathroom break. Something that was much easier in the woods for him than her – especially given her injured leg. He'd waited, trying to give her space and independence and had to grin when she'd returned slowly, painfully, but in one piece.

"Go. You're useless here anyway," Mason said in a hard tone but his eyes were twinkling.

Shadow gave him a flat look. But when he spun around to check on her the next time, Swede gave him a push in her direction.

"It's your turn. Go be a hero."

And he'd left. Now that she was safe again and he'd rejoined the men, it was as if he had an inner sense when she moved or needed something. Like what was with that?

"We're leaving in twenty minutes. We'll head to a town and see if we can get her a faster return trip," Mason said. "Her leg is healing, but I can't be sure there isn't muscle damage inside that she'd need a doctor to fix. And the sooner for that the better."

Shadow nodded. "Which rig? I'll get her settled in." He glanced around. "She had a pack at one time too."

Cooper nodded to the side. "It's over there."

Shadow caught sight of the red canvas pack. He waited to hear the end of the conversation then walked over and grabbed the bag. Returning to her side, he watched her face brighten. And inside he sighed. He had it bad. Anything to see her smile. Particularly when it was directed at him.

"Thank you," she cried. "I wondered if I'd see it again."

He laid it down beside her.

She opened it immediately and rummaged through. "I have spare jeans in here."

"Not jeans. Too hard to get on and off for cleaning the leg wound."

She frowned and plucked at the material on her legs now. "But these belong to someone. I have to give them back."

"They are mine and I don't need them right now."

With a gasp, she threw her arms around him and hugged him. Damn. He couldn't help wrapping his arms around her and holding her tight. For a moment, he glimpsed the sunlight as it broke through the shadows. Then she dropped her arms and the light disappeared.

But it was enough. He stared at her in wonder. Is that what it was like to not be alone? He couldn't ask her. Knew it wasn't the time for such a question and she likely wouldn't know as she lived in the sunlight and had no idea the world was cloaked in shadows like he did.

As he watched she went back to rummaging through her bag. She pulled out a chocolate bar in triumph. Then she stared at its size before shoving it back inside.

"You aren't hungry?"

"I'm starved," she confessed. "But everyone is, and I can't break a bar that small to give everyone a piece."

What? He studied her again. "You don't have to share with everyone."

"Have to, no I don't. But I want to. So it will have to wait until later when there are less people around so everyone can have a taste."

Not understanding her logic, he said, "We're leaving in the other truck." He watched as Swede started loading the back of their rig. "I need to get you over there now."

"Is it big enough," she asked in a low voice, mentally counting the men in the area. "Maybe I should wait here until later."

"For what later?" he asked. "This is your ride. Now or never."

She nodded. "Now then. If you have room for me."

He sighed and swooped down and caught her up in his arms, startling a squeak out of her as he carried her and her backpack to the truck beside them. Swede seeing them coming, opened up the back passenger door. "Your ride, princess."

She beamed at him. "Thanks, I appreciate it."

"Well, it's not a plane but we'll get you home one way or another."

Shadow helped her sit on the bench then watched as she scooted back so her leg was resting on the seat. She took up most of the back. That wouldn't last long. "Rest. We'll be leaving in just a few minutes."

She leaned forward. "But there's not enough room for everyone."

"There will be," he whispered back.

That she'd be riding on his lap was something he understood, but she had yet to figure out. He was looking forward to seeing her reaction when she finally did.

CHAPTER 12

S HE GAVE HIM a flat stare when she finally understood that his picking her up and settling her on his lap wasn't temporary. As in this was the way she'd be riding to the next town.

He grinned at her. She glared at him.

Swede, sitting in the front, chuckled. She wanted to smack him. Beside Shadow sat Cooper and then Hawk. Mason drove and Dane had been pinched into the middle in the front. Markus and Evan had stayed behind to help the Canadians out.

She turned her head toward Shadow. "I told you I wouldn't fit."

"And I told you, you would."

She sighed. "You're being difficult," she announced.

"No, you are."

"You can't always tell me I'm wrong." She gave him a curt nod for punctuation.

"If you are, I can," he countered.

She gasped. "Are you saying I'm always wrong? That's mean," she cried.

Shadow rolled his eyes and stared out the window.

She caught sight of Hawk's smirk. "He's being mean, isn't he?"

Immediately Hawk agreed.

Right. He knew what his role was. "You should tell him," she said with a nod.

"Shadow, you're being mean," Hawk instantly said.

A low rumble of laughter rippled through the truck.

She crossed her arms. "It's easy to see which of you have partners," she snapped.

Cooper eyed her curiously. "How's that?"

"All those men know better than to argue," she replied, glaring at Shadow. "Then there are those who haven't learned that lesson yet."

And this time the men cracked up.

Cooper immediately started whistling a tune she vaguely recognized. "What's that song?" she asked.

Straight-faced he opened his mouth to answer, but Shadow's arm straightened and belted him across the chest.

Cooper coughed several times.

Arianna rounded on Shadow. "What was that for?" she cried. "We were just having a nice conversation."

He glared at her. But never said a word.

"See, you're just being mean again."

The men in the truck were all trying to suppress chuckles. Cooper the most of all. She studied him suspiciously. "He didn't hurt you, did he?"

"Just my feelings," Cooper managed in a deadpan tone of voice.

"Oh, I'm so sorry. Shadow is like that," she explained to the captive audience. "He rarely explains himself. He probably just didn't want you to give the wrong answer and be embarrassed." She rounded on Shadow who was staring at her in apparent fascination. "If you'd explain yourself a little more it would be easier on everyone. Use those words I know you have inside," she said nicely. "It really will get easier over time."

"You talk too much," he snapped.

Her lower lip trembled.

An odd silence sounded in the truck.

Cooper nudged Shadow. "Fix it."

"It's okay," she said in a low voice. "It's not the first time he's told me that."

And she was jerked forward and kissed hard.

Eagerly she threw her arms around him and kissed him back only he suddenly pushed her back and jammed her up against his chest.

Happily she snuggled in close. "I'm sorry for calling you mean. You're really a pussycat inside."

SHADOW SIGHED. WHAT the hell was he going to do with her? Calling him a pussycat. Hell, he was a fucking panther in the dark.

"Isn't that nice," Hawk murmured from the other side. "I'm happy we have a pussycat in the truck."

The group sniggered.

Mason, who was driving, came to Shadow's rescue. "But as I recall we've all had similar scenarios happen to us."

"So damn glad that's over," Dane said with feeling. "What a confounding stage of life that was."

Confounding. Yeah, that was the word for it. Shadow stared down at the woman snuggled up against his chest. How could she be such a powder puff right now and yet be the same woman who'd signaled for help in the cabin window and crawled from tree to tree to knock an attacker down because he was hunting her brother? And that was without mentioning the three men she shot to death.

Now she was curled up like a baby as innocent as could be.

Yeah, he was confounded. Not only by her behavior but her thought processes. She seemed to think he was… Hell, he didn't know what she thought. He'd say wonderful but that was ridiculous. Yet by body language alone, he had to consider it. She didn't go to any of the other men on her own.

"Next time," Cooper announced, "there's a beautiful woman who needs rescuing, I get the job."

Several of the guys chuckled. But everyone in the truck knew what he meant.

Shadow wondered if fate played a hand in picking the rescuers. Then again, he'd rescued dozens of people and outside of normal gratitude they never seemed to show any interest in him. Yet every time lately they'd been on a mission and a woman had been in trouble, she'd hooked up with one of his teammates. And he might have had a hand in that last time too. He'd known Swede had been sweet on Eva for years. But she was – in his head – forbidden. Shadow had even helped send him to her rescue, hoping it would be enough to change things for his friend. And it had.

More than anyone had expected.

That wasn't the same thing right now. He'd never met Arianna before.

And there'd been more than just him involved in this rescue, but Arianna had apparently picked him. Shadow just didn't know to what extent she was favoring him.

But he wanted to.

He leaned back and closed his eyes. It was going to be a long trip. All the more so the way she slumbered. His body was more than aware of the feminine body on his lap. It didn't need any more incentive to wake up and pay attention.

Arianna shuffled slightly and moaned.

He groaned as her rounded bottom slid across his groin.

It was going to be one fucking long trip.

CHAPTER 13

S HE DOZED, SHIFTED to get comfortable, surfaced then dozed again.

When she finally woke it was to see a different terrain outside the truck window. She sat up and heard Shadow's gasp, then groan.

"Oh, I'm sorry," she cried out in a hushed whisper as she tried to wiggle into a better position.

He grabbed her hips and stopped her movements.

"Is that better?"

"Yes," he said between gritted teeth. Then he took a deep breath. "Just stop your damn wiggling."

She glared at him. "Are we back to that? Remember I said there was no room in here for me."

"Are we back to that," he said perversely enjoying getting her riled up again. "I said there *was* enough room for you."

She sighed and collapsed down again. "You're getting into your mean mode again."

He hugged her close. "No, I'm not."

She was quiet for a long time. "Where are we? I thought we'd have reached the next town by now."

"Shouldn't be much longer. Although there is some concern that there isn't much there. Apparently, small Canadian towns in the north are often only a collection of houses and not much else."

"I remember that from last time. Nowhere close

enough to drive to. It's like six hours to the main center."

"Right. If need be, we can do that."

She sighed. "I hope we don't have to. I'm getting awfully hungry."

"You've still got your chocolate bar," he reminded her. As she perked up and looked around for her bag, he added, "Don't bother. It's in the back with the rest of the gear."

He reached for her hips to stop her from moving too much, but she didn't notice. Her sore leg was stretched across Cooper's legs, giving him no room to go anywhere. Poor Cooper.

Shadow reached into his pocket and pulled out her bar. "Here. I pulled it out earlier."

With a beaming smile she took it, opened it, and carefully broke it into seven pieces.

He watched her as she handed out a piece to everyone. One piece was slightly larger than the others and one was slightly smaller. The small one she kept for herself, and she gave him the biggest piece.

Of course she did. He was looking after her so well. She wished she could give him more.

But there wasn't anything else to give him. At least not here.

She studied the small town as they drove past. There were a few houses dotting the highway from miles out. Normal in a way. If you were a loner and preferred wilderness to city, like these people did, they all wanted to live on the edge of town. No matter how small the town was. And as small towns went she'd have said this was the smallest she'd seen. Barely a community and not big enough to be considered a township.

There was a small store in the center and before they knew it they'd passed it. Mason slowed and pulled off on the side of the highway. "Did anyone see a store or medical center or…anything? What's the chance we haven't hit the main town yet?"

"I saw a store," Arianna said, twisting to look behind them. "But nothing else."

Several others confirmed the store.

Mason had the truck turned around and pulled up to the store, which appeared to double as a gas station, except from the ancient pumps in the back, she wasn't sure she trusted anything that came out of these machines.

But a bathroom would be good.

The door opened behind her, and Shadow exited with her in his arms, somehow making the movement natural and graceful.

"Any chance of a bathroom?" she whispered, studying the gas station.

"Likely inside." He held her steady as she regained her footing and hobbled around a few steps to keep the blood circulating.

The air had a freshness to it she loved. She took a deep breath. She hadn't had a chance to notice the air this morning with everything going on but now on the way home…she sniffed happily. "Smells nice."

"Not in here it doesn't." Mason stepped back out of the store.

She turned slightly to see him. The grim visage had her heart and stomach plummeting. "What's wrong?"

"The store owner is dead." Mason nodded to the interior behind him. "Been dead at least a day."

"Shit," she heard Shadow mutter. He dropped her arm that she'd been using for support and said, "I have to go look."

Arianna watched mutely as Shadow disappeared into the store. Swede, being the guy he was, had stepped into

Shadow's place, but he'd opened the back of the truck first and was now armed. She took a deep breath and let it out carefully.

"I'd hoped this was all over," she said in low tones.

"It was," Swede said. "Until we found another dead man."

"Do you think he was killed by the kidnappers?"

"Likely, but we need to find out for sure. Can't guess on this one. And that means talk to anyone here who is left to talk to us."

She gasped and turned to him. "You don't think they are all dead."

"No. I don't." He immediately shook his head. "But the storekeeper was killed yesterday, that's enough time for others to go into hiding."

Yet his voice didn't match his words. He stared behind the vehicle and studied the houses across the road. One small house on the corner in particular. And the fluttering curtains in the window. "Think they are in there?"

"Oh yeah, the question is who and are they wary naturally or did they see something that has terrified them," he muttered, shifting to study the other buildings.

She looked around. There were a dozen homes all centered near the store but not a sign of anyone. As her gaze swept past the store, the door opened and Dane and Cooper... Shadow walked out. The dark overcast and chiseled faces said so much. She wanted to hobble closer, reach out and let him know she was here, but the look on his face said he wouldn't likely recognize the support if she did. It made her sad. She watched him disappear around the corner of the building. That reminded her she needed a bathroom. She looked for a restroom sign but didn't see one.

"What are you looking for?" Swede asked, an intent look in his eyes.

She scrunched up her face. "A bathroom."

"I'll look." He motioned toward Cooper who walked closer. Then Swede took off around the building. She smiled at Cooper. "Hey."

He grinned. "Hey back. How's the leg?"

"Fine." Then she shrugged, admitting with a wry grin, "As long as I don't try to use it."

He chuckled. "You're coming due for more pain killers if you feel the need."

She frowned, considering. "I'm not too bad at the moment"

"Good, then we'll leave it for a little bit longer. What we don't want is to leave it so long that you end up suffering until the new meds kick in."

Yeah, that didn't sound like fun.

But the pain killers knocked her out and made her thinking fuzzy, forcing others to carry her sorry ass around until she was awake again. "Maybe when we get this mess settled…" She motioned to the town around them.

"*This* has nothing to do with you. If we can't determine that you're safe here then you're not staying. We'll figure out another way to get you home."

"Are you guys going home?" she asked cautiously. "Maybe I could go with you?"

"Maybe," he said cheerfully. "I'm all for it. Then at least we know you're safe. But you need medical attention now, not in a few days when we get there."

"Seems like we're always against the clock." She hoped the damage to her leg was minor but had no way to know. Cooper's good drugs kept her from having to worry about it too much. But she wanted to have the full function of it.

"So we need a hospital to check you over and then we can make plans."

Sounded good. But she suspected she'd soon be parted from these men. That was sad. She was so proud to have known them. They were heroes. And they'd done right by her. If they needed her to buck up and be left behind so they could carry on tracking her kidnappers then so be it.

Swede arrived. "Found it. It's at the back."

He didn't give her an opportunity to protest but swooped her up into his arms and carried her laughingly protesting around to the back of the building.

The door was open. He set her down inside then stepped out and closed the door. She wanted to laugh at the look on his face. He'd been dying to ask if she wanted help but knew she wouldn't take it kindly. He was a good man. Just like the rest of them.

Privacy and a real toilet, and look, running water. She smiled with joy. Oh the simple things in life. She quickly used the toilet then set about to wash the rest of her…at least what she could reach. The paper towels were scratchy on her neck and face but the warm water was a delight. When she finished she opened the door and hobbled out.

Into Shadow.

"Oh," she stumbled back and cried out as sharp pain radiated up her leg.

He reached out to help stabilize her. She took several breaths and managed a smile. "Sorry."

His eyebrow shot up. "For what?"

Yeah, she didn't know. For being an idiot and walking with her head down. For not seeing him standing there? For getting shot. "I don't know, it was a stupid thing to say." And fell silent.

Thankfully he let it go. "Ready?"

She nodded and took a step forward. And stopped, shuddering. Why the hell hadn't she taken the pain killers when Cooper had offered? She bit her lip. Now she'd have to wait for them to kick in before she'd feel better.

It was on the tip of her tongue to ask Shadow for help when he scooped her up into his arms. She looped her arms around his neck happily. "You're a good man."

He shook his head. "You have no idea what you're talking about."

"Really? Why, because I'm a woman? Because I'm injured?"

"Because you don't know me," he snapped, his voice harsh.

She stilled and stared up at him. What was going on inside that massive intelligence of his? And why?

"You don't scare me," she whispered, realizing that they had reached the truck. "No matter what you're thinking, you're not bad – you're good. Honorable. Stalwart. Capable."

He slanted her a long look of disbelief.

She beamed up at him. "It's true."

"You're living in that sunny world of yours again."

"I always live there," she said in a low voice as he set her down on the bench seat. "You could come visit me."

He went to back away, but she reached up and tugged his face down toward her and kissed him ever so gently. As she slowly withdrew she added, "You don't have to live in the shadows, maybe it's time to experience a little sunshine for yourself."

SHADOW RETURNED TO the dead man's side. He ignored the grins of his fellow SEALs. They were all idiots. Then, so was he. He didn't even know what to think about Arianna. He felt drawn to her side all the time. He needed to focus on his work, the job at hand, instead he found himself constantly looking at her, to check that she was okay. Be with her. There was a hunger inside he didn't recognize. Not a sexual hunger, although that hummed constantly below the surface too, and that's the part that surprised him. She was gorgeous and he'd do pretty damn much anything to take her to bed, but there was something else going on inside. This need, this wish to be with her, to understand her view and her life that she kept giving him little glimpses of. It was…different. He hadn't seen it right away. Then the circumstances were hardly normal. Then he'd thought she might have been joking about the sunshine and rainbows, but she really seemed to be like that, and he didn't get it. Didn't understand how it could be. She'd not had such a perfect life that she'd only seen the good in life. She'd been born unique, special, and somehow that part of her had survived the trauma called life.

He grinned at the phrasing. He didn't really believe growing up and surviving this world was a trauma. Neither did he believe anyone survived unscathed. But whereas most people might walk through life and hide away the hurts and hide away from those who hurt them, Arianna had this sunny, that's okay I know it won't happen again attitude.

It was likely to reach around and bite her in the ass sometime soon.

"So, buddy, that's quite the facial expression. Kind of like you don't know what hit you and not sure what to do with the blow," Dane said in a low voice. "You okay?"

Not wanting to get into anything personal – like hell he was going to discuss any of this – Shadow nodded.

"Fine."

"Right. So you're not but you don't want to discuss it. Got it."

And Dane gave him a mock salute and with a smile he walked toward Mason who was on his phone trying to make arrangements to collect the body.

Shadow studied Dane. He'd been struck by lightning on one of their trips. Been completely sideswiped by meeting Marielle and had been pretty grumpy about it for a while too. But he'd walked forward regardless, and now he was so damn happy it was sickening.

And made Shadow realize just how possible this all was.

Maybe.

Arianna might like Shadow as a rescuer – but as a man? That didn't mean there was anything more to it than simple attraction.

Shadow had been seriously disappointed in his life. He knew exactly how easy it was to *not* get what he wanted in this world, so he'd made it easier on himself by choosing to *not* want much. He kept his life simple now. Straightforward.

Until he hit a wall called Arianna.

Now he knew there was something he really wanted and most likely couldn't have. So he could go for it and possibly have his hopes dashed or not bother because he knew the outcome already.

He studied the interior of the store while his mind was already busy tracking the events of what had gone on, almost like a weird psychic ability, his mind could put the pieces together and show him what had happened. The store owner, living out where he did, had likely been too talkative on a day the kidnappers couldn't afford to talk to anyone. They'd taken the simple route.

And he'd gotten a bullet for being friendly.

Too bad he couldn't get Arianna to learn the same lesson. She was going to get seriously hurt one day.

Swede stepped in front of him with a determined look on his face as Shadow tried to refocus on their next step.

Shadow frowned. "What?"

"You're not going to break that girl's heart are you?"

"Of course not." He gave Swede a good frown. "She's not in any danger of having it broken."

Swede shook his head. "Don't be so blind to something special right in front of your nose that you hurt your chances at happiness because you think she's better off without you."

That made him step back mentally. Outside he narrowed his gaze at his best friend and warned him to back off.

The problem with Swede was now that he'd found happiness he wanted to see everyone around him happy. Well, given that only Shadow and Cooper were still single on the team… "Go tell that to Cooper," he snapped.

"She's not interested in Cooper," Swede said calmly. "Although he might be interested if you aren't."

"I thought you said she wasn't interested." Shadow could feel his shoulders hunching in on themselves. He hated this stuff. And never did heart to heart – especially not with his buddies.

"If he's there for her, and you've turned her away, then she just might head in that direction. It's natural to go where you are wanted. She can only keep butting up against the rejection for so long before she turns to another for comfort."

His gut twisted.

"You're gonna have to make a decision soon."

"No decision to make. She's a senator's daughter and sees me as her rescuer. Like anyone in her situation, she's grateful."

Swede studied him for a long moment. "And you don't want gratitude, is that it?"

Shadow shot him a hooded look. "Would you?"

"Nope. But I think you're wrong. I think Arianna doesn't give a shit about where you are from, or your lineage or lack of it, or that you saved her ass a couple of times, she saved yours a time or two as I recall, I don't see you bending over with gratitude..." Swede crossed his arms. "I do however think she sees something in you that you don't see yourself."

Shadow had already turned to join the others. At Swede's words, he froze. Slowly, he turned back to face his friend. "What is that?"

He hated that he could hear that tiny bit of hope weaving through his voice. But it was there damn it. Swede would know. He missed nothing. Shadow had been off his mark since he'd met Arianna. Like what was with that? He couldn't let her distract him so much but thoughts of her filled his mind. Wouldn't let go.

Swede walked past and reached out to smack him on the shoulder. "You'll have to figure that out yourself."

And he refused to say any more.

CHAPTER 14

ARIANNA LAY DOWN on the back of the truck, her leg throbbing. Shit. It was better, then worse, with the worse part building. She still hadn't gotten more pain medicine. And she was getting weepy. Was there anything worse?

She already felt so damn female when surrounded by all these macho men. And weepy just seemed to go along with being hurt. She wanted to be strong and capable beside them. Hated to think she was doing her sex an injustice. That all the women in the world were looking at her like she'd let them down. Everything had been good until she got hurt.

Cooper's head popped over the back seat of the truck. She wasn't even startled. There were so many men in and out and around always looking after her she never knew who it would be next.

"You okay?"

She nodded but didn't open her eyes. "Yeah."

"Liar. The leg is killing you, isn't it?"

Her lips twisted and she stared up at him. He was seriously gorgeous. Friendly. An all–around nice guy. So why couldn't she be hooked on him instead of Shadow. Shadow's darkness called to her. Reached into the deepest part of her and wrapped her heart up in caring and warmth. If only she could do the same for him and wrap his heart up in a loving hug.

Cooper shook out two pills from a bottle and handed them to her, along with a sealed bottle of water. He popped the top as she sat up. She stared at the pills. "I really hate that these help."

"No point in being in pain if you don't have to be. Your body needs rest. It can't heal if it's fighting the pain. We got to do what we got to do. And healing that leg is important. I wish we had antibiotics for it."

Shadow appeared at the truck. "We've got an antibiotic cream from the store for those scratches of yours though." He held it up, adding, "It's not much but it's something and we need to change that dressing too."

He disappeared then reappeared with a small medical kit. Cooper shifted back out of the front of the cab. "Let me know if you need any help."

She stared at Shadow and then the kit and realized what he meant, and her whole body cringed at the thought. "Oh no, Shadow, please not."

That stare of his didn't change. Her lower lip trembled. She took a deep breath, feeling the shudder of fear ripple throughout her whole body and regardless of the pain killers she'd just taken her leg started to boom in earnest.

"Sorry, Arianna," he said. "It's got to be done."

She sniffled back the pleas under her tongue. She knew it did. But she didn't want it to happen at all, didn't want them to think less of her.

She rolled onto her back, wincing as her leg was jarred, and crossed her arms over her chest. "Okay, I'm ready."

His regretful sigh filled the truck. At least he wasn't looking forward to this process either.

In fact, he was so gentle…it surprised her. Her pants were lowered to her ankles, like how embarrassing, and the bandage cut away from her leg. When he lifted the dressing off her skin, she was watching his face, trying to gauge his reaction to her wound.

When he didn't say anything, she whispered, "How bad is it?"

"Surprisingly good," he said and glanced up at her. "Are you going to look at it?"

That's when she realized she'd squeezed her eyes closed. She shook her head. "Nope. It's going to hurt more if I do."

"So if you ignore things they don't hurt you?"

She heard the humor in his voice and realized how silly that sounded. Right. Along with so much else of her attitude and outlook in the world. "It might be silly to you, but if it helps me get through this, then it's working fine."

Silence. Not that she cared. She was so focused on not blubbering like a baby this time she barely noticed. Besides, it was getting harder to sense that silence through the rest of the noise. The rest? Damn. She winced inside as she realized the other noise *was* her blubbering like an idiot. Tears pouring down her cheeks and she sniffed like a two-year-old. She'd always been a baby to pain. And here he most likely hadn't even started cleaning her leg. How totally unheroic of her. So much for wanting to make a good impression. She was acting the same as ever.

Well, it was for the better. Guys like Shadow didn't want watering pots like herself. She swiped at her eyes and tried to turn off the waterworks. It took a long moment before she mustered up the courage to peek out from under her lashes. He was likely disgusted with her.

Instead, he stood outside the truck and stared at her with such an odd look on his face. A look that said he didn't know what to do with her. Well, she didn't know what to do with him either.

But what if that look was about her leg? Maybe he'd lied earlier.

"Is it bad?" she whispered struggling to sit up. "Tell me the truth."

Immediately he shook his head. "No, your wounds are doing quite well." Then he shrugged and added, "At least as well as can be expected."

She frowned. "That means it's doing terrible."

He gave her a long look. "I said it was doing well, didn't I?"

"Sure." She struggled to sit, bracing herself for fresh tears when the pain hit, but was surprised to find that although it was aching and sore, it wasn't screaming at her. "But then you couched in terms that meant it would do better under different circumstances?"

"Sure, if you were in a bed and not trying to walk and had maybe a dose of antibiotics in you so as to not be in danger of getting an infection, you know…ideal circumstances. But you aren't, so given that you aren't, you're doing fine."

She blinked as she tried to process what he was saying. Then gave it up. It sounded reassuring and she was willing to trust him.

Besides, she needed something else from him. And he wasn't going to give it to her unless he knew she needed it. And he, big oaf that he was, wasn't going to know unless she told him. Only she didn't want to have to. "I'd be a lot better if I had one more thing," she announced expectantly.

"What's that?"

She gave him a big smile. Surely he'd be able to guess. "I'm sure you can figure it out if you put your mind to it."

There was that so very predictable frown. With a quick shake of his head, he said, "No, what do you need."

She sighed and wiggled to the open passenger door so her leg could hang down. Then she opened her arms. Immediately, he stepped forward to help her out of the truck.

Idiot. Sure enough he stepped back as soon as she was standing.

She shook her head. "No. That's not what I needed."

At his confused look, she motioned for him to lean down. When he promptly did so, she whispered. "I need a hug, please."

Instantly, he cuddled her close. Oh happy sigh. It's not that he didn't want to, or that he wasn't willing, he just wasn't much of a toucher and that was too bad, he was so, so good at it. She let out a big sigh and smiled up at him. He stared down at her, an unreadable look on his face. She smiled. "It's okay. I'll keep your secret."

His eyebrows shot up and a worried look crossed his face. "And what secret is that?"

"You're an awesome hugger." She reached up and kissed his cheek.

He shook his head, once again not sure what to do with her easy affection "What was that for?"

"As a thank you." Her grin deepened, her irrepressible good humor surfacing. "For letting me cry like a baby."

That brought a grin to his face. "You did much better this time."

"Right, sure I did." She rolled her eyes at his nice comment. "At least you're allowing me to save face. And the others?" She looked around and at not seeing anyone she added only half joking, "Did I scare them away with my bawling."

"You didn't bawl," he said seriously. "You were quiet

and tears are allowed. You're hurt and hurting and sometimes tears are the only answer. Don't be so hard on yourself."

His words surprised her but so did the warm caring way he delivered them. Much happier, she leaned against his chest just happy to be held. She wasn't clingy usually but she did love being close to him.

"Besides, most of the men have gone to find someone to talk to from the town."

"Hopefully, they found lots of people." She glanced around. "I can't imagine something like this being ignored." And that was another reminder. She tilted her head back. "Still no word on my family?"

He shook his head. She sighed. "How am I getting home at this point?"

"Waiting on orders to answer that."

Her lips curled. "If they are as good at making decisions as the rest of the government it will be Christmas before we get a solid answer."

He grinned. "True enough. But we're heading back to California and you're supposed to go to...where, Oregon?"

She shook her head. "We live in Newport Beach, CA."

"Really?" His tone held more than surprise in it.
She nodded. "Why?"

He was silent for a long moment then said, "I live at the base. Coronado."

She gave him a fat grin. They didn't live that far apart. She'd love to see him after this mess was over. But he had a life there. "I guess you'll be happy to go home."

"Always, but that doesn't change the fact that I'll likely be called out in another day or week or month."

"Always something needing your attention. My father

would say the same for him."

The two smiled.

"What do you do for a living," he asked her. "Our files didn't include much about you."

"What, not my education, favorite foods, past lovers, or the color of my underwear?" she asked in a mocking voice. "Who knew?"

"Pink."

She stared up at him in confusion.

"The color of your underwear is pink. You went to UCLA but I don't think the program you started in is the one you completed and you've had past lovers but not the right ones."

Oh boy. She tried to close her gaping mouth but it was damn hard. She *was* wearing pink panties, and he had no choice but to see them considering he'd removed her pants to clean her leg wound—twice. That he noticed brought a flush to her cheeks. But as for the rest… Oddly enough her mind latched onto the one thing he'd missed and the easier topic to carry forward. "And my favorite food?" she challenged, still trying to figure out what his comment about not having the right lovers meant.

He slanted her a devastatingly cute sideways grin that had her heart racing instantly and said, "Chocolate of course."

"Damn."

He laughed. "So what field of study did you complete?"

With a resentful look his way she said, "I'm a teacher. My father wanted me to be a lawyer and follow in his footsteps but…" She looked away. "I just couldn't."

"Of course not. You'd want to give the victim everything and be devastated when the victim turned out to not be a victim," he said promptly.

"Well, something like that." She wrinkled up her nose at him. "I just couldn't do that type of work. It wasn't me," she said, staring back at the long years of fighting with her father. "Father never understood."

"Of course not. First you were female and second you're a bleeding heart," he said, but the words were so full of warm laughter it took the sting out.

"Not in all things," she protested. "I also don't get along well with my father or my stepmother."

"Why would you? They are the opposite of you, aren't they? They give money because it's expected of them, a requirement of their social status and to make sure that they attend the most public of functions so that everyone knows they did their duty. You on the other hand probably give money to the local animal shelter and hand over money to the single moms and old folks in the area."

"Food. I take food to the old folks in my building. And shop for them sometimes," she said. "My father threatened to cut off my allowance when he found out I was doing that as a teen." She sighed at the memories.

"And what did you do then?" he asked.

"I told him to go ahead and I'd be sure to contact the local newspaper about the senator who cut off the support for those less fortunate," she confessed.

He nudged her chin up and searched her eyes.

"See," she whispered, needing him to see her as she really was. "I'm not a very nice person."

His lips twitched. "Sweetie, the world I live in – you're a pink puff ball full of niceness."

She blinked then narrowed her gaze at him. Was he mocking her? Hadn't he understood what she'd said? "I don't think you understand," she said earnestly. "I took advantage of the situation."

He snickered. "No, you did what you had to do."

Now she was getting mad. "No I didn't. I could have walked away and not said anything to him. But I was upset and angry."

But he wasn't listening. "You were not a bad person for what you did."

"I blackmailed him," she snapped. "Weren't you listening?"

Mason's cold voice cut through the conversation. "Who did you blackmail and does it relate to this case."

That did it, Shadow burst out laughing.

Arianna reached out and plowed her fist into his belly. The rest of the men crowded around. She couldn't figure out if they were stunned that she'd hit him or the fact that Shadow was damn near rolling on the ground in hysterics.

"You…you…" And words failed her.

The men were helpful though.

"Meanie," Dane suggested.

"Arrogant SOB," said Hawk helpfully.

"Asshole," said Cooper with a huge grin.

"No, I couldn't call him that," she said with a gasp. "But he is a meanie. And hurtful. And not very accepting of my faults."

That did it. The others started to snigger and Shadow fell on his butt to the ground, holding his head in his hands as he tried to stop the laughter rolling through him.

She stared at them and then at him. "Why won't he believe me?"

Mason, his voice desperately trying to quell the humor, said, "Then explain and we'll pass judgment."

She blinked at him suspiciously. The others were trying to calm down so they could hear. She sighed and quickly explained. She finished with, "So I blackmailed my father into continuing my allowance. See... I told Shadow here I was a terrible person, and he should find someone much better than me."

The men, huge grins on their faces all nodded. She wailed. "You all think I'm terrible too."

And damn if her lower lip didn't tremble.

Mason, once again the voice of reason said, "And after you blackmailed your father, what did he do?"

"He doubled the amount," she said with a small grin.

"And just for the record," Shadow said from the ground where Swede was offering a helping hand. "You never said I should find someone better than you."

"Oh, so you want to repeat that in front of all your friends? Just to humiliate me more."

He sighed.

"Look, they are laughing at me," she lamented.

He groaned. "They aren't laughing at you, they're laughing at me."

"What?" she turned to face all the men who were grinning or trying to hide grins but still nodding their heads. "You wouldn't..."

She spun so she was standing in front of Shadow, defending him, her feistiness rising to the surface. "You can't laugh at him, he's your friend. He's a good man."

"Oh for the love of Go–"

"Now what?" she cried out, turning to face him. "I can't have them making fun of you. That's not nice. Everyone thinks you're cold and mean. They don't know you like I do. You're a marshmallow inside."

"Marshmallow?" Swede asked in a barely controlled voice.

"Softie is probably good," Hawk suggested helpfully.

"I like the pussycat term she used before," Dane said. "Yeah, that's really a good description of Shadow."

"Exactly," she said earnestly, spinning to beam at the men. "Inside he's really a lovable person, even if he often shows a cold, detached exterior."

"Jesus," Shadow said and jerked her around and into his arms. "Enough already. You're killing my hard earned reputation."

She opened her mouth again to blast him, but he calmly picked her up. "Remember how I shut you up last time?"

And he kissed her. Again.

HE HAD TO stop doing that.

The rest of his team were cheering him on and he felt like a heel. Pulling back he studied the slumberous look she gave him. His lips tilted. She didn't appear to be bothered by the crowd around them. He'd hate for her to feel they didn't respect her because they did – if for no other reason than for taking him on.

Crack.

Shadow hit the ground, pulling Arianna over with him. He heard her cry of pain and hoped to hell it was because of her original injury and not a second bullet. He'd deliberately pulled her on top of him as he fell, but now he rolled, tucking her under the vehicle and came up, gun out and ready. His team had scattered, Cooper crouched beside him swearing in low tones but the language he used, yeah the air had turned ripe. There was blood on his shoulder, but it was only a scratch. Thank heavens, Cooper had just gotten back to Active Duty, he'd be pissed to be sidelined so quickly.

He peered around the grill of the truck. Mason had managed to get to the far side of the gas pumps, not the ideal location but he could maneuver around behind the neighbor's house if he got cover.

And Shadow could give him that. Catching his eye, they set up the timing and on the count of three, Shadow jumped up and started firing. When Mason was safe, Shadow popped back down and looked at Arianna. She lay quietly where he'd placed her, her gaze locked on him and huge.

He gave her a reassuring smile. "It's okay."

But her look said she didn't believe him. And considering more firepower was being exchanged she had good reason.

"Shadow…"

The hiss came from the store behind him. Dane was there, motioning at him to join him.

"Cooper," he said in an urgent whisper. "I'm taking her inside the store."

"Got it."

With a warning glance at Arianna, Shadow scooped her up in his arm and raced to the store and inside as Cooper covered them.

"Do we have any idea who or how many?" he asked when he came to a stop inside. Arianna had looped her arms around his head.

"No. Two for sure."

"Same group?" Shadow asked. He looked at the back door, in his mind he could see the layout of the other houses. And the distance he'd have to travel to reach safety.

"That amount of shooting I'm going to say yes." Dane motioned to the back. "Swede took off and went to the left, Hawk went to the right."

"Cooper is at the truck and Mason at the pumps," Shadow added filling him in. "Now Arianna is here."

"Keep an eye on her," Shadow said. He carefully lowered her to beside a wall full of ropes and other miscellaneous items. "I'll be back," he whispered.

At the next round of gunfire he bolted out the back door.

CHAPTER 15

ARIANNA HUDDLED IN the corner of the store, arms over her head as the gunfire rained all around the building. Shots hit the old wooden structure but didn't penetrate the thick walls. Smoke filled the air, making it difficult to breathe, but she honestly couldn't figure out if that was the panic or residue in the air. When there appeared to be a small break in the shooting, she slowly lowered her arms. And froze.

The smell hit her at the doorway. The storekeeper lay on the floor in front of her. She hadn't seen him before. Now the dead man came clearly into view. He'd been covered with an old plaid hunting shirt but laid up against the back of the counter. She had no doubt about his identity. The poor man.

"Arianna?" Dane's harsh whisper broke her out of her reverie.

"I'm here. I'm fine."

"Good."

"What's going on out there? Surely that's more than one man?"

"Yeah, looks like three."

Three. She shook her head. "Did the other prisoners get away from the soldiers and somehow come into town via a different route?"

"We didn't see a different route. Mason has been try-ing to contact the other soldiers. We could use the backup, and if they are traveling toward us, we don't want them to get caught in the trap."

"No, there're enough dead men already." Too many dead. Thankfully most of the deaths hadn't involved her.

She didn't count the guy she knocked out of the tree. He'd been going after her brother. Kevin. Thank God her brother wasn't here with her now. That would be terrible for him. He should be home safe and sound. But with both parents injured and in the hospital she had no idea where he'd go. Who'd look after him? He'd be with her if she'd gone home. If she was allowed to leave. Her leg didn't feel horrible but neither did it feel terrific. The hospital might have sent her home to heal or they'd have forced her to wait in the hospital a day or two longer. And Kevin would be in the same boat as he was now.

At least he'd escaped without physical injury, but she knew these past events would scar him for life. How could it not? He was a strong boy though and with help he'd get past this.

She just wished she was there with him now.

The silence outside continued in an elongated moment. She twisted to look up at Cooper. "Any idea what's happening out there?"

"No. Not yet. If our team can sneak up and take them out, this could be over in minutes."

"Or hours," she muttered.

"Hopefully not. We aren't into sieges."

"Good." As the words left her mouth a short burst of gunfire sounded behind the store. Shit. She'd feel better if that had been out front.

Cooper raced to hide behind the door. Arianna scrunched up as small as she could.

Slowly the door was pushed open and swung loose. No hand visible. Nobody walking inside. Her breath caught in the back of her throat, and she pressed harder against the shelves at her back. Now what the hell…

A man somersaulted inside, and with guns blazing, he spun and fired. She lay flat on the floor as the bullets rained over her head.

A single shot fired.

The gunman collapsed to the floor, a bullet between the eyes. Shadow walked inside the store, kicked the gun away from the dead man and nudged him with his boot. Satisfied the danger had been neutralized, he turned to study Arianna. "Cooper," he called out.

"Yep," Cooper said, "Right behind you."

"Anyone else in here," Shadow asked in a dark, flat voice that left Arianna breathless at the dangerous man in front of her.

"Only us," she whispered. "And now two dead guys."

He shifted to the window. "Mason took out one, this is two. We're looking for at least one more. Maybe two more. We're afraid they've holed up in one of the houses, possibly holding a family hostage."

"To what purpose," Cooper asked. "They failed in their mission. What's the point of attacking innocent bystanders?"

"No idea. They might have been holding them as insurance for the senator as extra leverage."

"Makes no sense," Arianna said. "If his own family didn't do it, a house of strangers wouldn't either."

"I have to agree," Shadow said. "It could have been insurance in case their group got into trouble."

"Or to persuade you to hand me over?"

Shadow shot her a hard look. "Not happening."

"I think once the plan blew up and they lost three family members, they realized the senator wasn't going to do what they wanted, so they looked to grab me to save something of the operation. Or maybe they needed me as extra insurance to gain their freedom." She shuddered. "You have to help the family."

"We are planning to. But that's not going to work out so well if we can't shut down the men hunting us." He spun around and crept to the open door. "First things first."

And once again he disappeared.

She looked from the second dead man to Cooper. "Do you want to go after Shadow?"

Cooper shook his head. "Shadow operates on a whole different level than the rest of us. He works best alone."

She nodded, trying not to worry about the man. If he was the best then he was doing what he needed to do. She glanced over at the killer's gun. "Can you give me his gun?" She pointed to the assault rifle Shadow had kicked against the far wall. "I don't want to be defenseless."

"It's not a beginner's weapon," Cooper said cautiously. "You could kill all of us with that thing."

She stared at it with misgivings. "I wouldn't want to hurt you… But I don't want to be a sitting duck for the next man either."

Cooper carefully closed the door part way and picked up the rifle. He checked it over then walked toward her. "I've put the safety on. If you click this," and he showed her, "then it's basically point and shoot. But you need to have a target in sight and it's going to fire multiple rounds as soon as you pull this trigger."

"Oh." She carefully looked at the mean looking weapon and realized she wanted nothing to do with it. Particularly if she did something wrong. Taking a deep breath, she said, "Take it away. I don't want it."

She ignored the relief on his face.

But she could understand how he felt. She didn't

want to be caught unarmed, but if she were armed and someone approached they'd kill her anyway. She'd be the one hesitating to pull the trigger so she'd be just as dead.

SHADOW'S HEART HAD damn near seized up when he saw the gunman sneaking around the side of the door. Too hidden for a clear shot, too far away for a tackle and too damn close to Arianna. Shadow was already on the run when the man had disappeared into the store. With the gunshots filling the air, he burst through to see the gunman lining up a shot. He couldn't see a target but there were only two choices and neither were ones he was prepared to lose.

He fired one shot to the head. The man fell and never moved again.

Thank God. But this was so not over. With relief coursing through his veins he'd raced back outside and to the house on the north end of town. The faster he traveled, the more he considered her theory. Would they be looking for hostages to get out of the country? With the resources available to them, surely they could have slipped away without this. He had to wonder if anyone lived here. Or was this place a ghost town. Then again, the store owner lived here. But there'd been nothing fresh in the store. So he didn't cater to locals as much as travelers, and there couldn't be many of them through here. The roads led to nowhere. Just more roads north. There wasn't any major center further past the cabin and the road into that place hadn't been traveled in many years. Mother Nature had tried to reclaim most of it.

The team had checked the south end of town already. There were four houses there. Two were derelict and empty. The other two vacant but in better shape. Now they were heading to the houses they'd passed on their drive in to town.

He moved and shifted with the changing landscape, blending in and out as required. In the distance he heard a dog bark. Then nothing. That wasn't normal. He shifted back a few steps and changed his angle. The dog barked again. Good. Dogs made great warning systems for both those he protected and predators. They let them know what the dog was sensing at what time. People never thought of that. Shadow caught sight of Swede two houses up. He motioned at Shadow to come closer.

Keeping low and moving fast, he quickly joined Swede.

"Hawk and Mason are on the other side." He pointed to the last house. "If there are more shooters here, they have to be inside this one."

"Where's the dog?"

Swede shook his head. "No idea. Haven't seen one."

Shadow frowned. "If it's not there, it's got to be somewhere close as I heard one. And dog means people."

"We haven't found more. But…" he motioned to the woods. "There could be more in there."

Shadow studied the thick trees that completely blocked any view of what was behind. "I'm going to scout that area."

"You're worried about the dog?"

"Yes, because he's not alone." And Shadow headed for the woods.

CHAPTER 16

S HE HATED TO sit and wait. There had to be something she could do. Something useful. The other military unit would be joining them soon – surely she could help the process of ending this mess somehow. She slid over to the dead kidnapper and struggled to remove his wallet from his pants.

Cooper, always on guard, asked, "What did you find?"

"His ID."

"Really?" He motioned at her. "Toss it to me."

She'd already done a quick search and hadn't found anything else. She flung it lightly in his direction and it was more due to his skill than hers that he caught it. She went back to searching the rest of the man's pockets. She didn't recognize his face but figured based on the khaki outfit he was part of the same kidnapper group. God help her if they ever decided to change those uniforms.

In the last chest pocket she found something harder and crumpled.

She pulled it out and gasped in shock. It was a picture of her standing outside her own condo.

"What is it?"

She struggled to reorient herself. Such a horrid thing to find but maybe not all that unusual given that she'd been on the trip. She used the checkout counter to pull herself to her feet and held out the picture for Cooper.

He studied it.

"It was taken outside my house," she said. "I know they already kidnapped my family and that's over and done with, but it's a little disturbing to know they were stalking me at home beforehand."

"Maybe and maybe not. They could be using this image to identify you as they know you're the one that didn't get on the plane." He nodded as if liking his hypothesis. "Explains why they are making a play for you here."

"They don't need me now," she exclaimed. "They never did." She shook her head. "Could these men have been here since yesterday?" She frowned. "Waiting for their team to show up? Then when we got here instead, all hell broke loose?"

As if the world had heard her, gunshots split the air again. "Oh God," she whispered. "I need this to be over?"

"Soon," he said standing right beside her, both of them peering out the window from the side. "At least it should be."

He turned to look at her. "They might have been using the town as a base. That makes the most sense."

It did. It also meant this wasn't over. The continuous shooting worried her. She'd known Shadow was safe when she'd seen him here, but with this new round... What if he'd been shot?

She hobbled toward the door.

"Whoa, where are you going?"

She waved her hand outside. "I wanted to look around."

"Bad idea," he said. "We wait until they come back."

"Aren't you getting tired of being the babysitter?"

He laughed. "Sure, but I was off active duty for a long time due to a bad injury, so I'm just damn happy to be back as much as I am." His grin widened. "If that's being your babysitter – no worries. I've had worse jobs."

She tried to study him covertly but couldn't see any physical injury on him. So whatever had happened, he'd healed. "I suppose they want to keep you safe as much as possible too."

His grin widened. "I doubt that's the reason as much as everyone wants in on the action, only someone has to stay behind."

"So you drew the short straw." She laughed at his look. "That's okay. I'm happy to have you with me."

"My pleasure," he said simply. "You're a special woman."

The glance she sent him said he was out of his mind. "I'm an idiot. I could have had an easy life but no, that wasn't good enough for me."

"I thought you were a lawyer. Or started as one."

"Sure, but before then my daddy tried to marry me off to a judge." She winced at the memory. "Told me it was the best he could do for me. And I should take the offer as I wasn't likely to get a better one."

There was an awkward silence. "And how old was this judge?"

"Early fifties I think. Back then that seemed ancient. I was in the last term of high school."

"Wow. Nice father."

"He is in many ways, but he has strong views on a woman's place. It's because of him I applied to law school. No one was more surprised than I was when I got in. But it was the wrong place for me."

He stayed quiet for a bit, then said, "Your father was also at an advanced age when he started a family."

"True enough. And even older when he fathered Kevin and yes, he is the father of us both. Insisted on DNA tests." She smiled. "He is consistent."

"Interesting. Maybe an effect of his career. Maybe his age."

"And the way he was reared by an older father himself. He didn't have my father until he was sixty–five himself."

Cooper's eyebrows shot up. "Wow. That would have an impact, I'm sure."

She nodded. "I don't blame my father, but it has made me head in the opposite direction. He's dark so I'm light. He's serious so I'm not. He's all about image…" She grinned. "And I'm not. As you can see. My father's clothes were the top casual for the man–at–the–cabin look he could buy." She motioned to her oversized black sweatpants. "And I'm wearing Shadow's pants and damn glad to have them," she admitted. "I think the biggest thing was he's all about image so I'm all about real." She sighed and leaned against the wall. "It's hard though as my mother was a watering pot and ditzy to boot. And I have way too much of that in me."

"No, you don't. You temper it with courage and independence and caring. You have to be yourself and given the two different people you came from, I think you did a wonderful job."

She grinned, feeling chipper in spite of everything. "Now tell me that Shadow believes the same thing you do, and you'll have made my day."

"Oh my broken heart," he said in a mocking tone. "You shot a single arrow and killed me with that comment."

"Nah, you might be interested in me but you're not *interested* in me."

His dancing eyes landed on her. "Even if I was, Shadow is the man in your heart and that guy deserves to have someone sweet in his world."

"Aw. That's so nice of you to say." She beamed up at him. "Now if only he'd get that message, too."

"I'd tell him but he needs to figure it out for himself."

She nodded seriously. "So true. And as I suspect that he'd be one of the last to go down in the line of fire, I think he'd be the same in terms of letting down the guards to his heart."

"But that doesn't mean you should give up…" he said in alarm.

"Oh, I won't give up," she said with a smile. "But I might just have to change tactics."

And she wouldn't say any more.

THE TREES WERE so thick and stick thin Shadow could barely make his way through the woods. The place was in need of a controlled burn before Mother Nature took care of it herself. The undergrowth was strewn with old broken sticks and dead leaves. Treacherous for walking and deadly to try and sneak up on anyone. He'd skirted the worst of the area and now peered down what appeared to be a dirt driveway. There were tracks at least. He slipped from tree to tree working his way deeper into the woods until it finally opened up to show a log cabin at least forty years old. Untreated, the logs had long ago turned grey.

There was a fenced yard with a dog run along the back. He could hear the snarling sound of canines fighting over territory. So there was at least one, if not two. But where were the owners? He'd have expected the kidnappers to shoot the dogs first. Unless something else was going on here. Then again shooting the dogs let the neighbors know something was up. Shadow quickly traced the perimeter.

There were no lights inside. No vehicles outside but a garage or workshop sat on the far corner of the property. He worked his way over to the back of the small outbuilding. There were windows but no lights. There was, however, a back door. He turned the knob. The door unlatched. Inside, he could see nothing but a row of white. His eyes slowly adjusted to add hair and glowing eyes to the row of teeth in the darkness. But the guard dog never made a sound.

Shadow closed his eyes and reached out to the dog mentally like he'd done many times before. All animals responded to him well but the wilder ones even more so. They might have seen him as an equal, not competition. He didn't know, but they generally had little argument over his presence.

Still, there was always going to be that one instance where the rule didn't hold true. He hoped it wasn't this one. The dog looked well cared for except there was blood on his haunch. His own or someone else's? He took a step toward the animal, speaking in a low voice. As he approached, the dog curled back his lip and showed fangs. Shadow stopped and searched for food. Behind the one dog, lay a second one. Injured. Or dead. Oh, crap. He shouldered his rifle and walked closer as if he had the right. The dog had been raised by people and likely a gun had been responsible for the injury. The dog growled deeper but let him pass. He crouched down beside the injured dog and gently ran a hand over the older lab cross. She was dead. A bullet square in her ribs. She'd not had a chance. Bastards. He hated anyone killing animals unless for food, and when it was a pet like this one—well there was no excuse.

Slowly, Shadow turned to the other dog, "I'm sorry,

boy. She's gone." At the sound of his voice, the dog lay down and dropped his nose on his paws. And whimpered.

Shadow gently stroked the young animal's head. "You already knew that though, didn't you? Sorry, buddy. There's a lot of pain going on around here right now."

He gave a quick search to the garage and found a truck parked on the side. He walked over. The engine was still warm. He popped the hood and pulled off the distributor cap. At least no one would be running away in this rig.

With a final glance at the dog, he quietly closed the door and left. The dog was safer inside right now. But he'd be sure to open the door before he left the property.

The house stood before him. Still no lights or sounds. He raced across the short distance until his back was up against the wall. He listened intently. Still quiet. There were a few basement windows, dusty and caked in dirt. He doubted they'd been cleaned in years. If the windows would open, he could get in that way. But if they were as unused as they appeared to be he wasn't likely to do so silently.

He slid around to the back of the house and the small porch. Also old and creaky likely, but the door was slightly ajar. He frowned, his senses on alert. A trap or someone in a hurry.

Then he heard it.

A tiny snuffle.

Not a young one either. An older woman with a cold came to mind. The proverbial hankie in her hand. And likely a captor at her side.

She sniffled again.

"Shut the fuck up."

Shadow smiled. Perfect. Now he had a target.

CHAPTER 17

ARIANNA WANDERED THE store feeling useless and hating the wait. Her mind spun endlessly after seeing the photo of herself in that man's pocket. To know someone had been taking photos of her without her knowledge. What a horrible feeling. Especially when she should have been safe now. This mess over and done with. Right? Her family was home safe. Right?

She spun to look at Cooper. "Has anyone had an update on my family?"

There must have been something in the tone of her voice because Cooper turned to her, his glance searching. "We know they arrived at the hospital in San Francisco."

She closed her eyes. "Okay, good. Just for a moment there, given that picture, I was afraid they might have taken my family again."

"We've had confirmation they arrived. We don't have an update on your father's condition, but you already know he's in critical condition and he's not expected to survive the head injuries. Last I heard, your stepmother was recovering."

She nodded. That's what she'd expected. Not easy to deal with given her current circumstances. She'd loved her own father but… For Kevin's sake, she hoped her stepmother survived and was capable of raising Kevin. He needed it. He'd had a cold childhood already. He needed so much more.

She needed to get home to him. "Is someone coming to help out?"

He nodded. "The other military team is on the way. And they have the hostages still. More soldiers are en route to help out." He glanced at his watch. "They should be here soon."

"Then what?"

He shrugged. "Good question. I'm not leading this and we're not on home territory. Quite likely we'll be sent on our way."

She brightened. "Perfect!" She glanced over at the man on the ground. "I wonder what happened to the leader."

"The man you sent the photo of?"

"He said something in passing that he was picking up someone." She shrugged. "I don't know who."

Cooper stared at her. "Interesting."

She nodded. "Maybe if we knew who and where they were we could grab both of them. But that was a long time ago. He's likely halfway around the world by now."

"Could be. Any idea why they targeted your father?"

"Something to do with needing his vote on something major." She studied the man on the floor. "But that made no sense to me. My father has always made his position clear."

"Is he close to anyone else in the House?"

She glanced over at him. "Close, no. Not really. He doesn't socialize with many and when he does it's usually for political or charity functions."

He wandered the store, never losing that alertness inside.

"What are you thinking?"

"Your father is well known to be a hard ass, correct?"

"Correct."

"So what if someone was using him to force other Congressmen to take a stance. Your father is known to never give in. Never break and what's happened to him sends a hell of a message to others."

"I don't understand exactly how the voting works but getting someone else appointed wouldn't be easy."

"But he's not out, is he? As long as he's alive they won't move to change the status any time soon. So in theory if he's used as an example, the others might cave in a lot earlier. You know when you're up against a street gang, if you take out the leader, then the others scatter."

"So you're saying that by taking out my father, the others are more likely to do what they are told to do." She snorted. "Now that could be. I've been tossing this all around in my head and coming up empty."

"We've got a good idea of how this went down but need the details."

"Like?"

"How they knew where you were going, why you were going, when you were going. And how did all of you come together." He walked the few steps toward her. "And we have to consider if there was anyone on the inside."

"Well, it wasn't me," she said with feeling. "The arrangements were made by my father's office. They'd know when and where."

"Anyone else?"

"I don't know who Kevin and Linda might have told but not likely anyone. It was a fast decision. In fact..." She considered the issue. "It was too fast."

"No warning."

"No, I wondered about that. I didn't hear about it until early in the week. And as soon as I did..." She peered out the window but didn't see anything but her memories. "I invited myself." She studied the dead man again. "And as that's the case, why would he have my photo?"

"Maybe you invited yourself, but it's also possible you were going to be forced to go regardless. They could have easily kidnapped you and held you somewhere else."

"I can't understand what makes people do things like this."

"Money and power." He held out the picture to her. "Any idea when this might have been taken?"

She glanced over at it. "I'm wearing the same coat I always wear so that could have been anytime."

"It's in the evening."

"Is it? Then that narrows it down as I don't wear that coat out for any evening functions. It's more for going for a walk or to pick up a few groceries."

"So when would that have been?" he persisted.

She looked at the image again. And saw her neighbor in one of her Old Russian day dresses she always wore. The old woman had passed away a couple of weeks ago. "I can say it's at least three weeks old," she explained.

"And did you know about the plans three weeks ago?"

"No," she said in surprise. "I only heard about it on Monday. We flew out on Friday."

"For the long weekend?"

She nodded. "It was a short holiday and a rather long flight. I think that was my stepmother's biggest issue. But then you have to understand, if a longer vacation was planned, she'd have bitched about it as well. She didn't like to travel."

"But your father insisted?"

She cast her mind back. "I don't know," she admitted. "I was never involved in the discussion." She clenched her fingers into a fist. "I only heard from Kevin that she hadn't wanted to come."

"Any reason to believe she'd be involved?"

Her head shot up and stared. "No. Why would she be?"

"Who inherits?"

That caught her by surprise. "I don't know," she said slowly, not liking his line of questioning. "Likely my stepmother. There should be something there for Kevin's education as well. My father is very wealthy, but I don't know what's in the will."

"What happens if all of you die except Kevin?"

Her stomach started to bubble with an overload of acid. "I don't know." Lord, she hadn't wanted to know. "His guardian would be responsible for him I'm sure."

"And who is that?"

She studied Cooper. "My father's aide. He's been with my father for decades. I've known him all my life. He's my step–uncle, actually," she confessed. "He introduced my father and my stepmother to each other way back when."

SHADOW PUSHED THE back door open with the toe of his boot like a strong wind would. The door swung open soundlessly. About time something worked out. He'd already contacted his team, letting them know where he was and what he was doing.

He slipped inside. And stilled.

The kitchen was empty.

And dark.

He studied the layout, his attention lingering on the chipped teapot and half cup of tea on the table, a single plate with crumbs and a bit of bread left. The decor was dated, unkempt. Not dirty but badly in need of repair. He studied the two doorways into and out of the kitchen. One on the left and one on the right. He shifted to the one furthest away. He could see a living room ahead, but it was dimly lit and held only shelving that he could see. He checked out the room moving silently forward. Whoever lived here had likely been here most of their lives. And had little money or interest in upkeep or modernization. Given the voice and sniffles he'd heard earlier he could see this being a pensioner, likely a widow left alone now and waiting out her last days. He hoped she had someone who cared close by. But given the age of the town and the lack of people living there, he doubted it.

Seeing the room empty and not connecting through to the other side he envisioned it as a parlor from days gone and then closed off later. It was the other side of the house he needed to reach. As he turned back to retrace his steps, he saw a huge cupboard. Weapon in hand, he opened it. And realized it was actually a doorway that matched the old wall panels. It led to the front entrance. He stood and listened. There was only one major room downstairs and whatever was upstairs. He glanced up the old staircase, but there was no way to make it up without alerting whoever was in the house that there was an intruder.

At the entrance to the other room, he could hear an odd sound. His mind raced to catalogue it. And realized it was the sound of someone playing cell phone games. The almost silent sound of the fingers tapping and his soft groans when he missed something and angry breaths as he lost, the muted music as the game played.

Good. Keep the asshole distracted. He slipped around the corner. An old woman huddled on an old dusty couch, her wrists bloodied from the ties on her paper thin skin. She raised her head, her mouth opening to cry out. Shadow placed his finger to his lips. She subsided, shaky but valiant as she glared at the man, dressed in khakis, playing his cell phone.

Shadow raised his rifle.

In a low deadly voice, he said, "Now you have to kidnap old ladies after losing the senator and his family. Is that a demotion?"

At Shadow's first word, the man froze. By the time he'd stopped talking, Shadow was staring into the glittering eyes of one of the kidnappers he recognized from the senator's cabin. So one had escaped and come to warn the men waiting here. Interesting.

"You have two choices. You can stand up and be taken as my prisoner back to Washington or you can reach for that weapon at your side."

The man glared at him. "My death won't matter. Another will take my place. We took money for a job. It must be done."

A spidery tingle shot down Shadow's spine. "Mercenaries. Interesting. We figured you for terrorists."

He shrugged. "We are. But sourcing money is always an issue. Mercenaries bring in good money."

It was and there was a never ending source of assholes who wanted shit done. "And the job?"

He laughed. "It was a double whammy. We got paid for two jobs."

"So tell me…" Shadow said in a conversational voice. "How do two jobs dovetail like that?"

"Some senators needed to make a decision and refused. We were supposed to make an example of Senator Stephenson so the others would cave easier. Beating up that old man felt damn good." He sniggered. "And the other job wanted the old man and the young woman dead. We know the old man isn't going to make it. The young woman, well, if you assholes hadn't rescued her we'd have been in the clear there too."

"And who wanted her dead."

The asshole laughed. "I'm not saying anything more."

Shadow expected as much. "Not a problem. We have a pretty good idea already. It always comes down to money, power or sex."

The man smiled. "Well, it's up to you to figure out which one."

"Not bothered." Shadow motioned to the man's gun. "Kick it over here."

"Nah. You come and get it."

Shadow smiled. "I don't think so." He lifted his rifle butt. "After the men you've murdered I'm totally okay with pulling the trigger right here and now."

The old lady stood up shakily. "He shot my dog," she said, tears in her eyes. "Both of them."

"The old girl didn't make it, but the young one is in the garage and still doing fine."

He heard the old lady's gasp of joy. She struggled to walk past him rubbing her sore wrists. "You be careful," Shadow warned.

"I will," she whispered. "Just please don't let him get away." She shot the stranger a scared look. "He said he'd do me a favor and kill me before he left. That would be an easier death than old age."

The stranger laughed. "Look at you, old and dried up. That's no way..." He scooped up his weapon.

And Shadow shot him.

Dead.

CHAPTER 18

COOPER'S PHONE WENT off. Arianna raced to his side to listen.

"Hey, Shadow. Yes, she's fine."

Arianna beamed. Cooper rolled his eyes at her. "No, I've been taking good care of her. No, I haven't had an update from the others. No, we haven't had anyone else in the store."

When he hung up the phone, Cooper was grinning. "Shadow has taken out one asshole. Now if only we knew how many we were up against."

"No," Mason said in a doorway. "We've taken out four now. Is Shadow on his way back?"

"Yes."

"Good," Mason said. "I just got word the military should be here in an hour to sort this out."

"Are we needed here after that?"

"Only to hand off the operation to them. If they need anything more one or two men can stay behind." Mason studied Arianna. "You're looking better."

"Feeling it too," she said with forced cheerfulness. "More than ready to leave."

He nodded. "Aren't we all?" And he turned and walked back out.

Cooper raised his brows. "Sounds like this one is almost wrapped up."

"I hope so. I just want to go home."

That happened sooner than she expected. With a speed that left her stunned, the military arrived by helicopter. They landed on the edge of town and were followed by a second and third. Soldiers surged through the tiny town, and she could only watch in awe as the military machine took over.

She was quickly helped into one of the helicopters and airborne before she knew it.

Cooper was the only one of the SEALs she saw at the end. She clung to him as they approached the helicopter. "Am I going alone?" she whispered, her eyes darting from one stranger's face to the other, searching for those she knew.

"Yes. They are taking you to the next hospital. You have to get that leg checked. Should have done that hours ago," he said in a reassuring voice.

"I know." She gripped her arms around his neck twice as hard as he loaded her onto the huge black machine. "Doesn't mean I want to go alone."

"If we can, we'll come by. I can't say if we're still needed here or if we'll be sent on our way, but home for us is California."

"Me too." She brightened. "Can they fly me there?"

He shook his head. "No, they can't."

Her face fell. Another soldier motioned at a seat in the helicopter. She swallowed and slowly released her arms from Cooper's neck. Just before he walked way, she called out, "Say good-bye to everyone for me."

He stilled, turned back, and said, "You'll see us again."

"Will I?" she said in a forlorn voice. "It doesn't feel like it."

"I promise."

And he was engulfed in chaos as men ordered him

back. The helicopter started up. One soldier hopped up beside her. Seconds later, she was airborne.

It looked like a bad movie as she was slowly lifted above the scene. She watched as the men scurried through every house and a stretcher was brought out for the storekeeper. Too quickly she was too high up to see anything or anyone clearly. She leaned her head back and tried to ignore the man beside her. It wasn't his fault he wasn't the man she wanted beside her. Then, no one was. Was it really over? How could she have connected with Shadow only to lose him at this stage?

"Miss, are you okay?"

She rolled her head to the side, seeing the worry on the soldier's face and tried to smile, realizing that once again a waterfall of tears rolled down her cheeks.

"I'm okay," she managed. "It was a very tough weekend, that's all."

"It's over. You're safe now."

And that was partly why she was crying. Stupid really. Still, she was going to miss those men. All of them. They'd worked their way into her heart in such a way she knew she'd never be able to forget. How could such a crazy weekend happen in the first place and then there was the way it all ended. At that, she started to really cry. The release of stress, the constant danger, the fear, and panic – it had happened in a short time frame. Like a small bomb going off inside, the tears and heartache burst free. The soldier let her cry. She appreciated that. The release was good but made her feel crappy at the same time. How did that work?

They weren't in the air for long before they descended.

The soldier noticed her interest. "We'll be at the hospital in just a few minutes."

She nodded, not caring which hospital. It wasn't the one at home and that's where she wanted to be. But she didn't have time to look at much as soon houses appeared below then a large roof with a landing spot came next. The helicopter lowered gently and landed easily on the spot.

Several people rushed toward her.

She was unloaded onto a stretcher and whisked to a door. Before she was pushed inside, she watched the helicopter rise up and disappear into the clouds above. With it went her dreams of seeing Shadow and his team again. She stared at the long white corridors as she was taken into an elevator and rolled down to the ER. There she was moved into a small curtained off room. She hated everything about it. Not logical, considering they were helping her.

Shadow was already gone, her world lost and empty.

Then the curtain was ripped back. The medical team poured over her as she was partially stripped, her leg poked and prodded, then cleaned. She lay there, vulnerable, as they did what they had to do. Already tired and worn out, she barely reacted.

A doctor leaned over her. "Miss Stephenson, how are you feeling?"

She raised dull eyes to him. "I'm fine. How is my leg?"

He glanced down at it. "It's going to be fine."

"Oh good." She knew it would be. After all, the guys had looked after it. They'd done their best and in this case their best was pretty fine. "Can I go home now?"

"We'll need to keep you for a day or two. Then there's a lot of paperwork to take care of. So should be sometime in the next couple of days."

Paperwork? Who cared about that right now? Without Shadow her world looked so dark and she knew her golden dream attitude wasn't going to pull her out of this one.

But her irrepressible positive thinking latched onto Cooper's promise that they'd see her again. And would try to come by the hospital if they could. Only…what if she was shipped out first? Then what? Then it didn't matter what he said, he'd have done his best and this time it would be that the wheels of bureaucracy had moved too fast. She brightened even more. That never happened. Paperwork…took forever. Right. She'd still be here when the SEALs got free of that town. She had to be…

The doctor stepped back slightly. "Now, there is someone I'd like you to speak with. You've been through a traumatic ordeal. And as you're going to be with us for the next couple of days, I think it would be helpful if you talked to one of our trauma counselors."

She was ready to agree to anything if it meant she could stay until the guys arrived but at his word, *counselor*, she froze.

"Is that like a shrink?" she asked cautiously, her gaze locked on his face. "Surely I don't need that?"

"Don't look at it that way. Dr. Mendelson is very good at her job, and in this case, her job would be to help you get over the horrific experience you've just been through." He straightened and walked to the doorway. "Now that we have that sorted, I'll let her know you're here."

And he was gone.

She stared suspiciously at the doorway, afraid the shrink would be popping through any second. She really didn't want to talk with her, but was it worth fighting over?

She was still mulling it over when an orderly came

and raised the bars on her bed. In alarm, she asked, "What are you doing?"

"Not to worry, your room is ready. I'm taking you down." He unclicked the brakes on the wheels and pulled the bed back out slightly. Then unhooked her IV bag to lay it on her bed. "Now we can get you settled in for a pleasant visit. You're only with us for a few days I understand."

He was really nice. Still, part of her was suspicious, was everyone like that here? And then the orderly nudged the curtain accidentally. "Oops, sorry about that. Here I was trying to be so careful."

"It's fine," she said, chuckling inside.

"Well, I'm still sorry. We don't want you to have a bad impression of us."

She counted three more apologies on the way to her room. One when they passed another orderly pushing a different patient in a bed, again as they turned the corner into her room and she moved her hand away even though there was lots of room and then because he couldn't set the bed up any closer to the window. She gave a happy sigh. He was a sweetheart. She was quickly falling in love with the country and the people.

After she was set up in her new bed, a move he made painless, and her IV once again hanging, her medication administered and a wonderful warm blanket wrapped around her, she lay in a haze of wellbeing.

Truly, she was safe now.

And she closed her eyes.

SHADOW MADE HIS way slowly back to the store. Soldiers had arrived at the old woman's house, but it had been

Shadow who had dug the grave for the beloved dog and had brought the young one back to the old lady. She'd had tears of gratitude in her eyes as she thanked him again. He'd patted her shoulder, put on the tea kettle, ordered one of the young men who'd arrived to make sure she got a hot cup of tea, had the medical team check her over for other injuries and see if she needed anything else. He made it quite clear that the cupboards were bare and the woman needed more help than a pat on her hand.

The soldier had assured him she'd be taken care of.

Satisfied, Shadow walked back into town watching the military in action as they did a house to house search. His team were standing talking with several military leaders. Good, maybe after the updates they could get back to their original mission. Helicopters had been arriving and leaving steadily. Also good. There were five dead men to take care of. And who knew how many living were in need of medical assistance.

Mason gave him a quick nod as he spoke with the major.

The two men saluted and the major turned to the rest of the team. "You have our thanks, if there is ever anything we can do…"

It wasn't meaningless either. The two countries had a great rapport and military alliance when times warranted.

"Cooper?" Shadow called and stopped. Cooper's shoulders hunched. Guilt? He searched the surrounding area, although he'd been doing just that since he'd seen his team. But there was no sign of her. He'd left Arianna inside the store. Maybe she was still in there. Or better yet getting medical attention. He twisted looking but couldn't see her.

"Cooper," he repeated in an ominous tone of voice, hating he was immediately thinking the worst. Surely she hadn't been killed. He'd left her alive and well in the store. But he hadn't actually checked her over to see if a stray bullet had caught her. "Where is she?"

Cooper took a deep breath but it was Mason who answered.

"She was airlifted out a half hour ago."

Shadow locked down inside. She was gone. He hadn't been able to say good-bye. There'd been no time. No one had let him know. He'd been busy helping the old lady and Arianna had been shipped out alone.

God, she'd have been a wreck. And he hadn't been there for her. Of course he hadn't. He'd done his job. Done what he was supposed to do. Damn it.

Mason, his gaze steady on his face while none of the others would look at him, said in a low voice, "She's at the hospital."

He nodded. "Good, that leg needs attention." He was damn proud of himself for keeping his voice steady. Inside though, he was shattering. And couldn't afford to let anyone know. He blinked and stared across the way, lost. The world of his, darkening. Shadows filling up the places she'd opened up, letting in the sunlight. Now the light was gone.

Foolish.

Cheesy.

Stupid.

But it was the way he felt.

Cooper spoke up. "She didn't want to go, but she didn't have a choice. Like you said, her leg needed attention." He raised his gaze to Shadow's dark hooded one. "I told her we'd go to the hospital to see her if we could. I promised her that she'd see us again."

And the shadows moved to the other side, letting the light shine once again.

"Good. That's important to her." Shadow turned and walked toward the store. Needing to leave. To get away. To be alone. Before the others understood just how much she meant to him. And how much her needing that promise did for his soul. It didn't matter that she'd made Cooper promise. It had been intended for him.

"We'll be leaving in ten minutes," Mason called. "We're hours from the hospital."

"I'll be ready," he said in a controlled voice. "Just want to make sure of something."

The men watched him as he strode inside. He could feel their scrutiny burning into his back. Once in the store, a quick glance confirming he was alone, he walked to the end where she'd been crouched the last time he'd seen her, and for just a moment he let down his guard, and whispered, "Thank God. Ten minutes. We're coming sweetheart. We'll be there soon."

CHAPTER 19

W AKING IN THE hospital sucked. Sure she was comfortable and she was feeling better and not being cramped in a back seat with her legs stretched out across the guys' knees but she was…alone.

Was there anything worse? She wasn't sure how she was going to be able to go back to her condo and her teaching job. She currently taught at a private girls' school. How bloody predictable was that? She loved her kids, but had thought often that she'd like to work with those less fortunate. Her father would have a heart attack if he knew what she was thinking.

Then again, her poor father wasn't going to be able to react to anything anymore. Even if he survived this, he wasn't going to be around for too much longer.

She'd love to teach the not so privileged kids. She wasn't sure she had the temperament for inner city kids, there was definitely a skill needed for them that she didn't think she had. The public system interested her though. Everyone seemed to think private school would mean she could avoid most of the problems prevalent in the public system. But she'd found growing up that the private school system had just as many problems. There were still drugs, booze, and sex at the younger ages. Cheating was rampant and the class eliteness was horrific.

Yet she'd followed the same path for teaching. Now she realized it wasn't enough. It kept her in her comfort zone when there was so much else available. She needed more. And if her mind suggested she explore opportunities in the direction of San Diego and a very large well known base there, well who could blame her?

Her stomach growled. She couldn't remember when she'd last eaten. The doctor's had given her a shot of something in her IV like vitamins or something, but she wished for food. Like a real meal. She'd missed lunch as it had been served while she'd been in the ER. Now she'd have to wait for dinner and her stomach was already weighing the odds between the value of a hospital lunch versus no food, and she realized it didn't matter how bad it was, she'd be happy to have anything. She yawned and snuggled under the covers again. She was still so damn tired. She dozed peacefully just under the surface. When she heard the louder footsteps on the hallways she figured it was the doctors on their rounds.

But there was something odd in the air. She opened her eyes. And smiled.

She didn't turn. She didn't trust her heart. It was doing the happy dance inside her chest. She knew exactly who was at the doorway. She said slowly in a low voice, without turning to look at him, "Hello, Shadow."

She sensed his surprise. He walked into the room a few steps. "May I come in?"

She rolled over, saw he was alone and beamed up at him. She opened her arms and was gratified to see him reach out for her. She hugged him closer. God she'd missed this. Him.

When she could trust her voice, she cried, "I hated to leave you without saying good-bye."

"It's what had to be done. Your leg needed care." He looked down at her sheet covered limbs and asked, "How is it?"

"It's great," she exclaimed. "The doctor said you guys did a wonderful job."

"Of course," he said casually. "Our medical training for field dressings is pretty extensive."

"Then why did I have to come here," she said, feeling aggravated at knowing she could have stayed with him.

He placed a finger against her lips. "In case there was more damage than we could see."

She kissed his finger and he smiled down at her. Such a warm caring smile, she sighed happily. "Are you okay? I know it got pretty hairy for a while there."

"It did. Everything is being mopped up now. We weren't needed at this stage so we're on our way home."

Her face fell. "Without me?"

"You are staying here until they can arrange for you to go home."

"On a commercial flight?" She hated the sound of that. "Can I go home with you? Surely I need to go in for debriefing. I'm a US citizen and the recovered victim of a kidnapping. The senator's daughter. Are you sure I can't come home with you?" she said in a wheedling voice.

"We could be going home on a commercial flight too," he said. "No idea what the plans are for the moment."

"Perfect. Let me come with you. Then at least if I am too tired or injured I can trust that you'll make sure I get home."

"Which is another good reason why you are staying here," he said.

Her face fell. For a moment there she'd so hoped.

"You aren't ready to fly yet," he added in a soothing voice.

"Sure I am," she said stoutly. "If I was ready for everything else that happened over the last few days, flying home with you guys is hardly an issue."

A voice from the doorway called out. They turned to stare as Swede carrying two large bags of something that smelled heavenly and the rest of the gang carrying coffee arrived. The last man in was Cooper, and he arrived a few seconds later, carrying a huge bouquet of flowers in his arms.

She cried out and reached for them.

"They are gorgeous."

"And they are from all of us," Cooper said. "Even the silent dude here. He just wouldn't wait for us to arrive together. He raced ahead."

She lay the flowers on her lap. "Thank you." And she reached up to hug him, then Swede, Hawk, Dane and finally Mason.

They all stepped back, grinning. She was so damn happy. "I missed you guys. I hated leaving without you all."

"Hey, it broke my heart to put you on that helicopter," Cooper admitted. "I knew Shadow here would shoot me for it too."

"He didn't though, did he?" She searched Cooper's face, saw the grin then caught Shadow rolling his eyes. "Of course you wouldn't shoot him, but that doesn't mean you wouldn't have smacked him around some."

"Not likely, he's bigger than me," Shadow said with a straight face.

The others snickered.

"That's only because he had to do so much physical therapy after getting injured," she explained. "I'm sure if you worked out, you'd get that size too."

The others laughed.

"I was kidding," Shadow said, shaking his head.

She sighed. "Right, of course you were." She winced.

"Speaking of which, the doctor wants me to see a shrink. Please let me go home with you guys. I really don't want to have to speak to anyone about what happened."

"Actually, I'm not sure that you should be speaking to anyone yet." Shadow turned to Mason. "It will involve her relationship with her father and family and the events leading up to this. As what that is isn't exactly clear at this point, should she be talking about any of this to someone without clearance?"

Mason pursed his lips. "A good point. But not sure it's enough to stop you from talking to a trauma counselor. You might need to do that at some point."

"Maybe, but at home would be better. Besides," she glanced over at Cooper, "I was telling Cooper some of the dirty family history."

"And I didn't fill you in on what the one kidnapper said, about this being a double job," Shadow interrupted her. "You and your father weren't supposed to survive."

She stared at him. "Just me and my father? Not all of us?"

"According to the kidnapper, you and your father weren't supposed to make it out alive. When we rescued you, it changed things."

"And I was explaining to Cooper that I believe if my father dies then his estate would go to my stepmother and if something happened to her then to my brother. And that means his guardian would have control."

"And who is that guardian?"

She sighed. "My father's aide. Who is also my step-uncle. My stepmother's brother. He's the one who made the arrangements for our trip."

The men gave several exclamations as they worked out the angles on the kidnapping and who could be responsible.

Shadow reached over and grabbed her hand. "We'll get to the bottom of this."

"I know you will." She reached up to stroke his face. "I just hate the thought that even though I'll be home in a few days, this nightmare might not be over. I really need it to be over."

"It will be," Swede said from the side. He moved a small swing table across her lap. "But before any of this can be over, we need food. So let's take a look at what we've got."

"I'm so hungry. That chocolate bar was a long time ago."

"Did you get anything since?" Swede asked her in shock. "Hell, you're skinny enough without losing more meals." He opened the takeout bag and proceeded to unload enough food for a dozen people. Or maybe a half dozen SEALs.

SHADOW HADN'T REALIZED how acceptance, approval, had such an impact on someone. Arianna blossomed with the men. They were all friendly and joking, gently teasing, but he knew the atmosphere, their actions for what it was. They all approved. Of her. For him.

How sappy. But it made him feel great. She was something. Not unlike the other women the men had paired up with. And yet, different. She was herself. Was he being foolish thinking that maybe they could try for a relationship? He didn't have anything good to say about the highbrow females he'd met in the past, and Arianna was definitely one of them.

But she was also herself. And very down to earth.

She had a lot of processing to do now though and not

the least was the death of her father. He had died, but had she been told? Everyone had tried to prepare her and she understood he'd had little chance of surviving, but that wasn't the same thing as hearing the definitive statement. He'd noticed that no one had brought it up, including Arianna herself. As if she knew but couldn't stand to have the truth voiced because then she'd be forced to deal with the emotional onslaught of grief.

And who was he to judge her for that? He locked everything inside. She let it all pour out. In public…that wasn't much fun. She'd try to wait for a private time to release all that pain.

That her own family might have had a hand in this nightmare was not hard to believe. He'd seen too much of the world to be surprised any more. Not to mention there was the stepmom in there too. If she lived through the trauma then she was the one who inherited it all. And that made their current theory implausible. But she'd still have to be careful. As in more than careful. At least until this mess was over.

With a full plate in his hand, he glanced around at the hospital room and smiled. His brothers in arms were men he could trust with anyone, but especially with Arianna. They'd bend over backwards to make her happy as Shadow had done for each of their partners.

Content, he picked up his fork. And stared at what was on the end of it. He was a meat and potatoes guy. Most of the men were. But this time they'd let Swede shop. And that was always a mistake. That man could eat. Like seriously eat. And never had a problem trying new foods. Often bought meals the guys didn't recognize. And while all SEALs ate healthy, Swede started at one end and ate his way through to the other end of his plate then started working on anything else close by. So Shadow had to make up his mind quickly if he wanted second servings – or it would be too late.

While the others wrangled gently there was a hard knock on the door and an older lady walked in.

"Excuse me. Are you supposed to be here?" she asked in a voice laced with the potential to breathe fire on their heads if they gave the wrong answer.

Shadow had had a teacher like her in school. With just one look you were cringing in your shoes.

They had the right to be here – sometime. He just didn't know when and from the look on Arianna's face, she didn't want them to go anywhere anytime soon.

Shadow stood and straightened his shoulders, and in a low lethal level voice, he said, "Yes, and do you?"

She glared at him, but he refused to back down. Arianna had been through enough, and if she needed him to defend her from one more assault then he was prepared to do so.

"I'm the trauma counselor," she snapped, her nose in the air and not backing down either. "I need to speak with her, assess her state of mind."

No one could miss Arianna's squeak of horror.

"I'm fine," she rushed to say. "These men are the ones who rescued me."

"That might be but after the trauma you've been through the last thing you need is a reminder of those events by having the same men surround you. They need to disappear and now." She waved her hand at them.

"No, you don't understand," Arianna said, her voice slightly stronger. "I feel better with them around."

"No. And no, and no. You don't. You are looking at these soldiers in the wrong light. They are not your friends. They were doing a job. It's over. Now your job is to heal and move past these events. You can't look at these men as your personal heroes forever."

Shadow opened his mouth to blast her.

Mason spun and glared at her.

Swede slowly straightened to his full height.

And not one of them got a chance to say anything as Arianna's voice cut through the tension in the room.

"I'm sorry, you appear to have been given the wrong information. I don't need trauma counseling. I'm fine. Also, I don't need to forget that these are my friends because you are wrong, they are my friends, and I'm proud to call them friend in return." Her voice rose as she fired the next volley at the woman standing frozen. "And don't you ever… And I mean ever, insult these heroes in such a way again. They are heroes. To me. And my country."

Arianna's chest heaved as she now stood at the side of her bed, and taking several hobbling steps, stood in front of Shadow. "No one insults my friends while I am still standing. So take that attitude and your counseling skills back out that door. You are not wanted here."

And if that wasn't going to get the job done, Shadow had no idea what it would take. The poor woman almost ran from the room.

Shadow grinned down at the injured sprite who'd taken on the dragon lady to defend her warriors. She'd love that imagery. And he was such a sap. He put down his plate of food, snagged her up in his arms and laid her back down in the bed. He kissed her hard.

When she opened her mouth to snap at him, he popped the mystery meat into her mouth.

"Chew on that and not on me."

She chewed but still glared. He added for all the men to hear, "And thanks for the defense, sweetheart. But you didn't have to. We have thick skins."

"You might, but I don't when it comes to others. So remember that." She narrowed her gaze and finally managed to swallow. "No one insults you while I'm here. Got that?"

Hiding grins of their own, they all nodded obediently. And Shadow realized something else. He was really hooked. He sat back down and picked up his plate and proceeded to eat, waiting for her to calm down. But he knew she'd be the talk of the trip home now. She'd defended all of them. Stood up and blasted back at some poor woman who'd insulted them.

Except the men had been okay with the insult. They'd heard worse. Arianna had been the one to take umbrage. Protective. Caring. The same as she was with her brother.

There was a commotion outside and they all looked at each other. Now came the big guns.

Instead it was the doctor. He walked in and smiled. "You are the heroes, I presume."

They all nodded, sheepish grins on their faces.

"Nice to meet you," the doctor said in an amiable, let's–all–get–along voice. "Now we do have a problem though. I'd suggested Miss Stephenson take some time to work with the trauma counselor—"

"And your advice was taken into consideration, and I've decided to refuse it," Arianna said coolly from her bed. "I do understand that I'll need to speak with someone. I'm sure my doctor at home has someone he can recommend."

The doctor studied her for a long moment then nodded. "As long as you do, my dear. It's important to keep it all in perspective so you can move forward with your life."

"No problem," she said, beaming at him. "I'm feeling wonderful."

"And you do look much better." He smiled. "So maybe reconnecting with your friends is the first step."

She nodded. "Thanks for caring."

He motioned to the plates of food. "I gather you won't be needing dinner either?" he asked in a dry voice. "You appear to have enough here for the entire hospital."

"Just Swede," she said with a straight face, pointing to Swede. "He's a hard man to fill." Swede once again stood up and dwarfed the doctor who laughed and shook his head.

"Sounds like you're in good hands." With a smile, he added, "I'll take my leave."

Mason hopped to his feet and handed his empty plate to Cooper. "If I could have a word with you, Doctor…"

Surprised, the doctor who already stood in the open doorway, said, "Of course."

Mason stepped outside the room and the door was shut, leaving the rest of them to stare and wonder at what Mason was up too.

Shadow hoped he knew, but knowing Mason as he did…it could be anything.

Still he caught Arianna biting her bottom lip in worry as she stared at the closed door. "Sunshine and rainbows, remember?"

With a confused look, she stared at him. Then a slow understanding dawned in her eyes. "Right. And don't forget the unicorns."

He laughed. The others looked at the two of them in confusion then shook their heads.

Shadow studied the containers of food stacked beside Swede and asked, "Any leftovers?"

"Nope." But Swede's grin was a mile wide.

"You couldn't have eaten all that already? Aren't you on a diet?"

At Swede's look of horror the others burst out laughing. Hawk reached for the closest stack of containers and passed them to Shadow. "Help yourself. You know he'll finish all of it no matter how much there is, so get yours first."

On that note, Shadow refilled Arianna's and his plates. Then handed the leftovers back to the big man who stared at the almost empty container like a puppy who hadn't eaten in days.

"You can have mine," Arianna offered with a big smile, handing her plate to Swede.

He gently pushed it back. "No way. You need to eat. There's more."

Happy and content for the first time in his memory, Shadow watched the rest of his team wrangle in fun over the food.

THEY WERE ALL little boys. Arianna watched the fun and games as the men ploughed through what was left to eat. Mason still hadn't come back. It was worrisome. Was it about her? What else could it be about? It wasn't like Mason knew the doctor. Then again, maybe he had medical questions. She couldn't second-guess this one.

When the door opened up to let Mason back in, they all stopped and waited.

"And…" Hawk asked. "What's the latest?"

"We're flying commercial all the way. If we can switch out in Seattle to a military flight then we will."

"Good stuff." Dane stood up and collected the dirty paper dishes in a big stack. He quickly bagged the empty containers next. "When?"

"Flight leaves in three hours. We need to return the truck at the airport."

Cooper hopped to his feet. "That means leaving now."

"Pretty much. We have just one more thing to do."

Arianna's heart sank. Her stomach wanted to revolt. In fact, she wanted to curl up alone under the covers and cry. Time for that in a little bit apparently. They'd be gone in minutes. Damn. She'd been hoping.

"What else is there to do?" Hawk asked impatiently when Mason didn't answer.

She glanced over at Mason, realizing they were all looking at him for that answer. She studied the twinkle in his eyes. And hope surged inside. "Me? Are you waiting for me?"

He nodded. "The doctor is going to put a thicker bandage on that leg so you can travel easier and the agreement is you're to check in at a clinic tomorrow morning. If you agree to those terms, you can fly home with us."

"Yes," she shouted. "Yes."

The men grinned.

"Good. In that case, I suggest we clear out so the doctor can do his thing. Then we have a plane to catch."

"Thank you. Thank you. *Thank you,*" she chanted as the men gathered up their coats and slowly walked out to wait in the hallway.

Shadow was the last to leave. She beamed up at him. Then her face fell. "Mason won't get in trouble, will he?"

"No. You were right earlier. All those reasons are valid for bringing you home with us. You are going to have to speak with the investigators when you get there though."

She nodded. "I know. That's no problem. I'd have to explain to someone. Several someone's most likely. You guys killed everyone else…"

"Not the one man. We never saw him again."

Right. That brought her up short. "Not a good reminder."

"No, but something we have to keep in mind."

The doctor walked in just then. Shadow leaned over and kissed her. "I'll wait outside."

And he left too.

The doctor smiled at her. "So that's the way of it."

She nodded. "I sure hope it is."

He laughed, pulled the sheet back and said, "Now let's take a look."

And take a look he did. After the check–up, he quickly bound her leg. "I'm not sure if your pants are here…"

"They should be around," she said, hating to think she might not be able to leave because she didn't have clothes. "I was actually wearing a spare pair of pants from one of the men."

He nodded. "I'll send one of the nurses in with your belongings."

He disappeared and a nurse reappeared with a paper bag and her pack. "Here's what we had for you."

Arianna opened the paper bag and pulled out the same black pants she'd been wearing. She had her spare jeans in her pack but the reasons for wearing Shadow's pants still held. She'd thought they were sweatpants but instead now that she had a chance to examine them she could see they were an underlay for the cold. No wonder she'd never felt the chill in the air when she'd been outside. These things were wonderful. With the nurse's help, she dressed in the same pants but with a clean shirt and her vest she had in the pack. She wished she had managed a shower but given the choices she'd forgo that for a ride home. She'd be able to sleep in her own bed tonight. And could shower in her own shower. Just the sound of that made her grin.

That was so worth being dirty for a little while longer. By the time she was dressed, her hair brushed and twisted into a knot and secured at the back of her head and her pack slung over her shoulder, she took a last look around the small room and gave a happy sigh. She was going home.

Picking up her bouquet of flowers and with a big

grin, she walked out to the hallway and her new friends.

Cooper said, "You look great."

She beamed. "I feel great. Dressed again, a full tummy and now on my way home. Yay me."

They laughed and said, "Paperwork then we're on our way."

The paperwork was just a few signatures then they led her, using crutches Shadow had found for her, outside to the truck.

IT BOTHERED SHADOW that there were doubts about who was behind the kidnapping. Could the kidnapper he'd talked to been serious? He'd sounded it. But that meant that someone who wanted the senator and his daughter dead, got wind of the kidnapping and might have made their own deal. Was that possible? Sure, but how *probable* was it? There were a lot of assholes out there but most people went through their entire life never brushing up against the seriously bad ones.

He could see setting it up so that the kidnapping was intended to go wrong and have the two – or more die. But never Kevin. If the entire family was wiped out, the money would not go to the right person. That was key. And narrowed the field.

The investigators needed to check out the senator's aide. And anyone else close enough to know the details of the will. Like the lawyers and the witnesses to the will. Not to mention, did anyone know who those people were?

"Arianna, have you seen your father's will?"

She shook her head. Not even the return to an unpleasant subject seemed to dull her good humor. She'd been smiling nonstop since they boarded the flight. The first one was taking them into Seattle direct, and they'd be home a second flight later. But he wouldn't be leaving her alone until she was safe and tucked up in her own bed.

"No. I haven't and he's never spoken to me about it." Pulling her attention from the window she turned to look at him. "Why?"

"Just wondering how many people know the details."

She wrinkled up her face. "No idea. No one has ever contacted me."

"And…" he hated to ask this, as it made him sound crass, "If you die, who does your estate go to?"

"Kevin," she said promptly. "There are other family members around but I don't know them. If I die then he's the one who needs the money the most."

Mason, sitting across from them, asked, "Can you give us a list of anyone in your family who might be in line to inherit?"

"Sure."

Shadow handed her a small pad of paper and a pen. She stared at the blank page for a long moment as if collecting her thoughts. Then the names showed up. Two then a third. She drew a line underneath and started writing other names down.

"I think we should look at the stepmom," Swede said from beside Mason. "It's usually someone who will inherit and she's the surviving spouse and will have her son's money to look after."

Dane agreed. He leaned across the aisle adding, "She didn't want to go supposedly, so just the right amount of reluctance. She was hurt but not badly. Her son was never hurt, which is what she'd want, and she gets rid of an aging domineering husband leaving her in the honey seat."

Shadow had to agree that in theory the stepmother was a good suspect. But did she have the stomach for killing her husband. Then again, she hadn't killed him, someone else had. And having a killer was a different story.

"What if the kidnappers contacted someone in the Senate, asking for ransom? And that person took advantage of the moment and turned the deal into something else," Shadow said slowly. "The only reason *we* knew who was involved was Arianna's photo sent to her father's aide."

"Which should in theory clear him of being a participant."

"Unless he knew how to contact the kidnappers and then made a deal for himself. Although, with the senator and Arianna dead, the money goes to the stepmother and the boy, and not him." Mason paused then shrugged. "Unless he can move up in his career from this somehow."

"But why Arianna?"

Everyone turned to look at her. She shrugged. "I have money from my mother's side of the family, but it's not much comparatively."

The others winced, a few sent side long glances at Shadow who slouched lower in his chair at the news.

"Your idea of not much isn't necessarily everyone's," he muttered. Of course she had money. Probably tons of the shit. Like why would he fall for a rich woman when someone who lived at the poverty line would suit him as well? He wasn't into glitz and glamour. Sideways, he took his first look at her clothing. Decent t–shirt, nice warm vest, probably expensive. Her pack had been a popular outdoor brand. A good brand for everyday outdoor people. They carried a die hard line that was hard-wearing and durable. Hers wasn't that level. Yet she wasn't carrying a glamor girl pretty version. So there was hope for her yet. Then he caught sight of her pants. And he barely held back his grin. She was wearing *his* pants still. And not only wearing. She rocked the look.

So what if she had money. She looked damn good in his underwear.

CHAPTER 21

FOR ALL HER initial exuberance at finally being on the way home, it was waning quickly. There was also a sense of melancholy. Arianna had been devastated at not saying good-bye to the men before, but now there were going to be plenty ahead of her. More pain. More loss. More to deal with.

She yawned. They'd boarded the second flight. This time a military flight as Mason had managed to pull his magic and get them onto one. They'd connected up with Markus and Evan at the same time. This type of flight didn't offer the same frills or extras but was more comforting to her own way of thinking. She leaned her head against Shadow's shoulder and closed her eyes. "Wake me when we land," she murmured, knowing that he had little choice but to do so.

Even though exhausted, she couldn't sleep. She drifted in and out, hearing the men talk. Bits and pieces of disjointed conversations all in a low monotone. She had hours of flying yet and needed to rest, but her own mind was caught on the problems. Anything to avoid looking at what her life would be like in a few hours. Alone.

She shifted restlessly.

"You're not sleeping," Shadow murmured for her ears only. "Leg bothering you?"

"No," she whispered. "Just life bothering me."

He reached across for her hand and grasped it gently

in his. "It will work out. Stay positive."

With a grin, she answered, "Really? Is that you saying that to me?"

A deep chuckle rolled out from his mouth. He was so damn sexy.

"Maybe some of that happy-go-lucky attitude is rubbing off on me."

"Oh dear. Your friends won't recognize you." She'd love to think some of her normally positive happy outlook on life was brightening up his world too. He was a sweetheart, but so didn't believe in all the things she wanted for her world. They were darkness and light.

"I guess we're opposites, aren't we?" she asked in a small voice. Was that a good thing or bad?

"In some ways. But in many no, we're the same."

"Almost home." She yawned again. "I should go to the hospital. See my stepmother." She paused. Then added, "And say good-bye to my father." She'd stomped on that inevitability until later. When she could deal with it.

He gathered her hand. "Your stepmother, she's not there. She's at home resting." He lowered his voice, and said, "And your dad…well, you can do that tomorrow."

Her breath caught in the back of her throat. She shifted so she could look in his eyes. She didn't have to ask, she could see it. Shadow shook his head. She bit her lip and let him tug her into his arms where he just held her. She already knew inside, yet getting that confirmation, well, that hurt. "He'd appreciate going out in battle. A martyr for his beliefs," she said in low tones.

He nodded. "Kevin is lucky to have you," he whispered.

"Not really." Arianna looked at him. "I should have called him before this."

"You haven't had time to do anything, especially to think about others. He's been told you're fine. That's the important part."

She offered a wan smile, determined to hold the tears back. There would be time to grieve later. In private where she could honor him the way he'd like to be remembered. She had to get home first. She stuffed the emotions deep inside until later. "Right. The rest is just time to heal and reconnect." She frowned thinking about all the suppositions they'd thrown out earlier. "Has someone warned my stepmother that she might be next in line to die?"

Shadow looked down at her. "No idea. Besides, whoever is behind this had a great way to get rid of her already. They let her live. There must be a reason."

"Right. More conspiracy theories. Hate them." She looked down at the lights below. It was late and the city was lit up like a beautiful Christmas tree of lights. She might not like all the nasty theories, but it didn't change the fact that because of what the one killer said, her world was even more unstable than before. And now her father had died. She knew it, understood it, accepted it and knew she wasn't even close to dealing with it. The tears rose. Ruthlessly. She shoved them back down until later.

She had to get through this next couple of hours. Then they'd be gone and she could deal with the loss. So many losses.

"What time is it?"

"It's almost eleven."

First she had to get from the airport home. She froze. She was in a military plane heading for a military airport. That meant outside San Diego most likely. The naval base where the team was from. She wasn't home yet. Newport Beach was at least an hour away. Likely two. And she had no idea how to get from the one to the other. Shit.

The plane landed with so little ceremony and custom hassles she wished she could fly this way all the time. There were quick good-bye hugs from the men and then there was just Shadow standing beside her.

Forlornly she stared at the men's retreating backs. "I'm going to miss them."

"You'll see them again."

She laughed. "I hope not if it means getting kidnapped again."

"It won't. Come on." He led her back outside to a large parking lot and a black Jeep. He unlocked it, threw the two bags into the back. "Get in."

Grinning, she hopped in. "Nice Jeep."

"Ha. Several of us own them." He turned it on and reversed out of the parking spot. "Now let's get you the last leg to your home."

HE'D SEEN HER worry over how she'd get home. He was hardly going to dump her at the airport. She was injured. He'd considered taking her to his place for the night and driving her home in the morning, but what she'd been through, he thought she'd rest best in her own bed.

She leaned back and closed her eyes.

He put on low peaceful music and drove down the highway. He was due some shut eye himself. But not yet. She came first.

At the outskirts to Newport Beach he brought up her address on his phone. She wasn't far from where he was idling on the curb. She slept gently. He'd have to wake her soon for the house keys. He hoped after all she'd been through she still had them. He pulled up in front of a small brownstone complex with wide lazy porches in the front. Nice.

"Arianna. Is this home?"

She murmured something unintelligible and opened her eyes. When she saw the building beside her, she cried out in joy. "Oh my God. I'm home."

And he realized he'd done the right thing bringing her here. He got out and grabbed her bag from the back then brought her crutches to her. On the sidewalk she looked up and beamed.

"You know how many times I figured I'd never see this place again?"

"Just goes to show you that life is full of surprises." He led her to the stairway then scooped her up, crutches and all and carried her to the porch level. "Have your keys?"

"I do." She rummaged around in her pack and triumphantly pulled out a set.

He took them from her and opened the door. And paused to let her go inside. She hobbled forward, her happy sigh making him smile. "I'm so damn glad to be here," she whispered. She stared at the stairs in front of her. "But doing those stairs with my leg is going to be a bitch."

He laughed and shut the door behind her. Turning, he swept her off her feet again and carried her to the second floor. And her bedroom. She flicked the light switch on flowing the soft colored room with warm light. "Oh my God. Even better, my bed."

Still grinning, he laid her down on the covers. She immediately bounced to her feet and threw her arms around his neck and kissed him. "Thank you for seeing I made it home."

"I told you I would." Hating to leave but knowing it

was time, and he had a long drive home, he hugged her close then stepped back. "Now get some rest."

And he walked to the door.

He glanced back to see her fighting to hold back tears. "Hey, it's going to be okay."

She shook her head. "If you walk out that door it won't ever be okay."

He froze. He wanted to stay. Of course he did. Any man would. And it would certainly be his desired next step but what about…her reasoning…

"This can't be just so you don't have to say good-bye."

She shook her head. "It's not," but her voice was low, soft.

He narrowed his gaze at her. He'd only stay for the right reasons.

In a low but more confident voice, she said, "Just stay the night, then. You don't want that long drive back right now. Sleep. Rest."

So had he misjudged what she was asking? Damn he hated this.

He was no good at pussy footing around the issue. Better to know now. "If I stay it won't be to sleep on the couch downstairs."

And her smile was breathtaking. "Then you'd better sleep here." She stood up slowly and in spite of her best attempts to not show it, winced. And he knew he shouldn't leave her alone to fend for herself tonight at all. She motioned at the bed. "With me."

"Come on. You're in no shape for anything right now."

She shot him a look. "Really? How do you feel about taking a shower with me?"

And that smile of hers set him on fire. He shouldn't.

She was hurt. But damn he wanted to.

She hobbled to the bathroom, her shirt tugged over her shoulder and tossed on the floor beside him. He hesitated.

"I haven't had a shower in days and I'm covered in blood." Her bra was tossed outside to land in the middle of the floor. He swallowed hard. Oh shit. There was only so much resistance he could put into place here, and knowing it wasn't in her best interest was fast waning as an excuse. When his pants and yes her panties were flung out the door, followed by two small socks, he couldn't think of anything else but her standing with that damn bandage in the shower. Alone.

When the water turned on he knew he was lost.

He stripped off his clothes and left them in a pile beside hers. And walked into the bathroom, already heavily aroused. Blood pounded through his body. He needed her. Like now.

Calm down, Shadow. She needed a careful lover not a fast, take her hard against the shower wall, type of lover. He stood outside the frosted glass doors and watched the water sluice down her slender from. He closed his eyes, willing his body to slow down, reaching for the last bit of control.

"Are you going to join me or just watch?"

And she opened the door inviting him in.

CHAPTER 22

S HE HADN'T WANTED him to leave. It was one of those moments where she knew that if she didn't say what was needed to be said then she'd regret it for the rest of her life. She wanted Shadow forever. If she only got one night then she only got one night. It was more than she was going to have if she didn't tell him how she felt. Even then it felt stilted, awkward. Partly because he didn't come rushing over to take her into his arms. Followed by her own realization of how dirty she was. And then she understood what she needed to do.

Now seeing him standing on the other side of the glass watching her… Oh God. She could be standing in ice water right now and she wouldn't notice. She needed him and now. She knew her leg was an issue. But she knew they'd find a way. And if she had a little pain to go with the joy, then that was all right too.

He stepped inside the large shower and picked up the bottle of shampoo. She couldn't see him clearly through the water in her eyes but when he turned her so he could shampoo her long hair, she could feel him hard and ready, nudging her hip. When his fingers slid through her locks and then dug in lightly to her scalp, she moaned.

"Feels so good," she whispered.

And he massaged her scalp a little more. When he turned her to face him, she leaned her forehead against his chest and accepted the ministrations. She loved the careful way he worked shampoo through her hair. When his fingers worked down to her neck and shoulder muscles she groaned and looped her arms around his back to snuggle up close. Her breasts pressed against his chest, his erection nestled against her belly.

She didn't want the moment to end. When those wonderful fingers slid down her spine carefully massaging the bank of muscles on either side, she whimpered in joy.

"How can I be so sore?" she asked. "I didn't do any-thing."

"Running and twisting, climbing trees, sitting in the truck for hours in a position not conducive to relaxing and then there were the hours in the store…"

"Well, if you're going to put it that way," she muttered with a small laugh, "I guess all of me is going to be sore."

His hands slid down to her hips and dug deep, working the muscles inside. She melted. When they slipped lower to cup her cheeks and pull her up against him, she shivered.

"Feels so good," she said.

"You feel good," he whispered against her ear, and the heat of his voice sent tingles down her spine. Then he kissed her ear, gently tracing the outside skin with his tongue and dropping kisses behind and below, his mouth tracing down her long neck to the curve of her shoulders. Her arms slipped up his hot wet chest, her fingers sliding into his thick hair. She clung to him as he retraced his steps, dropping kisses on to her chin and over to her mouth. He'd kissed her several times already but when he took her mouth this time it was like nothing she'd experienced ever before. It was heart stoppingly beautiful. And she couldn't get enough. When he withdrew his head she followed. She needed more. So much more. He kissed her again, tiny gentle kisses across her eyes and temple, all the while hugging her close.

So tender. So caring. So loving. She could feel his restraint, felt the shudders of thinly held control work their way down his strong body. He was afraid of hurting her. And she couldn't have cared less. After what she'd been through this…his touch…being here with him…heaven.

"Love me, Shadow, please love me…"

He slid his hand into her hair and tugged her head back. Something had shifted. This time when he took her mouth it was deep and dark and possessive. His other hand slid up her sleek wet body to cup her breast. She cried out, but he inhaled the sound looking for more. She whimpered as he squeezed gently, his finger rubbing the nipple, waking her body. She slid her hand between their bodies and found him. Hot. Hard. Ready. And she squeezed his length, her fingers sliding down then back up as she explored the size of him.

His groan was heaven to her ears. She slid her hand back down to cup the sacs below, he gasped and pulled her hand away.

"Too much."

"Not enough."

He gave a half groan. "Impatient."

"With you…yes."

His free hand slid down to cup her left cheek, in one scoop he bent, lifted her thigh over his arm and raised her high and using his body, pinned her in place against the tiled back of the shower. She gasped as he nudged up against her center. She wrapped her legs around his waist. So close. And so damn far away.

"Are you sure?"

She groaned in laughter. "Never more so."

But still he hesitated.

She dropped tiny kisses on his chin, his neck, her hands frantic on his back and arms. "I'm protected, if that's the concern."

A shudder rippled across his body. "It wasn't but it should have been," he said in a midnight dark voice. "You make me forget everything."

"Good," she said rubbing her breasts slowly from side to side against his chest. "It's only a fraction of what you do to me. And yet, it's not enough."

He kissed her again, his other hand sliding up and down, teasing, tantalizing, stroking her to a fevered pitch and just when she didn't think she could stand it anymore, he slid his hand down, grabbed her hip.

And entered her on a deep surge.

And stilled.

She gasped in shock and in joy, wanting to weep as emotions poured through her.

"Did I hurt you?" he muttered, his body shuddering in place.

"No, never," she cried. "But if you don't move, I'm going to hurt you."

And with a deep chuckle, he plunged again and again. Pinned against the wall, her feet not even on the floor, she was slammed by his passion, her need rising but her response stymied because she couldn't move. She was completely helpless. Left to his mercy. And his timing.

And Lord, he was good. Just when she didn't think she'd reach that peak, so damn close and so frustratingly far away, he bent and took one nipple deep into mouth and suckled hard.

The pulsations started deep inside and worked outward in ever increasing waves as the climax rolled through her. She cried out, her body lay in a state of wonder as he pounded and pounded and…ground against her, his own groan melding with hers as he found his own release.

She rested her head against his chest and grinned happily. When she could trust her voice, she said, "I always knew SEALs were good in the water."

He gave a great shout of laugher, wrapped her in his arms and pushing open the shower, he reached for the towel hanging beside the door and wrapped it around her back. Then, he carefully carried her to her bed and slowly lowered her down.

"Now sleep. I'm not going anywhere."

She reached up and kissed him, lovingly, pouring all the emotions that were overwhelming her and bringing tears to her eyes. "I don't want you to go anywhere ever again."

And she slept.

HE WATCHED HER crash, physically and mentally, emotionally. As if overload had happened and it had been too much. She literally closed her eyes and was out. He slowly withdrew and stood up. With the towel he dried her off. And wondered at the leg. Leave it wet? Dry it? Change it? Deciding that leaving it as is for the moment was likely to cause the least amount of damage in the long run, he gently tugged the bedding out from under her and covered her back up. He returned to the shower and cleaned up the bathroom floor as much as he could. They'd tracked a lot of water on the way to the bed and he didn't want her to slip and fall if she needed to go to the washroom in the night. She murmured in her sleep. He returned to her side and stood for a moment watching her. She shifted uneasily. He reached down and placed a hand on her temple. "Easy, sweetie, you're safe now."

Instantly, she stilled and fell into a deeper sleep.

He stared around the small room and wondered why he couldn't sleep. His instincts wouldn't shut down. He was tired. Could use a power nap but with no one to watch her back while he was out, he couldn't do it.

Something was wrong and he didn't know what. He grabbed up his phone and wandered the bedroom, his fingers searching for information that would shed light on this mess. He also sent a couple of texts. Had he spent too much of his lifetime looking for bad guys and competent ones at that…that the idiot bad guys seemed to be just too simple. Still, he had nothing to go on. But he hadn't been kidding when he'd said the reasons for doing this was going to boil down to sex, power, or money. And sometimes all three.

There was an odd looking couch bench chair thing at the window, he sat down and studied the information coming in. Everyone knew they'd planned to return this night. So the senator's office could know as well. If nothing else, Kevin had been told and he'd likely told several other people. How could he not? He was eight. And this was his adored sister.

But that didn't mean something nasty wasn't planned for Arianna's return. Especially if she stood between a killer and his prize.

With messages coming and going, he hated the warning sensation at the nape of his neck. Yet he couldn't seem to get the idea out of his head. If he was on the killing streak and she was on his list then he'd have made sure there'd be something or someone waiting for her when she got home. Like early in the morning. As their tickets out of Seattle had originally had them booked. But they'd caught a military flight out. Getting them home hours early. Cooper had made the arrangements. Had he canceled the original plans?

He checked the airlines. It still said Arianna was due to arrive at five-thirty am.

His instinct prodded him. What if someone planned for her to not make it home?

He wanted to take her out of here and back to his place now. He quickly dressed, that sense of something wrong riding him hard. He sent several more texts then turned his attention to sleeping beauty. Throwing back her covers, he went to the dresser and pulled out clothes for her.

"Arianna?" he said in a harsh whisper. "Get dressed. We're leaving."

Groggy after only a couple of hours sleep, she sat up and blinked at him.

He didn't waste any time with explanations but worked to get her clothes on her again. When she was up and ready to go, silent but awake, he carried her downstairs and out the back of the house.

She wrapped her arms around him and held on. He loved that she didn't bubble over with protest or questions. She trusted him at a level he'd never had anyone trust him before.

Outside he recognized the condos all shared the same backyard. He kept close to the buildings and worked his way to the right, around the last one. The room was tight, but the sky was already getting lighter. He peered out onto the street. Then raced to his Jeep.

He set her down on her feet and unlocked his vehicle.

"Oh, I don't think so."

Shadow froze at the foreign sounding voice. He glanced at Arianna to see the horror on her face. And knew.

It was the missing so called terrorist who had turned to exhortation and kidnapping to fund his cause. Shadow turned slowly to see a handgun pointed directly at him. Shit.

"If you don't mind, we need you to get into that truck. We have a bit of a trip ahead of us."

Arianna shook her head. "No, I can't. No more."

"I could put a bullet in your friend here? Would that make you more cooperative?"

"No!" she cried. "I'll come." She glanced around blindly. "Where do you want me to go?"

"That truck." And he pointed to a black vehicle to the far side of the road. "Now."

Arianna stumbled forward, her leg stiff and ungainly. As she came close to the kidnapper, she fell.

He swore and reached out to stop her.

And Shadow was on him in an instant.

CHAPTER 23

ARIANNA LAY ON the pavement, her leg throbbing and watched as Shadow kicked the gun out of the man's hands and pounded his face into the ground. She didn't want him to kill the enemy, he had enough to deal with in his life. But she didn't want the asshole to get up again. Only to see the gunman flip and deck Shadow with a right hook. Shadow dropped like a rock. Desperate now, she pulled herself along the ground to where the gun lay. She might not like them, but to save Shadow's life, she'd use it without a second thought. As she already had.

"Ha. Like you're going to get that."

And a foot stomped down on top of the gun in front of her.

She closed her eyes. Damn she'd been so close. She stared at her step–uncle. A man more a stranger than a relative. "Really? It was you all the time?"

He shrugged. "Well, not just me."

He nodded to the vehicle parked to the side. "Your stepmother might have had something to do with it."

If a heart could break, Arianna knew hers was at the point of trying. Her stepmother had her father killed? Together with her uncle? How…how…words failed her. With difficulty, she pulled herself up to stand then hobbled closer to face her stepmother. "You did that to him?" she said incredulously. "Why? You had everything."

"He was going to divorce me," Linda snapped.

Arianna shook her head. "So? That's hardly worth killing him for. He planned to divorce my mother, but she died before he could."

"And if she'd lived you'd have realized that he planned well for that contingency. She was going to be squeezed out completely. He wasn't going to give me anything either." She sneered. "You lucked out. Do you have any idea how shitty your life would have been if your mother had lived?"

"Money? This has always been about money? Not Father's job?"

The uncle shrugged. "Why not make it a dual purpose. There was a lobbying committee that did want your father to take a beating. But that wasn't enough for our purposes. He needed to die so we could have the inheritance."

She nodded numbly as if she understood. But honestly…there was no understanding this. "And Kevin? Did he not deserve a father?" She wanted to rail against a world that would now take Kevin's mother from him too. There's no way Linda could keep this secret. The SEAL's would hunt her down and take her out – one way or another.

Her stepmother's vicious voice snapped, "He was no father."

"Right, well he's the one Kevin had. Now he has to learn that his mother is a murderer."

"And who is going to tell him?" Linda said in harsh acerbic tones. "You won't be around to ruin him."

Ruin him. She'd have done anything to make that boy's life happy. Unlike his parents. "Is that why you needed me dead? So you didn't have to worry about Kevin loving me more than you?" she cried. "So you have to murder me?"

The stepmother laughed. "Absolutely not. I was never jealous of you, no need to be. Kevin doesn't love you," she said snidely. "But we need your money."

"My money?" Arianna stared at her in bewilderment. "I have some, but nothing like what you have now Father is dead."

It was her step–uncle who gave a bark of laughter at that comment. "That's where you're wrong. See, his estate goes equally to you and Kevin. And your estate when you die, goes to Kevin. So as his guardian, Linda and I will have complete control over all of it."

"And my brother?" She gazed from one to the other. "Will he ever see a penny of it?"

"Maybe. And maybe not. Depends on how long the money lasts."

She shook her head. She couldn't believe it. She'd been surrounded by the enemy. If she died, then there'd be no one there for Kevin. Did they know about her inheritance from her grandmother, on her father's side that left Kevin a sizable inheritance as well? If so they'd kill him too. She had little doubts that if it came to a competition between her son and money, Linda would choose the money.

She always had.

There had to be some way out of this mess. She glanced at the unconscious kidnapper on the street. "So is he a terrorist?"

"Well, yes and no. He bears a remarkable resemblance to a famous one so I knew the ruse would work." He sneered. "Sometimes you just have to act when you see the perfect opportunity." He lifted the hand gun. "The funny thing is, he's a little terrorist connected to a bigger one and they jumped all over this plan. Squeezed me about dry trying to get to this point. I'm happy there aren't any of them left. Less to pay at the end." He casually lined the gun up and pulled the trigger.

The unconscious man's body jerked.

Arianna cried out in a low voice, "He was unarmed."

"And now he's dead." Her step–uncle laughed. "Jesus, you're such a fool. None of you get to live this night out. Sorry about your boyfriend though. What did you do, pick him up at the airport?"

He laughed and lined the gun up on Shadow's head. "Now to make sure it looks like our terrorist shot your boyfriend first then killed himself."

He went to pull the trigger. Arianna screamed and dove in front of the gun but was slammed to the ground as gunfire lit the night.

Followed by a hushed silence.

Arianna lay on the ground, Shadow covered her as a blanket. Her stepmother was crying hysterically beside the vehicle. And her step–uncle…was lying in a pool of blood.

As sudden as the silence, there came the noise. Sirens, dogs barking, house lights came on.

And then the men.

Cooper. Mason. Dane. Hawk. Swede's big head above Shadow's.

"Arianna, you hurt?" Swede asked.

She shook her head, realizing she was bawling like an idiot. She sniffled and tried to stop the waterworks, but it wasn't until Shadow got up and hauled her gently up into his arms that she managed to slow it down. She wrapped her arms around his neck and squeezed tight.

"It's okay," he whispered. "You're safe."

She sniffled and looked at the men surrounding them. She let go of Shadow to walk into Swede's huge arms. Then each of the others as she hugged them hard.

Held safe and secure back in Shadow's arms, she said, "Thank you all so much."

"We were hardly going to desert you until it was over," Swede said. "Besides, Shadow here hasn't told us if he's keeping you."

"Keeping me?" she turned a puzzled look up to Shadow.

"Forget about it. It's a recurring joke among the men."

Shadow used such a dismissive tone, her suspicions were instantly aroused. She turned back to Swede for clarification, studied the huge grin on everyone's face, and thought about all she'd learned about the group. "As in a joke you all participated in and now it's Shadow's turn. Correct?"

Cooper laughed. "I said she was bright." And he nodded. "That's exactly right. Only Shadow and I are still unattached. So it's been a standing joke since Mason first met his partner. Now if anyone looks close to finding their perfect partner, we have to ask if he's keeping the woman in question. Because if not, there is always another one of us who might be interested." And he waggled his eyebrows in a mock leer.

She laughed. Then threw her arms around Shadow crying, "Keep me, please keep me."

"I never planned to do anything but that from the moment I met you," he whispered against her ear. "Some of us know exactly what we want and know to go after it."

With a happy cry, she hugged him tight. Then pulled back slightly and said, "I come with baggage, you know that, don't you?"

"Kevin?"

She nodded. "He's lost everyone else."

Shadow smiled. "No, he's gained six uncles."

She turned to look at the group of heroes smiling at the two of them. "He's going to love that," she said warmly. "He's had so very little male contact in his life."

"Oh," Mason said with a grin. "He'll get lots now."

Tears came to her eyes. It had been a hell of a trip. She'd lost her father, found out her stepmother had betrayed them all, and her step-uncle. Kevin would need years to get over this nightmare, and all she could think of as she stood there in Shadows arms – was that she was so damn lucky. She smiled up at him. "I'm so glad I went on that trip. It was the worst trip imaginable but as far as silver linings go… If I hadn't gone I'd have missed meeting you and that would have been horrible." She leaned up and whispered so only he could hear, "I love you so much."

"Not as much as I love you," he murmured and to the cheers of his team, he kissed her yet again.

COOPER

SEALs of Honor, Book 6

Dale Mayer

CHAPTER 1

L IKE HELL HE was going to stay behind.

Cooper Braxton slipped into the room and took a seat at the back. He'd come as soon as he'd heard. He didn't know the details but he was going on this mission. If he could. And he needed to if the rumors were true.

"Listen up, everyone. We have an unusual situation. Turkey has requested our assistance. Because we're in place, this one is ours."

Right. They were doing specialized training with the Turkish military who were facing a unique situation with the millions of refugees crossing their borders.

"We have intel that a medical team working one of the smaller refugee camps in Turkey is being targeted." He looked at the men. "Why them, we don't know for sure. But most likely because one of the two medical clinics are staffed with US citizens."

Copper winced.

Being one of the good guys trying to help those less fortunate was no guarantee of being safe. After a joint military push to move the Islamic terrorist troops out of one of their strongholds a few days ago, they knew retaliation was a given.

But doctors and nurses trying to help those displaced?

"Some of the team members are retired military – one, Dr. Landry, a retired SEAL – adding to the attraction."

There were several angry murmurs in the room. Cooper took a quick glance around. He knew them all. All good men. All men to have your back.

But he wasn't going to trust Dr. Sasha Childs' life to anyone but himself. Not after all she'd done for him.

The orders came hard and fast. They knew what they were doing. No one needed to be told twice. An eight-man team was leaving within two hours and he wanted in on it.

The men broke up and headed out.

"Cooper, hold a moment, will you," Levi called out to him.

Cooper nodded. Levi was a conundrum. One of the best SEALs here. He'd been on some of the worst missions and always on the most secretive. Even here amongst the elites there were layers with Levi as one of the most unknown and always one of the most dangerous. No one really knew what he did, but he'd disappear for days and when he came back it was as if the lines of his face had been carved a little deeper. There were others in his group. But no one knew who.

Cooper walked over, his mind trying to formulate what the hell he could say that would get him on this mission.

"I need you on this one."

Cooper's eyes shot up in surprise. "Good. Why?"

"Apparently you know several of the doctors, personally."

Cooper winced. "You could have said because I'm the best bomb man you've got."

Levi smiled. "You are the best EOD man here. But I can't tell you that so this works as well."

"Has a move been made against the medical team yet? Or does this remain at the threat level? Do we know if the doctors have been put on alert?"

"The Turkish military is on it," Levi said. "They have doubled security, but there are over fifteen thousand people at the camp. And it's one of the smallest here. The medical team *has* been warned."

"And they shrugged it off, of course." Cooper knew that both Dr. Landry and Dr. Sasha would.

"Right. I see you do know them."

"A little too well and yet not well enough."

Levi studied him for a long moment then gave a clipped nod. "Understood."

And he probably did. Levi saw…everything.

"We can't let them be taken." He kept his tone cool, controlled.

"We're actually sending you to escort them home."

Cooper narrowed his gaze. "A joint task, eight of our men – to escort a group of American doctors home?" He shook his head. "No. There's more to it than that."

A whisper of a smile crossed Levi's face. "It just came in a few minutes ago. One of the doctors has gone missing. As of forty-five minutes ago. She was seen at the clinic with a full roster of pregnant women waiting for her. Thirty minutes later she was nowhere to be found. No one saw her leave and no one has heard from her since."

And he knew. Inside he knew. Instinct. That's why he'd come racing. "It's Dr. Sasha, isn't it?"

Levi nodded. "It is."

Cooper's breath rushed out of his chest. "And the others?"

"They are accounted for at last check in. A search is underway for Dr. Sasha."

Cooper nodded but his feet were already taking him out of the room.

"Cooper," Levi called out. "Don't do anything stupid."

"Never," he called back. "She saved me. I'm not going to rest until I have returned the favor."

And if anyone suspected he had feelings for the sprite who had more dynamo and energy than any person he'd ever met, well, he had no plans to confirm it.

She was married.

And that made her off limits.

And didn't change his loyalty one bit.

CHAPTER 2

SASHA LEANED BACK on her heels, then slowly straightened, wincing as her back screamed. She smiled down at the young woman in the very early stages of labor. "Everything looks good, Yalta," she said in a cheerful voice, knowing the woman didn't understand English well but would recognize her tone. It was hard to keep the worry back though. The woman had an extremely narrow pelvis and could have a bad time of it. "But we need to get you to the clinic where we can keep an eye on you."

A series of musical voices rose above her as the driver translated her words to the men and women filling the small room. The accommodations were tight and there was barely enough room to give the woman any privacy.

From the dark looks and deep tones of those muttering around her, she figured it didn't matter what she said, her suggestion wasn't going to be allowed. In an ideal situation the young mother-to-be should have been moved to the hospital. But the refugee camp didn't have its own hospital and the closest one was overcrowded, short staffed. If Mother Nature wanted to, she could make things very difficult for this young woman. Therefore she needed to be where Sasha or one of the other doctors was close to keep an eye on her.

She didn't have much room at the clinic but instinct said this delivery wasn't going to be smooth or easy. She picked up her bag but that caused another uproar. She turned to the driver and asked, "What's the problem?"

"They want you to stay," Jamel said with a shrug. "They say you aren't allowed to leave."

With a sharp look she responded in a cool voice. "Yalta needs to be at the medical center. I have dozens of other people who need my assistance."

As she turned to walk out of the small shelter several men stepped in front of her. She pulled her radio out and sent a message back to the clinic. "I'm at Yalta's place. She has just started labor. I'm being *asked* to stay," but she paid careful attention to the word asked. There was no asking being done here. They were going to force her to stay whether she liked it or not. The young father-to-be sat beside his wife and didn't look ready to let Yalta leave. Sasha said, "Requesting assistance."

"Understood," cracked the voice on the other end of her radio. And she hoped they did. She wasn't into strong arming her way out of here, and if someone got hurt in the process, that wasn't going to help anyone.

A delay here was going to have serious implications for other patients at the clinic. She'd been forced here by the driver who was related to Yalta. He'd been adamant that she see his cousin. And she was glad she had, but they had rules here for a darn good reason. And safety of the medical team was one of them. With the rush to this spot, she hadn't had a chance to let anyone know where she went. Now, almost two hours later she'd been able to call through.

She returned to her patient's side. A film of sweat covered the young woman's forehead. She wasn't in terrible pain but was obviously discomfited by the situation. Sasha reached down and held her hand.

Yalta squeezed her hand tight.

"You'll be fine," Sasha said calmly and smiled at the young woman.

Only this would take time. Time Sasha didn't have. She checked her watch and mentally calculated. Security would be a half hour getting here. And then if everything went smoothly, it would be the same time to return to the clinic. If Yalta's family became difficult then well…it would take longer. The refugee camp solved many problems for these people but was a short term answer. When that short term turned long term the refugees became frustrated, and violence broke out. The atmosphere had been less than peaceful these last few weeks.

Her three-month stint here was almost done. She was ready to go home. But it made her feel guilty. These people needed her – in fact, they needed dozens like her. One doctor could only do so much. And with a dozen more refugee camps around the country, the government was calling out for assistance of every kind. The newest and largest camp along the border had two full hospitals and seven clinics. She didn't have anything close to that here. There were two clinics at opposite ends of the compound.

In the distance she heard the familiar sound of a truck. She hoped it was her security detail. She hadn't had to use one the whole time she'd been here, but things had gotten more difficult lately. And she was finding her sense of security had thinned.

Two more days left then she'd be safely back home in California. She gave a snort that had Yalta look at her anxiously. She squeezed the young girl's hand reassuringly. And tried to keep her reactions to herself. It was a little difficult though when she remembered that going home had its own set of problems.

Greg. Her ex-husband would be there.

They were divorced. The ink dry over nine months ago. She didn't want to see him. There was no reason to, he was living with Sasha's ex-best friend as well. Only they all lived in Coronado. Greg and Maureen were in the Navy and lived on base in the same house Sasha had shared with him. Nothing like catching the two of them in bed together to find out who was really there for her.

Of course listening to her husband blame her for being married to her job had smarted. She'd worked hard to get where she was. She completed her residency and went immediately into her specialty, all at a very young age. She had the brains and a talent for surgery, and now as she specialized in spinal injuries she saw more of those brave men and women in service than she liked. Coronado was big, but not big enough she wouldn't trip over them at any moment. And that was to be avoided at all costs.

It had been hard to live there. Even though she no longer lived on base, she was forever looking over her shoulder and avoiding her favorite haunts as they'd been *their* favorite haunts.

Leaving had been a good answer. When the call came out for medical volunteers here, she jumped at it. She'd hoped volunteering would help her gain distance and perspective. And it had. But it had also shown her the lost dreams that would never happen now. The cottage in Maine she and Greg had hoped to buy to be closer to his family. Or the three children they'd planned to have starting in a year or two from now. Something brought home to her even more with Yalta here beside her.

And that just sent her into a funk.

She was as much to blame as her ex was.

He had a right to make his own choices, but his methodology…well it sucked.

Then there was her best friend, Maureen. They'd

gone to school together and been there for each other ever since. Apparently she'd been there for Greg as well.

But as she stared down at Yalta about to give birth in the refugee camp, a young woman who'd lost so damn much due to war, and yet had gained an opportunity for a new future, she realized she was in a similar position herself. And that her trip here had done what it had been meant to do.

By taking her out of her own sorrows and placing her where she could see the reality of so many thousands of other people worse off than she was…she'd healed.

Raised voices at the door startled her. She could hear the kerfuffle as security came to retrieve her. She smiled down at the young girl. "Do you want to come with me?"

The girl's gaze slid to the side and the men standing glared at her.

"Right. You do but you don't think you'll be able to. Well, that's not necessarily their choice." She stood up and turned to speak with security. She motioned at Yalta. "She is coming to the clinic."

The men nodded. She was relieved to see four big men here to pick her up. And then she caught sight of the guns – the proof that there were bigger problems to solve here. The men transferred Yalta to a portable stretcher and quickly loaded her up on their vehicle.

Sasha turned to the driver who'd brought her to the home and said, "Tell them she needs more care than I can give her here. They can visit her in an hour at the clinic." And with a guard at her side, she walked out to the truck.

She hopped up onto the backseat where she could keep an eye on her patient, and with a still silence all around them, they slowly drove through the crowd. These people had lost everything. But they'd managed to retain who they were. She had no intention of changing that or the way they lived, but if there was something she could do to save a life or in this case two lives, then she was obligated to do it.

The vehicle slowly wound through the camp back to the medical center. She could wish for a delivery of more medical supplies, but that was likely dreaming. She missed the simple necessities of her medical world and the ease with which she could get them.

At the clinic Yalta was unloaded and carried into one of the small rooms. Sasha followed behind.

"Dr. Sasha?"

She turned, drumming up a tired smile. "Yes?"

She didn't recognize the soldier in front of her. He motioned her to come into the supply room. She'd been planning to go there anyway so she stepped through expecting to see the same person handling inventory as always.

Turning, she looked around and frowned. The room was empty and the back loading door open. "Where is–"

Something heavy slammed into her head. The force sent her to her knees then to the floor. Something was shoved in her mouth, a hood pulled over her head. Then she knew no more.

SALTY. THE WIND blowing in his face had a saltiness to it that was unmistakable. Cooper studied the waterfront shack in front of him. Did it hold Dr. Sasha and the three others his team was looking for? They'd barely landed when they'd heard four US members of the medical team had all gone missing. Not just Dr. Sasha. There was plenty of confusion at this point as to whether Dr. Sasha had been missing since morning or if she'd gone missing, been found and then had disappeared again.

Bottom line. None of the four could be located.

They'd been tracked this far. Now Cooper and his team, jointly with the Turkish military, were spread out in the woods around the shack.

Intel had led the teams here to the Turkish coastline a few hours out of Mersin.

But no one had confirmed the hostages were inside. The building was derelict, unlit with no windows, and showed no signs of being inhabited. He damned well hoped they were inside. They had no other information to go on.

He rubbed the scar across his back. Some things never changed. Some things one never forgot. He'd been a long time getting back to active duty and even longer back to his SEAL team. But it was Dr. Sasha that had made it possible. He loved the guys he worked with – trusted them all. Damn good men. Even after all he'd been through there was nothing else in the world he wanted to do.

His headset crackled in his ear. *All quiet.*

But the doc who'd saved his life and helped him make it back to the job he loved was supposed to be inside that hellhole.

Keeping low and moving fast, Cooper raced around the corner of the tree to the far side of the shack. Keeping to the shadows his eyes moved constantly, looking for something – anything – that would confirm the hostages were here.

Nothing moved. Now the moon was sneaking out from behind the clouds, and he wanted to take another look. He quickly relayed his new position to the others. Moonlight shone down, rippling on the waves as they lapped up against the long wharf.

There were no vehicles to show how the hostages had been transported to this point, and given the shack's location, they could only assume the hostages arrived by water. And would be taken out the same way.

And that couldn't be allowed to happen.

So far there'd been only silence surrounding the kidnapping. There'd been no demands made. No videos posted online. No boasting or laughing. Just an eerie silence that was more haunting than anything else.

Something caught his eye. He had no idea what he was looking at, but it was odd. He narrowed his focus, tried to identify the object and realized it was an older model army rig camouflaged in the trees.

Finally, a sign.

CHAPTER 3

SASHA HUDDLED BESIDE her three coworkers. They were squashed in the corner of the dilapidated building that smelled of old fish and…fear. This nightmare was entering the tenth hour. There'd been no sign of rescue. And once a boat arrived, they were being moved to a ship anchored offshore. Just the thought made her want to cry. Dear God. If they weren't rescued soon then the opportunity would be lost.

The gunmen had laughed and told them how they'd be made examples of, as a warning to the Western world. Made famous by YouTube. She didn't even know what terrorist group held them.

She'd woken with a headache and dried blood from a split scalp to find herself trussed up in the back of a truck. After what had seemed like hours of traveling she'd been dumped here. The air was damp, salty…

And the thought of being spirited away in the dark terrified her.

She couldn't stop thinking about the people they'd left behind. The patients. The need was great and the number of trained medical personnel were few. Now even less. Theresa, the only other woman captive, had flown over on the same flight with Sasha but had signed up for a full year.

Sasha didn't know if she could do that. David, the other member of their small group, was a retired military doctor and had devoted his life to helping others. The same as Dr. Ron Landry.

Five of them had been taken in all. Two women, three men. All had worked at the same clinic, all doctors except for the driver. That left two nurses behind. And neither were American. She groaned silently and took a quick look around. Her driver, Jamel, lay on the far side, most likely dead. He'd been shot while trying to escape. Ron had raced over to help him and taken a bullet for his efforts too.

The rest had been warned back.

She glanced down at Ron. The oldest doctor of their group by a couple of decades, he lay beside her, the sweat pouring off his face. He needed medical treatment, but the kidnappers refused to let them help. He didn't have long if he didn't get that bullet out and the bleeding stopped. To make it worse, he was in a great deal of pain.

She gently stroked his shoulder with one hand as she adjusted his makeshift bandage with the other. Anger burned inside. This was despicable. Ron had devoted his life to helping others. He'd always been one of those who stepped up and out to help anyone in need.

She could see the still form of the driver along the wall. She didn't know what role he'd played in this – if any. Had he helped the terrorists? Been killed for his efforts? But why? Surely, they'd reward him instead. He'd always stuck close to them at the camp – maybe too close now that she thought about it – moving the doctors from one area to another as needed. Was he a traitor and was possibly double-crossed and killed for his efforts? Or an innocent bystander?

Their kidnappers had shot the two men so fast, maybe they hadn't cared who they killed. They were all about fear, terror, pain, maximum damage.

She deliberately avoided looking at the gunmen. She didn't want to draw any attention her way. For the same reason she rested her head on her folded arm and kept her free arm on Ron. Keeping pressure on his wound, keeping him calm was all she could do.

Did anyone even know they'd been kidnapped? And if so how long before they were rescued? Or were they just going to be another casualty of war. A statistic. A number the world would glance past not really understanding what it meant. Who it hurt. There was no sense to it. She'd been shocked to see the size of the refugee camp. The sheer number of physical ailments and the injuries needing treatment.

She'd left behind four pregnant women due to give birth in the next week. She had managed to get one little girl's dislocated shoulder fixed before she'd been hauled out to attend to Yalta. She'd left behind a little boy with a broken leg. She hoped he got that leg set properly.

Ron's harsh breathing slowed. She eyed him carefully. At sixty-one, he'd been doing this type of work for over twenty years. How sad that there was twenty years of strife somewhere in the world that required his skill set. Now he was going to die for his efforts. She hated that. He'd done so much good in the world. He deserved to be treated better.

She closed her eyes and tried to sleep. Almost impossible to do with panic sitting just below the surface and her nerves, raw, screaming. But sleep was the only thing that would make time pass and even that was going to be painful. Her body ached after the long truck ride, and now they were sitting on the hard wooden floor. They hadn't had any food or water since leaving the camp either. Her throat was parched and the ocean breeze was making it worse.

The last thing she wanted was to dwell on their possible future. Yet it was hard not to after all the horrible videos that had been splashed over the Internet. Countries would only offer aid if it was safe for their people. Killing her group would send a strong message to deter more from coming. And that was too bad.

She'd heard about the videos of hangings, mass burnings, people being put into cages and drowned. What made these terrorists so angry, so full of hate? How could they do this to their fellow man? No respect for life. They didn't see their victims as people, only as bugs to be squashed.

A sudden spat in a language she didn't recognize between two guards made her peer through her hair to see what was going on. Two men raced to the door. Two others raced toward her yelling at them to stand up.

Bending over Ron, she tried to help him to his feet, but he was barely conscious and she couldn't hold his weight. David stepped in to help when a rifle butt hit him up the side of the head. David lost his grip and Ron collapsed to the ground.

He never made a sound. She cried out but Theresa held her back from going to him. The gunmen separated them from him and moved the group to the doorway and outside. The moon was high and shone bright overhead. She tried hard to look around. She wanted to leave a trail, a sign for someone that they'd been here. That they needed help.

The gunmen didn't give her a chance.

She cast one last look at Ron before she was pushed out of his sight. He needed medical attention, and if he didn't survive he deserved a proper burial. He was a hero. And should be remembered as such.

At gunpoint they were moved down to the edge of

the dock where a motorboat waited. She tried to take stock of their location in case she could send aid back for Ron. The building smelled like an old fish cannery. But it was too small.

The woods were dark. Shadows moved in the darkness. She caught the slight movement out of the corner of her eye. It was to be expected that they'd have other guards in the woods.

But no signs of a rescue.

Resistance was futile. Helpless, they were pushed on board. Two gunmen joined them. The powerful engine fired to life and slowly pulled away. They kept the lights off. Damn, she could barely see anything.

Offshore sat a large ship of some kind. She didn't know how international water laws worked here, and although she hoped she was still in Turkey she doubted she would be soon.

David reached over and grabbed her hand. "I'm going overboard," he murmured.

No, she screamed inside but didn't say a word. Silently she shook her head, her gaze pleading with him to not do this. He stood up as if shifting his position. The gunman hit him on the shoulder with his gun.

David grabbed for the gun but the second gunman slammed into him. David fell to the bottom of the boat. The gunman fell over the side. He splashed and cried out for help, but the weight of his clothing and gear quickly pulled him under. She watched in horror as the disturbance in the water diminished as he sank deeper.

The other gunman roared in outrage as the boat driver pulled the boat into slow wide circles looking for their fallen comrade.

After ten minutes of fruitless searching, the kidnappers, pissed, their faces ridged with anger, turned the boat back to the ship waiting for them.

Now there were only two of them, but the one looked all too ready to shoot. Shit. With only the three hostages left, their odds of overpowering these men and escaping looked worse by the moment. She stared straight ahead and tried to marshal her thought.

A blast exploded behind them. She spun around.

The remaining gunman shouted and waved at the pilot. She didn't understand the words, but she understood the urgency. The pilot gunned the boat. Good, that hadn't been part of their plan. Behind her gunfire blazed into the night. She smiled fiercely. Damn well time. These assholes they'd left behind had been found and were taking heavy fire. Not heavy enough for her.

She twisted in her seat to stare at the shack they'd left behind. A second blast rent the air, and the building where Ron lay burst into flames. She stared at the flames in horror, tears coming to her eyes. Theresa reached out a hand and grabbed her. Sasha sniffled.

She was torn between diving into the water and trying to reach land and the obvious rescue going on there or stay here and hope the rescuers realized where they'd been taken to. She *was* a strong swimmer.

"No don't." Theresa tugged her closer. "They'll shoot you too."

The lone gunmen clicked his gun against her shoulder and pointed it at her head. She realized they'd read her mind. She slowly sat back down, her gaze on the fiery scene behind them.

Please, dear God, please let somebody have seen them on the boat.

The small motorboat pulled up beside a larger vessel looming out of the water in the dark. Terrifyingly large.

She couldn't read the writing on the side. But the

letters looked Greek to her, which considering they weren't very far off the Greek coastline made sense. The motor boat drifted toward a ladder. At the gunman's prodding the three were forced up the ladder and onto the deck.

"Climb," said the closest male. He shoved her forward. She tripped, but David caught her before she hit the floor.

"Thanks," she muttered.

"Just take it easy," he said, helping her onto the ladder. Once on top, they were grabbed and dragged down another set of stairways, inside a hallway and down to a room. They were shoved and locked inside.

Grateful for the reprieve, she threw herself across one bed...

"What are they going to do with us," Theresa cried out, taking the second bed. "Does anybody know where we are?"

"I don't," Sasha whispered. "But the terrorists were fighting off someone on shore."

"I wouldn't count on that," David warned. "They could have been just burning any evidence they might have left behind."

"I heard gunfire," Sasha said.

"I did too." Theresa laid down on the mattress. "I hope somebody rescued Ron before they blew up that building." She rolled over onto her side and faced the wall. "He was a good man."

In a pained voice, Sasha added, "We have to stay hopeful. And we have to stay strong. It's the only way we'll survive."

"We have to find a way to get off this ship." Theresa sat up and stared at the others. "That's the only way we're going to survive."

"We're also not underway," David said. "That's a good thing. There are other boats on the deck. We could make it to shore. We don't need much time, but we do need that window of opportunity."

"I think our window of opportunity has already closed," Sasha said. "We should have overpowered them when the man went overboard."

David shook his head. "They'd have shot us." He groaned. "They'd have waited until we surfaced then shot us dead."

COOPER RACED ALONG the front of the wharf. Where were the boats? They were supposed to be here already. He glanced behind him but flames blocked his view. A boat carrying six had managed to escape. That there were two women in that group was great news. They'd rescued one injured man from inside the burning building and handed him off to the Turkish team.

He'd been in a bad way so they hadn't managed to get any information out of him, but they'd recognized Dr. Landry. That meant the others were close by. In the distance he could see a large ship standing silent in the dark – no lights – no noise.

Damn it, they should be out on the water already. The moon drifted behind the clouds casting a dark shadow over the water and highlighting the whitecaps.

Three sleek black watercraft pulled up. He and the other men climbed on board. The hostages had to be on this freighter. He couldn't stand the thought of losing her. Not when they were so close.

In the bottom of the boat was scuba gear.

He hoped it wouldn't be needed, but if it was necessary he was glad to have it. Mason leaned closer. "The Turkish underwater team is ahead of us."

"Understood," Cooper said.

"It still sucks though," said Swede. "I could use the swim." His grin flashed in the dark.

Mason laughed. "Maybe you could go for one afterwards. Just for fun."

Spray hit them in the face as the boat slammed down on the water. At the speed they were traveling in the dark, the rough waters, they were hitting waves face on. And dropping on the other side. They'd get a swim after all if this kept up. Cooper grabbed the side of the boat as it slammed down hard a second time.

By the time they came alongside the freighter, a storm looked ready to crack overhead. Knowing that the thunder and heavy winds would cover some of their approach but not all, the men silently unfurled grappling hooks.

Once on top, Cooper crouched low. With the moon playing hide-and-go-seek with the storm clouds, visibility was limited. Both good and bad. Outside of his own team, the deck appeared empty. There should be a half dozen people to man a ship this size, including the hostages, potentially twice that amount.

With the teams racing along the top and splitting to go down into the layers below, he took the first right and followed the hallway down and down. At each level they checked, looking for the enemy and the hostages.

Too often, on past missions, they found both at the same time – with shitty results all around.

Hearing a voice up ahead, he stopped outside a door and listened. A woman's voice. Motioning to Swede who was behind him, they stepped to either side of the door. He tried the handle.

The door was locked.

The voices inside stilled.

At a motion to move back from Swede, Cooper complied. With a sharp kick, the entire door knob snapped off and hung drunkenly to the side.

Cooper grinned ferociously and lashing out a second time the door opened.

Inside three terrified faces stared at him. His gaze went from one to the other and…stopped. One woman and one man and the elf in the middle, Dr. Sasha. He studied her. Traumatized but physically, she was fine. Something settled deep inside.

Swede quickly identified themselves then asked, "Are any of you hurt?"

They all shook their heads. Cooper studied the dried blood on the man's head.

The man stepped forward. "I'm fine. Just an argument with the butt of a rifle," he said.

Cooper nodded. "Are there any more of you here?"

"No," Dr. Sasha said. "Dr. Landry, who was badly injured was left behind in the warehouse." That there was a hardness to her tone didn't surprise him. This group had already seen enough of the war-torn country. Watching their friend gunned down would have finished the job.

"And our driver," said the tall, lanky woman. "Don't forget him. He was killed in the warehouse too."

"We found Dr. Landry," Cooper whispered. He peered into the hallway.

At the women's gasps, he held his finger to his lips. "He's alive but in rough shape."

Dr. Sasha whispered, "They wouldn't let us help him. They gunned him down when he tried to help the driver."

With Swede leading, he motioned at them to follow. One by one they raced behind his friend and teammate.

They made it topside without meeting anyone. That bothered him. Surely someone would be on guard.

Just as they raced to the side where he could help them down, gunfire filled the air.

One of the women cried out and the group hit the floor. He grabbed Dr. Sasha and maneuvered her toward the edge. "Go now."

She sent him a startled look then looked at the railing.

"Move it," he ordered.

She took a deep breath and grabbed for the ladder now hanging down over the edge. He watched her progress. When she was down far enough, he motioned at the second woman. "Hurry. We're out of time."

Sobbing, she struggled down the first rung. "I'm so scared," she whispered.

"No time for fear," Cooper said. "Keep your eyes on the rungs and go."

She dropped down several more rungs and finally it was the man with the head wound who stepped over the top rung and started his descent.

It had only taken four minutes.

To Cooper they were all taking too damn long.

CHAPTER 4

SASHA STARED TOWARD the shore from the back of the boat. The vessel was small, sleek and dark. Like the night closing in around her. The wind had picked up. She tugged her shirt collar higher against her neck. It was warm out, but her nerves were stretched taut and she had no stomach left – it had gone south along with her nerves. Add in the wind and spray, and the rising panic that they wouldn't be fast enough. That the enemy was racing behind them…closing in.

Please, God, let them get away safe.

Until she was a long way away, she wouldn't feel safe. Or until she saw the dead bodies of the terrorists. She dealt with death every day. It was permanent – final, and she needed to know that the assholes wouldn't be able to terrorize anyone again.

If she didn't get that closure she was afraid her nightmare would just relive this hell over and over again. These men could still pop out like the boogie man from hell.

And that she couldn't handle. She wasn't sure she'd sleep again.

But even if she confirmed these men were dead, there were always more men waiting to take their place.

Feeling safe would take time. Something she was going to have plenty of now that her time here was done. Or would be in less than two days. Was she supposed to go back right now? Finish the last day? But what about the patients, Yalta and her baby? The new doctor to take her place wouldn't be arriving for a couple of days, so if she didn't return she'd be leaving the camp in a tough situation. Not to mention there'd been no replacements booked for the other three doctors. The second medical clinic was just as overrun as hers had been.

Her gaze caught sight of and lingered on one of two soldiers who had found her. He looked familiar.

None of them seemed real considering what she'd just been through. She wanted to reach out and touch the soldiers. Make sure they weren't part of her imagination.

"You okay?" David asked in a low voice against her ear. Both women tucked up close to him. David was one of those big teddy bear kind of guys. Always a smile on his face. Even tempered. She'd never seen him angry. Frustrated yes…but given the shortages of medical supplies and long line of recipients for these medical supplies that was to be expected.

She nodded. "I will be."

"Are they Americans?" Theresa asked in a low voice as she cuddled up closer to David.

Sasha blinked in surprise. She hadn't considered the rescuers' nationality. The ones she'd spoken with had sounded American, but she'd also heard a group speaking Turkish. Then joint task force operations were the norm.

SEALs? Nah. Soldiers yes, possibly. If the American government had been informed but surely it would take longer to get here and help. Of course the SEALs were elusive and over-the-top miracle workers. Would they have come over to help? Why? Because she was American? Because David was? Or was Ron someone big in this world? She'd never be important enough for someone to stretch his neck out and save her. She'd helped a lot of people due to her profession, but she'd not been the recipient of much in return.

Then she hadn't gone into medicine for what she could get out of it.

She'd been all about helping others.

And she still was. But finding out your husband was cheating on you with your best friend – well that did tend to sour your outlook on life.

The three all huddled up close against the sudden bitter wind.

Sasha stared out at the darkness. The boat rocked with the heavy waves. She felt the hard glances of those soldiers, but no one said a word.

That worked for her. She just wanted to get the hell home. That meant on US soil. She needed to go home and spend time with her mother who was all alone now that her father had passed away.

So many people went home when they hit troubled patches, but she'd been raised to be independent and going back to her parents hadn't been an option. She'd happily visit, but she had an empty house waiting for her.

Fifteen cold minutes later they'd made it back to shore. Not once did she look at the freighter. She kept her eyes on the land but couldn't help that horrible sense of being watched. Surely all the gunmen had been caught *by now*.

She'd only seen the three men who'd forced her to the motorboat, but there had to be a dozen or more.

And as she stared at the blazing fire on the shore, she had to wonder how many of the others escaped? Terrorists never seemed to run out of willing men. Still she'd balance some of their lives for Ron's. That he'd been rescued and not burned alive was a miracle. Now they needed a second one that would save his life.

He was a tough buzzard and given a chance, he'd pull through.

The boat nudged up against the dock. The heat of the fire, although a good hundred yards away, was stifling.

One of the soldiers reached a hand to help her off the boat. Gratefully she accepted it and clambered up to safety. Once on the dock, she said, "Thank you."

She smiled up at him and recognized the man who'd kicked the door down for them. There was something about him that was familiar and the look in his eye was almost overly familiar. Did she know him? He seemed to know her. He grinned. "No problem," he said a low voice. "Glad we found you in time."

Tears burned the back of her eyes.

"So am I," she choked out. Then trying to hold back the tears, she started to walk away. Her mental state roiled with relief and fear. She couldn't help but search the shadows. What if some of the men had gotten away?

The soldier in front motioned at her to keep moving. So obviously they weren't out of trouble yet.

She turned back to wait for the others to catch up. The one soldier was speaking to Theresa.

Something about his voice caught her attention. She caught a glimpse of his profile, but in the dark, it was almost impossible to see his features. She had to be imagining him. Still, those electric blue eyes. She'd spent a decent amount of time in Coronado, so it wasn't out of the realm of possibility that she'd have seen him before.

And then there was her line of work…

Theresa said something in a low voice to him. Sasha couldn't hear the words, but she understood the tremor in her friend's voice. This had been a traumatic day for all of them.

These men had done a hell of a job. They deserved a

medal for freeing her group.

The soldier said in a louder voice, "You'll be fine now. We'll get you home in no time."

And she realized she knew that voice.

With the big soldier waiting for her beside the open door of a black SUV, the items in her brain clicked and she gasped. She did know him. And knew what he was – a SEAL. She spun and studied the soldier still standing with his head bent toward Theresa.

"Cooper?"

The soldier behind her froze. And damn it, the soldier in front of her did too. He turned to study her.

"Hello, Dr. Sasha," he said, his tone droll. "Nice to see you again."

COOPER STARED AT the tiny doctor in front of him. God he'd loved her since she'd done the surgery and given him his life back. Not only had she done the surgery, but she'd hounded him on his physical therapy too. He grinned. She wasn't bigger than a mosquito. That's why everyone called her, Dr. Sasha. Her real name was Sasha Childs. But given her five foot stature, her name caused her more grief than anything. So Dr. Sasha it was.

"It is," she said with a delighted grin. "Thank you for saving us, me."

He'd always loved that about her. So much spirit. Almost with an edge but she had a ready smile for anyone.

But then she surprised him and barreled toward him arms open.

He laughed quietly and held her close. "Glad to be able to return the favor," he said in a low voice.

"Now that's a fair trade," she whispered.

He knew what she meant. Swede made a harsh sound. Right. They needed to save the reunion for later. "We'll talk later. We have to go now."

She gave a quick nod, picked up her feet and ran back to Swede. She flashed him a big grin and dove into the back of the truck. Apparently seeing a familiar face had picked up her spirits.

Then again, seeing her had picked up his.

But what the hell was she doing over here?

And where was her husband?

Swede nudged Cooper, making him realize he was standing there like an idiot.

"You know her?"

Cooper gave him a sheepish grin. "Yeah, long story. The surgeon on call that day I was shot collapsed in surgery. She was there for some special training at the time and took over. She saved my life."

Swede's eyebrows shot up to his hairline. He turned to glance back at Sasha then snorted. "You got all the luck. When I got shot, I ended up with that old geezer Mahoney."

Cooper snickered. Mahoney was close to seventy and had the bedside manner of an old goat. "I lucked out," Cooper said. "The nurses told me about what happened afterwards. She not only saved my life, she saved the doctor's life who'd been working on me."

"And you let her walk away," Swede said with a note of incredulity. "Haven't you learned anything from the guys yet?"

"Yeah well this was before Mason found Tesla," Cooper protested. "And besides, she's married."

Swede frowned. "Are you sure about that? I wouldn't want my wife over here in this troubled time while my fat ass is back home."

"You don't know, they might be happy with that arrangement," Cooper said in exasperation. "Besides you won't let Mia out of your sight for five minutes."

"Have you seen the guys on base? Hell," Swede said, "I'd lose her in a heartbeat if I did leave her alone."

He had a point.

Their team had gotten a hell of a name for themselves. Not only were they SEALs, but they were hell on wheels in the love department too. Somehow his buddies had all found love – often in the most unexpected places. The base had dozens of nicknames for the team. Only one they were called to their face. The Keepers. But there were rumors of others. Love Boaters was the worst. The guys hated that one. Some were cruder but no one ever made mention of the names around the team. They wouldn't stand for it.

And dare anyone say anything against any of the women, the guy would be knocked flat in no time.

But on the other side of that coin, there'd been dozens of requests for guys to work with The Keepers in the hopes that the luck might wear off on them. The love vibe was a hard thing to miss out on if you were looking for it.

Many SEALs were already happily married. And some were in the middle of ugly divorces. Still others hadn't recovered from breakups and had no plans to.

The military was hell on relationships.

CHAPTER 5

"**H**OW DO YOU know him?" David asked when they were settled in the back of the SUV. Theresa turned to listen when Sasha answered.

"I did surgery on him a lifetime ago – about a year ago," she said with a smile. "He was a decent size back then but not like he is now," she admitted.

"Looks like he recovered well."

She laughed. "He had to do a fair bit of physical therapy as part of his recovery. He wanted to return to work and was chafing at the bit, so I pointed him toward power lifting. The man was a SEAL and in incredible shape anyway, but all that downtime while his team was on active duty pissed him off. He needed the outlet."

"Well, I'd say it worked out," Theresa said admiringly. "How come I never get patients who look like that?"

"Hmm, maybe because you specialize in pediatrics," David said with droll humor.

Theresa nodded slowly. "I'm sorry about the divorce, Sasha. They suck at any time."

"They do indeed," Sasha said in a noncommittal voice, hoping the conversation would move on.

They were stuck in the SUV, waiting for something or someone. She studied Cooper outside the vehicle. He stood beside her door with his back to her.

Could they leave already? This might be safer than before, but it sure as hell wasn't safe yet. And she didn't do *unsafe* right now. She needed it locked down – to know for sure she wasn't going to be spirited away. She'd been okay with the edge of uncertainty while married. Not now. Now she had to know where she stood at all times.

Was there anything more devastating than betrayal – especially times two?

She sank down into the seat aware of the stilted silence around her. Then David, dear David who wouldn't hurt anyone piped up. "The first thing I want is a hot shower."

"Food," said Theresa. "I'm starved."

"Water for me," Sasha admitted.

Cooper popped his head inside. "That's one thing I can help with." He opened a pack from the front and handed around several bottles of water.

Sasha smiled her thanks when he gave her one. His searching gaze made her realize he might have heard some of the earlier conversation. That was okay. If he didn't hear it now, he'd hear it soon enough. Divorce was like that. Not that he'd care. He hadn't seen her on anything other than a professional footing and likely didn't know her ex anyway.

At least she hoped he didn't.

Divorce was hard on everyone, not just the couple involved.

Then again a dead love was just that – dead. She almost laughed. Talk about being morose when it came to her marriage. Not bitter, but sad. Knowledgeable about hurt and pain in a way she'd never experienced before. And not sure she liked the way she'd changed. But once a hard lesson is learned well, you do anything you can to avoid being forced to learn it again…

And now here on the other side of the world, the size of the planet was brought home to her again.

Cooper was a good man. She'd seen him when he was down and he'd never given up. A smile broke free and made her laugh. The smiles had been coming on more and more. Good thing. Her family hadn't known what to do with her. She'd lost her sunny disposition when she'd lost her husband.

It had taken a long time to get over him, she wasn't proud of that, but she loved very deeply and any deep wound took time to close.

Now, she realized she'd hit a turning point.

One she'd been waiting for. It *was* time to go home.

Not because of the hostage taking. Not because of the volunteer work – but because she could.

She'd healed. Become whole again.

And now she could return to her old life.

COOPER TOOK THE driver's side and started the engine. He glanced behind to make sure all passengers were buckled in. His gaze lingered on Dr. Sasha's profile as she stared out the window. Fatigue lined her face, but there was a small smile playing at the corner of her mouth.

He'd heard the others. But wasn't sure if he'd heard right. The good doctor was divorced?

Good.

If the man couldn't make her happy then he didn't deserve to have her.

She was a hell of a doctor. Of course that didn't make her a hell of a woman – but he'd love to find out.

They had several hours ahead of them. He'd heard the comment about needing food, but they didn't have anything with them. He figured they'd get a few hours under their belt and then stop. They were heading deeper into Turkey. But would have to go past to the camp the team had been snatched from. Behind him the rest of the men were in the second vehicle. Backup had arrived to help the Turkish team handle the scene. Cooper and the rest of the SEAL team had the three doctors and were taking them back to safety.

He'd hope for a military helicopter and maybe a quick exit to Germany, but that hadn't pulled together. At least not yet. Still they were a short distance away. Good enough for him.

Swede motioned at the turnoff for the highway. "Once we're on the road we'll need to stop for gas."

Cooper nodded. "Coffee and food too." He nodded to the back of the vehicle. "With any luck they'll sleep that far."

Swede nodded, but he'd turned and was studying the passengers. "They aren't out yet, but will be soon."

His headset crackled.

"That's Markus checking in. Says the Turkish team have searched the freighter. They've picked up three men only."

"Damn."

Swede nodded. "Should have been twice that many."

"Not our problem." He knew that's what the bosses would say. But he hated to leave a job half finished. "And our orders?" he asked. "Did Mason get any update?"

"No change. Get the hostages to safety."

Cooper glanced in the rearview mirror. Dr. Sasha's eyes were closed, her head learning against the window. He'd have hated to find out that Dr. Sasha perished because his country hadn't done enough to save her when she'd done so much for her countrymen. He wasn't the only military man to end up on her table. He didn't know what had happened to her a year ago, but he was damn sorry for it.

She was good people.

CHAPTER 6

S ASHA'S NECK ACHED and her butt throbbed. For a
moment she was afraid she was still in the hands of
the damn terrorists. But a quick glance around reassured
her she was riding in the vehicle and Cooper was driving
her and the others to safety.

The vehicle slowed yet again and made a turn.

The change in the engine had woken her. They'd taken a ramp off the highway and were now rounding a large
corner to a gas station and restaurant up ahead.

Even SEALs needed gas.

She smiled as the large SUV pulled up outside a
pump.

Twisting to look behind her she saw David and Theresa both slumped in their seats sound asleep. There was
no sign of the second SUV and the rest of them. But they
were out there somewhere.

Swede and Cooper hopped out. She opened her door.
Cooper was there in an instant.

"I need a bathroom," she confessed. "And if there's a
chance of a coffee…"

Cooper nodded. "I'll escort you in."

She beamed. "Thank you." With a backward glance
at the other two still sleeping, she walked with him to the
restaurant and on to the ladies room at the back. There,
she used the facilities and washed her hands, staring at her
face in the mirror. She looked like shit.

No, actually she looked like she'd been attacked and grabbed, a hood thrown over her head and tossed in the back of a vehicle then held hostage for several hours before being forced out to a ship.

And subsequently rescued. Thank God for the last part. Her face looked pale, but her eyes twinkled so something had improved.

She grinned.

At least she hadn't lost her sense of humor.

She took advantage of the hot water and towels to do a quick wash. She ran her fingers through her hair and froze. She'd never once considered her personal belongings. Her purse, wallet. Passport. She groaned. Replacing that stuff was going to be a bitch.

After freshening up as much as possible, she straightened her clothing and went back out to the restaurant.

Cooper stood outside the door.

"Hey, thanks for waiting."

He hooked her arm in his. "I won't be leaving your side until I know you're home safe and sound, Doc."

She laughed. "It might have been doc before, but do make it Sasha now. I don't plan on cutting up your muscled body any time soon."

"I should hope not." He grinned. "I went to a lot of effort to put this body back together again."

She poked him. "So did I, so did I."

Laughing, he led her to the front counter where a large paper bag and a tray of takeout coffee sat waiting for them. As he paid, the door opened letting in a large group of men dressed like Cooper. Instinctively she wedged up beside Cooper and the counter.

He glanced down at her inquiringly. She nodded to the noisy group.

Cooper spun, his stance alert, wary.

And then Cooper relaxed. "What kept you so long? Markus, you drive like my grandmother."

At that, the guy standing on the left looking like a cross between a Hell's Angel and a real angel snorted. "Maybe so, but you've never driven with my granny and you drive like her. Those *were* speed signs back there, you know?"

Cooper's voice was wry as he answered, "What signs?"

The guys smirked. Then their gazes shifted to her.

One after another they tilted their heads and said, "Ma'am."

She raised an eyebrow and studied the group. They were all Americans and likely Cooper's team. She nodded back to them and said in a low voice, "Thank you for rescuing me and my team."

They nodded. She walked forward carrying the coffee tray. They instantly moved to the side. She beamed in thanks. They were extremely respectful. Maybe too much so. It raised her suspicions. But then again there was a feeling of walking a gauntlet as she exited the restaurant.

Cooper walked behind her, and a few of the men made some kind of comment but in a low voice. Cooper snorted and raced to catch up. "Hey, wait for me. How can I protect you if you race ahead?"

"I'm always racing around," she said with a grin as he caught up to her. "You should remember that."

"I remember. You ran from point A to point B without ever slowing down."

She laughed. "That's about the sound of it."

"You don't have to rush here. We're not going anywhere until the others are ready."

At the SUV, she found David and Theresa standing outside the vehicle stretching with Swede standing guard.

His eyes lit up at the coffee in her hands. "Is one of

those for me?" he asked hopefully.

"Actually Cooper has yours." She smiled up at him. "And he's got food."

Swede spun toward Cooper, hands out.

"Oh no you don't." Cooper backed up slightly, holding two bags of food. "You're driving from here on in. Keeping your hands on the wheel is the only way the rest of us are going to get any food."

Sasha handed out the coffees to the others as she listened to the men's banter. It added a sense of normalcy to a very non-normal situation. She appreciated it.

Swede growled. "If that's all the food you got, I'll go order more when I take these two in."

And true to his word, he shepherded David and Theresa into the restaurant for their own bathroom breaks. Sasha placed her coffee on the hood of the SUV then turned and did a couple of stretches. She was sore and bruised but knew she needed to stay active. She'd already stiffened up more than she was happy with.

As she straightened from touching her toes, she winced.

"Shit," she whispered under her breath.

"Are you okay?" Cooper asked in a sharp voice.

COOPER STUDIED HER wan features intently. "Did they hurt you?"

She shook her head. Then shrugged. "Maybe a little. I'm stubborn."

"I do remember that part." He smiled at her. "But just because you are a doctor, doesn't mean you can't be injured."

"But it does mean I know when the injuries are something to worry about."

Silence.

She smiled. "Besides we all got beat up a little, it's not just me."

He spun to look at the others, visible in the restaurant window. "Anyone need medical care?"

She laughed. "We're all doctors. We can manage."

He frowned. "Maybe, but you haven't got any medical supplies."

That wiped the frown off her face. She blinked rapidly and stared at a point over his shoulder as she struggled to regain control.

He reached out a hand and placed it on her shoulder. "I'm sorry."

She sniffled once and gave him a watery smile. "Let's just hope he survives. Ron is a good man."

Cooper nodded. "We did get him to the medics, but I haven't heard an update on his condition yet."

"Then we'll stay positive."

Cooper waited a moment. "After they shot Ron what happened?"

She winced. "We ran to help him, but that just angered them more and they started yelling at us. Kicking and hitting us with their rifles."

"Anyone get knocked out?"

"No, thank heavens." She took a sip of coffee and recovered her composure. "We were just beaten up a bit. A small price to pay for helping Ron."

"And could you help him?"

"Not enough," she said candidly. He raised his eyebrows at that. He suspected there was a lot more to the story that she wasn't sharing. That was okay, he'd get the information from the others.

Eventually.

He doubted anyone wanted to talk yet, but the details had to come out. They needed every bit of information available. No one realized how important their information was until someone else heard it. "Would you recognize the men if you saw them again?"

"There was six of them. I'd recognize three, possibly four." She frowned. "Not sure about the others considering I tried to avoid looking at them too closely. Also one flipped overboard and drowned while they were taking us to the ship."

"Right, one less to worry about. And three or four is better than none."

Loud noises erupted from the restaurant as the door opened to let more people in and out. He reached out a reassuring hand to Sasha as she studied the new arrivals.

"Where are we going?" she asked him. "My purse and passport are back in the refugee camp, and I have patients who need help."

"They're going to be picked up for us. You're all going to be debriefed at the Turkish base then again in the US."

She nodded. "My contract was up anyway, but we've left them shorthanded. Can I get a call through? There's a young woman in labor I want to check on."

Swede said from behind, "When we get to our rendezvous."

"I don't think that your contract would hold anyway if the camp can't guarantee your safety," Cooper added, pulling out a muffin from the bag. He handed one to each person.

"It's too bad. This will impact the aid the camps receive. And they need way more than they have now."

"Not our problem," David said. "Remember that. We can't save the world. Only one patient at a time."

Theresa smiled her thanks and said, "I think I've heard that saying at least once a day for the last three months. Not sure what I'll do when I'm back home again."

Cooper could feel the air lighten.

"I'll be turning around and heading right back again," David said. "This isn't likely the last incident like this." He shrugged. "There are still a lot of people to help."

Cooper admired that they were all doing what they loved and obviously shared a common outlook toward humanitarian work. The world needed more people like them.

The rest of his team joined them. Markus walked beside Evan, Mason bringing up the rear. It was Mason who motioned Cooper to the side. "Let's split the numbers up better," Mason said. "I don't like having them stacked the way they are now."

Cooper understood. All the SEALs in one vehicle meant that they could be taken out in one event, leaving the doctors alone with only two men to defend them. He nodded. "I'll take Dr. Sasha and Theresa. You can take Dr. Monroe."

Mason grinned. Cooper glared at him.

Swede and Shadow made no attempt to hide anything. They beamed.

Swede said, "So where do you want me, Cooper, with you or with Mason?"

"They are comfortable with you, so with me."

He meant Sasha of course and they all knew it.

Swede nodded. "Sounds good to me." He smacked Cooper on the back then strode quickly to the driver's side. "I'm driving."

Markus stepped up and said, "I'm riding shotgun."

Damn it. Cooper frowned at him, but Markus ignored him and hopped into the front seat.

"Evan," Mason said and pointed to the backseat where Sasha sat.

"Sure." Evan walked to the other side and got in to the middle seat.

"Hey," Evan said. "Don't I know you from Coronado?"

Sasha smiled up at him. "It's possible. I've lived and worked there for years."

"Yeah? Cool. Where are you living now?"

And just like that Evan and Sasha were laughing. Cooper, still standing outside, glared at them both.

Shadow walked over to Cooper's side and in a low tone said, "That will push her away. That's the last thing you want to do."

He smacked Cooper on the back and said, "See you at the next rendezvous spot." He turned and helped David into the second SUV.

That left just Mason. Mason studied his face. After a long uncomfortable silence, Mason asked, "You good?"

"Of course," Cooper said in a clipped tone.

"No you're not. But if you're lucky you will be."

And with that cryptic remark, Mason sauntered over to the second vehicle and took the shotgun position.

Sourly Cooper got into the last seat beside Theresa.

She smiled at him. "Sorry," she said. "Seating arrangements not to your liking?"

He realized how churlish he was being and smiled back holding up the two bags of food he'd collected. "I've got the food, so it doesn't matter where I sit."

And that's when Swede and Markus realized they might lose out. Swearing and cussing at Cooper for tricking them, Swede pulled out onto the highway, and everyone settled into the next part of the journey.

CHAPTER 7

THEY STOPPED TWO hours later at a rest stop. Sasha welcomed the chance to stretch and breathe the morning fresh air. The sun had crested over the horizon, but her eyes watched as the leader, Mason, walked toward them.

"As we have to pass close by, we're willing to swing into the refugee camp and give you time to collect your belongings and transfer cases off to other doctors. You can thank Dr. Munroe for that. He's very persuasive."

At David's "Whoop," he added. "We're talking an hour, two at the most."

Another of the SEALs stepped forward. "We're expected at base in two hours. We made good time so far and can extend that slightly, but that's all. Are we clear?"

Sasha nodded. "Thank you," she said. "My passport and personal belongings are still there – at least I hope they are."

"Mine too," Theresa said. "Plus I have some keepsakes I'd like to not lose."

"You will have two escorts each. Remember, we don't know how you were selected or why, but you were kidnapped from the camp. There is an ongoing investigation, but it hasn't gotten very far. Some people will know you went missing and others won't. No talking about it. No details. Stick to the plan, and we'll get through this fast and without any trouble."

But his tone of voice made it clear they were going to follow his rules. He studied each of the three of them in turn. "Be alert. If anyone acts suspicious tell us."

She had no problem with an escort. In fact, she preferred it. The last thing she wanted to do was find herself thrown in the back of a truck for a second time.

They reached the gates a half hour later. The security was tight but finally they parked off to the side of the medical clinic. She hopped out and took a look around.

She'd been gone less than a day but it seemed like weeks.

Yet in many ways it was as if she'd never left.

The small audience they'd garnered, even though it was really early, had the same look of hopelessness on their faces as always. Intermixed with anger and relief the cracks and crevasses said much about this stage of their lives.

And how they were handling it.

She smiled at them and turned toward the door of the clinic. With Cooper and one of his team she walked through the entrance, her mind already consumed with what she needed to do. She'd check the clinic first then grab up her few belongings. Home, such a magical word. Right back to California.

The place was dim, but in the back she could see lights. And hear crying.

Voices she recognized.

She raced to the commotion and found Yalta in the middle of a contraction. A nurse stood at her side. When the woman looked up, there was such a wealth of relief on her face, Sasha knew the situation was dire.

"Update," she ordered as she quickly washed up.

"She's been asking for you for hours," the nurse murmured. "The baby isn't moving. We've requested an ambulance to the hospital for her, but so far there's no sight of it. It's been two hours. The hospital is over-whelmed as well."

"Of course it is, isn't it always? That doesn't mean they can ignore our needs. We bother them the least we can but…"

"I know."

"Go check on the ambulance. I'll give the hospital a call in a minute." Sasha walked over to the weeping woman. "Easy, Yalta, take it easy."

The woman broke into tears and words poured forth. Words Sasha couldn't understand.

A male voice answered Yalta from somewhere behind Sasha. She twisted to see the man with Cooper answering the woman. She thought his name was Markus.

"What is she saying?" she snapped.

"She's been calling for you. Where were you? She is all alone." Markus gave her a crooked grin. "And more of the same."

"Right. I had moved her to the clinic and that's when I was snatched," she murmured.

"From this point?" Cooper asked, his voice hard.

She nodded. "From the small room on the side where we store our medical supplies. It has a door directly to the outside, and I was taken out that way."

"Did you see the person who kidnapped you? Was it one of the men that held you captive?"

She frowned, but her attention was on the irregular heartbeats from Yalta's belly. "No, not really. I was hit from behind."

"So you didn't catch a glimpse of anyone."

Her frown deepened. "A soldier called my name and he motioned toward the supply room, which is where I'd been heading anyway. There was supposed to be someone inside."

Cooper cut in. "Anything you can remember will help. We'll check out the supply room ourselves."

She heard him, but she wasn't listening as she checked her patient over. She straightened. "We need that ambulance. If it doesn't get here fast we'll have to try and save the baby, but I'm not set up for it," she muttered, turning to look around the small room. As clinics went the place was decent. As a surgical delivery room, hell no.

She turned to Cooper. "I need one of the other doctors here – now."

The two men turned to look at her then at each other.

"It's not a request," she snapped. "This is an order."

And she turned back to her patient.

The nurse came running back in at that moment. "The ambulance hasn't even left yet," she cried. "There's been a big accident, and they are shorthanded themselves."

"That means we're on our own."

She spun to make sure one of the men had left, and sure enough Cooper was gone. Good, the one left behind spoke the language. "Markus," she asked. "Can you tell her that we're going to have to do a cesarean to save the baby?"

"Can you do that here?"

She shrugged. "Sure I can. Is this ideal? No. She might survive the wait to the hospital, but her baby won't."

He walked closer to the young woman and spoke to her in a low calm voice that Sasha loved. He had a great bedside manner. And there was something about his voice that oozed caring.

The woman started weeping but she clutched his

hand tight.

When his voice fell quiet she glanced over to see him gently stroking her hand before speaking to her again in that same low tone.

Whatever he was saying to her was helping. She was curious though. "What are you telling her?"

"I'm telling her that she's lucky to be here and that you're the best. If you can save her baby then you will."

"How do you know?" Sasha stared at him in shock. "I haven't worked on you before. I'd have remembered."

"No," he said with a gentle smile. "But you saved Cooper. I heard about the doctor you saved at the same time, too."

She shook her head. "That's not fair. I was just doing what needed to be done."

"And did both jobs well." He grinned. "I know many a man who says they owe you big time."

Discomfited, she returned to her patient.

A moment later she asked, "Can you ask her about her family? Does she have anyone she'd like here with her?"

The musical sounds erupted again as the two spoke. "Her mother is ill and the rest are men."

"Husband? Does he want to be here?"

"Custom won't let him," Markus said. "And that's something you and I aren't going to be able to buck today."

"No, I guess not." She walked to the small cupboards and pulled out a tray. They didn't have an incubator for the baby either. She could hope they didn't need one. As she set up a bassinet for the baby, David came rushing in.

"What have we got?"

"Cesarean," she said quietly. "No progress for several hours. Baby is in fetal distress." She showed him the woman's chart. "No ambulance for at least an hour, then the return trip, and we'll lose the baby in that time."

"Crap."

"Right." They smiled at each other. They'd been required to pull a few miracles out of their respective hats these last months. "Let's have at it."

With David handling the drugs, Sasha sorted the tools while the nurse prepped Yalta. She glanced over to find Markus staring at her, his gaze wide, his lips pinched. It was probably the first time anyone had asked him to do what she was about to ask him to do, but heck, he was a SEAL, he could handle anything. "Can you stay for her?"

He glanced at the scalpel in her hand, his eyebrows raised. Then gave a grim nod. She nodded at him once, waiting until he turned his attention to the poor woman. It wasn't going to be fun, but she'd make damn sure it was fast.

And it was. She was holding an unhappy newborn male in her hands in minutes.

She laughed as his angry cries filled the room.

With Yalta's happy tears and cries of joy she handed the squalling boy off to the nurse and turned her attention back to the patient.

"We're almost done," she said, more for Markus's benefit than anyone else's. Yalta wasn't feeling anything other than the overwhelming emotions that overtook every woman at this moment in her life.

Sasha had helped deliver any number of babies but wasn't sure she'd ever done a cesarean under these circumstance. The reality was it didn't matter. The joy was the same for everyone, no matter where in the world it happened.

What she wanted to know was would it ever happen to her? She'd had no doubt a year ago. She'd been happily married and completely in love with her life and knew the time for her own family would be soon. After that dream had blown up in her face, she'd avoided facing that question. It was too painful.

"Done?" David asked at her side. He looked at her over the mask in question.

She realized she'd been standing there staring at the woman. She shook off the reverie and nodded. "I am. She's in great shape."

"And you're a great doctor," he said seriously. "Love that you're so calm and controlled."

"Always," she said with a smile at Yalta. "It's all about the patient."

She hopped off the stool and walked over to the water to wash up. The nurse was taking care of Yalta while David studied the little boy now swaddled in towels. "He's beautiful," he announced to the new mother.

Markus quickly translated. The mother beamed and held out her arms.

They shifted her in bed so she could meet her new son.

The nurse came over to Sasha and gave her a big hug. "Thank God, you got back in time," she cried. "I wasn't sure what I was going to do."

"I did, so it's all good, and you did wonderfully," she said warmly. The thought of not having made it back made her nauseous. "David, anyone else in dire need at the moment?"

"No, Theresa has done what she needs to do as well. We can leave."

Sasha was undecided. Her patient needed to be watched carefully, and she hated to leave her like this. Just then she heard the sirens. A big grin broke across her face. "That's music to my ears."

"Isn't that too little too late?" Markus asked.

"In this case, it's perfect. Yalta shouldn't be alone."

"How long will this take?" Cooper asked from the doorway.

She spun in surprise. She'd forgotten he was there. "About twenty minutes for the paperwork and to get her transferred, then I'm free to go."

Markus nodded. "We're going to hold you to that."

"I promise," she said. "You can see why I needed to be here."

"I do." Cooper nodded. "Markus?"

Markus took off. With Cooper at her side, she walked to her quarters to pack up her few belongings. Only as she stood in the doorway to the tiny room, she realized her room wasn't as she'd left it.

"WHAT'S THE MATTER?" Cooper asked, studying the bare bones closet of a room. There shouldn't be much wrong as there was nothing here to go wrong.

"My stuff has been rifled through," she said shortly.

He gave her a side long glance. "You can tell?"

She reared back slightly and looked at the room again. Then laughed and relaxed slightly. "Absolutely but then when I do surgery I want my tools in a specific order and at a specific distance from my fingers. In other words everything is placed exactly where I want it. These…" she waved her arm at the shelf of folded clothes, "Are not the way I left them."

"Anything missing?"

She stepped inside and did a quick search. "Not that I can see." She pulled a bag out from under the single bed and opened the zipper. "I don't keep any valuables here.

They are in the office safe."

He frowned. "In a place like this, that's hardly safe."

"They aren't criminals here. They are families looking to start again."

"And many families in that position will do anything to make it happen."

She stood up and gathered the closest stack of clothing. He noticed that meant several pairs of jeans and a couple pairs of shorts. He'd love to see her in shorts. Then she'd be gorgeous in anything. While he watched, she quickly finished packing. Within minutes she straightened and looked around. "Do you see if I missed anything?"

"Looks cleaned out." But he dropped to the floor and looked under the bed. He almost laughed at the militant style the bed had been made up in. "I think you're good to go."

"Then to the office for my purse and passport. Not to mention the contract for being here."

She led the way with Cooper on her heels. They passed the room with mother and baby and Markus back standing watch. The ambulance could be heard outside. In the office she quickly opened the safe and withdrew a brown envelope and a small purse. Then closed and locked it again. They raced back to the patient where he watched as she efficiently managed the transfer.

She gave the young woman a hug before releasing her to the paramedics. Cooper immediately ushered her toward the SUV.

"We're here, Mason," he said to the silvery eyed man she'd assumed to be the leader of the group.

"There's one more thing…" she said to Mason. "And it's something Markus can help with. Plus, we'll all be together."

Mason narrowed his gaze at her and waited.

"The mother and son are safe, but no one has informed the family or the father that he has a healthy son or that his wife is going to be fine."

Cooper caught his breath behind her. She turned and glanced at him and Markus at his side. "I'm sure you can understand."

"A driver took you there, can you find the location on your own?" Mason asked.

She nodded. "That I can do."

"Even though this place is a maze?" Mason asked, one eyebrow raised.

She laughed and handed over a map and a piece of paper. "That's where they live and this is a map of the camp. I might not be able to figure it out, but you big bad SEALs will be able to."

She grinned as he rolled his eyes at her, but he took the sheet nonetheless. Cooper looked down at her in bemusement. Keeping his voice low he whispered, "I didn't know angels came in pint size."

She froze in shock then laughed. "I should punch you for that."

He snickered. "Go for it. I have a fly swatter around here somewhere."

Mason shook his head. "Let's go you two. We will travel together."

"Fun." She hopped into the back of the big black SUV. Cooper sat beside her. Markus took the passenger seat. With Mason driving the lead vehicle they slowly wound their way through the camp that was just waking up. Several people dashed inside their small shelters in fear. Many others came running out. Sasha waved at them.

"Smile, Markus. They are scared of you."

Markus shot her a look of surprise. "Me?" he protested. "Why me?"

"It's the look. So dour and dark. Smile a little and make their day instead."

He snorted in disgust, but he plastered a smile on his face anyway.

Cooper chuckled.

When Markus shot the bird at Cooper, he whooped. Lord, this was good to see. Sasha was such a breath of fresh air. She was bringing even Markus out of his shell. Evan was on the far side of her being uncharacteristically quiet. When Copper twisted enough that he could see Evan's face it was to realize he was studying Sasha's profile as if fascinated.

He glared at him but Evan didn't lift his head. Cooper reached along the back seat and flicked his arm.

Evan raised his gaze in surprise, and Cooper deepened his scowl. Evan narrowed his gaze as he studied his friend and then glanced from Sasha to Cooper and back again – and his face lit with unholy mirth.

Cooper knew he was going to be bugged forever.

He subsided in his seat and glared out the window. Only to see Markus's smirk in the rearview mirror.

"Shit," he said under his breath. They'd never leave him alone now.

Just as they reached the correct sector of the camp, a large group of young men stepped out in front to stop the vehicles.

And Sasha gasped in recognition. "Oh my God," she whispered. "That's my driver. The one we thought was shot dead."

CHAPTER 8

THE VEHICLES ROLLED to a stop. Sasha peered forward to see Mason speaking with the men. "Markus you need to help him," she ordered.

That he opened his door and hopped out immediately caused a snicker from her left. She eyed the man whose name she didn't know and asked, "Do you speak their language?"

He immediately shook his head.

"Exactly." She turned to Cooper. "Let me out."

He shook his head, his gaze never moving from the man sitting on a chair. She followed the same direction as he was looking and studied her driver. His skin pale and his features drawn. Without a shirt the bandage around his ribs was easy to see as was the blood seeping through it.

"Cooper…" she said in her most imperious tone. "He needs to be questioned and his injuries looked at. We also need to be asking if the other medical personnel here are in danger. Did he have anything to do with my abduction or not?"

In the lead vehicle she could see David and Theresa arguing with the men as well.

"Why do you guys have to be so difficult?" she muttered.

He slanted a gaze her way and she glared at him. Then in a move that surprised everyone, she hopped onto

483

her seat and scrambled into the front and was out Markus's door before they had a chance to grab her. Outside she raced to Jamel. It wasn't his full name but it was the only version she could enunciate.

When he saw her, he bounced to his feet and gasped, his face going sheer white.

"Easy, Jamel, sit down."

He collapsed back again. But whether it was from his injuries or shock, she didn't know.

He appeared agitated when he saw the SEALs surrounded them.

"It's okay. They are surrounding me. Not you."

"You think?" Cooper said in a cool voice. "We've been looking for him. He was at the same cabin, he gets shot and yet somehow you are moved and he escapes and tells no one."

"They said they'd kill me," he cried out in fear. "I was injured. Couldn't move. I waited until everyone was gone. And then tried to move. Only I wasn't alone. The gunman told me if I lived I had to keep quiet or they'd come and kill my family." His voice shook and his body wracked with tremors. She knew the signs well.

"I have to check your ribs. You're running a fever and that is not good."

"Doc," Evan said. "Aren't there others around here that can help him?"

"Yes," she said without looking up. "Go find me one." She shot Cooper a stern look. "But I assume people want to talk to him."

"No, no," Jamel cried. "No want to talk."

Several of the other men surrounded them.

"Back up and give me room," she ordered. "You can ask him questions, but I don't want him doing more damage to his injuries." She bent down and reached out to open his bandage, but he shook his hands at her. "No. No," he cried. "They will take me away."

"If they do," she's said, "I'll be with you."

He stared at her with hope. "You would help me?"

"I'm trying to help you now," she said gently. "Sit still so I can look."

He stilled long enough for her to unwrap the bandage. She sat back on her heels. This was what Ron had taken a bullet for. He'd been grazed. That was all. They hadn't intended to kill him or even maim him. "Did you clean this out?"

He nodded. "My wife."

Sasha sighed. "But you didn't go to the clinic to get help, did you?"

"I was afraid. Everyone knew I had been taken too."

"Did they?" Cooper asked in a hard voice. "How is that?"

Jamel shrank back at his tone of voice. Sasha was about to admonish Cooper when she thought better of it. The camp needed doctors. The doctors needed to be safe. Therefore Jamel needed to give a good accounting of his actions. So she bit her lip and studied the wound. It would benefit from a good cleaning and a new bandage, but other than that it would pain him but it wouldn't kill him. She looked at the leg but decided it didn't likely require any emergency attention from her. But the wounds bothered her. "What happens with him?"

"He comes with us." Mason held up his phone. "The Turkish want to have a talk with him."

Jamel cried out.

She stood up. "You took money for taking those men to where we were working, so they could kidnap us, didn't you?"

He looked at her in shame and then nodded.

"Well, that answers that question," she said quietly. "Of course the Turkish want to talk to you. They need to know who the men were and why they wanted us in particular."

"They wanted the Americans. Just the Americans they said."

"Which is what we figured?" She looked at Cooper, one eyebrow raised.

Cooper half lifted and half carried Jamel to the SUV.

"Good, now we can finally get to Yalta's family and finish this," she muttered. As she walked back to the SUV with Markus she realized that Mason might have changed his mind about letting the father know. She raced over to where he stood with the huge mountain man that seemed to be everywhere and nowhere. Along with his sidekick she barely saw clearly. Talk about living in the shadows.

"Mason," she interrupted when there was a break in his conversation, only to realize she was the reason for the break. They were all looking at her. She brushed her hair back off her head self-consciously. "Sorry for interrupting, but I want to confirm that we're still heading for Yalta's family?"

She stared directly at him.

His gaze narrowed as if hoping she'd relent. Instead she straightened her back and jutted out her chin. "Nothing has changed," she said.

"Lots has changed," he countered. "We now have a person of interest that we need to take in for questioning."

"And that doesn't change the need to let a young man know that his wife and son are alive and well," she said gently. "It's only a few minutes from here," she said persuasively.

"Might as well do it," Markus said when Mason looked over at him. "Doc here is a mite too stubborn for her own good."

"Exactly," she said with a beaming smile at him. "Thank you for explaining, Markus."

Markus frowned at her. Mason just narrowed his gaze.

"I'm even more stubborn when it's for the good of others," she said in response to Markus's irritation.

He rolled his eyes at her.

"You should get that problem fixed," she said earnestly. "One of these days your eyes are going to stay in the back of your head and you'll be blind."

He snorted.

She raised an eyebrow and stared calmly back.

He started to look worried.

She snickered. "Gotcha."

And she ran back to the SUV laughing. Cooper shook his head at her. "Still up to your bad jokes, huh?"

"That was a good one," she cried out.

"If Markus was six, maybe," Cooper said.

"Well…" she chuckled and walked to the open passenger door. She stood up on the running board on the side of the truck and as he was close enough, cute enough and the idea just seemed good enough she leaned over and kissed his cheek. "You're a sweetie to be so worried about your buddy."

And she scrambled into the back seat where she'd been sitting before.

COOPER DIDN'T NEED to see that the others were staring at him with smirks on their faces. He understood the awkward silence well enough. He sighed and was about to climb in beside Sasha when Markus opened the front passenger door and asked, "Sweetie?"

With a glare, Cooper got in and slammed the door.

There was an odd silence inside as well. He turned his dark gaze on Evan who was desperately trying to hold back a raucous laugh. Sasha, however, seemed completely calm. She fussed over Jamel.

"They won't hurt me, will they?" Jamel asked.

"Nope," she said cheerfully. "They just want to talk to you. It's important we catch these guys. They shot Dr. Ron because he went to your aid." Her voice deepened. "I still don't know if he's pulled through."

"He's a good man," Jamel said with tears in his eyes. "I only wanted to save my family. They kept saying they would kill my little Jakel. She's only eight. They said they take them for the men at that age." His shoulders started to shake. "I couldn't do that to her. Not to my baby."

Sasha's lips turned down, and Cooper could feel his own anger rising. It was so typical of an army particularly the ones they were facing in the Middle East now. The little girl wouldn't likely have survived and would have died a horribly slow death.

He could understand Jamel's actions, though he couldn't condone them.

But he could sure get behind Sasha's exuberant show of affection.

CHAPTER 9

SASHA WATCHED AND wondered at the speed they were traveling through the camp. Or rather the lack of speed. What was Mason looking for? And why wasn't he finding it. The stares were getting uglier the deeper they went. The camp was full of issues and tolerance was needed. A lot more than tolerance.

"I'm not really looking forward to seeing Yalta's family," she whispered to Cooper, not wanting Jamel who'd slumped down on the seat beside her to hear.

"You won't be alone this time," Cooper said in a low tone showing that he'd understood what she meant.

"Well, Jamel was with me," she added. "So I wasn't really alone then either, still…"

The lead vehicle pulled to a stop up ahead. Swede parked behind it. Sasha loved to see these men do everything so…effortlessly. They were so capable and wore their self-confidence like a mantle of power.

Very sexy.

She waited for Swede to turn off the engine and for Cooper to let her out of the vehicle. She motioned to Jamel. "We need him."

"No, we don't," Cooper said.

"I think we should get his help anyway. He knows them. If he were to say anything wrong, then Markus could tell us."

Cooper frowned. He turned to look at Jamel but the

man had shrunk deeper into the SUV.

"See," she announced. "He needs to come."

"Jamel, come with us."

He shook his head, but the door at his back opened and Swede tugged him out. With Jamel between Markus and Swede and looking more terrified than she could remember seeing him before, he led the group forward. She walked behind with Cooper and Evan. There were a couple more men around, but she didn't know their names. Cooper had spoken to them earlier but hadn't introduced her. He was always making eye contact as if they had a way to communicate silently.

She wished she did. She also wished she understood the underlying threats going on.

Why did Jamel not want to come here? She normally wasn't a suspicious person, but there was something about the way he was acting. As if he were afraid but not so much of the men they were going to see but…well she didn't know.

As they approached, men stepped out of the shelters. She could understand.

She'd brought a large group of strangers all dressed in military gear, and they appeared threatening. Many of these people had fled persecution in their homeland and came by fear naturally – particularly of the military.

"Yalta is okay," she cried out.

The men stood arms across their chests, their hard gazes on her.

As she was about to step forward, Cooper grabbed her arm to hold her back. Together, they stepped up beside Markus. "Tell them please, Markus."

He immediately started speaking. The men stared at him in surprise. One gestured to the large group and Markus shook his head. He seemed to be explaining the group's presence and obviously convinced them that they weren't in trouble because they all eased back. She studied their faces, but the one young man she'd seen holding Yalta's hand wasn't there.

"Ask for Yalta's husband," she said.

Markus spoke again. Two men stepped back and pointed to a shelter beside them. She bolted inside, Cooper and Markus on her heels. Inside lying down in the shadows was a young man – the one she'd been looking for – despondent and grieving.

"No," she cried, dropping to his side. "Yalta is fine."

But he wouldn't listen.

Markus crouched down beside her and grabbed the young man's shoulder and gave it a shake. He snapped at Markus and Markus snapped back. Then spoke slowly and carefully.

She waited and watched.

And finally the young man sat up, shock on his face. Words poured from his mouth as he grabbed Markus's shoulders and gripped them so tight his knuckles turned white.

And finally he seemed to believe – his face lit up in joy and he shouted out. Just as suddenly he burst into tears and hugged Markus.

Markus grinned at her over the young man's shoulder.

"It took a bit," he explained.

She looked up to see a half a dozen men and then an older woman slowly enter. And she realized that with the father crying, they thought Yalta was dead. She motioned to Markus. He slowly stood up and helped the father to his feet.

More conversation, then the father turned to his friends and family and beamed. He shouted out something and the chaos started.

She was picked up and hugged several times as the place came alive with joy.

The shelter filled with well-wishers.

It was all she could do to sneak out.

And came face to face with Jamel as he slipped around the back of the building.

WHERE HAD SHE gone now? Cooper raced outside, there were so many damn men cheering and slapping each other on the back it was impossible to maneuver. And impossible to keep track of Sasha. The do-gooder who always seemed to find trouble. And not for doing anything wrong, just for trying to help. That was the problem. For all he knew she'd found someone else in need and raced over to give aid. He could just imagine what her life was like here. For three months she'd have worked herself to the bone and never taken a break.

Until the kidnappers stopped her.

American she might be and therefore a prize to the terrorist, but if they were smart they'd have taken her for her medical skills. She was a doctor sure, but she was a hell of a surgeon too. He stood outside the shelter and made his way to the SUVs, his gaze whipping from one corner to the other. When he reached the vehicle and realized she wasn't there, he roared. "Sasha!"

His men turned to look at him.

"I can't find her."

The group spread. By now the joyful news had spread with even more people arriving. It was possible Sasha was in the middle of it, but Cooper couldn't see her. Anywhere.

Ten minutes later his worst fears were realized.

"Damn it."

David and Theresa were out of the vehicles and standing beside the SUV. Theresa was crying quietly as a grid search was quickly organized.

"Where's the driver?"

Markus came outside, his face dark.

Cooper said in a hard clipped voice, "He's gone too."

"And likely with Sasha. The men here say he's well-known for selling medical services. That's why they'd been angry when Sasha came the first time to check on Yalta. Jamel wanted payment or he wouldn't return with the doctor when Yalta really needed her."

"Oh, Jesus," David said. "That's despicable. Everyone struggles to survive here. Jamel is probably not alone in his actions."

"Well, if he's got her now, then we'll make sure he's stopped." Cooper's gaze never stopped surveying the crowd. "Markus, I think we need to let everyone here know what's likely happened and see if they will help."

"We don't know that he had anything to do with her disappearance," Mason cautioned. "She could be any-where."

"True, but the men want to help and they know the area, so ask if anyone has seen her. We have to find her fast. If it's the same people that kidnapped her then it could already be too late."

CHAPTER 10

SASHA STARED AT Jamel while inside she realized that by sneaking out back she'd left herself alone and exposed to trouble. The look on her Jamel's face wasn't that of a man seeking medical help.

"What's going on, Jamel?"

He shook his head. "I don't want to do this."

"Then don't do it, whatever it is," she countered. "And definitely don't do it if it's wrong. You're already in trouble, don't make things any worse."

He gave her a hangdog look that made her even more suspicious. "I need you to come over to another house. To help someone else."

"No. I can't do that," she said firmly, her feet already moving backwards. "I have to leave. You know that."

"No, these people need you," he cried.

She frowned and studied his face. He looked beat up, bruised, but more than that he looked different. Or maybe she was different. Because he had a slyness to the furtive way he looked around as if expecting someone to jump out from the shacks. And she realized he likely was. He definitely wasn't acting like normal. She gave a quick glance to the quiet area as everyone was still partying on the other side of the row, and without giving herself any chance to think, she bolted.

But wasn't fast enough. He grabbed her, a gun suddenly appearing from nowhere, and he pointed it at her head.

She took a deep breath and let it our shakily. "Jamel, what are you doing."

"What I have to do," he cried. "Do you think I want to do this?"

"I don't know," she said in a soothing voice, needing him to stay calm. If he got frightened then his finger would get trigger happy. And she'd be history.

She groaned. "How the hell do I always end up in the shit?"

"Move. I need you to come with me," he said, tugging on her arm. He kept glancing around knowing that she'd be missed any moment. When the SEALs found her, she was going to get it. She shouldn't have snuck out the back. Especially not telling anyone… But it had seemed like a good idea at the time. Of course knowing what she knew now…

She could scream for help but the noise from the front was loud, boisterous. "You only pretended to be dead, didn't you?"

He shot her a scornful look. "Of course I did, what would you do in that situation, stand up and let them shoot me again?"

"You could have done something to help us," she said, feeling the sting of more betrayal. "Did you do anything after you escaped?"

"What would you have me do?" he cried. "I saw there was a rescue happening, so I stole a truck and came home."

"Just like that, you stole a truck?" Still being tugged in the direction he wanted to go, she said, "That's not good."

"I was just trying to get home."

And she realized he likely made that excuse any time

he was caught doing what he shouldn't be doing. It somehow justified his actions. As if doing anything for his family made it okay.

"Where are you taking me?" She recognized the sudden silence behind her. Her absence had been missed. Good. The sudden pause in the noise was then broken by a shout followed by sounds of confusion.

"We must hurry."

She dragged back on his arm. "No. I don't want to go with you. You're the one that helped the terrorists before. Like hell I'm going to go with you again." And she jerked on his arm hard and broke free. She fled around the first corner and kept weaving through the rows upon rows of temporary housing.

Jamel was weasel thin and small and now that she knew him better she understood it described his behavior as well. She kept trying to dodge behind the buildings and circle back and around to where the men had to be waiting for her. In fact, she damn well hoped they were out looking for her. If she could get close enough she'd start screaming, but there was no point in alerting the enemy to her position if she also couldn't alert her rescuers.

She barreled around another corner, took a right and started running back toward safety.

And got two steps in before she slammed into a huge man. With her breath knocked out of her, she tumbled to the ground.

Before she had a chance to say or do anything she was picked up like a rag doll and squeezed.

COOPER WAS PISSED. At himself. At her. At the little rat

driver. He stormed through his section of the camp, one of the refugees who spoke a little English was at his side, asking anyone they came across if they'd seen Jamel or Dr. Sasha. They'd had a stream of *nos* so far and it wasn't doing any good to panic, but he wanted to. Damn it. Where the hell was she?

She knew it was dangerous here. She had to know that it was possible the kidnappers lived here – still lived here. If they saw her…

He should never have let her out of his sight. He cursed yet again to let off a little steam, but his mind was organized and reaching for answers.

"Anything?" he said into his headset.

"No. No one has seen her. Most weren't awake as it's early and many were hiding as they didn't understand the commotion, but not one has seen Dr. Sasha and she's well-loved here."

She was well-loved by everyone who'd been lucky enough to have her work on them too. She was just that kind of person. His translator stopped at a shack and sent out several questions.

A little girl with a cast on her arm smiled and nodded. The translator crouched down and talked to her. She nodded again and smiled up at him. Then she pointed past her home. Even Cooper understood that. And he ran down the direction she'd pointed out. The translator called up again, but Cooper's feet didn't want to slow.

"She turned left here."

Damn it. He turned and backtracked a few feet and followed the man who was now heading down a different lane. This place was a maze. How could anyone keep track of it? There were tents everywhere.

"Did she say anything else?"

"Yes. Dr. Sasha is with Jamel."

Of course she was. Well, she wasn't going to stay that way.

"She was running with the driver chasing her."

"So she's trying to escape from him. Damn it."

He studied the faces as they peered through the doorways. *Sasha, where the hell are you?*

The pathway ended abruptly and he came to stop. There was nothing ahead of them. Except tire tracks.

Shit.

"Mason?" At the quiet affirmative he quickly explained what he'd heard and found.

"Security gate is locked down. No one is going in or out. There aren't many vehicles here at all and none will get outside."

That helped but not by much. He turned to study the tracks. "Where's Hawk?"

"Should be thirty-seconds away."

Sure enough when he lifted his gaze a second time it was to see Hawk coming from the side, his gaze on the ground. "Her tracks stop here."

"Likely after getting into the vehicle."

Hawk nodded. But he didn't stop reading the ground and what it would tell him. "No. She fell here."

He pointed out a series of smudges on the ground that didn't tell him anything. "Then she got to her feet, and bending over she raced that way."

"What way?"

Suddenly, Cooper could see her childlike footprints racing down the path. He took off in pursuit. Hawk right beside him.

"Let me go in front."

Because that made the most sense, Cooper eased the pace back slightly and let Hawk take the lead. Hawk suddenly took a right then a left and came to a stop at another of the many identical tent homes. "Their tracks went in here," he said in a low voice. "But I can't tell if she's still in here or not."

"Not likely. She'd be trying to make her way back to us."

Hawk went around to the back of the tent, gave a shout and took off. Cooper was right behind him.

Just as suddenly as they started this second chase it came to an end as they found her and a huge young man who was holding her.

Of Jamel there was no sign.

Not that he'd waste time worrying about him. Sasha cried out, "Oh thank heavens. Jamel forced me to go with him again."

Cooper nodded but didn't take his eyes off the massive man who held her in his arms.

The man's gaze was hard, cold.

"Put her down."

The man never moved.

"I said put her down."

Nothing.

"I tried to talk to him, but I get no response either," she said apologetically. "He won't do anything."

"Where is he taking you?"

"I don't know."

She struggled to free herself. And couldn't move. The man held her tight.

Hawk shrugged. He walked closer as if to walk past. Then in a smooth movement he jumped and hit the huge man in the neck. Sasha tumbled to the ground. Cooper raced to help Hawk and between them they subdued the man long enough for the others to arrive. Camp security forces came swinging up behind them. When Cooper could, he stood up and spun around. When his gaze landed on her the tension eased. He swung her up in his arms and held her close. "Jesus," he whispered. "I was so damn afraid."

His heart slammed against his ribcage and the acid in his stomach threatened to overflow – especially now that she was safe.

It took a few moments to realize she was hugging him back just as hard, and that her body was shaking in reaction.

"God, I'm so sorry." She leaned back to look at him, her hands reaching to cup his face. "I just slipped out the back of the tent to avoid the crush with all the men cheering and shouting."

"I don't blame you for trying to get away, but you can't be anywhere alone. And the sooner I get you back stateside the better," he growled, worry threading through his voice. He slowly let her back down on her feet. "Don't do that again."

Cheeky as ever, she grinned up at him and said, "Don't what? Don't go missing? Don't make you worry? Or don't–"

"Bolt–"

"Return your hug…"

He glared at her. She smiled at him and slid her arm through his to cuddle closer. "Thank you for rescuing me again."

He wrapped an arm around her shoulders and led her back to the truck. The crowds around them separated to let them through.

He glanced over and caught the look in Hawk's eyes. That surprise and knowing mixed up with a big dose of humor in his friends gaze made Cooper realize how this exchange must have looked to anyone watching. He shook his head at Hawk as if to say, it was nothing.

Hawk's grin widened.

Not wanting Sasha to see their exchange he led her to the SUVs where David and Theresa cried out and ran to her. He waited patiently as they talked and hugged, then separated them. "Let's go. We need to get you out of here before something else happens," he muttered.

She gasped as she was forced to the other SUV. "You're not saying I'm to blame for everything, are you?"

"No, not everything. But too damn much of it, yes." He glared at her. "I want you safe."

That urchin's grin popped up. Damn he was getting foolish. All he wanted to do was repeat his actions so he could see it again.

"Get in, Doc."

She frowned and opened her mouth.

"Don't do it," he growled, fed up and frustrated that he couldn't whisk her away some place safe, strip her naked and make mad passionate love to her. That it was not going to happen – likely ever – just added to his pain.

Her frown deepened. She opened her mouth to blast him and this time he placed his finger against her lips and shook his head. "Don't do it."

She growled deep in the back of her throat.

And then did something that sent his blood quaking in his boots.

She bit his finger.

He pulled his hand away, swearing.

She grinned up at him unrepentantly. "That's what you get for trying to shut me up."

"Like anything would do that," he scoffed.

She laughed then leaned forward, and the look in her eyes had him thinking about that whole plan to get her naked again. And there was nothing he could do to control his train wreck of thoughts. And then she made it ten times worse.

"There's one thing that would work," she whispered.

He narrowed his gaze, knowing he was in quicksand and unable to ask for a handout.

"What?" Barely able to breathe, even less able to believe she was being as teasingly playful as she was, he hoped for one answer. The one he wanted so desperately to hear…

"A kiss."

Bingo.

CHAPTER 11

S ASHA CURLED UP in the far corner of the SUV and closed her eyes. She didn't understand the lighthearted exchange of the last few moments, but she understood one thing – it wasn't normal behavior for her.

So she was either more disturbed by this last attack than she thought, or she'd finally gotten over the breakup of her marriage.

Because there was no way to call that exchange anything other than flirting.

Something she couldn't ever remember having done before. But it was fun. Outrageous – then so were her circumstances. She'd come to Turkey to get away from all the drama and heavy emotions, and instead she ended up in danger in a world of violence. That's not what she wanted either.

So what did she want?

She stole a look at Cooper's thunderous face and smirked. He'd be a great place to start.

But not here or now. Home first. And didn't that have a delicious sound to it. She closed her eyes and let herself daydream.

The miles passing had a hypnotic motion, and it wasn't long before Sasha closed her eyes and leaned her head back. This would be over soon. Surely?

A full stomach, warm and safe with the nightmare several hours behind her she'd relaxed enough to be

505

comfortable and sleepy again.

"How much longer?" She twisted to look at Cooper.

"Not much. Maybe twenty minutes."

She nodded and leaned her head back and closed her eyes. "Maybe I'll nap then."

The vehicle slowed.

"Cooper." Swede's sharp voice had everyone leaning forward. Markus had his weapon out.

Sasha slid down on the seat, her hand to her throat. *Dear God, now what?*

The vehicle slowed to a stop. Evan was studying the traffic behind them.

"Everyone down," Cooper snapped. He had the door open and his gun out. Markus was at his side.

Theresa reached over and grasped Sasha's hand. "Now what?"

Sasha winced. "I have no idea."

"I don't want to leave the vehicle…" Theresa took a deep breath. "And I really don't want to venture out there." In the horizon red hues promised a storm in the making. But the sun was up, just sending off a weird light. In front of the SUV's she could see several damaged vehicles on the side of the road.

"It's an accident," she cried. "Oh no. Is anyone hurt?"

She glanced to the other SUV parked on the road. "David is there already."

That was good enough for her. Sasha bolted out of the vehicle, realized Markus had been standing behind the vehicle watching over them.

"Don't leave here, ladies," Markus warned. "There are a lot of people over there."

"But they might need our help too," Sasha said, studying the accident. "This isn't likely to be a trap, is it?" she murmured in a low voice as they approached the accident scene. In the distance sirens ripped through the air. So there was help coming.

"Not likely but we've seen all kinds of decoys."

"Maybe," she said doubtfully. "I doubt at this point. We've already been rescued. And none of us are so important that they'd continue to come after us."

She felt his sharp look but didn't have a clue what was behind it. He was a nice man. Quiet, dark. Easy to tease. She hadn't had time to get to know many of the men, she'd only been with them for a few hours, but they were all the same – dependable and dangerous as hell.

She thanked the Lord that they were on her side. She didn't ever want to see the terrorists again.

She glanced around at the dozen vehicles stopped on the road. There was hardly access for the ambulance to get in. David was working on one young man. "David?"

He looked up at her and smiled. "It's all good. No critical or life threatening injuries."

He straightened and glanced at her as the sirens grew louder. "Looks like the authorities are here."

"That's our cue to leave," Markus said at her side.

Cooper walked toward her and motioned back at the SUV. "Back you go. Time to get moving."

She turned obediently now that she knew she wasn't needed. "Are we on a deadline?" she asked Cooper.

"We are." He glanced at the sky. "In fact, we're late."

Now awake and alert after the stop, the miles flew by.

Theresa asked abruptly, "Are you going to go back to the refugee camp?"

Sasha shook her head. "I'd considered renewing my contract but hadn't made a decision. This just made up my mind."

"It does that, doesn't it?" Theresa stared out the window. "I'm not sure what I want to do. I want to go home but don't really know where to go."

"I told you before you're always welcome to stay with me until you decide. I have an empty house."

"Thanks." Theresa smiled at her. "There's a part of me that feels I should go back to the camp. There's no doubt they need us, but..." Her voice caught in her throat. "I just can't."

"I know. I almost feel like I've pushed my luck," Sasha admitted quietly. "I don't know how I'll feel as time goes on." But she did know. She wanted to go home. She'd left for a reason, and it no longer applied.

She could go home again.

She needed to go home again.

She'd been running for long enough.

COOPER LEANED FORWARD as Swede turned the vehicle into a large military compound. After a formal exchange at a guarded gate they were allowed to enter. Sasha straightened. "Are these our allies?" she whispered to him from behind.

"This is one of Turkey's military bases." He nodded. "They were part of the team that tracked you down. A group is even now turning the camp upside down to find Jamel."

She leaned back and released a heavy breath. "They have my thanks."

They were escorted to a series of buildings that wound through to a large office. There, courtesies were exchanged and two men turned to study the three visitors.

"Do any of you need medical attention?"

They all shook their heads.

The boss nodded. "We have flights arranged to take

you home soon."

Sasha smiled, and asked, "When."

The commander looked at his watch. "You'll be leaving in just under six hours." He looked at the three of them. "Before then, I'm sure you understand we have questions."

Cooper watched the relief on her face. She'd been through an ordeal and until it was over, she wasn't going to relax. Hell, neither was he.

The group was escorted into a waiting room and offered refreshments. One at a time they were led back into the office where they were asked for a full accounting. Sasha did her best. But outside of being forcibly taken to the gang's side, it had been a routine day. "Did anyone know who you were then?"

She shook her head. "Not really. But they were waiting for me when I got back." Then the questions centered on the driver.

Cooper stood guard as they each went in and out of the interviews. Mason who was speaking with members of the Turkish military at the other end of the room. After several nods and few a short questions and responses, Mason joined him.

"We're escorting them stateside."

"Good." Cooper didn't want Sasha to go home without him.

Only it didn't happen that way or that easily. The questioning took longer than expected. Apparently Theresa had seen several men skulking around the camp. At the time she hadn't thought anything of it, but under the intensive debriefing she'd known more than she realized. Cooper had seen it happen time and time again.

When the questioning was done, or at least the doctors were done, he was called in. He gave his accounting in a short terse few sentences. There wasn't much to add. No, he hadn't seen more than four at the shack and they'd seen three onboard. One man had gone overboard apparently but no he hadn't seen him or known if the man had survived. Same in regards to the driver. The medical team said he'd been there but unmoving, but he hadn't seen a body when the shack was trashed. No, he hadn't torched the place. He'd figured the kidnappers might have done so to clean up their tracks.

As it went on and on, he realized they were looking for something specific. "What's the matter?" he asked. "Are you missing men?"

"We're missing several that were hired for security at the camp. They are unaccounted for at this time. We are looking for a connection."

"You think they were a part of this?" He frowned, hating the sound of that but realizing it had to be checked out. "Did you question the doctors about these men?"

The men on the other side of the table shook their heads. "We're investigating it now."

"Possibly they've been kidnapped themselves." Cooper frowned. "My government needs to be informed."

The Turkish commander nodded his head. "You'll know when we know."

Then the questioning turned to the remaining personnel, the medical teams at the camp. Security had been beefed up, but that still couldn't guarantee the safety of anyone at this point. Cooper knew that. There were no guarantees in life and certainly not in war. There was a discussion on the nationalities of the volunteers at the camp.

He walked out of the room disturbed at the idea of the refugee camp having American citizens potentially involved in the kidnapping. The concept had been bantered about.

He sat down beside Sasha and tried to marshal his thoughts. He didn't want the traitors to be Americans or be seen posing as Americans. In fact, he wanted nothing by deed or rumor to taint the American name. He was proud of his country. He defended it with his life. And the thought that an American might be a traitor was more than he wanted to contemplate.

"Problems?" Sasha asked.

He shook his head then twisted so he could see her face. "Did you get to know any other Americans at the camp?"

She frowned slightly. "Good question. There were definitely a number of them. Some working as volunteers in the medical world, but there were many others as well."

"Any come to mind?"

She nodded. "The other driver. He was one. Young, carrot top, and he always had a bright smile. He was from Turkey originally, but his family moved to the US when he was twelve." She remembered, her smile widening. "He knew some people here so when they were looking for help, he signed up."

"He's a volunteer?"

"His was a paid position I think. But not much. He always made a few extra bucks giving rides in the camp. He wasn't supposed to, and he'd been told off a few times but…" She shrugged. "Commerce in a place like that happened."

"True, but that doesn't mean we have to like it or condone it."

"No, but it would be almost impossible to stop."

He nodded but stayed quiet. What could he say? Just then a soldier arrived to lead them out of the room, out of the building and toward the waiting plane.

Soon Sasha would be safe at home.

Then she could put this behind her and move on.

Now he had to find a way to stay in touch with her.

Before she got so deep back in her life, she forgot he existed.

CHAPTER 12

HOW LIFE HAD changed. And not necessarily in a good way.

What she needed was something to do. A way to move forward.

But now, seven days after returning home, she still felt paralyzed. Incapable of doing anything. She hadn't returned to her clinic – technically she had another week off. She'd told her story to so many people she was starting to hate the sound of her voice. At least Ron was alive and slowly healing, but she hadn't been allowed in to see him yet.

What did she want to do from here? She stared out the window of her mother's kitchen. It was nice to visit family now. Something she treasured after her kidnapping.

"You could just have a vacation you know?"

Sasha turned to look at her mother. "I am," she said with a smile. "I'm here with you."

"And planning to leave the minute you got here." Her mother's tone was rueful. "You can't seem to settle down."

Sasha winced. "I know, I'm sorry. I'm still not sleeping at night and although I've recovered physically, it doesn't feel like I've made any great strides emotionally."

"Do you have to go back to the base?"

Sasha nodded. "I still have to do one more QA session

and have a mental health checkup then I should be done with it all." She also wanted to go back to the base — maybe she could reconnect with Cooper. She hadn't seen him since she'd gotten home. It never occurred to her that she wouldn't. Why hadn't he called?

"I don't think you'll ever be done with it," her mother said. The words were delivered in an even tone, but there was something odd tucked inside. Sasha had heard something similar from her earlier but now wondered if what she was hearing was correct.

"I'm fine, Mom."

Her mother lifted her head from the pattern on the table and studied her features carefully. "Are you?" she asked. "I don't want to say the wrong thing and send you off to the other end of the world again, but you've been off since..." Her voice faltered.

"Since Greg?" She groaned. "I know. But can anyone go through that experience and not be affected?" She lifted her shoulders. "I think that's partly why I'm having trouble settling now. Last homecoming. It had been to find Greg and Maureen together."

"And now without a husband to come home to and no longer having the same best friend who you did everything with, trying to fill your days..."

"And nights..." Sasha filled in wryly. "Yeah, it's like my life is empty."

"And yet it's not."

"No, it's not, but it feels like a void has been created and I have done nothing to fill it."

"And do you still feel like someone is watching you?" her mother asked abruptly, her worried gaze studying Sasha.

"I forgot I said that to you." Sasha smiled at her mother and lied easily. "It was only in the first day or so. I think it was the fear that I'd be kidnapped again."

"With good reason." Her mother took a deep breath and words poured out. "I know you feel you need to help others and that's very admirable, but could you please stay on US soil? I don't think I could handle it if you went overseas again." Tears shone in the corner of her mother's eyes.

Sasha reached out to hold her mother's hands. "I'm so sorry. It was never you I was trying to get away from."

"I know, sweetheart, but as a mother we want to heal all our children's hurts. And when we can't, we sit by and watch helplessly as you make decisions that have a huge impact on us too."

While she was trying to figure out how to answer her mother, a text came in. She read it and frowned. "Theresa wants to move the meeting off base. She's still having a hard time and doesn't like the military aspect of the location."

Her mother frowned. "That makes no sense. It's not like you were kidnapped from the base or by the military. You were rescued by SEALs so that should make her feel better?"

There often wasn't much in the way of rhyme or reason for feelings. Sometimes one had to just go with their gut. "I'm okay with it either way," she said. She quickly texted Theresa back. After several more rounds of messages, they set it up for noon the next day.

"Good," she said, putting her phone away. "That's done. It should be the last step then I can forget about this mess too."

"Is the media calling you?"

"All the time," Sasha said cheerfully. "And I'm ignoring them all."

"Greg called while you were overseas, did I tell you

that?" she asked abruptly.

"No you didn't," Sasha said. Outside of an inner disquiet she was happy to note that the news didn't cause her any distress. Greg was over and done with. She didn't want anything more to do with him.

"And he called the day after you returned," her mother added quietly.

Sasha took a deep breath. Typical that her mother hadn't told her right away. Always waiting for the right time to slip those little zingers in. Then again, until Sasha had a new partner, her mother would consider the old one better than none. Unlike Sasha. Greg was no longer a part of her life and never would be again. "Odd, I wonder why?"

"He wanted to see you," her mother said. "He was really distraught to hear about the kidnapping."

"I wasn't impressed myself," Sasha said with a smile. "Just glad it's over with. If he calls again, just tell him I'm fine."

"Tell him yourself," Mom said. "You need to face him."

"Maybe, but I don't have to do it while I'm facing other stuff," Sasha said firmly but gently. "He had lots of time to see me before I left."

"Did he or did you push him off every time?"

"What would you have me do, Mom? Forgive him?"

"That would be a start. You loved him deeply."

"I did." Sasha stared at her hands, surprised to find that the phone was back out of her pocket and being turned over and over again in her fingers. "That was before he betrayed my trust."

"We all make mistakes."

Sasha smiled. "Forgetting your homework on the desk is a mistake. Calling a friend a bitch when you're upset with her is a mistake. What he did was make a decision."

COOPER WALKED THE fitness room, swinging his arms back and forth to loosen them up. Since returning from Turkey he'd been keyed up. As if waiting for the other shoe to drop, which was stupid. He was always going out on missions and never had this feeling. He didn't know what was wrong this time, but the more he looked at Dr. Sasha's kidnapping he had to wonder what the terrorists planned to do with her and her colleagues? Kill them as an example to the rest of the world? Sell them to the highest bidder? Or use their skills for their own people?

And why this group. There were a lot of volunteers at the refugee camp. Interesting that they kidnapped only the US medical staff. Maybe they thought by taking out key personnel their actions would have more impact.

His movements slowed as his mind twisted and turned on the problem.

"Now what's on your mind," Evan asked as he adjusted the weight on the barbell he was working with. "You look like you're trying to solve the problems of the world."

"Why only medical personnel?"

Markus sat up as he recovered from doing his crunches and said, "Good question."

"Maybe that was random chance, and they were just taken because they were American?" Evan said as he turned to look at Cooper. "Although to randomly grab four doctors seems not random at all."

He studied his two friends. "And they were snatched from different parts of the camp…"

"Wait, how do you know that?" Markus hopped to

his feet and grabbed his towel to wipe his face.

"Sasha... Dr. Childs said she'd been working in the one area but on the opposite side of where David and Theresa had been working. They did have a schedule at the clinic but her day was shot to shit as she was basically kidnapped and forced to go see a young pregnant woman who was too scared to go to the clinic."

Markus frowned as Levi, who'd been pumping iron on the far side, walked closer. "Yalta?" Markus asked.

"Yes," Cooper answered. "Jamel obviously had something to do with it. But why these four?"

"I heard your question." Levi wiped his face with the towel in his hands then threw it around his neck. "The only reason to steal medical personnel is if you need their skills. If they just wanted to make an example of these people, any American volunteers would do."

"Or because you want the refugee camp to suffer as well," Markus suggested.

"Which if they'd taken *all* the personnel it would have, but they only took, what, a third of them?" Cooper stood with his hands on his hips. "But losing that many doctors was obviously hard on those left behind, and how hard would it be to attract more if they can't keep the ones they have safe?"

"None of this answers the question as to why these medical personnel were snatched versus others."

"Someone knew who they were, where they'd be working and determined they'd be the easiest to grab," Levi said. "Jamel was paid to keep his clients informed of the doctors' whereabouts, but they did the choosing. In order to choose, they had to know what the choices were. That Jamel couldn't help with."

In a grim voice, Cooper said, "So in other words, someone knew who was at the camp – and he chose the ones he wanted."

CHAPTER 13

THE NEXT DAY was bright and sunny. Then she lived in California where it was either sunny or sunny smog. Today there were blue skies and that was a blessing. It also did a lot to lighten her mood. Her mother's words about Greg calling had drifted into her dreams making her toss and turn all night. She'd woken in a sweat.

Stupid. She pulled into the coffee shop that had a back room to rent for meetings and parked. This location was much nicer than the base where she'd be looking over her shoulder, afraid Greg had somehow found her. It's not that she was afraid of him but neither did that mean she was looking forward to seeing him again.

And the last thing she wanted was a confrontation.

She locked her car and walked into the front of the restaurant. A hostess greeted her.

"I'm having a meeting here today. Not sure if the back room is booked or not."

The hostess said, "I'll go check." And she hurried away.

Sasha surveyed the patrons wondering if Theresa was sitting at a table waiting for her. She hadn't recognized any military vehicles outside. Then again, they should be only meeting one person after all the rounds she'd done so far. She was surprised she needed to see anyone anymore. Surely she'd answered every damn question imaginable already.

The hostess returned. "The back room hasn't been booked yet, do you want to do it now?"

She waffled. "I'm not sure what plans Theresa has made already. Maybe just give me a table for four and we'll make that decision when the others arrive."

"Sure. Follow me." The hostess led the way to a table by the window.

"This is perfect. I can watch for the others this way. Thanks."

"Can I bring you a coffee while you wait?"

"Thank you, that would be lovely." The waitress hurried off, leaving Sasha studying the other patrons. Theresa should be here soon. She pulled out her phone and checked for a text. Nothing.

The coffee came immediately. She sipped it while she waited. The time passed slowly but she was in no rush. She'd known the appointment would take an hour or so. It would be nice to see Theresa again too. She hadn't gotten to know her well at the refugee camp, but they'd naturally gravitated toward each other over there. Although Theresa wasn't the easiest person to get along with. Then neither was Sasha at that point in her life.

She drank her cup of coffee and waited.

Theresa never showed.

Neither did the interviewer. An hour later, after several texts having been sent and none returned, she got up and paid for her coffee. She stood outside and studied the parking lot. What had happened to Theresa? She walked to the back of the lot, but it didn't offer any clues. Feeling like she'd mistaken the time or date, even though she'd read the texts several times, she walked to her car.

Once again in an odd mood, she drove slowly back to her house. Empty and alone, she wandered through the main floor wondering what could have happened. If only

Theresa hadn't shown up then Sasha would have assumed she'd forgotten or had something delay her. But for both to not show meant it was likely her mistake. Surely that had been the correct place? But again she'd checked the texts. Feeling like an idiot and sorry as now she'd have to finish the interview on the base, she walked into the kitchen to make herself some lunch.

She should have just eaten at the restaurant. She hadn't been hungry then and still wasn't, but it gave her something to do while her mind stressed over the missed meeting.

Opening the fridge, she pulled out the fixings for a sandwich. She grabbed a board and reached for the knife in the butcher block.

To find it missing.

Her heart stalled.

She snagged up her keys, purse, and phone and bolted outside to her car. She hopped in and hit the locks. Then she turned on the engine and backed out of her driveway without even thinking about it.

She never questioned her intuition. Her mind said, *Run*. She ran. Once out of the driveway, she turned the car around so she was on the far side several houses down where she could look at her house.

Inside she could hardly breathe. Her fingers shook on the steering wheel. She gasped for breath and desperately tried to calm down. What the hell was going on? She felt like she'd fallen down a rabbit hole.

She stared at her house and had to question what she'd seen. Then there was her over-the-top reaction to a missing knife. She'd only been home a week so knew it was likely a PTSD response, but that didn't explain the instant warning to run.

Images of the terrorists shooting their driver, the ensuing panic – Ron. She rolled down her window, took large gulps of fresh air.

Who could she even call? Not the police – not when the knife was likely in the dishwasher. Oh God. What if that's all it was? But there was no way she was going inside to check.

Cooper? Could she call him?

Maybe.

He might think she'd overreacted. Then again, did she give a damn?

Hell yes, she did. She liked him. A lot. He was a good man. She'd seen inside him a year ago in more ways than one. Seen his insecurities. His worries that he'd never regain his full strength. Never be able to return to the work he loved.

He'd worked his heart out to get back into the best shape he could. He'd called her after passing his physical and being back on active duty. He'd been so damn happy.

She smiled. And stared down at the phone in her hand.

To call him would be to ruin that. He'd see her as she really was. Someone who wasn't perfect or anywhere near as wonderful as he'd made her out to be.

And although that might hurt and be a demoralizing scenario it was nothing to the cost of her life.

Was she sure her butcher knife had been in that block? Why hadn't she checked the dishwasher?

Because it never went in there.

It wasn't supposed to go in because of the wooden handle.

That didn't mean she hadn't done it without thinking. She wasn't herself these days. She knew that. She was running on no sleep and her nerves were strung out. She'd avoided self-medicating herself but was one small step away from sleeping pills. She had to get some rest. But when she closed her eyes and slept, nameless faceless thugs threw hoods over her face and carted her away.

Everything in her world stemmed from that experience.

She opened her phone and called the receptionist at her office – the one she had yet to return too. They knew she was back, but not more than that.

"Cherry, this is Dr. Sasha. Can you look up a patient's record for me? I'm looking for the contact information for Cooper Braxton."

Her receptionist squealed. "Oh my gosh. It's you. Are you okay? We heard about you being taken hostage."

"I'm fine," she reassured the young woman who'd worked at the clinic longer than Sasha had. "I'll be in next week, but in the meantime if you could get me that information…"

"Oh, I'm sorry. Hang on…" Cherry bubbled away with the news as she searched for the information. "Sandra is pregnant and due in three months, Chelsea is engaged, and I have a new boyfriend," she spouted out randomly. "It's been an exciting couple of months for all of us."

"Yes, very exciting." Sasha missed the office staff. They were all generous, outgoing people. And had yet to step inside the building to let them know she was fine – because they'd ask questions she didn't want to answer.

"Okay, I have the information."

"Email it to me, please," Sasha said. "Sorry I don't have time to talk, I'm in a hurry." And she didn't want to chit chat about her adventures.

She hung up.

It took less than a minute for her phone to beep with the incoming message. "Thank God." She opened the message and clicked on the phone number inside.

It started to ring. And ring.

Shit. She stared at it, frozen.

His answering machine kicked in.

She made a strangled sound and hit cancel.

And breathed deep.

She was overreacting.

Just a stress induced panic attack.

She should go inside and forget this foolishness. She actually got as far as opening her car door, but the thought of going inside her house made her stomach heave.

Crap.

She collapsed back inside the car, tears starting to burn in the corner of her eyes.

Her phone rang.

She stared down at it.

It was Cooper.

Shit. Shit. *Shit.*

COOPER LET THE phone ring through to voicemail. He wasn't sure of the number but someone had called him. It could have been a pocket dial, but he figured in his line of work it was better to be safe than sorry. He waited for the voicemail to kick in. When it did he couldn't believe what he was hearing. That muffled exclamation had to be Dr. Sasha's voice. He was sure of it. Dr. Sasha had called him. Hope tempered with reality as he immediately called her back. "Sasha? I see you called, but I missed it. Call me back please." He left it at that. Terse but friendly. Concerned but not worried.

At least he thought so. But her voice had been

strange…

"New girlfriend," Markus teased.

Cooper studied his phone, wishing he'd managed to reach her. "I wish but this one is a little out of my league."

"Oh, who is it," Markus said with a frown. "Don't think of yourself that way. You are second to nobody."

"It's Dr. Sasha."

"Did you say Dr. Sasha called?" Levi asked.

Evan joined them then. And Cooper realized there wasn't going to be anything private at this point. He explained.

"She's a hell of a doctor," Levi said in a respectful tone. "She's helped a lot of men here."

"I heard that," Markus said. "I haven't had to see her professionally thankfully."

"You have her number, do you?" Levi asked, a quirky grin on his face. "Are you into sharing?"

"Hell, no." Cooper's response was instant and heartfelt. The other two laughed.

"Besides," he said. "You two aren't looking for permanent and the doc, well she's no one's plaything."

"No, she isn't. The doc is good people," Markus said quietly. He slapped Cooper on the back. "But if you ever change your mind… Or if it doesn't work out for you…" And he took the closest exit. "I'll see you two tomorrow."

Levi nodded at the direction he went. "Markus is good people too. He needs someone in his life again."

That's when Cooper remembered Markus's first wife died in a diving accident. She'd gone to Hawaii to scuba dive with her sister and had drowned on their second dive. He winced. "Yeah, he does. He's come a long way." Markus had been so dark and morose before but had apparently found some measure of peace.

"We'll need to see if we can hook him up," Cooper

said speculatively.

"Ha, he's only interested if you've got some of The Keepers type of magic. He's looking for what Mason and Swede have."

"Aren't we all?" Cooper shook his head. "And it's not just those two, it's all five of them. I'm starting to feel like there's something wrong with me, and I'll never get the same chance."

Evan snorted. "I saw her cling to you." He tapped the cellphone in Cooper's hands. "This is your chance." And he walked away too.

Levi nodded. "Don't mess it up or else a few of us will step up and try our hand."

Evan was single. Levi was divorced. Same as Sasha. Cooper had avoided that pain by avoiding getting married. The trauma hurt. At least that's what he told himself. In truth he hadn't met anyone he wanted to go that distance with. Cooper had had several long-term relationships, but that was before he joined the SEALs and way before his injury.

He was staring at his friends when his phone rang in his hand.

Dr. Sasha.

"Sasha?" he asked. "Are you okay?"

"No," she whispered. "I'm afraid not."

CHAPTER 14

S HE SHOULDN'T HAVE called him back. She knew that but she hadn't been able to resist. He'd been good to her so far. Then she hadn't asked anything of him personally.

"I..." and she fell silent. "Damn it. I shouldn't have called you."

"I'm glad you did," he rushed to say, his voice just concerned enough but not over the top. "Is something wrong?"

She could see his frown in her mind. Hear the worry in his voice. "Maybe."

"Maybe?" His tone rose. "What do you mean maybe?"

She took a shaky breath, trying to calm down the panic and fear inside. "I might be just overreacting."

"Overreacting to what?" Still sharp but now there was a direct business manner to it. That dependable can handle anything attitude. And it helped to stabilize the roller coaster of emotions roiling inside her.

"Okay, first off..." She took a deep breath and said, "Maybe this is all unrelated and maybe not. Let me explain." She started and once she didn't hear any sense of disbelief coming through the phone, she explained about feeling like she was being followed, then the restaurant meeting today and going home to the house and making her sandwich. When she finally wound down, she could feel the weight slide off her shoulders.

"I'm making too much of this, aren't I?" Lord, she was such a fool.

"I'm not saying that," he said cautiously. "Have you contacted Theresa since leaving the restaurant? Have you heard from her?"

"No. Not at all. I only have her cell number but she hasn't answered."

"And who were you meeting from the base?"

"I don't know his name. She just wanted my permission to rearrange the meeting so I agreed. She texted me the new arrangements, and I showed up there as planned."

"But neither of the other two people showed," he asked in surprise.

"Not that I could see. And I waited for an hour."

"And it was the right time?"

"Yes," she said tiredly, rubbing her temple as she slumped down in the car. "I checked and double checked. The right place at the right time."

"Then she's the one we need to check on first."

"Fine, but I'm not going back into my house. I'll go find a hotel or something for the night. I can't force myself to step back inside."

"Don't go anywhere close to your house," he snapped. "I'm in my vehicle. I'll be out your way in a few minutes. Stay in the car."

She stared down at her dead phone. "Wait. You don't know where I live."

But of course he didn't answer. He was already driving.

She groaned, leaning her head against the headrest. As a precaution, she hit the lock on her doors, hearing the reassuringly click as all four doors locked. She was reduced to being a prisoner in her own car.

Not a good sign.

Given that she had no idea where he was in relation to her, but it was heading into rush hour traffic, she figured she had at least a twenty-minute wait. She opened her phone and tried Theresa again. No answer. She left a message again.

A vehicle drove slowly past her on the street. The man driving looked at her house and the car slowed yet again. She studied the vehicle, but she didn't know it. Or the driver. The driver stuck his head out of the window and twisted to look behind him. His gaze caught sight of her in the car.

She slunk lower. Instantly he withdrew inside and gunned the car.

And raced away.

Shaking, she stayed low and wrapped her arms around her chest. Jesus, what the hell was going on?

When a Jeep drove past and slowed, she pushed herself up again and watched as Cooper parked in her driveway and got out. He took a quick look around, caught sight of her and motioned with his hand for her to stay there. And he disappeared around the back of her house. Leaving her to wait.

COOPER WALKED STRAIGHT to the back of the house, his gaze intent on the window fastenings, the door lock. Neither appeared to have been tampered with on this side. Didn't mean an intruder didn't break in on a different side. At the kitchen door, he paused. The door was ajar. Not by much, and it could have easily been from Sasha's quick exit from the house. He applauded her common sense and intuition.

Even if this was a false alarm, it was better than finding her dead.

He nudged the door open and stepped inside. There were no footprints or other obvious signs of an intruder. And the knife she'd mentioned was missing from the butcher block.

But had she misplaced it?

Or had someone picked it up. He searched the downstairs, but there was no signs of forced entry. And the silence in the place was deafening. The house had an unlived look to it. Then she'd been gone for three months leaving it empty. Possibly it had been broken into during that time and her knife stolen then. Although a thief wouldn't likely take the one knife from a set. Not if they were looking to pawn items.

His gaze landed on the new television. If there'd been a thief, they'd have taken the television. As they hadn't, then a break in wasn't the likely answer. The downstairs appeared to be empty and undisturbed.

He looked out the living room window to see Sasha outside in the car watching the house, her face creased with worry.

She'd been through a hell of an ordeal already. She appeared to be handling it – until today.

Then incidences piled up and pushed her to react in fear. Maybe justified. Maybe not.

He wished she'd called earlier when she first thought she was being followed. He understood. He'd been weeks looking over his shoulder after getting shot. It was something only another survivor would understand.

He'd been there and done that.

He was sorry she was here now.

Upstairs in the small two-story house he checked out

the second bedroom first, but it was completely empty. He opened the closets anyway. Empty.

The bathroom was the same.

In the main bedroom he stopped, his breath caught in the back of his throat.

The bedding on the double bed had been shredded. By a large knife. And it was still on the center of the bed. Beside the knife was a picture of Sasha and her ex-husband Greg. The picture had been cut in half too.

Shit. Thank God Sasha had raced out of the house.

He checked that the bedroom was empty, his mind consumed with "what if" scenarios. He gave the rest of the room a cursory look to make sure it was empty. Then checked out the bathroom. On the way downstairs, he started the first of several calls. The police would have to be called in now. What if Sasha had gone upstairs? Would she have found the intruder?

He moved through the downstairs thinking about the minimal damage. Someone had been intent on scaring her – not hurting her.

Yet.

He took several deep breaths to try and still the anger coursing through him then carefully walked outside to her car.

She lowered her window. "Well?" she demanded. "I didn't see anyone leave."

"No, there's no one in there."

"Oh thank you!" she cried. "I was so worried when you didn't come back out." She smiled up at him, relief wreathing her face.

"And you should be," he said in low tones. "Because someone was in the house earlier."

She stared at him, then swallowed hard. "How do you know?" She clutched his hand. "Did you see them?"

He shook his head. "No, but they were in your bed-room. The missing knife was used to cut up the bedding."

Her jaw dropped. "What? That's just…" She shrugged. "Why? It makes no sense."

"On top of the bedding, with the knife was a picture of you with your ex-husband. And the picture had been cut in half."

She slumped into her seat. In a shaken whisper, she said, "I don't understand."

"It's a message," he said carefully. "Are you sure you have split completely with your husband? It's like some-one is telling you it's over."

"I know it's over." She stared at him earnestly. "I ha-ven't seen him since I got back. And he certainly wasn't anyone I saw in the months before I left."

She frowned. "But he did call my mother and ask her how he could reach me and told her how thankful he was that I'd survived the kidnapping."

"That's normal, if it was an amicable split." He'd have done the same, maybe in a slightly different way, but if he'd been married and found out his ex had been through a traumatic ordeal he'd have called too. Not everyone hated their ex-partners.

"And you have no intention of going back to him?" he asked slowly, trying to read her facial expression.

She took a deep breath. "It wasn't completely amica-ble," she said in a low tone.

And he saw the pain, the anger. And the pride as she lifted her head and tossed her hair back. "No, I won't be going back."

"I hate to ask…" He winced. He really did hate to ask her for the details. Still the police would ask and pry and dig for more answers.

"I found him in bed with my best friend," she said,

staring straight ahead, her voice carefully devoid of any emotion. "I haven't seen her since and my ex only when I couldn't avoid it."

Shit. As reasons went that was a good one. "I'm sorry."

"Thanks, but I'm not the only one to find a good marriage was only a pipe dream," she said bitterly. "Unfortunately I was blind to what was going on behind my back. I'm a workaholic, and he needed more than I could give him. At least that's what he said."

Cooper snorted. "He's a child, not a man."

She snickered. "Yeah, he screamed like a two-year-old afterwards as well."

"Why is that?"

"My income is several times his. He thought he should get a portion of it, but the judge didn't agree."

"I should think not." Cooper frowned. "Do you think he's holding a grudge?"

Startled, she looked from him to her house then back to him. "I wouldn't think so. He was pissed at the time, but I figured it was Maureen who was the angrier."

"Your girlfriend?"

"Yeah, she has an expensive lifestyle."

"And she'd have been happier if he'd made out better?" he asked slowly, considering if a woman could be responsible for what he'd seen. And realized it had all the earmarks of a pissed off woman. Or someone tried to make it look that way.

Sasha shrugged. "Sure. I married for life. Not until someone better came along."

"Right." He really liked that statement. "The police are on their way."

"Damn." She studied the house. "I'll go to my mother's house for the night."

He shook his head. "I wouldn't do that. You don't want to bring her in to this." He motioned to the house behind him. "If they know you well enough to attack you in your space here, you don't want them to think the next step is to go to your mother's house to get to you."

Her face blanched. A police cruiser drove down the street toward them. Her fingers trembled on the steering wheel. She dropped them to her lap and clenched them tightly.

When the cruiser stopped and parked on the driveway of Sasha's house, Cooper gave her an admonishment to stay in the vehicle and he went over to talk to them.

CHAPTER 15

I T WAS HOURS before the cops left.

They'd brought in a crew to take pictures and dust for fingerprints. There'd been many conversations about the events overseas as the police looked for a connection. Cooper had answered most of the questions for her.

She didn't know what all they were doing now. She tried to keep out of it and was currently on her kitchen chair hugging a cup of coffee that Cooper had made for her. She had enough on her mind. She had to find a place to stay for the night, a few days maybe. She wasn't staying here. She would also have to get the locks changed, but all she could think about was moving. She'd originally wanted to buy a house after the divorce but had been too unsettled and the prices were so crazy she didn't want to make a snap decision.

Good thing she held off.

Now all she could think about was getting the hell away. If she owned the property, it would take much longer to get out.

She also wanted to move quietly so the intruder wouldn't know. And that was foolish. He had likely been watching the house since the beginning and would be expecting exactly that. He'd just follow her to the next house.

The cops had asked her so many questions, and after all the questioning she'd been through already, she'd quickly slipped into monotone answers to get through the process as quickly as possible.

"We'll need your contact information."

She pulled out her cellphone and gave him her number. While in Turkey, her phone had been in the safe most of the time. Now she wondered if it was part of the problem. But to think someone had gone through her phone and tracked her to her home was over the top. Yet this wasn't a random attack. Restless, she wanted to pack up a bag and leave…and run a long way away. Last time she'd left the country. And look at how well that had worked. She really needed a safe place to hole up and think.

She had lots of decisions to make, and no idea how to make them. First things first… "Can I go into my room and pack a bag?"

"Yes, I'll take you up."

She nodded and walked upstairs to her bedroom. Her mind busied, cataloging what she needed to pack. That made it easier when she arrived in her bedroom. She took one look at the bed and blanched. Then turned and hurried to the closet and pulled out her single bag. She quickly packed the bulk of her clothes before collecting the toiletries from the bathroom. As she stuffed what little she had, she realized how meager her personal possessions were. She'd done a major clean out of her belongings when she left her husband. That left her very little to move to this house. Being unsettled and needing a change, she'd avoided buying much after setting up on her own and then she'd gone overseas. Her clothing requirements, although more now than in the refugee camp, weren't extensive. She cast one long look at the bedroom she knew she'd never sleep in again and picked up her bag and walked downstairs.

"I'm leaving now," she said to the last officer standing at the door. "You have my cell number. Please keep me updated. Otherwise I'll become a nuisance asking you for updates."

He nodded. "Will do. Stay safe please."

She nodded. "I'll try."

"She'll be safe," Cooper said, appearing at her side, a protective arm around her shoulders. She smiled up at him.

"I really appreciate that you came when I called."

He laughed and reached out to pick up her hand and tucked it under his arm. "Good. I'm glad to hear that because I have a place where you can be safe. Come to my place," he urged. "I have a spare bedroom, and the guys and I will keep an eye on you."

She froze. Then shook her head. "Oh no. I don't want to live on base again."

He frowned that all too perceptive gaze, seeing more than she wanted. "Then come for the night so you have a place for now, and then we'll come up with a better plan."

She stared at him suspiciously. Then shook her head again. "Thank you but no. It's better that I go to a hotel for the next couple of days. I need time to think."

He stared at her, his gaze gentle. "You might need time to think, but no one said you had to do it alone."

He knew.

She stared into his dark eyes and realized he under-stood. He knew she didn't want to be alone. That the idea, in fact, terrified her. She wavered between feeling like she had to stand on her feet and wanting desperately to throw her arms around his neck and hug him close. Dear God, she didn't want to be alone tonight. She wasn't sure she could do it tomorrow either, but after a good night's sleep things would look better.

They had to. They looked like shit from here.

COOPER WANTED TO leave her car at her house and take her home in his, but she was clutching to her bit of independence with a fierce intensity he knew had more to do with the need to be able to flee then the need to stand on her own two feet.

He had seen her off and on in the months he'd been healing. The woman before him wasn't the same one.

She was different now. Harder. Leaner. Wary.

Before she was all smiles and laughter.

But she'd been through a betrayal, an ugly divorce, then kidnapped and terrorized, and watched her friend get shot. And now she was under attack again – this time it was personal.

She might be putting on a brave face for the rest of the world, but he'd seen underneath.

He led her out to her car then handed her a small piece of paper with his address on it. "Do you know this street?"

She studied the address then nodded. "I do."

"Good. Then follow me there and we'll get you set up for the night."

"I can go to a hotel."

"No," he said. "With me tonight. We'll talk tomor-row."

She gave a shuddering breath and gave him a dipped nod.

He waited until she was buckled into her car and the engine on, doors locked, then he returned to his Jeep. Careful to keep her in his rear sight, he drove to his small bungalow, keeping an eye out in case they were being followed, but discerned nothing. Just to be on the safe side, he had her park outside a set of apartments at the end of the block and walked her back to his small house.

"You're taking precautions," she said, her gaze searching his. "Are you expecting trouble?"

"No, I'm not expecting it, but I don't want to be unprepared just in case."

Inside the house he showed her to her bedroom and then walked back out to the kitchen. As he put on coffee his cellphone rang. Markus.

"Anything?" he asked his friend.

"Not much available. The divorce was not contested. They had a prenup in place, Greg comes from a wealthy family who have since lost more than half of their net worth. She came from middle class but of course does well now. She was in school when they first met and married."

"Did he put her through school?"

"No. Doc is gifted and was granted scholarships the whole way."

"So she has no debts and doing well. Good for her."

"And that's where the problem comes in. He wanted her to pay him for having been there while she'd been going through school. Something about wanting a payment for his support against her future earnings. As in if they'd stayed married then he'd be expecting a higher quality of living."

Cooper snorted at that.

"The judge said that if he'd kept his pecker in his pants then his complaints might have more grounds. As it was the assets since the marriage began were split as evenly as possible. She got her car. He got his Jeep. There was minimal cash but that was split as well."

"All common in today's world."

"Exactly. Greg also broke off with his girlfriend a few

months back."

"So he's reassessing his position and might want to try his hand with his ex-wife." Cooper snorted. He doubted Sasha knew. Typical. "Where did you get this by the way?"

"A combination of public documents and gossip. He's navy. Nothing is secret here."

"So true." He tried to keep his voice normal, but his tone ended up cool, detached. Maybe Markus would let it pass.

"Cooper…" Markus hesitated. "What's up?"

Damn. Of course he'd notice.

Cooper hated to bring it up. Markus had lost his wife and they'd been terribly in love. He'd been devastated. That hit had taken him years to get over and said much about the relationship.

Cooper rubbed the back of his neck. "I just wondered, is this really the state of today's marriages?"

"Not all of them but too many, yes," Markus said. "You never got married?"

"No, I haven't found anyone to go the distance. And I have no intention of getting married until I find one who will," he said. "It's not that I don't believe divorce is the best or in some cases, the only answer, but I don't want it to be *my* answer."

The passion in his voice was hard for him to not hear himself. "I want to know she will be there for me, capable of handling the times I'm away, and not complain if I work too hard, that she'll be there when I come back." He sighed. "Sorry, didn't mean that to come across so vehemently."

"Understood. With so many of your friends finding partners the issue becomes a hot button."

"In many ways." Cooper groaned. "My brother has

been divorced twice already, and he's paying child support for four kids. Now, he's looking at doing it a third time."

"It's more common than you'd think," Markus, said. "Unfortunately."

"I know and if he's happy then good for him, but I want something different for myself."

"I do too, but I have to admit to being concerned that having found love and lost it that there won't be a second time around for me." His smile came through the phone as he added, "But having known the joy once, I am definitely willing to try again."

"There will be."

The phone call ended soon afterward. As the coffee dripped beside him, Cooper stared out the window.

"Problems?"

He smiled and turned to face Sasha, giving her an improvised version of the conversation. "No, just one of those philosophical issues. Markus lost his wife in a diving accident, and he's concerned that was his only chance at a perfect love."

Sasha nodded and walked to the coffee pot. She filled the cups he'd set out. Cooper hadn't even realized the coffee was ready.

"I've seen a lot of that. The shock and the fear after a traumatic loss. It's always difficult to move on."

"Do you agree with it?" he asked curiously.

"Agree that there is only one love per person?" She shook her head. "No, not at all. I think we have multiple chances at love. We also change and grow and what we wanted at sixteen is very different than at sixty. And the type of love or even our definition of what love is changes with time and experience."

"So we can all have someone…"

"I've seen proof of that over and over again." She

smiled at him. "I might deal in the medical world and see death on a regular basis, but that doesn't mean I don't see the good side of it as well." She stared down at her cup. "People are resilient and the human spirit even more so. Given the right conditions we can all be crushed and the opposite is also true. We can all thrive."

"Sounds like you've thought about it a lot."

She laughed and walked through to his small living room. "I was always one to question the universe growing up. Medical school showed me we have so few answers, that all possibilities must be examined to find the right solution. Divorce taught me…" Shadows came into her eyes. "…that two people can have very different perceptions of the situation."

"I'm sorry for that. I don't know your husband."

"Good," she said. "One of the hardest things about a divorce is the friendships, and the splits that happen as a result of it."

He nodded, having been a friend to various halves of relationships. "It's hard on the friendships as well," he said. "We visit both people. I have several divorced friends. We often did barbecues at each other's houses, yet suddenly, we're placed on a side." He shrugged. "I've really liked several wives that put me on the husband's side. It's a rejection of us too. And it's painful to watch friends split. Sometimes it's easier to back away."

"I found that as well. Greg was Navy with navy buddies. It seemed like everyone was uncomfortable around me so I'm the one who backed off."

"And maybe they were uncomfortable because their friend had done wrong, and that's something they had trouble with."

She tilted her head to the side. "It's possible. Several didn't believe it, or not at first. I'm not sure when the details came out as I left." She sighed. "If the details came out."

"No regrets about leaving?"

She shook her head. "None. It's over."

"He's broken up with his girlfriend." He hadn't meant to let her know. Still he found himself watching her face intently.

She laughed. "Okay, now that explains why he contacted my mother. I didn't see why he'd give a shit if he was still with her."

"You don't think he'd care about you getting kidnapped?"

"Maybe. We were together for years so you'd hope he cared enough to be concerned. But if he's broken up with Maureen then he's looking for a replacement." She grinned up at him. "I'm not it."

"Good."

He left it at that. But he could feel her speculative gaze. And ignored it.

He'd be a fool to not be interested. And he didn't just want her…he wanted so much more.

CHAPTER 16

SASHA FILLED THEIR coffee cups as Cooper's phone rang. She carried hers out to the back deck to give him privacy. And to give herself a moment to just relax. She didn't want to consider all that had happened so far today, and if the media found out about it, her life would get even more difficult.

That was not the way she'd like her mother to hear the news. She quickly dialed her.

And got no answer. She redialed, hoping her mother was out shopping and not hiding from reporters. When there was no answer, she left a voice message with a short message to call her back.

By the time she'd done that, she picked up her empty coffee cup and wandered back into the kitchen to refill it. And found Cooper still on the phone.

She topped his coffee cup up and placed it in front of him then refilled hers. She sat down and waited, her mind consumed with her mother. If it was any other day she'd not be so worried but after everything so far, well… She dialed her again. This time her mother answered.

Jesus. Sasha calmed down and had a short conversation with her, letting her know what happened. "I'm staying at a friend's house. I'll let you know what I decide to do from here on in."

"And please call Greg," her mother cried. "I know he's been missing you. He called again this morning. He's really sorry for what he did. Please phone him. You need help. Even after everything, I know he'll look after you."

Sasha rubbed her forehead. That was not going to happen. After saying good-bye she hung up and stared down at her phone.

"Problems?"

"No new ones," she quipped. "My mother. She thinks I'm better off with a man. So she wants me to call my ex. She thinks he's a great guy whose fall from grace is forgivable. Apparently he called just after I left her house."

"Interesting timing."

"What does the timing have to do with anything?" she asked, studying the look on his face.

"If he'd done the job, he'd have known then that you were on your way home and to get out of there." He pulled out a notepad and said, "We should have the police on the case pull the phone records and see where he made the call from."

"Well, we know it was Greg calling," she countered. "My mother knows him very well."

"And loves him too?"

"Yes," she said with a shrug. "What can I say? She doesn't know all the details, and I don't want to get into it with her."

He grinned. "Hey, I can't blame you. Who wants to air the dirty laundry?"

"Not me." The last thing she wanted to do was go into detail about how her mother thought Greg was the best son-in-law ever. There was a part of her that still wasn't sure if her mother blamed her. As if she hadn't been wife enough that poor Greg had been forced to find another woman to take care of his needs. Her mother had been very happy with her father all those years so tended to look at relationships with a bright happy innocence.

But with the understanding that being a wife came with specific responsibilities to keep her man happy. Sasha didn't have the same perspective. Especially now.

"The officer you spoke with before did not request the meeting."

She stared at him, the warmth draining from her face as a rush of white ice raced in. She swallowed. "What?"

"You heard me."

She shook her head. "I heard you but I didn't quite understand. Why did Theresa tell me he did then?" She knew her voice was rising but she didn't get it. "Why would she do that?"

Cooper reached across and covered her hand with his. "I don't know," he said in a careful calm tone. "But we will find out."

She stared into his gaze, trying to find a secure footing in the rocky foundation. "I wonder if she wanted to talk but thought I wouldn't take the time unless there was a reason?"

"We also have to consider that it wasn't Theresa contacting you to change the meeting."

She frowned and glanced at her cellphone. "We have to find her."

Cooper nodded. "The police are looking." He stroked the skin on the back of her hand. She swallowed hard as she thought about all the things that could go wrong with someone like Theresa. The events that had already taken place.

"I hate to think of her in trouble," she confessed. "We've already gone through so much."

"And she might be just fine," he said quietly. "What do you know about her?"

"She flew over with me and we sat together. I got to know her a little, not that she was very forthcoming," she said candidly. She studied the kitchen table thinking of all the conversations she'd shared with Theresa.

"Theresa was always depressed, despondent," Sasha said abruptly. "She worked hard, but the conditions were difficult for her. The pain and the suffering. The sheer hopelessness of the numbers just added to it. There might have been something going on in her personal life too, but I avoided those conversations because of my own situation."

"Was she ever suicidal?"

Sasha frowned. "I don't think so. We were friends but life was busy. I was dealing with shit myself and when there was time that wasn't the topic of choice. I told her if she ever needed a place that she was welcome to stay with me. But we were so busy…"

"So there wasn't much time to sit about and socialize." He squeezed her hand. "I get it. But I also work with a team, several teams of men, and I do have a basic understanding of who they are inside."

"Like what?" she challenged.

"Like Mason is an honorable leader. Swede would carry me through a jungle to save my ass, Hawk is a man to call on if you need help, Shadow is…well it's hard to define that guy, but he's the one that does the worst of the jobs and never complains. Dane is brilliant and sees things others don't. Markus is all bleeding heart although he does his best to hide it, and Evan has a bitter edge but it hides a man just waiting to be called in to help. I could tell you about so many more. Levi…Chase…Brett…"

"I get the idea," she said laughing. "I could say something about everyone too, but I didn't spend much time with them. I worked, then slept and got up and worked again. I was only there three months and got thrown in the deep end from the first day. Not sure I ever had a chance to socialize, but yes, I do get an impression of everyone." She marshaled her thoughts.

"David worked hard but needed his downtime. I can see him at home doing a full day then coming home to the beer on the deck. He's social and would have a core group of good friends. It hurt Theresa to see the children suffer over there. She did her work then walked away as if that was the only way she could keep doing the job."

He nodded. "That type of work is hard on some people."

"Ron handled it just fine. And energy, man he could work. He never complained. He was always there organizing more help and fundraising for medical supplies and specialists." She smiled. "I'm seriously delighted to hear that he's going to be fine."

"Anything to add about Theresa?"

"Not really, other than I think she's very unhappy and whatever sent her to the volunteer position, it didn't help her underlying issue."

"Did it help yours?"

She smiled. "Well, I'm feeling much better these days so maybe. It also created a new set of problems. There is always that sense of guilt for wanting to leave. I have skills to offer and to not offer them caused conflict."

"We see that aspect a lot too. We're often sent to regions in need of aid, including our skills, and when the orders are given to withdraw, we withdraw."

His phone buzzed. He released her hand and checked it. "Mason says the police did check your neighbors and no one reported seeing any strangers around your house. There was a delivery vehicle in the area during the day, but no one saw him go to your house."

"So we're no further ahead."

"Any idea where Theresa might be living? Did she

mention her family, friends?"

"No." Sasha looked surprised. "I'm not even sure I asked her," she confessed. "Good Lord, I'm a terrible person."

"Except we know you're not so maybe there's a reason why you didn't."

"She wasn't a terribly fun person to be around—or maybe it was me who wasn't. Coming home was traumatic for me too." She sighed. "Outside of the meetings I had little contact with her."

COOPER STUDIED HER face. She'd had a rough time of it these last few months, but she'd held up like a trooper. "It would be helpful to know more about her friends and family."

"We'll ask Ron. Maybe you could call David and ask him, I haven't seen him since the last interview."

"He's already gone again," Cooper said. "But we can follow up."

She nodded, hugging her cup of coffee. "I need to look for a place to live."

"Are you sure? It's a fast decision."

"With a fast reason." Her jaw locked. "I don't want to go back there."

"Do you have friends or family you can go visit with for a few weeks? Make it a holiday at the same time?"

"Maybe?" But she didn't look at him. He waited. She sighed. "I'd have to deal with Greg then. And my mother."

He grinned. "Gotta love family."

She pursed her lips, then her gaze lit up. "I have a friend who is traveling right now. I might be able to contact her about staying at her place."

"And the invitation is open to stay here."

He could see her open her mouth to refuse then she closed it and nodded. "Thanks. I'll see what I can make for arrangements."

"What are you going to do today?"

"It's a Sunday, right?"

He nodded.

"Do you work today?"

He shook his head. "No."

Her phone rang suddenly. He watched as she opened it, checked the number and winced.

"Does it help to avoid him?"

She raised her gaze to his. Then shrugged. "No. I guess not." She slid her finger across the screen of her phone. "Hello, Greg."

She left the phone on the table so he could hear too. There was a shocked silence then Greg rushed to speak. "Sasha?"

"As you called me, I'd think so," she said in a dry voice. "What do you need?"

Not what do you want? Interesting. Cooper sat back and wondered.

"Are you all right? I heard the news. I was really concerned."

"Thank you," she said calmly. "But I'm fine. Mom told you that I was okay."

"Sure," he said, his voice infused with caring. "But that's not the same as hearing your voice."

"Right. I'm fine though, thanks."

And she raised her gaze to Cooper. "How's Maureen?"

There was a harsh gasp then Greg rushed to say, "We broke up. Months ago."

"Ah. Sorry to hear that."

"Have you heard from her?" he asked quietly. "She'd planned on contacting you."

"No, I haven't. And I won't," she said with a note of finality.

Silence.

"I'm sorry."

Cooper listened intently, and there actually seemed to be a note of regret in his voice – or he was a darn good actor. He frowned, not liking the idea he was sincere about getting back together again. Sasha didn't appear to be affected by Greg's tone though. Thankfully.

"I am too."

Cooper listened to the painful conversation and tried to be detached. Was there anything in Greg's voice that said he'd have done that to Sasha's house? At this point he wanted to talk to Maureen. He wrote her name down and texted the information to the cops. Maybe they'd be able to track her down. At this time, nothing suggested she'd have come back to vandalize Sasha's house. If the breakup had been months ago there'd be no need.

Apparently, Sasha had the same thought. "Why did you and Maureen break up?"

"She moved on," Greg snapped. "She was there one day and gone the next."

"And you've spoken to her since, or has something happened to her?" she asked in alarm.

Cooper gave the phone a hard glance.

"I spoke to her sister, and she said Maureen had taken a job on the East Coast and she had left without wanting to get into it with me."

"Oh." She relaxed back. "Then she's moved on?" She smiled up at Cooper.

Good. The last thing he wanted to do was deal with

Greg. And realized he could put a stop to it right now. He grinned. Walking over, he plucked the phone out of her hand and said, "Sorry, Greg. Have to cut this short. She's a little busy." And he closed it. Then gave her a wicked smile and dropped a kiss on her shocked lips.

"You're welcome."

And loved it when she burst into laughter.

CHAPTER 17

S HE SLEPT SOUNDLY. Enough that when the birds first started singing outside her window at five-thirty she was happy to lie there and listen. She did have decisions to make and a little peace and quiet was perfect. She'd watched a movie and had a beer with Cooper last night. Two friends thrown together by circumstances and had enjoyed herself. He was the all American male and a pleasure to be around. That he was sexy as hell and a gentleman just added to the attraction. Make that a gentleman hero.

This morning life looked brighter, and she was able to view yesterday in a different light. Obviously someone had more than a little dislike for her if they'd shredded her bedding. Maureen? Why though? She'd broken up with Greg and already moved on. Yet, it was such a female thing to do… But how would she know where Sasha lived?

Had her mother told Greg?

Hearing a door open she hopped up to look out the window and saw Cooper doing a few stretches. He was dressed for a jog.

She called down, "Want company?"

Surprised, he looked up at her, a wide grin splitting his face. "Sure," he called. "But I figured you'd be still sleeping."

"Woke with the birds. Give me two minutes."

She dressed fast, loving the idea of going for a run. She'd been an obsessive jogger during her marriage and had used it as an outlet to deal with the fallout of the divorce. The refugee camp experience had changed her schedule, but she'd still managed to get in a few. The week back in the States, she'd run every day. It filled her heart with a lightness she couldn't express.

As she barreled downstairs and out the front door, laughing at him, she called out, "Come on slow poke."

And hit the sidewalk running and never slowed.

He shouted with laughter and raced to catch up. She was gratified to see he did so easily. She knew he was in great shape, but that still didn't make him a runner.

"Where to?" she asked.

"Trails or roads."

"Trails every time."

He motioned to a side street. "Then let's go this way." And he veered off. She followed. "How long do you want to run for, so I can determined the best route?"

She frowned, pondering his question. "I'd say I'm good for five miles easily, could do seven for fun and ten in a stretch. I normally do ten twice a week but haven't since going to the refugee camp." She glanced at him. "You?"

"Same roughly. But I run daily so let's settle in the middle and pull through the seven mile mark."

"Done." She quickly settled into a rhythm, and he matched his pace to hers. She was happy to see it didn't take much adjusting. He was a powerful man and could outrun her in a heartbeat but to keep up the endurance of a long jog was a different story altogether.

The trail was a series of paths winding through green space with the ocean on her right. She'd lived in a different location altogether and knowing that she'd not likely ever see Greg here helped her relax. She shook out her tense muscles.

They kept up a light teasing conversation the whole way and the trip passed in half the time she'd been expecting. Back at his house she ran inside and called out behind her in a teasing voice, "I get the first shower."

"Ha." He called behind her. "Leave me some hot water."

"Nope, going to drain the tank…" She dashed into the bathroom stripping off her clothes as she went.

COOPER LOVED THE teasing and admired the can-do attitude. That she'd raced ahead of him said much about her energy levels too. He'd enjoyed this morning's run but it hadn't worn him out. Neither had it worn her out.

Good thing.

They had a few things to deal with today. And not the least of which was to find Theresa. He'd sent several emails out last night looking for answers to the restaurant meeting. Sasha had shown her the emails and texts from Teresa about the meeting, but there was no name or department of who she'd be meeting. And that concerned him. He was more worried that the texts might not have come from Theresa herself. If her phone had been jacked it would have been easy to send a message to Sasha under the assumption she'd recognize Theresa's name. But why?

To create an opening to go into her house? Fairly complex maneuvering to go and rip up some bedding.

Too complex.

Unless Theresa had been snatched and was in danger even now. That didn't explain the setup for the restaurant though. He checked his laptop to see if new information had come in. He'd kept the others in the loop the whole way.

If this was related to Theresa and the mess in the refugee camp then he'd get lots of help. But if it wasn't then it was a local police issue, and they'd have to wait and see.

Markus had already checked on Greg's location, confirming he was in town.

He read through the other emails and found nothing helpful.

Damn it. He checked the time. Shower, breakfast then he'd call the cops who'd been at the house and see if they'd found anything.

He sent off a quick email to Mason asking for an update on Ron's condition. Sasha wanted to see him if she could.

Then he closed the phone down and headed to his bathroom.

His turn for a shower if she'd left him any hot water. He grinned. If she hadn't he'd have to dream up a way to retaliate.

He was loving this playful side of Dr. Sasha.

CHAPTER 18

S ASHA GRABBED HER phone while she searched the refrigerator for food.

"Hello."

"Sasha?" She closed her eyes. Shit. Why hadn't she checked the number first? She didn't want to talk to him again.

"Hello, Greg." She rubbed her temple. "Oh, sorry really bad timing," she lied. "I'm on my way out."

"Wait, where are you going?"

She frowned. "None of your business. Why?"

"No reason, just curious," and that voice was back to being warm and friendly. "I was thinking we could have coffee somewhere."

She narrowed her gaze, trying to figure out what was behind the suggestion.

"I doubt it's going to work out," she said smoothly. "I have a lot on my list."

"You still need to take a break, don't you? I'd love to see you." His voice deepened. "I missed you."

"Oh, do you miss Maureen, too?"

"What I had with her was nothing like what I had with you." He took a deep breath. "I'd hoped to do this in person but if you won't give me a chance to see you…" There was an odd silence then he continued with, "Look, I was an idiot. I shouldn't have done what I did. I don't have an excuse other than to say I was lonely as you were working so much."

"So it's my fault?" She'd heard this all before. "And your excuse is still as poor as it was the first time I heard it. Obviously, you tired of our marriage and no longer cared about me."

"I do care. I don't have a good excuse. I can only tell you over and over again that I'm sorry and it won't happen again."

"Except you never said that while you were happily playing house with my best friend," she snapped. "You're only saying it now that you're alone again. I'm not interested in filling Maureen's shoes. I'm happy to be friends, but that does not include benefits."

She hit the end call on her phone. And realized Cooper was leaning against the doorframe. He'd probably heard the entire conversation.

And damn it – her fingers were trembling. "How long does it take for someone to get the message? We've been split for over a year."

"But like you said, he's lost his current partner and is alone now," Cooper said quietly.

She nodded. "His problem. Not mine." And not Cooper's. She shouldn't be dumping all this on him. She stood up. "I need to eat then I need to do something."

"As in excess energy and you need to go for another run to de-stress?"

"As in my life has been out of control for too long, and I need to grab ahold again."

"Shall we go see Ron?"

She spun, her face lighting up like a light bulb. "Yes. Can we?"

"Yes." He smiled and held up his phone. "Just got permission. He's been asking about you."

She grinned. "Now that is a man to have your back.

He's been huge for getting help for those in need."

"Then let's get something to eat and go see him."

And he was true to his word as he quickly scrambled up eggs. She made toast and within a few minutes they were sitting down and eating.

A half hour later they pulled into the naval hospital parking lot.

She shook her head. "I forgot he'd spent so many years in the service."

"And been awarded many medals."

"Is he the reason we warranted the rescue?" she asked. "I'd been holding off asking why we got such attention. Don't get me wrong, I'm so damn grateful for it, but I'm curious."

He laughed. "He's one of the reason's your plight was brought to our attention, but not the only one. We were already in Turkey doing training exercises."

"Ah, makes sense." She smiled and walked ahead of him slightly. At the reception she stood off to one side as he talked to the woman. The hospital was huge, but she'd worked here before.

"He's down this way." Cooper held out his hand. "Follow me," he said.

She laughed and reached out for his hand. "It is visiting hours, right?"

"It is," Cooper said cheerfully. "He's on the second floor."

And he led her right to Ron's room.

She stepped inside and saw him. He saw her at the same time and opened his arms. She raced into them. "Oh my. I was so afraid we'd lost you." She hugged him gently.

"I'm fine." He grinned. "Now, at least. I wasn't so sure a week ago. Figured I'd pushed my luck for the last time."

"I hated to leave you in that damn cabin…" she cried, settling back on the edge of his bed to study his face critically. But the twinkle in his eye and returning color to his skin reassured her.

"And I hated to see you go." He smiled up at her, his face crinkling with wrinkles. "But I was out of it at that point, so the timeline of events are a blur."

"It wasn't long after Sasha and the others were hustled onto the boat that you were rescued and the shack was torched," Cooper said from the side of the room. Ron's face lit up when he saw Cooper. The men shook hands.

"Thanks for the rescue." Ron sighed. "I'd wondered at the time if the driver had been a part of it."

"Really? I'd considered that someone on the inside must have known where to find us." She studied his pale face. "We weren't even all on the same side of the camp."

"I know." He coughed, his face rippling in pain. "But I can't say I'm too surprised to hear what he was up to. Terrible circumstances bring out terrible actions. Most of those people are still in survivor mode."

Cooper said, "We think someone hired the driver. It's that man we want."

She understood what he meant but that didn't mean it was an easy concept to accept.

"And does it do any good to find the person now? We are free."

"As long as it's not followed us home," Ron said quietly.

She was silent until they walked out of the naval hospital toward Cooper's Jeep. "Is there any chance it followed me…us home?"

"I can't answer that, but considering your situation, we have to look at it." Cooper opened the passenger door to the Jeep. "It's possible, but why?"

"I don't know." She shrugged. "There are doctors everywhere. There's no reason for them to want to find us now. It's not like we heard or saw anything useful. They didn't discuss bigger plans with us." She smiled at him as he got inside the driver's side and closed the door. "I really can't see it."

"Good, then that's one less thing to worry about."

She smiled. "Besides, I should be safe. I'm on the base with the big bad SEAL."

He snickered. "There are dozens of us here."

"And except for a random shooting by a naval discontent, I should be safe."

He glanced over at her. "Got to love how everyone hears about the bad shit."

"We also hear about the good shit." She grinned. "And the very good shit. Like rescuing me and mine."

"Happy it was a rescue and not a recovery."

"Where to now?" she asked.

"Sasha?"

She froze and turned in her seat.

Of course. Her ex-husband.

"Hello, Greg."

Cooper placed an arm around the seat back and her shoulder in silent support, his warm breath hot on her neck as he whispered, "Easy."

She nodded slightly in acknowledgement.

"What a surprise," Greg said with a bright smile.

"It is. Sorry I can't talk now, we're late." She glanced at Cooper. "Shall we go?"

"No wait." Greg leaned in to see her. "It's a nice surprise to see you."

Cooper wasn't going to let this asshole get any closer to Sasha. He turned on the engine and shifted the Jeep into gear.

"Bye, Greg," she called out.

As Cooper drove the vehicle through the parking lot toward the exit and away from Greg, she let out a shaky breath. "I should have spoken with him."

"Do you still care for him?"

"No." She shook her head. "There is nothing more deadly than a dead love."

"And are you sure the love is dead."

"Oh yes," she said. "I'm sure."

He fell quiet. "Then it shouldn't bother you to see him." He turned the Jeep out of the parking lot and onto the main road.

"It's not the fear of seeing him because I loved him and I'm afraid to lose him, it's the betrayal that hurts. The fear that inside I'm really as he sees me."

"And that is?"

"Not enough," she whispered. "That I'm the one to blame for everything. That I wasn't a good enough wife, a good enough woman to keep him. No one likes to see themselves in a harsh light."

"You know that's garbage, right?" His voice was harsh, his tone piercing.

"In my head I do. But my heart says I'm equally at fault for what happened. I can see he might have needed more time with me. That he couldn't handle the demands my job required of me. Still, he didn't have to do what he did."

"I'd forget about him completely if I were you." Cooper pulled the Jeep into the mainstream traffic. "He's a child in a man's body. Men don't sit there and whine. They do something about the problem."

She laughed. "How true." She watched the traffic meander through town. "Why is the traffic so light?"

"No idea but it's nice. Then again it is Sunday." He turned down a second corner and pulled into one of the large hangar looking buildings.

"Why are we here?"

"We're going to meet the rest of my team."

"Are you sure I should? I'm a mess."

"And that's why you aren't making any decisions to-day or tomorrow," he said firmly. "Too much is going on."

"And then what," she said softly. "Stay with you?"

"That's hardly an imposition," he said quietly, reaching across and holding her hand. "You're special, Doc, we all want to keep you safe."

She slowly turned her head. "Do you think I'm not safe?"

He glanced at her and shook his head. "No," he said seriously. "I don't."

Hell.

HE WAS NEVER one to deal in lies and innuendos, and given the strange circumstances surrounding her, he'd really like to keep a close eye on her. He needed to keep her safe.

"Up ahead." He pointed out a huge flock of birds rising from the sands on the left.

"Wow. That's a lot of birds," she said, studying them. "I don't remember seeing them in such a large group."

"Just another day in paradise." He grinned as he turned off the Jeep and hopped out.

He came around to her side and helped her down. "Let's go see the gang."

She smiled and walked into where a dozen men pretended to be busy doing something and yet nothing at the same time. They stopped and watched as Cooper slipped Sasha's hand into the crook of his arm and brought her over to them.

Her footsteps slowed as she studied the faces of the team. She recognized a few faces. But only a few.

She gasped when she saw Markus in front of them. She slipped her arm free and ran to him.

Cooper could only watch as she threw herself in Markus's waiting arms. He swung her around before placing her back down on her feet again.

She laughed in delight. "Looks like you ended up all right after all," she teased.

"Hey, I was never the one in trouble," Markus protested. "It was you who caused us the grief all the time."

"And you who kept scaring those poor people," she cried out, a big smile on her face. "What did they do to you?"

"Ha, they wouldn't show us where you'd gotten too fast enough," he growled but there was no heat in his voice.

Good thing or Cooper would have to step in but instead he watched her easy camaraderie as she went to the others she greeted one by one and gave each a big hug and a thank you. When she reached Swede she shook her head and held up her arms waiting like a two-year-old. He chuckled and picked her up so she could reach around his neck.

Markus murmured at his side, "If you are letting her walk through your fingers…"

"Hell, no I'm not," he snapped.

Markus held up his hands in surrender and added, "Just saying…"

"Just saying what?" Cooper dared him to continue.

And he did, but it wasn't quite the angle Cooper expected.

"I guess I'm saying that I'm feeling a whole lot better about my future after all."

"Meaning…" Cooper wasn't going to let this drop until he knew exactly how Markus felt. Especially in regards to Sasha.

"That I think I'm ready to look around for someone again."

Cooper was silent for a long moment as he watched Sasha greet Mason.

"And no," Markus said. "I won't trespass. But if you and she don't work out…"

"There is no her and me," Cooper snapped but his voice was low, tinged with regret. "At least not yet."

"Bullshit. It's there. You just don't believe she'd want someone like you."

Cooper frowned. He hadn't considered that as a reason. He wasn't lacking self-confidence and his ego was extremely healthy. Did he think he wasn't worthy of her? No, it was more a case of him putting her so high up that there was almost a bit of star power there. Something he'd never have thought to see as a problem before. She wasn't a celebrity. But she was highly regarded in her profession and well-loved everywhere. Look at the easy way she'd just worked into the guys' hearts. He knew what they were all thinking.

The guys stared at him, speculation in their gazes as Sasha went to Chase and Brett and introduced herself. He didn't think she knew them but that wouldn't stop her from reaching out. She checked to see if she'd missed anyone and walked to Hawk.

Cooper didn't know what she said to him, but he was grinning like a fool.

Then in a surprise move she reached up and kissed big silent Shadow on the cheek and whispered something in his ear. He smiled down at her so gently Cooper knew he wasn't the only who wanted to know what she said.

She threw out her arms and turned in a big circle. "I am so damn glad to be home."

They smiled at her, but the air had changed to a sense of waitingness. Cooper knew she'd picked it up.

He waited for her to turn that steady gaze his way.

She studied the men one at a time then narrowed her gaze and looked at him. "Cooper – what don't I know?"

He didn't want to tell her. But she needed to know.

"David went overseas again."

She nodded. "We knew that. He'd planned to turn around as soon as he was allowed."

"And he's gone missing – again."

CHAPTER 19

HER CHEEKS TIGHT, her shoulders tense, she said in a curt voice, "Why?"

"Why didn't I tell you before we got here?" he asked in a calm voice, not pretending to misunderstand the question. "Because I wasn't allowed to tell you."

She studied him for a long moment and realized he was going to do what he needed to do regardless, and she really wouldn't want it any other way.

"Are you going after him?"

There was a group hesitation then Cooper shook his head. "No. We won't be."

Her shoulders slumped. "Of course not." She looked to be ready to cry then shoved back her shoulders. "And Theresa, is her disappearance related?"

Mason answered, "There's no evidence to say they are connected, but it's hard to imagine how they can't be."

"Theresa was terrified of going back. She was desperate to not have to complete her contract."

"There was a justified reason to walk away. No contracts will force her to finish if they can't protect her."

"And some of the people are diehards and say that they have to finish because the people need the help." She rubbed her temple. "David was a diehard. That's why he couldn't wait to go back. As for Teresa, well I suggested a colleague to help her deal with the trauma of the kidnapping."

"And did she contact your colleague? Do you know?"

"I don't know," she said. "I can call and see." As several of the men nodded, she pulled out her phone. "Simone? Hey…" Sasha smiled as her friend babbled in joy at her voice. "I'm fine. Yes, I know it was pretty rough for a while, but I'm doing better. That's actually why I'm calling. I referred a coworker to you. She'd been kidnapped with me. Theresa Guild."

Simone said, "Yes, I've spoken with her."

"Oh good," Sasha said. "She was supposed to meet me at a restaurant yesterday and never showed. I've been trying to contact her but no luck. When did you see her last?"

"Two days ago. We had a normal session and she booked another appointment for next week."

"You haven't spoken to her since? Did she give you any indication she might be leaving? Going away for a few days? Something?"

"No, I'm sorry but she didn't." There was a fraught silence as the other woman considered the issue. "Honestly it was mostly the trauma she'd been through and her broken marriage."

"Damn it." Sasha rubbed her temple. "I'm really worried about her." And she explained what had happened to her.

"I'm so sorry to hear that," Simone said. "I'll let you know if I hear from her."

Sasha rang off, explaining to the men who'd been listening in.

"Broken marriage?" Cooper said. "Hmmm. Now why did I think she'd been happily married?"

"How many happily married women do you know that spend a full year in a refugee camp without their husbands?" Swede asked.

"None," Evan answered.

There was an awkward silence as the men looked at each other. Sasha stared at them suspiciously. "What are you thinking?"

"Just wondering if she went over alone or with a partner, and if she went with a partner who he was."

"Do you think it makes a difference?"

"Information," Mason said in that strong quiet voice she always associated with him, "is always helpful. We can't make decisions when we don't have the information we need."

"But even if she was married, what would that have to do with her disappearance now?"

No one answered.

Her breath gushed out in a whoosh. "I don't remember her ever mentioning a husband. Neither did I see her with anyone else but our team..." She frowned as she dredged through the memories in her mind.

"Sasha...?" Cooper studied her face. "What are you thinking?"

"It's just she spent a lot of time with David. They were about ten years apart and spent a fair bit of time together. But we all did, so I can't see why that would be anything different."

"It might not be." Markus studied her. "But you seem to notice it as if it was something different."

"I don't know what it is though," she continued. "Honestly I worked all the time so haven't a clue what was going on around me. I was healing from my own divorce and deliberately didn't want to see what others were doing," she added the last note defiantly. "If others were involved in a relationship, I didn't see it."

"So let's reverse that then. Do you know who David hung around with?"

She hated prying into personal lives. This dissection of others. Because in its deepest form it was a dissection of herself. Why hadn't she noticed more? Because she didn't want to see. She didn't want to see everyone else happy and moving on – when she was still hurting. No, maybe not hurting…but not ready to venture out into that dating world again. It hurt to be out there. Such a meat market sound to it. She wasn't like that. She was shy inside. Reserved. She worked. That's what she did. She didn't party, go to the bars or hang out with many friends. She had her husband and they had their friends. She'd been content. Content as in seriously happy, wallowing in her own muddy pigsty.

Only it hadn't been the same for Greg.

As she'd found out too late.

It hurt even now but not from the lack of love or the loss of her life partner but the betrayal – why hadn't he said something to her?

"Sasha?"

She threw her head back. "I hate meddling into other people's lives."

"And how do you feel about kidnapping?"

She glared at Evan who smiled at her as if that would take the sting out of his words.

"David never seemed to be short of friends." She took a deep breath. "He's a lovable character with a great personality, and if he wanted a partner for the night then he'd have had no shortage of offers from the staff or anyone around for that matter."

She could sense the curiosity in their gazes and was determined to forestall the next question. "No, not me. I never got involved with anyone there. I don't do hookups," she said coolly. "And because I don't, I don't follow what other people do."

"And yet you know more than you thought," Cooper said.

"Maybe." She thought about the gentle interaction she'd seen. The tiny touches that happened between lovers and realized she did know. "He was likely having a relationship with her, yes."

"And do you know how her husband would have reacted?"

"No." She stared at him, shadows in her heart. "But if she was married, I can only imagine."

COOPER HEARD THE pain in her voice. Understood what was behind it. There was nothing he could do but hope she wasn't still in love with the guy. Because Cooper knew he was half in love with her himself. Always had been. She was…well he had no words to describe her. He admired her energy and compassion. He already knew she was dedicated and hardworking and caring. He'd thought she was a sexy bomb back when she was doing surgery on him. They'd connected – he knew they had but she'd been married. Which explained that although there'd been a connection between them, she'd always been proper. There'd been no other option. Not for her or for him.

And he admired her all the more for that.

She'd never made him question her motives or integrity and always made him stop and wonder at the person she was. Especially when she'd done that C-section at the refugee camp. He'd watched from the doorway. She hadn't hesitated. He'd seen the disbelief on Markus's face when she'd held up the scalpel – and her giving him that moment to turn away before she took that first incision.

Just as he knew his abilities and his strengths, so too did she.

He was damn proud of her.

And he was such an idiot.

"Cooper?"

He turned to look at Markus and raised an eyebrow. "What?"

"Thoughts?"

He shrugged. "I'm just wondering what lengths Theresa's husband would go to to punish his wife and her lover."

Sasha gasped softly as he reached out to her. "Not saying that it's related in any way, or that you'd be involved somehow, but we've all seen how love brings out the best and the worst in people."

A rather grim heaviness settled in the air.

"What nationality is he? And would he have any connections to pull off that original kidnapping or only possibly this second one?"

"She mentioned something about having connections, if she was married that could explain it," Sasha said. "But she was always vague and refused to give details." She frowned at Mason. "She was moody and often depressed, so I didn't get into too many discussions with her."

"Not to mention if she was having an affair that might have contributed to her depression. Sounds like we should be putting these questions to David."

"Sure," she said candidly. "It would affect anyone. And if her husband was there or came and went it would add to the stress. Maybe he found out about it or maybe he broke it off, and she just pretended to still be married." She shrugged as if she'd seen too many strange circumstances for it to be anything of interest. And given her profession he could imagine. "That's Simone's department. Give me broken bones and sliced tissue any day over broken hearts and shattered egos."

The others laughed. "Good enough."

Shadow said without lifting his head from his cellphone, "He's Turkish. They were married eight years ago in Turkey. Now to find out where he's been these last couple of days." He frowned, clicking away. "He works for the Turkish military."

"That doesn't explain how I'd be taken at the same time. It's not as if my kidnapping was random," she exclaimed.

"No, there will be a reason. We haven't found it yet, that's all."

"Neither does it have anything to do with the break-in at my house," she cried. "Why would it? It wasn't Theresa staying there with me." And she gasped, the color fading from her skin.

"What?" Cooper asked.

"We had to give our contact information when we returned," Sasha said. "So we gave our cell numbers and in my case my house. I gave her my address if she ever needed a place. She'd planned to stay at a hotel but wasn't looking forward to it."

"But she could have just as easily given a hotel and a room number."

Sasha shook her head. "They wanted next of kin, permanent address, and family member contact information. Things like that."

"It will be easy to find," Cooper said. "All that information will be on file."

"It is," Swede announced holding up his cellphone. "She gave 430 Cypress Lane."

Sasha cried out, "That's my address."

CHAPTER 20

SASHA SHOOK HER head. "Is it that simple?" No, it couldn't be. "That doesn't make sense. What about the picture of me and Greg cut in half? The intruder would know that image had nothing to do with her."

"I wouldn't be at all surprised if that's exactly what it was all about. The fact remains that your house was given as a permanent address for someone else, and that person has gone missing. Your house was broken into and vandalized. They have to be connected."

"And David?" she asked in a small voice. "He's a good man."

"He's a good doctor," Mason corrected. "You don't know the man himself."

She blinked. "Maybe I don't, but I can tell a lot about people by working with them. David was a dedicated vagabond. He loved women and he loved life and for him they didn't go together. His mistress was his work. The rest were and always would be playthings. And while he was there with a woman it would be a hell of a ride. Only Ferris Wheels are a treat and the view is special when you get to the top but like all these kinds of relationships, the wheel always comes down."

"Wow."

She smiled at Hawk who studied her intently like he hadn't quite seen her species before.

"It's not that difficult. You work with someone for a

long time and you get to know who and what they are. Look at you guys. Although there are going to be some in this group you are closer to than others, you wouldn't have a problem turning your back on any of them because they'd guard it for you, not stab into it. It's the same in the trenches of an overcrowded refugee camp. He had my back and I never doubted that he'd be there when I needed him. The same in reverse." She took a deep breath and added in a lower tone, "I didn't have that same feeling with Theresa."

"What was she like?"

"Besides despondent, depressed, and then switching to deliriously happy? It's as if she were two people. Very high energy then dragging her ass. No one knew which way she'd be on any given day. She worked hard and put in a solid day, but we all know the type that watch the clock to leave the minute the work day is done. But at the camp, the day was never done."

"So how did she de-stress in order to go from deep depression to deliriously happy?"

She stared at him. "Likely in bursts with David."

Silence.

That was something they could all understand. There was nothing like an affair to remove the drudgery of the day and give you something special to look forward to.

"Where is her husband now?" She studied their faces. "Can't you find out?"

"According to his commanding officers he's taken a week's leave."

She shook her head then said, "So he *could* be behind all this?"

"In theory, but that still doesn't connect him to you or to Ron. Neither does it connect to the driver."

"Maybe someone should be asking that weasel those

questions."

Cooper glanced at his watch. "We'll have to contact the Turkish military. We don't know if they're holding the driver in custody."

"I can't say I'd want to go back and face him, but I would if need be."

"Face who? The driver?" Cooper asked. "He's a no-body. Just a scam artist looking to make a living off the blood and sweat and tears of others."

"The husband."

They stopped and stared at her. "Why would he be interested in talking with you?" Mason asked.

"If he's got David and Theresa then he might be interested. I don't know," she cried. "I'm grasping at straws here."

Cooper walked over and placed an arm around her shoulders. "Come on. Time for a meal and maybe an evening jog. Let some of this tension out."

"We should go back to Ron – ask him about David and Theresa. Ask him about her husband."

"We will. You don't need to get involved."

She wasn't sure who said that but it didn't matter, the answer was the same. "I might not need to," she said. "But I am just as involved as anyone. More so as I was kidnapped and had my house vandalized. Thank you."

She studied the men who had done so much for her and her country and softened her tone slightly. "I know that's your job, just like I don't like anyone interfering in my job. But if there is anything I can do to help, I'd like to."

COOPER TOOK HER home after the meeting. A restless

energy simmered inside. He wanted to do something constructive and couldn't see any way to move forward. "How about barbecue steak and Greek salad for dinner."

She froze. "You cook?"

"As often as possible." He laughed at the interested look on her face. "You don't?"

"I do," she said, her smile flashing. "But my ex didn't."

"Ah." He hopped out of the vehicle and walked to the front door of his house. "Good thing I'm not your ex. And more things for you to change next time around."

"What next time?" she asked. "I'm not sure I'll go there again."

"You will," he said, a serious tone in his voice. "You're the kind of woman who likes to know she has her life in order so you can work on the areas you love."

"I had that, remember. It didn't turn out so well for me."

He unlocked his front door. "And that just means it's time for a progress check. In the years you were married, you made huge strides. You finished med school. Completed your specialty. Worked in your field. If your marriage didn't quite work out the way you expected then analyze why, tweak, and move on."

"Marriage is hardly a strategy."

"No, but life is. You can go through it and make decisions on the fly or you can look a few steps ahead and work toward them. You already did that by picking a profession and back tracking to see what you needed to do to achieve it – and you did that and so much more."

"It doesn't feel like an achievement. It feels like…" She frowned as if uncertain how to answer.

He waited, interested to see how she'd respond.

Only she didn't answer as her phone buzzed. She

pulled it out. "It's David."

She read the text. "He wants to meet." She looked at Cooper. "He says come alone. He's in trouble. No explanation."

CHAPTER 21

"**I**'M GLAD HE contacted me," Sasha cried out. "I was so worried."

"I'm still worried," Cooper said carefully. "Think about the message, come alone? He's in trouble. We can't confirm it's even from him. We'd thought he'd left the country."

She froze. "I forgot about that."

"We will go but we're taking precautions." He turned around in the hallway as if trying to pull his thoughts together.

"It's a public place," she protested. "What could possibly happen?"

He shook his head. "That's true as far as that goes, but we need to have backup just in case."

She glanced down at the text. "I could change the location and make it one closer."

"No, let's not do anything suspicious." He pulled out his phone. "Mason, we've had a development."

She listened while Cooper explained. Her stomach growled reminding her food had been a long time ago. Walking over to the sink she got a glass of water. All the information they'd gone over this morning roiled around inside her head. Nothing made any sense.

"Mason said no one can confirm that David left the country."

She spun to look at him. "What? You said he went

overseas."

He nodded. "That's what we heard. However, his passport was last scanned when he came home with us and hasn't been used to leave. According to Turkish officials, he hasn't re-entered Turkey. Now he may have another way to travel and once over there he could have entered via another way, or gone to another location altogether but..."

"But he's likely still here." She held up her phone. "So chances are this is from him. And he *is* in trouble."

Cooper nodded.

She drank her water, hating the bubble of acid in her stomach. "Let's go." She placed her glass down on the counter. "Do you want to drive or will I?"

She headed to the front door, not waiting for him to join her.

"Hold up," he said. "You're going to be a few minutes late for this meeting."

"Why's that?"

"Because Mason is grabbing a couple of men and he's going to join us."

She shook her head. "That won't work. If it's David it might spook him, and if it isn't David then they could be looking for a trap."

He smiled. "Sweetheart, we do this shit all the time."

She growled at him. "Maybe, but I don't. I deal with the people after you have done your shit."

He laughed. The sound was so unexpected she found herself grinning in reaction. She sighed happily. "Being around you has been good for me."

"How's that?" he asked as he unlocked the Jeep.

She got in and waited until he joined her, trying to formulate her thoughts.

"After the divorce I changed. Became quiet. Depressed. Some said I was morose. I knew I had to do something and running away to help at the camp suited my change of lifestyle." She slowly rotated her neck, even now struggling with the pain and suffering she'd seen.

"Only there wasn't much to smile about there. Sure these people had escaped persecution. They were so damn thankful to be alive. But they were in a holding state. They had no place to go and no way to get to this hoped-for future. Of course I buried myself in work and although the depression eased, the lightness inside hadn't returned. I didn't analyze it. I had no time for such things but since being back I've gone through a complete overhaul of the experience..." she took a deep breath, "and realized that the lightness wasn't so much gone but had been toned down by circumstances, yet it was there ready and willing to be turned back up."

She smiled at him. "I've seen it pop up more and more in the last ten days, but there'd been no real reason that I could pinpoint other than the fact I was alive." She laughed. "And that's a huge reason, but I've come to realize the marked improvement is due to you."

"Me?" he asked in surprise.

"Yes you. You make me smile." She said the words simply. There was no reason to adorn them. They were the truth and so much more powerful because of that.

"Thank you," he said, his voice warm and so damn caring.

She needed that. Needed to know that someone cared. That she wasn't alone in this messed up world. That someone understood what she'd been through and wouldn't judge her or expect more of her than she could give.

"No," she said with a big grin, "Thank *you*."

Now he laughed. "I don't think it was me as much as

your stress easing. A painful breakup hurts. We shove a lid on top and try to deal with every day. And if we're lucky while the lid is on, some of the pain eases. Time is good for that. And if we're really lucky some of the issues resolve in other ways. But when the time is right, you can open it up and find out that you've moved past every-thing."

"So you just accept that you're a good guy, huh?" she teased.

"I'm a good guy, yes. But the healing is in a large part due to your own hard work." He shot her a wicked grin that started in his eyes and made her heart beat faster. "And I'm happy to know you like being around me. Just as long as you don't pin a hero complex on me, I'm fine."

"Like you did to me?"

She heard him suck in his breath. Then he winced. "Ouch."

"Just figured while we're clearing the air that maybe we should *be clearing* the air."

He took his eyes off the road to study her for a long moment. "In one way I suppose but that begs the question, what are we clearing the air for?"

Her turn to suck in her breath. "Ouch." And she laughed. "Nice turning of the tables by the way while deflecting the questions."

"And exactly just what you are trying to do yourself." He pointed out with a grin.

"So what we're clearing the air for is to see if there is anything between us that needs an open pathway to proceed."

At the surprised silence in the vehicle she shrunk back against the passenger door and wished she'd kept her mouth shut. She added in a low voice. "Or not?"

He shook his head.

"Sorry I misunderstood," she rushed to say, wishing she could go back five minutes. How mortifying. "I said it had been a while, and I wasn't good at this to begin with. Forget I said anything. Let's focus on David."

She didn't say the next words out loud but she thought them. *Let's focus on David so I can get past this and get my life together. Something that was past time.*

Cooper pulled the Jeep into the parking lot and turned off the engine.

"YES, IT'S BEEN awhile for you and maybe that's a good thing. I do prefer to have an open conversation than not. I was just surprised," he said calmly as he twisted in his seat to look at her. "I'm more used to mind games. Something I hate in a relationship."

She reached for her door handle to get out, but he caught her chin up in his fingers. "So just for clarity because it feels like things got so very muddy all of a sudden," he leaned forward, "yes, we are clearing the air to see what there is between us. No, I don't have a hero complex, but I did and maybe still do have an angel complex. Don't make me out to be anything more than a flesh and blood male and we'll do fine."

She went to tug her chin free but he wouldn't let her. He'd waited too long to respond to her earlier comment, and now embarrassment had set in.

"I wasn't rejecting you. I was surprised. Plain and simple. And just in case you have any doubts."

He leaned forward and kissed her. It was a light searching kiss, looking for a response and wondering if he'd find one.

He started to pull back, but she threw her arms

around his neck and kissed him back. And that's when he realized that Dr. Sasha, the tiny dynamo who raced from one place to another with so much energy and compassion was going to be exactly the same in bed.

Just then that passion boiled over as if a lid had been removed and quickly threatened to consume them.

A heavy knock on the window as a large male walked by brought him to his senses. She was sitting in his lap and his hand was under her shirt, cupping her delicious breast.

"Jesus," he whispered in shock. "What the hell was that?"

She buried her face in his neck, her body trembling in his arms.

He held her close and rocked her gently. "Lady, I don't know what you've been doing with all that passion, but holy shit…"

That gurgled a startled laugh out of her. She lifted her head and there was that cheeky grin he'd first seen right after his surgery. That was the doctor he'd fallen in love with. He rested his forehead against hers.

She took a second shaky breath. "That was…"

"Yeah, I know. Jesus."

He lifted his head, not wanting the real world to interfere with the haze of intimacy they'd found. "We have to go."

But he couldn't release her, instead he cuddled her close.

"I suppose the others are here."

"Yeah, that was Swede who pounded on the window." Thank God the guys understood. Too bad he didn't. He'd wanted a relationship, wanted to see what they could create. It never occurred to him that this heat simmered beneath the surface. And now that it had, there was no way in hell he could ignore it. All he wanted was to take her home to bed. She was already staying with him. At his house. And if they were lucky, in his bed.

"We need to go in," she murmured, shifting back to her seat. "I can't say I want to now."

He winced. "The guys won't say anything to you."

"Maybe not, but that doesn't make it any less embarrassing."

He watched her slip out of the Jeep and slam the door.

"But it will make it that much harder to take you back to this point," he muttered.

He exited and locked up then hurried to catch up with her. She might want to put a little distance between them, but he'd do his damnedest to remove the little bit that was already there.

CHAPTER 22

INSIDE THE RESTAURANT, she stopped and assessed the patrons. The hostess walked toward her, a big smile on her face. "Dr. Childs, I believe?"

Sasha nodded. "I presume my other party is here and waiting."

"Yes, please come this way." The woman walked Sasha toward the back. Cooper was just a pace behind. She refused to look around at the full tables. There were some men she knew but the last thing she wanted was to be any more embarrassed than she already was. Making out in the front seat of the Jeep. Like high school all over again. And wasn't it supposed to be the back seat? Then again she didn't think the vehicle had one of those. The hostess motioned to a small meeting room.

"I'll bring the menus and would you like coffee?"

Sasha nodded, her gaze on the lone person in the room. She walked forward. "David?"

He froze then turned toward her. And she saw his haggard face for the first time.

"Oh my God, what's wrong?" She ran to the table and sat down beside him and wrapped her arms around him.

"They have Theresa."

His words were said so simply she didn't know what to say in response.

Then Cooper sat down beside her and David cried,

"No, you can't be here." He placed his hands on the table flat and pushed himself. His gaze zinged to Sasha. "I said come alone!"

Cooper was there instantly. With a hand on David's shoulder, he settled him back down. "I am here. No games. What the hell is going on?"

With a shaky breath David sat down hard. He shook his head. "They said they'd kill her if I brought in the authorities."

"Kill Theresa?" Sasha cried out softly. "Why, what's going on?"

He gazed at her with a tortured look.

Her heart bled for him. "David talk to me."

"I can't," he whispered. "I can't be responsible if they hurt her. I thought if I talked to you, we'd be able to find a way to help her. But if they see these men…"

"They aren't the police but they are the men that can help," she said forcefully. "So please…"

"Start at the beginning please," Cooper said. He brought out his phone and laid it on the table. "I'm going to record this."

But David stared at the phone as if it was going to bite him.

Sasha reached across the table. "David," she said in her no nonsense tone. "Talk to me."

His breath released in a long shaky movement, and he gave her an abrupt nod. "Theresa and I were an item in the camp. We didn't expect it to happen. Nor did we realize just what the relationship meant." He splayed out his hands. "I didn't know she was married."

Sasha raised her eyebrows. "She didn't tell you, or things blew up so fast that she was caught up too?"

"The latter – at least I'm presuming so. They had been having trouble for a long time so she joined the volunteers for the year so they could rethink their relationship. The camp was close enough they could go back and forth. But in the meantime she was there – on the spot – and missing out on one of life's biggest glory moments – love." He scrubbed his face with both hands.

"But she was still married," Cooper prompted.

David nodded. "And no longer wanted to be married. Then the kidnapping happened. We almost didn't make it and that brought us both a chance to rethink what we wanted."

A waitress walked in with their coffees and several menus. Sasha thanked the woman.

David stared out the window until she left.

"And then," Cooper prompted.

"I've never been married before," David said. "I've been involved in lots of relationships but none that mattered more to me than my work. Until I met Theresa."

"And did she reciprocate the feeling?"

Sasha listened to Cooper's questions, but she was trying to reconcile the woman she'd known briefly. This explained the woman's depression. Her melancholic state. But then why not get a divorce? "Was she going to get a divorce?"

"Yes, she planned to tell him that weekend, but it didn't work out that way. Then when we returned stateside she acted oddly. I wasn't sure what was going on. I tried to talk to her but she wouldn't talk. She just kept saying things were different now."

"So she wasn't going to get a divorce now?" The kidnapping had been traumatic. Maybe it had been enough to change her mind, but not necessarily. Sasha had gone through a period of determining what was important in her life. Now she was getting back to living. Hence,

Cooper at her side.

"She said she loved me more than anything, and she'd do everything she could to keep me safe. Then she walked out the door." He shook his head. "I should have questioned her. Pleaded with her to explain. To tell me what was really happening."

"Then how do you know she was taken?" Cooper studied David's face. "Maybe she returned to her husband and is breaking contact with you."

David shook his head. He pulled out his cellphone and slid it across the table.

Cooper opened the phone.

"Look at the last text. It's from her."

The text opened up.

"Help me please."

COOPER PARKED OUTSIDE the hangar and with Sasha at his side and David dragging his heels he waited until the truck pulled up beside them. Shadow hopped out with Hawk. Another vehicle pulled up right afterwards. This time Swede exited along with Markus.

Sasha beamed at them all.

David shrunk into his jacket.

"Are they ready for us?" Hawk asked.

"Yeah." And Cooper ushered David into the hangar where the others who'd been in Turkey waited.

Levi stood, his face cold and hard and so damn dark that Cooper was even feeling it. Levi was above all else a fair man. But this situation was so not normal.

"Local police?" Mason asked from Levi's side.

"Not yet." Cooper pulled out a chair for David to sit down. "And you're right. They are likely the ones to handle this, but I'm not sure. You'll have to hear the rest. David believes she's being held on a tanker in international waters out of the bay."

Levi barked, "Why?"

David waved his hand around as if they'd all go away, then he said, "It's something she said. Her husband's brother worked on a tanker. And Harken threatened to take her out and deep six her in the ocean at one point in time when they were fighting."

"Anything more?" Levi's tone was low and deep. His gaze was locked on the doctor.

"I said she mentioned having connections. That could have been because her husband worked for the Turkish military," Sasha said quietly. "I don't remember her talking about the shipping industry though."

David twisted so he could look at her. "She didn't talk much but there was one thing that wasn't allowed and that was adultery."

The air filled with the question of why she'd taken that step then…

"So she has an affair, the husband finds out and gets angry and punishes the wife. Makes sense. But then why try to kidnap the other three doctors?" Swede pondered out loud.

But Cooper got it. "Camouflage." He studied David. "Even better, he could make this into a terrorist hit against the Americans at the same time."

There were several sighs as everyone fit the pieces together.

"So wait, Ron and I were taken to hide the fact that David here was the target?" Sasha said in outrage.

"And Theresa. She'd have been killed. It's the only way the husband would be free of her permanently."

Sasha shook her head. "It's too elaborate."

"Why? He had access to the camp, knew he could find someone there like Jamel to help. All Harken needed was a way to arrange your transport after you were picked up."

"It's just too…" She didn't have words.

"David?" She turned to him. "Is this what you think happened?"

He frowned. "I know she was terrified of her husband. Worried what he might do…worried he might have been behind the kidnappings. One of the reasons we'd meshed so well was she went along with my passion for work. She'd be able to travel with me, and we'd be together all the time instead of apart most of the time. But that's all changed now, she was terrified of leaving the country again," he admitted. "She's really traumatized. And not thinking straight."

Cooper interjected, "When did you last see her and what was the conversation like?"

"It was yesterday," he admitted. "Late in the afternoon. I'd hoped to spend the night with her, but she got a text from her husband and became very antsy. She told me it was all over and to leave. So I left. But I didn't go far. I took another room in the same hotel, as I had no place to go, and drank myself silly." He stared at the men. "When I got up this morning she'd checked out already."

He handed over his phone and said, "Then I got a text from her."

Swede picked up the phone and quickly clicked through it.

"So was she just avoiding me all this time," Sasha asked. "Why set up the meeting with me and not show up."

"She got cold feet," David said.

"About what? You're both adults. If you choose to

have an affair that's between you two."

"I told her to let you know she was okay, but she was scared as she couldn't explain her behavior without taking that irrevocable step. She wasn't sure what to do so did nothing."

"So I worried when I didn't need to."

"That's not true," Cooper said. "What about your house?"

"Oh my God, I forgot about that." Sasha stared at him then slumped in place. "Was I being followed? The house watched? But for what purpose. None. So why vandalize my house?"

"What's this about your house," David asked, puzzlement wrinkling his forehead.

Markus quickly explained, adding, "Unless once again her house wasn't related to this issue."

"Yet the destruction sent her racing out of the house. Leaving it empty. Where had you planned to go before Cooper stepped in to help?"

"To my mother's house most likely." At their nods, she said, "Or a hotel."

She studied their faces and saw something move behind Cooper's gaze as he shifted from her to the others. He asked, "So it is him?"

Markus nodded. "He'd be my number one choice."

"And mine," Swede said. "We've all seen it before."

"Okay, enough of this talk." Sasha hopped to her feet, walked over to Cooper and stood in front of him. "Who do you think broke into my house?"

"Greg."

CHAPTER 23

S HE GASPED. "WHY would he do that?"

"Because he figured it would send you back into his arms."

She shook her head. "I wouldn't go."

"But did he know that? How big is his ego? Would he have believed you'd go back to him when you were in need? Didn't you say he was close to your mother? And your mother wanted you to get back together with him?"

She stared at Cooper, her thoughts moving at lightning speed. "That's awful."

"But believable?"

Shadow stepped up. "What is his ego like? Does he think you'd go back to him if you had the chance?"

Her throat closed up. "But he was unfaithful. Why would he think I'd sign up for that again?" She shook her head. "I wouldn't."

"Did you love him?" That was from Swede.

She nodded and bit her lip. "I did. But he betrayed me, so obviously he didn't love me. And if I did give him another chance I could never trust him. In many ways that would be so much worse. I need to know he'd be there for me all the time not just until someone better came along."

At that she heard the strangled gasp from behind her. David.

"I'm sorry, David." She walked over to give him a

hug. "That didn't come out right."

"No, maybe it's true though. I don't know. She was hot and then cold and then… I don't know."

"So is she missing or is she just avoiding you?" Levi asked in exasperation.

"Maybe the better question is, is the husband in town?" Swede said, walking over from where he'd gone to look at the computer. "His brother's ship is out in the bay. He's registered as being on board."

There was an awkward silence as everyone turned to look at David. He shrugged. "I can only tell you what she said to me."

"Would he really kill her because of an indiscretion?" Evan asked.

"Absolutely," Levi said. "It happens all the time. That truth, however, does not make it a fact in this case. She might have changed her mind and returned to Turkey. I presume that camp was close enough that she could hop back and forth to see her husband, but why then did she leave from the US?"

"We were hired through an organization Ron is associated with. They handle all visas and the agreement covers airfare to and from the US. Maybe she was planning for the future. By signing up from here, she had a guaranteed escape from the camp – and therefore from her husband. That way she could get away in case she needed to."

"A company here?" Cooper asked. "What's the name of it?"

She frowned and turned to David. "Do you remember?"

He shook his head. "My contract is different. I work with Ron and he runs so many projects I tend to move from one to the other. Theresa might not have been hired through there either. Her husband is a Turk and quite likely she received priority placement as well."

"Did you know her before going to the refugee camp?"

He nodded his head. "Yes, I did. Saw her a few times but not in years."

Sasha stood up. "So we're getting nowhere again. I'm going to go see Ron. Maybe he can shed some light on this mess."

"Just so you know," David stood up, his throat working, "Ron is Theresa's father."

"What?" Sasha stared at him in shock. "I didn't know that. Okay, so this is officially a soap opera." Sasha sat down hard. "I'm presuming Ron was against her marriage and didn't like her husband?"

David stared at her in surprise. "No, he didn't. They couldn't stand each other. Why?"

It was Cooper who answered. "Because it was Ron who was shot. As if there was something personal behind it."

"But it could have been any of us," Sasha murmured, her thoughts flinging backwards to the nightmare as it happened. "*If* her husband was in the group, Theresa didn't appear to recognize him or anyone."

"The terrorists might have been primed ahead of time as to who he was. Maybe targeted him for that reason," Cooper added in a quiet voice.

"Why didn't she say something," Sasha asked, tears filling her eyes. "Even when he lay dying, she didn't let on that Ron was her father," Sasha cried.

"She was devastated but was afraid of bringing attention to herself." David flipped his phone back and forth several times. "Her stress level was off the wall. She'd planned to see someone for counseling."

He studied Sasha. "I would have backed off if she'd told me what was going on. I only wanted to keep her safe. Keep her alive and healthy until we could be together." His gaze turned hopeful. "Maybe she's gone into hiding to avoid her husband. If he's here, he can't stay indefinitely."

Sasha had no words of wisdom to offer. There was so much going on. Information they needed and didn't have available.

"She's a good doctor," David said. "Not brilliant, but solid. There are few enough of those out there."

Sasha stood up abruptly. "I'm going to go see Ron. If anything develops, then please tag me so I'm in the loop."

"No you won't, at least not alone," Cooper said easily. "No being alone until we get to the bottom of this."

There wasn't any point in arguing, and truthfully, she was happy to hear that. She nodded abruptly. "Fine, be a hero."

She smiled at the others. "Good-bye."

The chorus of farewells had her grinning. Until she got outside and saw the Jeep – and the reminders overwhelmed her. "What will happen with David?"

"He's free to go. He didn't do anything. He's worried about Theresa with good reason."

"But there's nothing I can do right now and I need to just…do something normal."

"I understand. So we'll go and see Ron, maybe visit your mom and then figure out what's next."

And damn it if his voice didn't turn smoky and dark. She shivered and wondered briefly if they shouldn't divert to his house instead.

He turned on the Jeep and drove to the hospital. "Let's go see what he has to say."

"I doubt he knows anything…"

"We at least need to check it out."

Ron was awake and happy to see them. Until he heard the news. His face took on such a gray cast Sasha wondered about contacting the doctor on the floor. She had no idea what medications he was on, but the last thing they needed was for him to have a heart attack. Theresa was his daughter and finding out she was in danger had to be a blow.

"Have you seen her since our return?" Sasha asked.

"No, I haven't," he said softly. "She's not happy with me."

Ron stared out the window. "I didn't approve of the marriage and knew she wasn't happy. But neither did I approve of her hooking up with David. Don't get me wrong, I really like the man, but I didn't want her to be another of his short relationships and neither did I want her breaking her vows." He turned to face Sasha.

"I would, however, condone a divorce. Her husband is an ass and treated her terribly, but she wouldn't see it. What was I or anyone else going to do? She always treated me as a casual friend rather than her father in public." He shrugged. "I wanted her to return to the US with me but she refused."

"Maybe she changed her mind." Sasha explained their working theory.

He frowned. "If she was short on money, I'd have helped her out. Would have happily bought her a return ticket."

"But the contract gave her a flight home, allowing her to leave without him knowing…" Sasha frowned. That flight home wasn't going to help much if she had nowhere to hide. "Of course, this is only conjecture."

"No, it makes sense," Ron said. "Her husband can't travel to the US. Not legally, so he wouldn't be able to follow her. When she was here for a visit, I took her over to the office. I'm sure that's when she considered the notion."

"He can't come here?"

"No, he has a record. So he's not allowed in the US."

"And his brother?"

"He has two. The middle one works in the shipping industry and he travels the world on freighters. I think the younger one has worked with him but not sure that he still does."

Cooper opened his phone and texted Swede. "Let's make sure they know he can't come over here."

"But that doesn't help get her back," Sasha added quietly. She glanced at Ron and added, "Her brother-in-law's freighter is docked in the bay."

"We have to help her." He tried to get out of bed and groaned.

"Right idea, wrong pronoun," Sasha said. "*You* have to heal. She'll need you to be there when *we* get her back."

"Right idea and wrong pronoun," Cooper calmly repeated. "*I* will be helping to get her back again. *You, however,* will not."

She glared at him.

Ron chuckled. "I'm so glad to see you found someone, Sasha. You look very happy."

She snorted. "Then you're blind."

Ron grinned. "Generally I see people very clearly."

COOPER WATCHED RON, looking for any deception. But he couldn't see any. A man dedicated to his work and likely at the expense of his family. Then again his daughter was in her late thirties and well past the point of needing a father to be there at every corner.

He nudged Sasha toward the door. The hour was late.

"Bye, Ron." She smiled at him as they walked out. "What's the rush?"

"I thought you wanted to go to your mother's as well tonight."

"Not sure I do," she prompted. "I'll have to explain your presence in my life, and that won't be easy as she's still looking for Greg to return."

"Maybe having me there with you will help to change her mind," he suggested, liking the idea for that reason alone.

As they walked toward his Jeep she appeared to reconsider and pulled out her phone. "Okay, I'll see if she's going to be there."

"Or just arrive unexpectedly so she doesn't have time to let your ex know you're coming."

Sasha laughed. "That works too."

They arrived at her mother's place twenty minutes later to find her sitting outside in the lawn. She beamed when she saw her daughter.

Then her gaze caught on Cooper and she frowned. "Hello," she said slowly. "Who are you?"

Cooper stepped forward and held out his hand. "I'm a friend of your daughter's."

Instantly the other woman's gaze turned speculative. "Nice to meet you."

"It should be," Sasha said. "He's one of the men who rescued me, Mom."

She turned to Cooper and said, "This is my mother, Caroline."

"Nice to meet you, Caroline." He put on just enough charm to smooth the awkwardness but not enough to make her suspicious.

"I see," her mother said, but it was obvious she didn't see at all.

"We were at the hospital visiting Ron and thought we'd stop by to say hi," Sasha carried on breezily.

Her mother smiled warmly. "And I'm so glad you did. Can I make you some coffee?"

"Sure, that would be lovely."

Caroline got up and went inside leaving Sasha and Cooper alone. "That went well," he murmured, barely keeping his grin back.

"Like hell," Sasha muttered in response. "Well, I'd best go face the music. She's motioning at me from the window."

Cooper glanced over and sure enough she made a hard motion to her daughter then seeing Cooper watching, she gave a small wave and turned away.

"I can go, talk to her," he said.

"No, you can't," she hissed. "How do you explain this?" She motioned between the two of them. "Us?" She stood up, shaking her head.

"I could explain," he said.

She spun around and studied him. "How? What would you say to her?"

Her mother stepped out at that moment. "The coffee is dripping."

"Thanks, Mom,"

"I'd hoped you'd have come inside with me so I could show you my new dishes," Caroline said, a faint rebuke in her voice.

"Sorry." But Sasha's voice was completely unrepentant.

Cooper decided they could do this dance forever or he could shake it off. "She was afraid you'd ask questions. So I'd just like to clarify that we are seeing each other. I care for her very deeply. Your daughter is a very special woman, and I feel very blessed to have her in my life."

Sasha stood frozen beside him. Caroline stood with her mouth open in shock.

"I met her over a year ago. She helped put me back together again, and it was because of her that I would return to the work I love. She was happily married at the time, so I walked away. Neither cheating nor breaking up a marriage is something my sense of honor or integrity would allow. I found her again." He reached across and lifted her hand in his. "Literally, as it were, and when I realized she was single, I knew I'd do anything for a chance with her."

"What kind of chance?" her mother asked, clearly torn.

"As in, permanently. She's a very special woman, as I'm sure you agree."

"Yes, of course." Caroline said slowly. "She's my daughter."

"And deserves to be treated with honor and re-spect…and of course given a whole heart, not just a cheating heart," he added calmly.

Her mother sat back, a lemon slice look on her face, then her shoulders sagged and she nodded. "Yes, she does."

She turned to her daughter who'd been sitting immobile at his side. "And is this what you want?"

Sasha squeezed Cooper's hand and said, "I really want to see where this is going."

"And Greg?"

Sasha laughed. "Greg is a deceitful, lying, two-faced, son of a bitch. He betrayed me. I will never get back together with him. He burned that bridge permanently. I need to know my partner has my back, not targeting it."

The coffee maker inside beeped. Caroline quickly stood up and rushed inside.

"Did you mean it," he asked, trying to keep his voice neutral.

"Mean what? What I said about the relationship with you – absolutely." She studied him. "Did you mean what you said?"

"Absolutely."

She smirked then said in a wicked tone that caught him off guard, "Does that mean we can go to bed now that we have all the basics out of the way?"

"I sure hope so," he whispered fervently, heat rippling through him. "Can we skip coffee?"

A giggle escaped. Her eyes widened, and she slapped a hand over her mouth and stared at him. But her eyes were twinkling with mirth.

"Sasha, are you all right?" Caroline called from the kitchen.

"I'm fine, Mom," she managed to get out, but her shoulders still shook. He loved that lightheartedness in her. In fact, he was pretty darn sure he loved her. Period. And likely had for a long time. Now to get her out of here and back to his place – fast.

CHAPTER 24

"I THOUGHT WE'D never get out of there," she whispered as she buckled up her seat belt then waved good-bye to her mother.

"Do you think she believed us?"

"I'm sure she did. We were giggling like two-year-olds."

"With good reason." He pulled the Jeep into traffic. "So a quick stop at your place then mine?"

"Hell no."

He glanced over at her in surprise. "Sorry."

She leaned closer and ran a silky hand down his thigh. "Your place then mine."

"Shit," he whispered in a strangled voice. "You do pick your times, don't you?"

"Not intentionally, but right now, I do wish we were at your house and tucked up in your bed." And she let her fingers slide down the inside of his thigh.

He made a strangled sound and switched lanes. "Your empty house is closer."

"No, never there," she said. "I want to be in *your* bed."

"And that's where I want you," he said when he could, his voice a hoarse whisper. "You're a hell of a tease."

"No way," she said. "I'm making promises."

When he groaned, she laughed. When he wove in and

out of traffic and managed to get them back to his house in record time, she knew he was as anxious as she was. She tumbled out of the passenger side and ran around to his side where she threw herself into his arms.

He picked her up and pinned her against the hood of the Jeep, her legs wrapped around him and his erection exactly where she wanted it. Minus the clothing.

She wanted this man with an overwhelming passion. She couldn't imagine that ever changing. With tears in her eyes, she kissed him. She poured her feelings into that kiss. Emotions she'd worked hard to heal over the last year. He was so damn honorable. And that mattered.

Hell yeah it mattered.

He'd never cheat on her. He'd never hurt her deliberately and he'd never act like a kid with his hand stuck in the candy jar when he got caught. If he did wrong he'd stand up and take the punishment like a man.

A man. Jesus. A fucking big man. She rocked against him, her thighs tightening around his.

He flung his head back and thrust against her.

"Jesus," he cried as if seeing where they were standing. "What is it about you that I lose all sense of awareness?" He hitched an arm under her hips and walked into the house, the door slamming behind them.

She pressed frantic kisses on his cheek and jaw and neck, her hands running under his shirt while he growled. And then he ran up the stairs to his bedroom. She giggled.

He flung the two of them on the bed but twisted so he landed on his back – even now looking out for her.

She sat up and rode him through his jeans.

"Fuck," he roared, his hands going for the snap closure. She immediately shifted so he could open his pants and helped him drag them off. His boxers went with them. She pounced. But he wasn't having any of it.

"Hell no, fair play."

She shot him a frustrated look and stood up then whipped her shirt over her head and stepped out of her Capri length pants. She stood in her thong and bra and stepped up on the bed. He immediately stood up and placed tiny kisses over the lacy triangle. His fingers slid underneath the elastic edge to find the dampness inside. She cried out, her knees buckling. He flipped her to the side and quickly reversed their positions. Now it was his turn. His tongue tasted and stroked and sucked then delved until she was a writhing mass of nerves on the bed.

"Cooper, now," she cried out. "I want you inside of me."

He slid one finger down through her damp curls. She opened her legs wide. "Yes," she hissed. "More. More."

Carefully he worked one finger inside, and she realized he figured she might struggle with his size. And she might, but it was a challenge she was more than up to.

She pushed up on his shoulders and he willingly rolled over. She grinned. "You'll fit, no worries there."

He shouted with laughter. "You are awful tiny…"

"I am, and you're awfully big," she whispered, stroking the full length of him. "But we're made for this."

She threw one leg across and straddled him, her hips almost shaking with need. She gave him a saucy smile as she placed him at her entrance and slowly sank down – but not all the way.

His breath caught in the back of his throat as he tried to lift his hips up, his back aching as she rose slightly above him to keep him where she wanted him.

"Witch," he said in a thick voice.

"Never," she whispered and relaxed, feeling the stretching as he filled her completely and still there was more of him. She let herself sink lower.

He groaned.

She moaned. And shuddered when she took all of him.

She sat in place for a long moment as she reveled in the sensation. It had been a long time. And never this perfect. This man had snuck into her heart and soul, and she'd welcomed him into her body with joy. "God I missed this," she murmured.

"Not as much as I missed you this last year," he whispered. "I was heartbroken to find out you were married. Then I was heartbroken for you when I heard about your divorce."

"But not for yourself, huh?" she said, loving the moment. And needing so much more.

"No, you are mine. Have been since I first saw you," he whispered, reaching up to cup her breasts. "Don't ever doubt it."

She placed her hands on his chest and leaned forward to stare into his eyes and started to ride.

Gazes locked, she took them both to the edge of the precipice. He slid his hands down to her hips and held her in place as he ground up hard against her and sent them both over the edge.

Collapsing down onto his chest, she lay against his heart, hearing that rapid beat against her ear. His arms gently stroked down her back, tremors still wracking his heavily muscled frame.

"We're so damn lucky to have found each other," she whispered.

"YOU'RE SO DAMN special," he whispered.

Still recovering, she propped her head on her hands

and smirked. "Does that mean you're ready to go again?"

He gave a shout of laughter and hardened up perfectly – already inside her.

"Good thing," she said. "I've been abstinent for a long time."

"Planning to make *up* for it?" he asked suggestively.

"Depends, are you *up* for the job?"

Not only was he up for the job, he was bound and determined to give her a night she'd never forget. And he was *very* goal oriented.

CHAPTER 25

THE NEXT MORNING, true to his word, Cooper pulled into her driveway just before noon, and said, "Here we go. If we make it fast we can head to the beach afterwards."

She reached over and kissed his cheek. Something she'd done dozens of times already this morning. There was nothing like a night of hot passion to make for the best moods.

"Perfect." She really could use more clothes and she had a few plants she didn't want to see die because of neglect.

They walked up together, holding hands. The house was dark and silent but with Cooper at her side, the edgy fear wasn't there. She loved not having to face this alone. She unlocked the door and walked inside. Her huge fern on the front window was crying out for water.

"You go pack what you need, I'll water this guy."

She smiled at him. "There are two more in the kitch-en."

His phone rang as she ran lightly up the stairs, bracing herself for the reminder of what her bedroom had looked like last time. She could have asked Cooper to accompany her upstairs, but that seemed a little silly. Outside her door she took a deep breath and walked in. Then averting her gaze she went to work. She had a small suitcase in the closet that she pulled out and opened.

Quickly she emptied her drawers. There were more clothes in her closet. She rifled through them, choosing a dress and a sweater. That's all she had room for. With a quick walk through the bathroom she collected a few more toiletries and added them to the growing pile.

With the suitcase in hand, she walked out of the room. There was a second bathroom, but it was empty of everything but what a guest might need. The spare bedroom door was closed. She dropped the suitcase at the top of the stairs and pushed the door open. Walking inside her nose caught the scent of something strong. Something foreign.

And something that didn't belong.

She spun around to run out of the room but strong arms grabbed her and a hand slapped over her mouth. She struggled, panic overtaking her normal judgment and she went wild kicking and twisting to get free. To let Cooper know she was in trouble.

"Stupid bitch."

She shuddered. She didn't know that voice. But she understood one thing. He was big, strong and determined.

Her energy drained quickly and she hung limp in his arms. She could barely hear the voice in the background as if he whispered something to someone. And she was pretty sure it wasn't to her.

COOPER ANSWERED HIS phone as he filled up a large mug of water and walked from plant to plant.

"Mason, what's up?"

"The middle brother, Marten, was granted shore leave. He's due back today."

Cooper's breath released suddenly. "Anyone go with him?"

"Yeah, the younger brother called Yarnel."

Cooper's mind suddenly filled with possibilities. "Do you think that could be the older brother Harken? Using the younger brother's passport to get into the country? He is on a week's leave."

"And the freighter picked up several men down the coast four days ago. Supposedly Yarnel was one of them."

"So Harken travels as the younger brother, joins the freighter and lands in the US illegally. And it just so happens that his wife who's been having an affair disappears around the same time."

"We've contacted the freighter. They say the brothers aren't due back until later today, but they have given the Coast Guard permission to board." His voice turned dry. "Of course that could mean nothing."

"It means they either don't have her or don't know she's onboard."

"I vote the latter. This is a vendetta of the brothers against the wife."

"Do we have any information on the brothers?"

"The younger one is clean of any violations. The middle brother is divorced. The wife had a restraining order against him. He was accused of domestic violence but the wife refused to press charges. She is currently living in Germany. All three brothers reside in Turkey."

"So a predisposition for violence, particularly against wives."

"Exactly."

"Okay, keep us posted." He went to close the call, then remembered. "Mason, can you shoot me a picture of the brothers. Just in case."

And he suddenly realized that it was quiet upstairs. As

in too quiet.

"Shit," he whispered in a low voice.

"What's the matter?" Mason said in a terse tone.

Cooper whispered, "We're at Sasha's place."

He slowly turned to face the empty doorway. "She went upstairs ten minutes ago and now it's quiet." And his instinct kicked in. "Damn it, it's too quiet. Give me two minutes, if I don't call you back..." He hung up and slipped the phone in his pocket. He shifted to the base of the stairs. Studying the layout of the house, the stairs and the flooring, he realized that because it was hardwood it would be impossible to make it up without the wood creaking.

Unless... He hopped onto the railing and quickly pulled himself up to the second floor, his gaze on the level above him as he landed like a cat in the hallway. Could Sasha have lain down? Fallen asleep?

Her suitcase stood at the top of the stairs. He peered into the master bedroom. It was empty. Doing a quick check, he checked the ensuite bathroom and moved back out to the hallway. The second bathroom stood wide open. He stuck his head in but it was empty. The spare bedroom door was closed. Shit.

With his ear against the wood he listened.

Breathing.

Behind the door.

Well, that answered that.

He stepped back slightly and took a running jump, slamming against the door. It held. He hit again, focusing on the latch. The door popped open.

To show Sasha against the headboard, her arms tied behind her back.

Unconscious.

He searched the room but her attacker was gone. The

window curtains fluttered in the breeze. He growled deep inside his throat as he stared out into the afternoon sun. Outside of indents in the soft ground below showing the intruder had exited that way, there was no sign of him in the yard. He opened his phone. "Mason, Sasha was attacked. The intruder got away. I'm checking her now."

When the pulse beat strong under his fingers he closed his eyes and collapsed onto the bed. "She's alive."

"Thank God for that."

He could hear voices in the background, but he was so overwhelmed he couldn't speak.

"We're five minutes away. Hold tight."

And Mason hung up.

Cooper leaned over the bed and stroked Sasha's face. "Wake up, sweetheart. Wake up."

She muttered something unintelligible and her eyelids fluttered. She sighed then opened her eyes. When she saw him tears filled her eyes. "Cooper?"

"I'm so sorry, sweetheart."

She blinked in confusion. "What happened?"

"Don't move." He pulled a pocketknife from his pocket and cut the bindings holding her arms.

"That hurts," she cried out as her arms rolled forward. He picked up her closest arm and rubbed some life back into it.

"Do you remember what happened?" he asked gently, dropping a kiss on her wet cheek.

"Attacked from behind. Why does this keep happening?" Her voice was low and pained, breaking his heart. "At least it wasn't Greg."

"Even worse, it's not about you."

"Thank God. Imagine if it was." And she realized what she'd said. "Poor Theresa."

"The Coast Guard is on its way to search the ship for

her."

But Sasha was shaking her head. "I doubt she's there. The guy that's after her was here."

Her gaze widened and she cried out, "Look–"

And he knew.

He spun and lashed out but took the blow on the side of the head. The last thing he heard was Sasha's voice crying out to him. "No… Don't hurt him."

MASON KICKED THE truck into speeds he had no business using as he barreled toward Dr. Sasha's house. They'd tried to call Cooper's phone several times and no answer. The Jeep was parked in the driveway. Mason pulled up behind it, Shadow raced out to the front door. It was locked.

Mason beat him to the back door. The door was open. Mason backed up and looked at the second floor. There were no sounds and no windows open on that side. It was also a long drop. Not an impossible one but…

Motioning at Shadow, Mason slipped inside.

With one ear cocked, Mason watched as Shadow joined him. They did a fast sweep of the downstairs but the upstairs needed to be checked. Taking the stairs two at a time, he was on the second floor in seconds, Shadow at his heels. They checked the rooms where the doors were open, then centered on the one room with the closed door.

And reassessed. It wasn't closed. It hung drunkenly as in someone had already kicked it in.

He knew the damn place was going to be empty.

At his signal, the two entered low and swept the room.

"Shit."

"What was there – a four minute window?"

Mason nodded. "Just about." He had his phone out and called the others. "Markus. They're both gone and the Jeep is here."

"Hello? Anyone home?" A wavering voice from downstairs called, "Hello?"

Mason exchanged a look with Shadow and walked down the stairs. At the bottom was an older man.

"Hi. Can I help you?"

The man looked at him suspiciously. "Maybe we should be asking you that? What's going on over here? Martha sent me to check on that young girl who lives here. Said she just came back and left, only there's people here all the time. You got to have special license to run a bed and breakfast you know."

"Really, well maybe you could describe what you've seen. Particularly in the last few minutes."

"And why would you care?"

Mason didn't have time for this shit. He gave the man the short version of who he was and why he was there. "We suspect that one of my men and the young woman you mentioned were taken out of here against their will."

"When was there time?" the man said in a querulous voice. "First she was gone, then she's home, then she's gone. And she lets a friend stay here." He shook his head. "We're a quiet neighborhood but he's creepy. Then she rolls in today when the guy is here and now you, but I didn't see anyone leave."

"Have you been watching?" Mason snapped sharper than he intended. "All the time."

The older man looked discomforted. "Martha watch-es." He pointed to the house beside Sasha's. "That's our place and Martha is handicapped you know. She can't move much and has such fun watching what goes on in the neighborhood. Not in a mean way of course, but trying to be a good neighbor. But there's times I've got to take her into the doctor, and she frets then. Might miss something important."

And likely hadn't been home in the hours the house had been vandalized in the first place. Meaning she was nosey as hell when she was here. But that worked in their favor. Quickly he learned the men looked like brothers, and Martha thought she saw a woman once. From the description she could be Theresa. "But you didn't see anyone leave."

"No, Martha and I had our dinner and when we came back there was no change, but a panel van did drive away come to think of it." He frowned. "I suppose I might have missed them. Then you guys did too because you arrived right after."

"License plate?"

"No, didn't see it."

"Color."

"White?"

"Make?"

"Nope."

"What can you tell me about it?" Mason asked, barely keeping his exasperation at bay.

"It had backed into something. Rear right taillight was gone and the bumper and corner crumpled. Already rusted so not recent." He leaned forward and said in a low tone, "They should have gotten that fixed."

"Yeah they should have, but they didn't." And now he'd get them.

MARKUS WAITED AT the docks for the Coast Guard to return. He'd wanted to be on the boat heading out to the freighter but had missed it. He stomped his feet, still pissed. They could have waited five minutes.

"Markus, get in."

He spun to look as Evan and Dane pulled up in a powerboat. "About time."

"You don't know the half of it. One of our own is missing," Dane snapped. He pulled the speedboat out of the harbor as soon as Markus jumped in. Evan quickly shared the latest news.

"Cooper is missing? Jesus." Markus stared at the freighter in the deep water. Was his friend on there?

"I know. A search is on for the van." Evan motioned to the wharf. "Hawk is handling the surveillance on the dock and Mason is on his way here with Shadow."

Markus nodded and thought about the tiny doc and what she'd done for so many men.

"I'd change that to two of our own are missing."

"Agreed," Evan said. "Let's get these assholes."

CHAPTER 26

Noo. SASHA STARED at the tiny room and the bunk overhead. What had happened? And why? As she lay there she could feel movement under her. A ship. She was once again on a bloody ship.

She rolled over and gasped in shock. Cooper lay unconscious beside her, blood oozing from a head wound. Immediately she tried to reach over for him, but her hands were tied in front of her. She glared at the rope only to realize they'd been tied in a hurry with a thick rope that couldn't be tightened enough to hold her small wrists. Immediately she twisted her wrists free and slid the rope to the floor then scrambled over to Cooper. The bleeding had slowed, and there was no softness to the bone below. Some swelling had set in but it wasn't much yet.

His pulse was strong. His color good.

She shook him hard. "Cooper, wake up," she whispered, "We've been kidnapped."

And his eyes popped open.

Talk about instant awareness. She bent over and kissed him. "Love that about you."

His gaze flashed in her direction then around the room. Instantly assessing. Instantly seeing the details she'd taken several minutes to understand. She appreciated that nimble mind. His awareness of the danger they were in. And while he was doing that, she pulled the knife out from his ankle sheath.

He stared at her in surprise as she cut his bonds but accepted it back when she handed it over to him. She stepped out from the bed and straightened. And gasped in shock.

"Theresa." She reached up to shake the woman lying on the top bunk. No reaction. "I've got a pulse."

"Good." Cooper was at the door checking the knob. "Locked."

"Of course," she whispered. "Just the three of us, no windows. And the floor is moving. We're on a ship."

"A freighter more to the point. And likely we both know which one."

She nodded. "Why would they snatch us?"

"Wrong time. Wrong place," he said, staring at her. "Either they kept Theresa there until they could move her to the ship or had moved her and were cleaning up so they left no evidence that they'd been there. Or they forgot something and returned."

"You mean they were living in my house?" She gasped. "That's not something I want to imagine."

"Think about it," he said, "it's the address she gave. They probably cut up your bedding to send you running out of the house. It gave them a place to hide out, or to hide Theresa out or both. And no one would know you weren't there."

The door burst open.

Several men rushed in with big batons and wailed on her and Cooper. She cried out and tried to fight back, but she was picked up and thrown over a man's shoulder. They were so strong.

"Cooper," she cried out, but there was no response as she was turned to get through the narrow door. Cooper was fighting hard and taking a beating.

"No," she screamed. "Let him be." And she did the only thing she could do – she sank her teeth into her attacker's neck. The man roared and threw her to the ground. She was up in a flash, his baton somehow in her hand, and she wielded it with a ferocity she'd never felt before, hitting him and any of the others she could reach.

An anger, once unleashed she couldn't stop, and she beat the men attacking Cooper until she couldn't lift her arms anymore.

"Easy. Stop, Sasha. Stop."

She bent over gasping to find men flat on the floor unconscious and her hands covered in their bloody spray. She struggled for breath.

Cooper's voice finally penetrated the red haze in her head. "Come on, we have to get out of here now." Cooper dragged one man lying half in and half out of the room all the way in, then motioned at her to go ahead of him.

"Not without Theresa," she said fiercely, her mind cataloging the bloody cuts and welts on Cooper's face and neck. Bruised and bloody, he gave her a fierce grin and nudged her toward the door.

"I'm getting her, you get moving." He reached up and snagged the unconscious Theresa, pulling her over his shoulder. "Go, go."

"Where?"

"Stairs. We need to find the stairs up."

She bolted forward.

HE'D TAKEN WORSE beatings and kept going. He wasn't about to stop now. Their lives depended on it. He followed Sasha down the narrow hallway to the closest exit and up the stairs. They met no one on the way up.

He hadn't had a chance to look the four men over but didn't think any were the ones they suspected of kidnapping Theresa. However, given their recent actions they were all complicit in the crime.

Sasha opened a door. Daylight shone in. "Stop," he hissed. "They could be out there."

Too late, she was already racing across the deck toward the ladder. Only men were boarding and flowing across the deck now.

Coast Guard.

Thank God.

"Stop or I'll shoot," roared a voice behind him. Cooper didn't know if the enemy had seen the new arrivals, but he wasn't going to stop. He raced forward. Shots rang out behind him.

He ducked and bolted behind the lifeboats.

The Coast Guard had scattered but someone returned fire.

Likely, all of them.

He lowered Theresa to the deck and tucked her under the suspended boat. A hawk's cry soared overhead. Only it originated too close by to be a bird. Cooper gave a fierce grin. That was Mason's voice. On the other side of the lifeboat.

Cooper's voice hissed. "Mason?"

"Yeah," Mason whispered back.

"Sasha and Theresa are with me."

Gunfire split the air around them. Sasha clutched his arm tight. "What do we do?"

"Stay hidden and wait it out. Mason is here. And if he is," he whispered peering around, "so are others."

A gun barrel suddenly pressed against the base of his neck.

The man holding it said, "Get up, slowly."

Cooper, his gaze locked on Sasha's terrified face, rose.

"Walk forward. Bitch get up and follow him."

Forced to leave Theresa behind, Cooper snagged up Sasha's hand and dragged her close.

"Walk," he whispered.

She followed. He could feel her tremble. Feel her tiny frame shake as she tried to hold it together. He walked deliberately close to the rails and kept his gaze forward, his mind racing for options. A bird soared overhead. A second hawk cried in the sky.

"Now stop there."

"Shit."

He froze and glanced around. Six feet to the railing. A hundred feet to the water. He'd take the chance but with Sasha?

A single shot fired. Sasha's knees buckled. "My leg," she cried out.

Decision made.

He caught Sasha up in his arms and in two steps he sprung up and soared over the railing.

Shots spat around him. He felt one tug his shoulder. He cradled Sasha close.

And they fell.

Sasha whimpered and clung to him. The landing was going to hurt. He wrapped his arms around her tight. Pinning her against her chest.

With his other hand he held her neck and said, "Hold on."

He took a deep breath and sealed her lips with his own.

And they hit the water…hard.

CHAPTER 27

SASHA FELT THE hard force of the water try to separate them as they slammed into it, but Cooper held her against him so tight she never felt any pain. They sank for a long moment then he kicked up hard and they started moving to the surface. His mouth still on hers. Several more hard kicks and they broke the surface. She gasped for air. The shock of what just happened argued with the shock of the cold water.

"You okay?"

"Yeah," she said crying, blinking to clear her vision. "I'm okay."

"Just hold tight," he whispered as he struck out strong. "The Coast Guard boat is close by."

"Oh thank God."

He swam strong and she kicked every time he did. It hurt but it felt good. She couldn't believe this had just happened. "What about Theresa?"

"The men will look after her."

She kissed his cheek, the water splashing up between them. "Thank you for saving me."

"Really?" He chuckled and snuggled her in his arms. "I threw you off the ship."

"No, you didn't. You carried me off. Different story."

He laughed. "Any way you like to think of it."

"There is the Coast Guard."

She twisted and looked. "Good thing. I'm getting

cold."

"Shock," he said striking out again.

"Yes, doc," she said.

He grinned. "You are very cheeky considering that you just got shot."

"Hopefully just a graze," she whispered. "Besides I had a guardian angel who could fly." She smiled and wrapped her arms tighter around his neck. "Starting to feel a little woozy."

"Hold on. Don't give in just yet."

HE REACHED THE boat to find several men reaching down for him. They had Sasha up on the deck and wrapped in blankets before he made it onboard.

Safe finally, he stood and stretched. He accepted a blanket and wrapped it around his shoulders. There was a commotion above. He turned.

The bullet hit him square in the belly.

He was lifted up off his feet and slammed back down on his back.

Where he stared at the sky.

"Cooper!"

He could hear Sasha cry out. One of the Coast Guard men bent over him.

He could hear voices, could see faces. But there was ice in his veins. His blood pumped out across his abdomen, dripping down his side.

Then pressure. So much damn pressure.

CHAPTER 28

S EVERAL SHOTS SLAMMED into the side of the boat. Everyone scattered.

Sasha ignored them as she worked frantically on Cooper. The blood was welling on his lower abdomen. "Get me a helicopter," she screamed at the men under-cover.

"Ten minutes out."

She nodded. "Good."

She worked to stabilize Cooper, but the bleeding was heavy. She used part of her shirt to fold up a wad of dressing, and using his knife, she cut away his shirt and tied the pad around him. The Coast Guard vessel would have a medical kit on board but with the bullets pinning them in place no one was moving. His heartbeat was strong. But his color was poor. His temperature, low.

"Cooper, you stay with me," she cried.

"Sasha?" he whispered.

"I'm here. Save your strength," she whispered, leaning over him. "We've got a helicopter coming for you."

"Only if you come with me."

"I'm fine," she cried. "It's you."

"I'm fine." But his voice was fading. "I didn't go through everything I did to lose you now."

"You haven't lost me!" She leaned over and placed her lips against his. "Never."

"Are you sure?"

"Jesus, Cooper. You know I love you."

"No." He squeezed her hand. "I didn't know that. But I'd hoped."

And he fell silent. His head rolling to the side.

Shit, *shit.* She lifted the dressing, but the hole was small and nasty. They needed to get that darn bullet out. She was more worried about what damage it might have caused inside. She studied the sky. Where was the damn helicopter? Finally she heard the whup whup as it spun closer, the noise loud in the sudden silence. The gunfire above had stopped. Good. Maybe this was over now.

"It could land up top, couldn't it?" But then she'd have to move him up the ladder, and she didn't want to do that if not necessary. Not anymore than was necessary.

The Coast Guard brought a stretcher to her side. It was amazing to see how efficient the professionals worked to transport him. Without ceremony Cooper was transferred to the helicopter. She watched in amazement as he was whisked away.

"Not to worry." Mason spoke at her shoulder as he helped her to sit down. "Cooper is strong. He'll be fine."

She knew all too well that even the simplest of wounds could be the downfall of the strongest of men.

In Cooper's case, his injury wasn't even close to being simple.

COOPER OPENED HIS eyes to a room that he'd seen too much of already. He was in the hospital. Again.

Shit.

Anger and disbelief overwhelmed him. He didn't want to be here. He didn't want anything to do with being injured.

"How are you feeling?"

He smiled, his gaze following Sasha's voice. Inside he relaxed. It was her. She lay stretched out on the bed beside him. "You're supposed to be in the hospital," he snapped. "You were shot in the leg, weren't you?"

"Just a graze. Besides I'm in the hospital," she said with a smirk. "And as I'm in bed I'm resting too."

"But you're in my bed."

She leaned forward, heat in her gaze. "You don't want me in your bed?"

"Ha, it's all I can think about," he said, feeling his insides ease as he realized they were both going to be fine and that she really was there with him.

"Well, you're not *that* badly injured," she whispered, dropping kisses on his temple, her fingers trailing across his chest.

"Really?" he asked in delight.

"Nope. You'll be down for a few weeks at the most."

Relief overwhelmed him.

"Then maybe that's too bad," he whispered, tumbling her into his arms. "I'd love to spend a few weeks in bed with you."

"You should be so lucky."

"Oh I plan to get lucky – often."

She laughed and kissed him. "Sounds good to me. Maybe I'll keep you after all."

"You'll keep me?" His grin split across his face at her wording. "You know, that's a great idea."

"You think so?" She studied him suspiciously. "Why is that?"

"Because I always aspired to be part of The Keepers." He took a moment to explain how the group of SEALs earned the nickname.

She blinked at him in surprise then understood. Her

laughter peeled out, filling the room with sunshine. "You are now a bona fide member."

He tugged her down and kissed her.

And knew he was the luckiest man in the world.

This concludes Books 4–6 of SEALs of Honor.
Read the first Chapter of Markus: SEALs of Honor,
Book 7

SEALS OF HONOR: MARKUS
BOOK 7
CHAPTER 1

S HIT HE WAS tired. Not that Markus Donner would let anyone know.

Not bone weary. That implied he could feel his bones. And that was beyond him. This last mission had been hell. But he'd made it home. Enjoyed four days of rest. Not that enjoyed was quite the right word. Maybe survived?

Now back to training. In Alaska this time. The military base here was huge and he enjoyed coming to this part of the country. The north offered unique geographical challenges for them. In a way that was a relief. He could use something to beat down. Home was empty. Lonely. He'd slept the first day away. And the second had been like moving through treacle. His body was recovering fine. His heart, his mind…not so fast.

Yet the melancholy had nothing to do with his work. Lord he loved his job. Loved his chance to serve. Especially in this capacity. He gave his all every day. He'd buried himself in his work for years. And it had helped him to heal.

Only now there was just a hole in his heart. A void in his life.

One he wasn't sure how to fill.

Life wasn't the same when you came home to an empty house. An empty life. More than that it was hard to come home and know it wasn't going to change – if he didn't change it.

And that was a mission he wasn't ready for.

When he'd found out they were heading to Alaska for wilderness training, he couldn't wait. He'd had enough of his own company by then and needed to focus on something he could grab onto and do something about. Not stare at this emptiness inside. How could something that didn't exist hurt? It made no sense. But it was a reality that he'd lived with for several years now.

God he'd loved Fiona, his wife of five years.

Losing her had been the toughest thing in his life. He'd gone off the wall for a while. It was the guys who'd reined him back in. He'd have died happy on a mission. He'd been crazy and on edge and had pushed the edge farther. He knew he'd been out of control for a time. He hadn't cared. He'd needed to die in action. It was the only way he could live. But the guys had knocked some sense into him.

Levi had finished the job by making him realize that his death would be on his team. That's what Levi had finally gotten through to him. And that was something he couldn't do. He knew the guilt, the pain of losing someone – how could he force that onto them?

So he'd forced himself to deal with the new reality of living without Fiona.

But damn it, it hurt.

Still, he went out, gave his heart to the mission and came home. Alone.

It had taken months before the guys let him do that alone thing. For the longest time he was babysat by one or the other as they kept a watchful gaze on him. He'd both hated them and loved them for it.

As he healed they'd eased back.

In a way that was worse. Now he was always alone and he didn't want to be. Not any longer. The emptiness clawed at him. Now he craved more.

And buried that need in work – again.

Alaska was good. Tons of rough territory. His muscles screamed to run free. He loved to feel his heart pound, his muscles burn. It was beyond anything.

And he enjoyed every minute of it. Soaking wet, mud in his face and his heart pounding in his chest. The hunt. There was nothing like a good chase to keep him alive and moving. This training exercise was man against the wilderness and man against himself. And of course man against one another. Sure there were always bad guys, but right now he was after another SEAL team. And he wanted to beat their ass. He grinned ferociously. Was there ever anything more primitive than being pitted against an enemy that was equal to you? That age old fight for dominance. To find the alpha between them. The thing was his buddies were the best of the best and they were *all* alphas. This wasn't so much about being the top as much as it was about knowing that in real situations he would be top, regardless of who stood with him.

There was no room for error in the real world, and that meant there was no room for error here either.

Shots fired, whizzing past his head.

Shit. He ducked and was moving before his mind had registered that someone had snuck around and seen him.

He zinged to the left and then right as he slipped through the wetlands. The river water was high, the ground soft and marshy. And the clumps of wild grasses deceptive. The ground was so rough with hillocks he could lie flat behind one and be completely hidden.

Movement on the right had him sliding to his belly as he waited and watched. The ground cover was such it was damn near impossible to see anyone. It became a waiting game. He knew the drill wasn't over until the other team was caught. There was no surrender in this instance.

The training area was forty square miles. He had a lot of ground to cover.

He slowly lifted his head and looked around. And heard a rifle click behind him.

Shit. Shit. *Shit.*

He hated to lose.

Slowly he raised his hands, considering his options. He wasn't going to get taken. No way in hell was that going to happen.

"Move."

Markus froze. He didn't know that voice. But making these practices real was what it was all about.

Only this training session was on taking out snipers. Not plaid wearing grizzled hunters.

Wearing a bright orange cap and with chew in his mouth, the man nudged him hard with an old 30:30 lever-action rifle.

Markus almost smiled but the rifle looked too well used for humor.

"I said move."

Not sure how this was playing out, Markus followed the orders. This was not public land, and no one but military should be anywhere close.

People did sometimes accidentally trip into the region though. It happened. And to give the old man the benefit of the doubt, maybe Markus had stepped onto private land. Not sure how possible that was considering the area, but he'd been wrong before.

He turned and walked forward as ordered. He looked

around hoping to see one of his men sporting a huge grin.

"Don't know what the hell you think you're doing here," the old man growled, "but I am not going to find out."

Markus shook his head but stayed quiet. What the hell just happened? Or was he part of the practice session?

That was the best explanation given the circumstances. Then again, there was nothing normal about this guy. Trying to wrap his head around the sudden change, he knew one thing – the old rifle in the guy's hand was non-military, but it had a serious end and lots of years of use.

So an old geezer who lived alone and hunted when he pleased and where he pleased most likely. Still Markus's job was as it always was…to escape and take down the sniper.

But not at the expense of getting shot. And never by hurting a civilian – unless he deserved it.

And if this guy *was* a civilian, the last thing he wanted was for his team to find out he'd been given the shake down by this guy. Friend or enemy? Too early to tell. They hadn't been aware of any friendlies in the region – even confused ones.

But that's what a real-life session was all about. You couldn't plan for every contingency. It wasn't possible.

And this was just another example.

"Where are we going?" he asked in a low conversational voice. He was in full combat gear so it was impossible to not understand who he was on one level. He was obviously a soldier. That he was a SEAL wasn't something he planned to divulge.

"Don't matter to you none."

The serious end of the gun nudged his back.

Still confused and half afraid he was being taken for a ride while the other half worried he'd stumbled into something much more serious… Markus kept on walking. But he reached up his hand to his ear and under the pretext of scratching he sent out a series of taps on his earpiece asking for help. He had a cellphone but that didn't mean he had service.

Books 7–10 are available now!
To find out more visit Dale Mayer's website.
https://geni.us/DMSSoH7-10

Author's Note

Thank you for reading SEALs of Honor, Books 4–6! If you enjoyed the book, please take a moment and leave a short review.

Dear reader,

I love to hear from readers, and you can contact me at my website: www.dalemayer.com or at my Facebook author page. To be informed of new releases and special offers, sign up for my newsletter or follow me on BookBub. And if you are interested in joining Dale Mayer's Reader Group, here is the Facebook sign up page. http://geni.us/DaleMayerFBGroup

Cheers,
Dale Mayer

About the Author

Dale Mayer is a *USA Today* best-selling author, best known for her SEALs military romances, her Psychic Visions series, and her Lovely Lethal Garden cozy series. Her contemporary romances are raw and full of passion and emotion (Broken But ... Mending, Hathaway House series). Her thrillers will keep you guessing (Kate Morgan, By Death series), and her romantic comedies will keep you giggling (*It's a Dog's Life*, a stand-alone novella; and the Broken Protocols series, starring Charming Marvin, the cat).

Dale honors the stories that come to her—and some of them are crazy, break all the rules and cross multiple genres!

To go with her fiction, she also writes nonfiction in many different fields, with books available on résumé writing, companion gardening, and the US mortgage system. All her books are available in print and ebook format.

Connect with Dale Mayer Online

Dale's Website – www.dalemayer.com
Twitter – @DaleMayer
Facebook Page – geni.us/DaleMayerFBFanPage
Facebook Group – geni.us/DaleMayerFBGroup
BookBub – geni.us/DaleMayerBookbub
Instagram – geni.us/DaleMayerInstagram
Goodreads – geni.us/DaleMayerGoodreads
Newsletter – geni.us/DaleNews

Also by Dale Mayer

Published Adult Books:

Psychic Vision Series

Tuesday's Child

Hide'n Go Seek

Maddy's Floor

Garden of Sorrow

Knock, Knock…

Rare Find

Eyes to the Soul

Now You See Her

Shattered

Into the Night…

Psychic Visions Books 1–3

Psychic Visions Books 4–6

Psychic Visions Books 7–9

By Death Series

Touched by Death – Part 1

Touched by Death – Part 2

Touched by Death – Parts 1&2

Haunted by Death

Chilled by Death

By Death Books 1–3

Second Chances...at Love Series

Second Chances – Part 1

Second Chances – Part 2

Second Chances – complete book (Parts 1 & 2)

Charmin Marvin Romantic Comedy Series

Broken Protocols

Broken Protocols 2

Broken Protocols 3

Broken Protocols 3.5

Broken Protocols 1-3

Broken and... Mending

Skin

Scars

Scales (of Justice)

Broken but... Mending 1-3

Glory

Genesis

Tori

Celeste

Glory Trilogy

Biker Blues

Biker Blues: Morgan, Part 1

Biker Blues: Morgan, Part 2

Biker Blues: Morgan, Part 3

Biker Baby Blues: Morgan, Part 4

Biker Blues: Morgan, Full Set

Biker Blues: Salvation, Part 1

Biker Blues: Salvation, Part 2

Biker Blues: Salvation, Part 3

Biker Blues: Salvation, Full Set

SEALs of Honor

Mason: SEALs of Honor, Book 1

Hawk: SEALs of Honor, Book 2

Dane: SEALs of Honor, Book 3

Swede: SEALs of Honor, Book 4

Shadow: SEALs of Honor, Book 5

Cooper: SEALs of Honor, Book 6

Markus: SEALs of Honor, Book 7

Evan: SEALs of Honor, Book 8

Chase: SEALs of Honor, Book 9

Brett: SEALs of Honor, Book 10

SEALs of Honor, Books 1–3

SEALs of Honor, Books 4–6

Collections

Dare to Be You…

Dare to Love…

Dare to be Strong…

RomanceX3

Standalone Novellas

It's a Dog's Life

Riana's Revenge

Published Young Adult Books:

Family Blood Ties Series

Vampire in Denial

Vampire in Distress

Vampire in Design

Vampire in Deceit

Vampire in Defiance

Vampire in Conflict

Vampire in Chaos

Vampire in Crisis

Vampire in Control

Vampire in Charge

Family Blood Ties Set 1–3

Family Blood Ties Set 1–5

Family Blood Ties Set 4–6

Family Blood Ties Set 7–9

Sian's Solution – A Family Blood Ties Short Story

Design series

Dangerous Designs

Deadly Designs

Darkest Designs

Design Series Trilogy

Standalone

In Cassie's Corner

Gem Stone (a Gemma Stone Mystery)
Time Thieves

Published Non-Fiction Books:

Career Essentials
Career Essentials: The Résumé
Career Essentials: The Cover Letter
Career Essentials: The Interview
Career Essentials: 3 in 1